PETER ESSEX was born in Hong Kong and educated in Australia, Great Britain and South Africa, where he now lives. He has been involved in military operations on the Namibian-Angolan border, where he gained an insight into the brutal Namibian bush war. *The Exile* is his first novel.

PETER ESSEX

The Exile

FONTANA/Collins

First published by William Collins Sons & Co. Ltd 1984
First issued in Fontana Paperbacks 1986

Copyright © Peter Essex 1984

Made and printed in Great Britain by
William Collins Sons & Co. Ltd, Glasgow

OVAMBOLAND,
SOUTH WEST AFRICA

CHRISTMAS EVE, 1930

*When the lion kills it is because the spirit
of a departed elder has demanded the sacrifice.*

OVIMBUNDU LORE.

Birth of a Chief

The rains were coming and that was good. The winter had been long and the land was parched. The rain wind from the north, groaning like a thousand whirring bull roarers, hurtled on to the mopani pole stockade, sliced through it and lashed the tribesmen huddled in its sanctuary. Not a man moved, though. The old baobab tree, the guardian of the kraal, as heavy, thick and gnarled as a bull elephant, reared up against the wind, convulsing in the grip of its invisible enemy, but not one blanketed tribesman as much as shuffled.

They had waited all day and now it was night. But no matter – they would wait until morning if need be. They were listening, too, not just to the song of the rain wind. As important as that was, it was as nothing compared to the sound they were expecting, the sound that would come from Onema's lodge.

Onema was an *akwanekamba*, a royal woman. A male child born of her would one day become a chief, their chief; and Onema had been near to birth since sunrise. In the circumstances, the weather was of little concern to Dula, Onema's husband, and to the waiting elders of the tribe. Dula was closest to Onema's lodge. That was his right. It was also his right to communicate through the latticed window of the hut, to find out how the birth was progressing, but for a while now he had not done so. That was because for a while he had not been rewarded with a response to his enquiries. Grandmother Osieta, supervising the birth, a wasp of a woman, made her own rules. The censorship from the interior of the royal dwelling was final.

'*Ondi nelao*! I am happy.'

Dula was first to hear grandmother's words. He turned

7

from the hut, raising his kierie in exuberation and striking the head of it into the soil. Then even above the roaring storm wind the others could hear Osieta's shout, '*Ondi nelao! Ondi nelao!*' and the lusty bawling of the boy born to be chief.

The rain began then and that was a good omen. The water pelted down in big cold stinging globules and the people in Onema's kraal rejoiced in it. The chant was '*Omupangeli unomuenjo*' – Prince, you have come to remain with a long life – and their kieries shook the ground. No amount of rain would stop them. A vein of lightning, splitting the blackness with its blue-white rage, hit the baobab tree. That stopped them.

It stopped them long enough for them to realize that grandmother was no longer calling gladly. It stopped them in time to hear Onema's scream gash the night; in time to hear that not one child, but clearly two were bawling from the interior of the royal quarters. Had Onema given birth to a stillborn child this would have been more welcome than twin babies. Dula hung his head, glad then for the kaross of darkness that hid his shame, his uncleanness. The *Okushatua*, the ceremony of drawing blood, would be his redemption.

Onema's sobbing cries went on long after she had flung up her arm to try to block off the nightmare that had issued from her womb; long after she had pushed the second infant to the extreme stretch of her legs; long after the tribesmen had dispersed to their huts, drenched with rain and misery. Grandmother did not try to comfort her. Comfort would come after her grand-daughter's blood had been cleansed by the *Ongonga*, the tribal witch-doctor. She pushed her daughter's blocking elbow to one side and peered closely into the girl's eyes.

'Onema!' She shook the girl. 'Onema! Hear me, daughter. You are of the ruling family. Now behave like an *akwanekamba*. Lift up your head! The whole tribe is ashamed of this event. You must be cleansed. Do you hear me?'

Onema nodded. She had heard . . . The first-born

suckling at her breast did not seem evil, though. He was beautiful. The other baby she did not wish to see. He was the one with the bad blood, she was sure of it.

'You will have more children, my daughter.' Grandmother was talking again. 'You will bear a man-child who will become chief. Many, many children will be yours and the tribe will be proud of you.'

Onema nodded again. She wanted the tribe to be proud. They were a proud people.

'You know what has to be done, my daughter.'

Onema stood up shakily. Cold shivers racked her body. She knew what had to be done, she was an *akwanekamba*. She could do anything. She lifted both offspring, carrying them to the rear of her quarters. For a moment all three bodies were in contact. Little heads turned by instinct, mouths groping for her full nipples, tiny fingers closed on her hand in total trust. When she laid them both down it was with the care of a normal mother. She stood back and watched their seeking limbs. To give them her sweet milk would be wrong. Their mouths would soon be forced full of earth as the *Ongonga* choked them with the substance of their sovereign inheritance – that was tribal law. She watched her babies and her soul wept. For the first and only time in her life, Onema of the ruling house had doubts then, terrible doubts, about both the wisdom and morality of a law that could bring death to two infants before they had seen a single golden sunrise. She was an *akwanekamba*. She turned her back on her babies – and there he was . . .

The tribal *Ongonga* was small, old and bent but standing there in Onema's smoky dwelling that night, wearing his age-old leadwood ritual mask, his shoulders cloaked in the mane of a lion, he was as close to the god Kalunga as any man could ever be. He was all-powerful, he was Onosi the lion. Rolled under his arm he had brought with him a hide, a freshly slaughtered black ox hide. He unfurled it, laying it on the floor next to the twins and carefully tamping down the edges.

The smell of blood on it permeated the air. The

9

Ongonga stood up and stretched his shoulders like a man awakening, his arms and legs working into a shuffle that brought the shells and rattles about his body into the cadence of his chant, the rhythm of his dance. His terrible ceremonial razor, his '*oshimbi*', swirled from a wrist thong like a silver moon. As suddenly as he had started he stopped and when he stopped Onema did not have to be ordered or lead. She walked boldly on to the hide, the upfacing skin tissue velvet soft and damp underfoot. Then, head high, she kneeled. 'I am ready,' she said. 'I implore you, be quick.'

'Onema, my child, take my hand and step with me and I will cleanse you of the *oshithila*. The evil will flee. Close your eyes and do not open them until I permit it, close your eyes and step with me. Step with Onosi, the lion.'

Onema felt herself being led. She walked and as she walked the knife blade began its work. It grazed down her neck, shaving the skin, then moved on to her chest and down to her breasts. More brutal slashes scythed her navel and stomach, her groin and her thighs. It seemed the agony would never stop. She was walking and though she was walking her feet did not step from the hide, she was always conscious of its softness underfoot.

'I cleanse your body, I cleanse your body.'

With each stinging stroke the *Ongonga* chanted the words. Her skin was burning, her body cringing with cold and weakness. He moved to her shoulders, then down her back and deep between the creases of her buttocks. All the time he chanted. Her endurance was gone. She had no strength to walk, but she walked and all the time she walked the babies, seemingly sensing their mother's hell, lifted their voices in a piercing interlocking scream. But she kept silent. And then the knife was still.

'Kneel, Onema.'

She did as she was bade.

'Open your eyes.'

She was at the main gate to the kraal, and still in the centre of the oxhide. Her offspring lay at her knees. The *Ongonga* was at her side. Several large fires were burning nearby, lighting the night. But their warmth did not reach her. She was shivering uncontrollably. Onema looked down at her injured breasts. The rain, suddenly no more than a misty drizzle, washed little rivulets of diluted blood down to the crest of her nipple and on to the hide. No one was there to see her shame and that was some consolation.

The lion *Ongonga* had more instructions for her. Her ordeal was not over yet.

'Open wide your mouth and rest your tongue on my hand.'

She hardly had the strength to do it. The knife blade bit into her tongue twice and her mouth welled with blood. Quickly he tilted her head forward.

'Now let the blood of your mouth fall upon the offspring of your womb. Their time has come to die. Let the blood fall and the tribe will be clean again.'

She closed her eyes and the *Ongonga* withdrew the support of her head. To save herself from falling she buckled on to her elbows. When she felt for her babies they were gone. The last thing the *Ongonga* said was, 'Stand back, Onema, your maids will care for you.'

She was aware of a great gentleness then. Her hand-maidens lifted her, supported her, sung soft songs of her courage as they washed her, smoothed healing *omugolo* balm on her wounds and led her on the stipulated route from the main gate to her dwelling. She stumbled, as she was intended to do, over the wooden corn-stamping pestle, and consequently upset the pail of water, as she was supposed to do, spilling it over the fire that had been arranged there. She walked unaided through the steam as it hissed and whirled, taking with it the last of the evil spirits that had caused such adversity for her people.

Cleansed, forgiven and accepted, Onema was helped to her quarters. Had she had the strength to cry, she would have cried. As they laid her down, Onema fainted.

Chapter 1

Freckled and tanned, her shock of travel-twisted blonde hair whipping in the evening breeze, Dr Heidi Mueller was driving her Model A Pickup truck the only way she knew how – too fast: Owamboland was so big, and as for time – there was too little of that! There was no pretence about Heidi Mueller. The Owambo sun rouged her cheeks, hard work-a-day muscles stayed her waist. The only piece of jewellery she possessed was a heavy gold ring, set into which was a splendid bright blue dome-cut sapphire. Her ring hand was engaged in wrenching the steering wheel into a series of bends at lunatic speed . . . Always there was too little time and too much to do. But she tried, she never stopped trying – and her motor vehicle and her manservant were expected to follow suit. Mostly they did.

There must have been Owambos who had not heard of her, mostly young healthy ones. The sick ones knew where to find her, though. They came in droves, burning with malaria, wasting with sleeping sickness, with dengue crippling their muscles and joints and trachoma eroding their vision. From the Ruacana Falls in the west to the Mengetti forests in the east, after the witchdoctors had made their incisions and sucked stones and dead lizards and pieces of animal tissue from their patients, and failed to cure, they sought *Ondoktola*, the healer; more often than not were healed.

So the *Ongongas* hated her with a collective hate that should have been sufficiently crushing to beat her and her medicines into the hard Owambo soil. They had burned her in their *oupule* fires and they had tied her fallen blonde hair to the genitals of dead and rotting hyenas and achieved nothing. She was protected. She lived by a praxis that many pretended to hold, or did indeed use, as a sham cripple uses a crutch. She lived by the written word of the Holy Bible. It was her sole protection and apparently it was enough. She seemed unstoppable.

On this Owambo evening Dr Mueller was stopped. She had no choice. The storm bludgeoned her and her Model A and her manservant to a halt. 'It won't last,' she said, her words intended as encouragement to the struggling ignition. They made no difference. The trembler coil gave a last surge of voltage and petered out.

'It won't last!' echoed the lanky young Owambo huddled into his blanket on the passenger seat. He did not believe it, though, not for a moment. *Ondoktola* was unbelievably clever. She could cure diseases or sew up wounds that had the touch of death on them. Five years of his tutelage, however, had taught her less than nothing about the weather. He had lost count, many rains ago, of the number of times, he, Ezekiel, had had to plead with the local common tribesmen to bring their oxen and save her motor machine from drowning. He had given up explaining that rain didn't just come: it was summoned by the Chiefs *Ekanjo*; men with ability to talk to the winds and call the water clouds. The proof was manifest. Had they not that very morning seen just such an *Ekanjo*, an old man walking towards the rising sun, whirling his special lash that made the noise of a giant bird as he passed through the kraals, and had he not then warned *Ondoktola* that the rains would start that day – and indeed had they not? Ezekiel clicked his tongue reprovingly and shook his head. He had lost patience with *Ondoktola* in that respect, and that was a pity because apart from that shortcoming she was a wonderful person; and notwithstanding that weakness in her, he loved her, he worshipped her.

He had become a Christian because of her, had he not?

'It won't last. The first rain never lasts,' she yelled again, but this time there was no response. Heidi Mueller was careful to hide her smile from Ezekiel. She was fully aware of his frustration regarding her *modus operandi*. He

14

was the one, after all, who usually ended up cold and muddy . . . She had in fact seen those hungry anvil-headed thunder clouds, shouldering out the afternoon sun, consuming the golden rays in their fat black bellies. If she had had time, she would have stopped and they would have made a safe camp and she would have captured what she could of the lowering menace on a sketch pad. But there had not been time. A royal babe was going to be born at a kraal some thirty-five miles to the west. So in spite of distant booming clouds, the oncoming storm and in spite of Ezekiel's obvious disapproval, they had driven westward, no thought for anything but the destination; the birth.

And a while later – Ezekiel had not had time to check just how much later – their impertinence to the *Ekanjo* had been punished. The storm had hit them with the ferocity of a charging buffalo, overwhelmed them, trampled upon them and stopped them dead in their tracks. *Ondoktola* had reacted in frustration; '*Ovambolosi otave ka tokolelua ekano la luse!*' The ignition had been cursed to eternal damnation.

'The engine's dead, Ezekiel. Now what are we going to do? It's no good trying to start up in this infernal rain – and don't look so smug, young man, or you'll get out and push!'

It was black everywhere apart from the snapping light-ning, but she did not have to see his face to know that it was set in his martyred 'I told you so' expression. In turn he knew her well enough to realize that her wrath was contrived. She was low on his list when it came to weather prophets but there would not be any pushing, not then – she was not mad.

'Ezekiel, how long do you think this will keep up?'

'It is a great storm.' He had the African knack of talking politely around a question he could not answer. The rain was streaming through the windscreen now as if the glass were absorbent. The hammering on the roof of the cab was deafening. At any moment it seemed it must tear apart. She shouted, 'How far do you think the kraal is? We've already crossed the Odila river. It must be very close now.'

Ezekiel thought about it. If he said the kraal was close,

15

she would probably try to walk the distance. 'I do not think we are meant to reach that place tonight.' He emphasized 'Not tonight.'

As if in concurrence, as if to reinforce his wisdom, a brilliant thunderbolt exploded so near that they could smell the ignited air before it was blown away. The track ahead, visible in that amethyst instant, had transformed itself into a river. The deluge thrashed on and on.

'The kraal must be close,' Dr Mueller shouted, 'very close.'

Then, with African suddenness, it was all over. Above them a sickle moon glowed and all around them water vapour from the still warm earth rose in a mist that cut visibility to only a few paces. Dr Mueller lifted the celluloid side curtain, and the night sounds of the bush greeted her. She could hear a lone hyena heckling the rearguard wind squall, the octave-hopping notes of a hungry spotted owl. She kicked off her shoes and splashed down into the mud stream flowing past the truck, feeling its invisible ebb against her ankles, not able to see it. Perhaps the headlights would work again. She reached into the cab and worked the control toggle. The lights came on at once, cutting a yellow cone ahead of them into the soggy misty woodland . . . Ahead of them, on a slight rise, a diorama was illuminated that should never have seen the light . . .

Half man, half lion, a figure knelt there, mane lank with rain, a mask for a face. It was killing a baby. Arched across a muscular thigh, suffocating in a clutch of oozing choking red mud, was an infant. As light trespassed, the mask lifted, seemed to draw back into a snarl, then burst into a roar of fury. Then the figure was running, scrambling and slipping in a muddy panic, the infant grasped by the ankle like a rag doll.

Heidi Mueller knew the devil when she saw him. She was on to the apparition with falcon speed, tearing, hitting and pulling. Beneath mane and mask was a man, an *Ongonga*. He flung out his right arm to ward her off. In his left he held the prize, the infant, extended away from his challenger like a disputed trophy in some satanic fairground. And all the time they were edging away from the haven of the headlights.

Then the *Ongonga* faltered and she gained a grip on the baby. With all the strength she had left she shoved the *Ongonga*, and slipped. The wiry old body was wet and slick. The *Ongonga* twisted like a snake and recovered. She was down when he came for her, this time with a knife. The blade burned across her defending forearm but she still had the child, a boy child. She lifted herself, punching out with her bleeding arm, and retreated backwards towards the light. Then she turned and fled.

She was tired and the light seemed so far away. Mud dragged at her feet, invisible branches lashed at her body. She could hear the *Ongonga's* squelching footsteps as he rushed up behind her, keening and grunting. She heard him fall, splashing into the mud. Then she, too, lost her foothold and went over, grasping the child to her chest protectively, and twisting sideways into a skid that crashed her against the wheels of the truck.

'Ezekiel!'

The doctor arched herself on to her knees, probing to free the infant's air passage. The little body felt slippery and cold.

'Ezekiel, stop him!'

But her Owambo servant could no more lift a hand to an *Ongonga* than she could reverse an aeon of ingrained barbarity with hypodermics, sutures and Sunday Mass. She was alone! And then it was that she heard the swish of a thrown hunting spear, the sharp smack of rupturing flesh and the indrawn scream of the lion man, as, tugging at the cloth of her dress, he fell.

The spear was embedded high in his sternum, up to the copper wire binding. Heidi Mueller paid no heed to him; there was no medical help for a dying *Ongonga* as she laboured over the bundle in her hands. The little body was deadly cold.

'Ezekiel!' she called, 'bring me a blanket, quickly, from the back of the truck.'

17

Ezekiel was hearing nothing but the gasping, bubbling noises of death his spear had caused; his spear thrown with his arm. The *Ongonga* was choking in blood – but the *Ongonga* had a message for them, hollow gurgling words from the mask:

'You can run. You can hide, but my eyes will see you . . . my mouth will say to you . . . you are cursed . . . by Kalunga . . . your ancestors are arrayed against you . . . oh, yes, but mine will be the hand that rises up to kill you *Omukuita* . . . in agony you will die, warrior . . .' He beckoned Ezekiel closer with one finger and Ezekiel obeyed. Now the voice was no more than a failing gasp. 'I will reach out for all of you . . . every living person here tonight will die by the hand of Onosi the lion . . . there is agony for all here . . . agony for all of you. You are cursed and *Ondoktola* too . . . and your offspring and their offspring too . . . all of you here and all still to come will . . . be stained with the blood . . . of my wound . . . The mark will never wash away.'

Heidi Mueller looked up from the infant, the tears of ten heartbreaking years blurring her vision.

'Murderer!' she screamed.

But the *Ongonga* did not hear the accusation. He was dead.

'Why Ezekiel, why, why, why did he do it? Ezekiel, this was Onema's child. I know it.'

The big Owambo raised himself from his knees and turned to *Ondoktola*. In the oblique glow of the headlights he looked ghastly.

'It is a terrible thing that has been done. We were not meant to be here. I know that. I told you that, but it has been done and cannot be changed. Now I am cursed and you, too, *Ondoktola*, and our children and their children's children. Now I must bury the *Ongonga* and the baby too, for no one must ever know of this or you, *Ondoktola*, will be hunted and killed by the tribe. Be sure of that.'

'Bury him then, Ezekiel, for I have a lot of work to do among these people. Don't be afraid. You are blessed for

18

what you did, not cursed. You are safe with my God, and on Christmas Eve, too, Hallelujah.'

Terror withdrew its sting then. For her it did. She'd been damned by the witchdoctors of Owamboland a thousand times before. A dying *Ongonga*'s curse would have no greater potency . . . How could it?

A bright moon had crystallized and brought with it a soft cool breeze to blow away the mist. The bush veldt was breathing again. But Ezekiel had picked up a tremor in the voice he knew so well. He didn't feel safe or blessed. He felt terrible.

The ground was waterlogged, but a short distance from the truck, next to a lone tree, he found a peninsula of ground dry enough to dig a hole. With their storm lantern hanging from a bough, and ringed by pools of mirrored night stars, he cut the graves, and when they were occupied and covered he stood back. Vomit was pushing its way hotly into his throat, had been for some time. He bent his head and as quickly as he could let his stomach heave. But he felt no better. He felt alone, unprotected – and there was something else. There was someone watching him, he was so certain of it that he looked around, peered into the darkness beyond the storm lamp, his back sprinkled with cold apprehension. The walk to the Ford lasted for ever. He forced himself to walk. If he ran he would never stop running. He cranked the engine, then, climbed deliberately into the cab, thankful that his back was no longer exposed. When *Ondoktola* engaged first gear and the truck lurched forward he breathed again. Then she stopped. God she mustn't stop! She wanted to talk . . .

'Ezekiel, before we drive from this spot there is something I must say. You destroyed an evil thing here, a murderer. If you wish to go to the police, do so. I will stand by you and you will be released. On the other hand, if you wish to remain silent then I will stand by you also. Do you understand? The decision is yours.'

'No police,' Ezekiel shook his head. 'No police, *Ondoktola*.'

'Good, then it is over. We will never talk about this place again. Did you throw away your spear? We must have no reminders of tonight.'

It wasn't to be that way, however, because at that moment the miserable survivor of Onema's offspring, tightly secured in the black ox burial hide, began to cry quietly, the sound muted and not carrying far. It did not have to. Heidi Mueller heard it instantly, as did Ezekiel. To her it was the sound of life; to him, in some inexplicable way, the opposite. Not for the first time that night he felt real fear. He had guessed it. Now he knew it. Onema had had twins – *Oshithila*, unholy twins – they were to have their reminder after all. A living reminder.

The rest of the night Dr Mueller drove the truck in a sliding, bumpy, wheel-spinning run along the mud-bath trail of the Angolan border. No more rain fell so the track was usable, but only just.

For Ezekiel the journey was an endless, punishing exercise in digging, axle-winching and pole-cutting. It seemed every few hundred paces he would be called on to deliver the truck from the sucking, devouring mire, and thus he kept them mobile and safe from the lapping flood waters. And every muddy inch of the route the survivor screamed. Wrapped in a soft wool blanket on the seat between them, nothing seemed to pacify him. He cried when they were moving. He cried when they were bogged down, with *Ondoktola* lovingly holding him to a teat bottle of body-warmed milk. It was not until the kindled flames of dawn licked the clouds on the earth's edge and delivered up the sun that the child fell silent.

The rising sun was blinding. Dr Mueller shielded her eyes and persevered onwards, but the lakes of water on all sides had ignited into a blaze of blinding orange light. They were forced to crawl along, then to stop. She laughed exhaustedly and peered forward to the dashboard. 'All night,' she said. 'All night to do sixty miles. Ezekiel, we'll never make it at this rate.'

'*Ondoktola?*'

'Sixty miles and a bit, that's all we managed.'

To him it felt as though they had gone 600 miles. Some time during the night he had hurt his back. He felt lame right down to his feet. They unpacked and had breakfast there, *Ondoktola* constantly watching the infant in the cab. Ezekiel preferred to look anywhere but at the child. Her arm was still bleeding, he noticed. It would need rebandaging.

'Isn't he beautiful, Ezekiel?'

Ezekiel did not answer. There was nothing beautiful about that morning that he could see, and no prospect other than that of sadness, and the promise of more. He turned with pretended interest to the re-packing of provisions and cooking gear. There was a large wicker basket for that purpose.

'Ezekiel,' the doctor asked softly, 'come over here.'

It was his practice to move quickly when *Ondoktola* called. That day, however, he waited mutely for a further summons.

'Ezekiel!'

Avoiding her eyes, he came.

'Ezekiel, I know of the tribal laws and prohibitions when twins are born, but I've taught you other ways, haven't I?'

He kept his eyes averted. She had indeed taught him other ways and he had believed in them, almost, had thrown his spear without hesitation for her protection and would do so again. Cursed, however, in both life and death, how then could peace ever be recaptured?

'Ezekiel, you took an evil life. You were forced to, in order to save an innocent: Exodus 2, verse 11. Let Moses be your example.'

Would she ever understand?

'The *Ongonga* was carrying out our law, *Ondoktola*.'

'Yes, an evil law.'

Ezekiel ignored the interruption. 'He was doing as the tribe wished him to do, as it has always been done. Kalunga is their god. He was doing the will of Kalunga, of the ancestors.'

21

'There is only one God!' She almost shouted the words.

Ezekiel shook his head bitterly. 'No matter what is written in the Bible, all Owambos know that a twin birth in the royal household is unholy and unclean. The survival of such babies is prohibited. So I have killed a man doing the will of the people and their god.'

'Kalunga,' Dr Mueller asserted, 'is not God, never will be, never was God. You know there is only one God, the God I have taught you to pray to.'

'I will pray, *Ondoktola*.'

'And your prayers will be answered, Ezekiel.'

The baby started crying then, sharp furious little screams that had *Ondoktola* running to him. Ezekiel slowly finished re-packing the truck, deep in thought. What if Kalunga had a mind to punish him, whose side would *Ondoktola*'s God take then? Would his words to *Ondoktola*'s God help him if that happened?

He wondered, too, where they were heading then. They had crossed the Owamboland border at the little village of Onjoba early that morning. They were therefore now in neighbouring Kavango. He had been too proud to ask *Ondoktola* what their destination was. If she wished to keep that a secret from him, so be it, but it hurt him that he was not trusted. The rising sun was now slightly to their right and therefore their course, if kept up, would bring them to the mighty Okavango river. Along the banks of the Okavango were many church missions, any of which would provide a foster home for the child if *Ondoktola* so requested. She only had to ask and they would do it. Tondora, Andara, Sambyu, Nyangara – she was known all along the river.

He heaved the provisions basket back under the canopy and the blade of his hunting spear caught in the basket work. He had cleaned it in the earth but there were still traces of red on the metal. Never would he throw that blade away. It had been his father's reward to him after his initiation. He recalled how hard it had been to tug it from the *Ongonga*'s dead body. What a spear it was, long and sharp! Several times he had been forced to catch back

22

his throwing arm as the *Ongonga* and *Ondoktola* whirled in the semi darkness. When his chance came, his throw had been perfect, as straight and as hard as any warlord . . . Warlord? Ha! He had taken up the spear with courage but what was left of the warlord now . . . a banished man with a banished spirit?

'*Mine will be the hand* . . .' What had he said? Yes . . . '*the hand that rises up to kill you. You will die by the hand of Onosi, the lion.*'

He recalled Onosi's bloody mouth working behind the rage of the wooden muzzle. Such yellow old teeth the *Ongonga* had had . . . He remembered the shaggy lion-maned shoulders, the upturned face at the bottom of the grave. Wrinkled it had been, with the liability of a century of death. The belching inhuman groan the body had emitted as the weight of shovelled soil had squeezed the air from it; he remembered all that.

Ezekiel shuddered and rubbed the morning chill from his forearms. The lamp-lit picture of the *Ongonga* in his grave: he thought about that again. He had the feeling that something was absent from that recollection. There was something wrong about it. *Ondoktola* was calling him now. The baby had been pacified. The provisions basket had been loaded and the sun was shining from a kindly height. He squinted into it, his brows tangled into a frown. What was it then? He closed the tailgate, bolted and locked it, then took his seat.

There like an *eonga*, like a spear twisting in his own gut, realization came to him. When he had buried the *Ongonga* it had not been the ceremonial mask that had glared up at him, daring him to pitch the muddy soil down. It had been an old, very old and very vindictive human face. The lion mask had not been on the witchdoctor, nor had it been anywhere in the grave. It was so obvious, so clear to him now, he wondered how it had escaped him until then. The mask was alive, the mask was the old *Ongonga*'s *efano la njola*, his image, and his means of revenge. It would kill them: 'the mask'.

The clouds that day had no real substance to them and

23

by mid morning, with a fierce sun heating the cab to untouchable temperatures, they had reached the mighty Okavango river. Following the banks of that massive inland river was a road as yet untouched by the rains. *Ondoktola* pressed the truck to the limit. All day and into the evening they drove, through the lush bushveld with the river close by on their left, strongly flowing and as yet unaffected by the western rains, enchantingly bluer than even *Ondoktola*'s magic paint brushes would have been able to portray them – the majestic Okavango.

The track, used mainly by traders and the police, was good in spite of its bends and dips where magnificently horned buck, even buffalo and elephant, seemed to enjoy passing the day. *Ondoktola* drove skilfully in spite of her bad arm and apart from one close encounter with a trumpeting bull elephant they had no more problems and made good time.

Right through the day they drove and through the following night, only stopping to refill the petrol tank with the drums they carried on the back of the truck, and for one meal. Coffee, the doctor drank incessantly.

'Talk to me, Ezekiel,' she demanded for the hundreth time.

'What shall I say, *Ondoktola?*'

'Just talk to me. Don't stop.' So he had spoken to her, had told her the story of '*Nangumbe*' the first man alive, and she had said his name was really 'Adam'. He had told her of the omens, the *oshipue*, and she had said *oshipue* had no power against prayer. He had told her of the Owambo ceremonies of pregnancy and birth. She had no answer for him then. She had been either too sleepy or too deep in thought. He had spoken about a thousand things and told her a thousand legends. After many hours, for an Owambo has much to say on such deep subjects, when he was dry of tales, she had said simply, 'One day I too will have a child.'

Then her hand strayed across the seat and ran across the blanketed infant between them; the exile. They did not say much after that. They just drove, drank more coffee, drove on through the night. He hoped that *Ondoktola* never did

24

have a child, for it was cursed, '. . . *and your offspring and their offspring too . . .*' If she did have a child, he, Ezekiel, would take that infant and hide it somewhere so far away that the spirit of the lion *Ongonga* would never ever find it . . . He made a solemn vow to himself then, that was what he would do.

By morning they were there, winding through the cherished green vegetable gardens that encompassed the Andara mission. *Ondoktola* drew up in front of the weathered brick basilica, cradled her arms over the steering wheel and with a soft sigh, almost lost in the hissing of the over-heated radiator, slumped her head forward on to her knuckles. The dust plume that had trailed them for so long wafted past, settling over a group of *Umbukushu* nuns standing in the shade of the vestibule. 'We,' her voice was thick with exhaustion as she turned to Ezekiel, 'have been driving for two full nights and a day.' Then she rested her forehead again. 'It's over, Ezekiel. We are here.'

The nuns came over to the truck quickly, in a cluster. Concerned eyes took it all in. *Ondoktola* was hurt. There were no questions. Quick gentle hands helped her from the truck, plucked up the baby, then carried them both to the nearby clinic building.

It was over. Ezekiel could not believe it was over. His legs and body were aching. He wanted to walk about, stretch his sore back. He wanted to sleep. How he wanted to sleep! But first he had to pray. There was a mattress in the back of the truck. He opened up, and climbed in, wondering if *Ondoktola*'s God would mind if he lay down to make his missal . . . He lifted his hands to his face – and woke up again that afternoon. It was the mission bell that had awakened him. The bell high in the basilica was being tolled in long, evenly spaced fluid peals that transfused the stillness of the late afternoon and reminded him of his commitment, his new greater commitment to *Ondoktola*'s God.

Ezekiel prayed then, not much of a prayer, nothing approaching *Ondoktola*'s wonderful style, but considering

25

that it had been his first unaided try, he was not unhappy. After that he eased himself from the baking confines under the truck canopy and, quite naturally, thought of water: water to wash his body and soul in, water to quench his great thirst – the Okavango. Coolly he allowed the river to take him, his clothes, his shoes, his body. Pockets of trapped air bubbled past his shoulders as he lay rubbing the mud and grime and smell of death from his skin. It felt wonderful, unbelievable, like traders' velvet. It touched him, flowed over him and through him. He would have liked to stay there much longer but now some young girls with their cone-shaped *shikuku* fishing baskets were thrashing the topaz-shaded shallows nearby and he was in the way. Reluctantly he stood up and trudged dripping to the bank. The girls, as girls will, were giggling, and Ezekiel turned. Then for the first time since that night his face broke into a smile. Yes, there was peace to be found at Andara if you knew where to look – or was there?

He found himself shivering slightly and it was not the coolness of his wet clothes that was causing it. It was coming from deep inside him, wave after wave. Conscience with the suddenness of a *makalane* cane lash caught him and Ezekiel groaned aloud. For the second time the spectre of the carved wooden ghost had caused his gut to plunge in alarm. The eyes, the ears and the mouth of the *Ongonga* were not buried. Indeed they seemed more tangible than ever with the bell for evening Mass.

'*My eyes will see you. My ears will hear you. My mouth will constantly bear these words to you . . . you are cursed.*'

Ezekiel turned away from the basilica and, head drooping, began to walk up river, close to the bank. Cicadas screeching brassily for the rains soon drowned the ringing of the bell. Long legs began to stride irritably and soon he was loping at a good rate through the dense river undergrowth, springing through green shrub walls, beating the waterberry thickets aside, challenging everything in his way to stop him. A narrow footpath ran winding to his left but it was not for him – the chastisement of the low branches and the stones underfoot was what he craved. A startled grey hornbill swept up just ahead of him, calling plaintively as it dipped away in its peculiar swooping flight. Attracted by the mournful sound, envying its freedom, Ezekiel followed. The ground was becoming heavier, big grey boulders, lichened and veined, blocking him sternly. From their summits the hornbill called *'peeue peeue ila!'*; come, come, come, and he responded, pursuing the bird like a klipspringer, clambering higher and higher.

Now soaring rocky barricades were squeezing the river unwillingly into narrows. Roaring in turbulent protest, the Okavango speeded up and thrashed violently through. He envied it its power. Then a rugged rock cliff, amber in the fading daylight, checked him. Above, the hornbill still called encouragement. He looked towards it, sweat-stung eyes focusing slowly. Strutting on the boulder barricades the bird seemed to be mocking him as he peered back. But there was nothing left in him, certainly not strength enough to heft a pebble at the tormentor. He scarcely had control over his limbs as he sank to the ground; and presently, as he knew he would, the mask crawled up to meet him. *Mine will be the hand that rises up to kill you, omukuaita.*

Ezekiel clawed himself to the time-worn rock face, pressed himself against its surface, still warm from the afternoon sun, but from the deep shadows of the caves and clefts came no comfort, only the voices of ancestors, crying rejection. Not since he had been a child, a little herdboy, lost in the massive elephant grass oshanas, had he wept as he wept then.

'Kalunga, li-dilulala, I am sorry.'

After a while he sat up and watched the orange ball of the sun plummet towards the horizon. It always speeded up impatiently at day's end. The hornbill gave one more call, then, with a flutter of wing feathers, it swooped off westwards, leaving him alone to face the night.

Two hundred and fifty miles to the west by road (if one could credit the speedometer reading of Dr Mueller's old Model A truck) and about thirty paces from the track the crown of a lone tamboti tree glowed golden in the same rays. As tamboties went it was a fine specimen, craggy-barked and gnarled, its lower branches sweeping well outwards over a healthy colony of thatching grass at its base. At the edge of its reach the grass was scarred raw in two adjacent places. There Ezekiel's spade had cut the previous night.

Tambotie trunks could not be used for dug-outs. They caused ulcers on the rowers' arms and buttocks. Likewise, ox yokes made from the wood produced painful sores on the beasts' necks. It could not be burned as firewood as the smoke, treacherously aromatic, brought about bad headaches and vomiting. Termites and borers which attacked almost every other tree that grew left the tambotie strictly alone. Even the flowers, small spiky catkins, weren't worth a glance. Thus, being so obnoxious, so toxic, the tree had survived among the wood-hungry Ovambos for almost two centuries. An outcast of legendary status, it was a natural lair for reprobate spirits. To the kwanyama tribes people therefore it was *Othila*, taboo, its shade was evil.

A warm breeze was gusting, just enough to stir the tree's limbs, ruffle the foliage and gently rock the leadwood mask caught on a lower branch like a bizarre Christmas tree decoration, a yuletide monstrosity. It swayed and bobbed as though alive, vacant eye sockets lowering over the darkening *omifutu* veld, hate-drawn jaws picking up the lament of the evening breeze in a slithering low-toned whistle. No one would come near the *osinima sii*; the evil thing, the tree and its secret were safe.

'*Wa tokelwa po*? Onosi the lion . . . has it become night for you?'

Chapter 2

The good sisters christened him Moses, which in a biblical sense was not altogether inappropriate. They knew just who the foster parents should be, too. The Kopers were childless. They had been praying for a child for years. They were good people, and their time had come to be rewarded. Moses was given into their care and everybody was happy, extremely happy – for a while.

The boy grew rapidly and healthily, in fact at ten years he was already handling woodworking tools and helping Johannes Koper, the mission handyman. He could hoe a straight furrow and was strong enough to take a dug-out clean across the Okavango and back. There was school, too, a little brick building close by the church where forty pairs of eyes and forty pairs of ears followed the squeaking chalk and listened to the gifted instruction of gentle Pater Wagner.

Young Moses found school easy, so easy that it bored him. The constant repetition of work he understood with ease that was irksome, and ranked as being a distraction. He simply could not wait for the last song to be sung, the last slate to be handed in so that he could tear out of the hot classroom and make for the river, and from the river to the *mahango* fields to ride the young oxen into mock battles with mock spears and mock enemies. That was what he liked best. He could outride boys years older than himself and his spear always carried furthest. He should have been happy.

The white traders who trekked up from the south with their truck-loads of cloth and flour, knives and mirrors and beads and sweets and the million other items craved for by the civilization-hungry people of the Kavango always stopped at Andara. It was a profitable port of call. When they were about, Moses was always to be found there too, crawling into the back of the trucks or fiddling with the goods on the trestle tables. They called him *Mazambaan*, which could have been a play on the name Moses or could have been from the Zulu word for potato: they were a rough bunch and did not give reasons. It did not matter to Moses. He liked them. He was proud of his nickname and would have liked everyone to use it.

Koper was a religious man. It could not be proved but it was said in the household, and generally believed too, that his maternal great-grandfather had been among Heinrich Schmelen's Oorlam pilgrims in the early 1800s. And no one could dispute the fact that he, Johannes Koper, had been right there among those pioneers who had kneeled and prayed with their spades and their trowels on the bare site Chief Andara had bequeathed to the Catholic missionaries. He was a good man, one who lived by the Scriptures and ensured that the reading of them took precedence to any activity under his humble roof. Moses did not therefore lack for religious instruction. He had an abundance of it. The sisters approved. Pater Wagner approved. And from far off Owamboland, Dr Mueller approved. She never returned to Andara, there just was not time, but she was kept informed and she followed the boy's progress with pleasure and pride. Moses was growing up well in spite of the occasional academic backsliding, and great things were being planned for him, unheard of things for a boy of those parts. Perhaps that was the trouble . . .

Moses had an inkling that he was not from those parts. There was little mistaking it. The Kopers were Hottentots. They had the typical features of members of that race, the lighter skin colour and the finer bone structure. Moses was dark and was big-boned, and even his hair seemed different. He was not Kavango, either, although he looked more like them. If he had been born Kavango, he realized, even if his parents had both died, he would have been raised by an uncle. The Kavangos were fanatical about caring for their own. He knew what he was not. He did not know, however, what he was. Perhaps it was this confusion that led to the tragedy one afternoon soon after his thirteenth birthday.

That day the sky was as blue and clear as any boy could wish for and naturally after school there was a scramble for the coolness of the river before the long hot trek to the kraals and the waiting chores. Bare-buttocked and yelling, all the boys took to the sandy shallows, all of them except Moses and another big youth called Kungwa. The shallows were not for them. They launched a dug-out and headed for the hippo pools. The water was cooler there. They could swim and, best of all, it was forbidden territory.

Kungwa was a few years older than Moses and between them there was constant rivalry and challenge. Their rough-and-tumble fights always went further than either of them really intended. Always with them a push became a shove, became a fight before either of them knew it. Both of them were big and robust and usually both of them ended up hurt.

Kungwa was the only boy who had ever dared to call him a Hottentot. They had fought each other to a standstill the day he did that, and Moses had gone home to his parents ashamed and unwilling to explain to Johannes Koper that he had fought because he had found it humiliating to have coffee-coloured parents; and more resolved than ever that he was not one of them.

Lately both youths had observed an unspoken but satisfyingly pain-free truce, each allowing the other space, like fledgling eagles, to stretch their wings. So how both came to be in the same dug-out that same sunny afternoon neither of them understood. It was just there, the dug-out, and they took it, paddled it to midstream – and then, of course, someone had to mention the rapids. The rapids: each of them was certain the other would funk out first as the river picked up pace and thunder and the sand banks, soft grass and wild date palms changed to sheer unclimb-able hostile rock.

Neither of them said a word as the current inexorably picked up their craft and bore it downstream past a group of amazed schoolmates, boys and girls playing safely on the bank, past the mission outbuildings and onwards. Kungwa was in the nose of the dug-out, Moses in the tail. Both had their long punting poles in their hands and either of them could easily have brought the craft up by simply bending their poles into the bottom. Neither did.

The water became glassy and then quickly turbulent. Kungwa looked back questioningly. It was not enough for Moses. Later he would have been able to claim that the look had meant nothing. Kungwa would have to use his pole. He, Moses, was not going to, not for anything. They could hear the rapids now, there was no mistaking the sound. They were both river boys, both had thrown sticks into the current from the very rocks they were now passing, to watch them snatched away by the angry water . . . If Kungwa looked around again he would call to him, arrange something that would leave them both their pride. But Kungwa did not turn.

They were in the rollicking white water and still it was not too late. There was a bend in the narrows ahead. Once they were in the pull of those waters it would be too late. Execution Rock was what it was called and there was a reason for it: the water there was a torrent, a maelstrom. It passed over three main ridges, hit a cliff, then bent itself backwards into a tortuous dog's leg. It was just ahead. Kungwa turned at last. This time there was alarm in his eyes and probably he saw the same in the face of the boy behind him. As one they lifted their poles and stabbed for the bottom. They had left it too late. Two adults could probably have brought the craft up, three or more would have had no trouble. The two boys did not have the leverage, the strength or the expertise – they did not have a chance. They hit the first ridge with a shuddering crash that spun the dug-out sideways and miraculously right side

32

up on to the step. The second ridge was not so kind. Something hit the dug-out with a smash that slammed them into the air. Moses saw Kungwa fall backwards into the belly of the craft. There was a moment when the air turned to murderous water, then they hit the third ridge at Execution Rock and the dug-out broke its back.

Kiaat wood is buoyant and that characteristic saved Moses. The half of the canoe he had was still floating and he hugged it with every bit of strength in his arms as the thundering Okavango tried to pry him loose and drown him.

Moses beat the river. Once through the Andara rapids the Okavango quickly regains its even temper, broadens out into flat sandy shallows where hippos and crocodiles bask, where wild geese of every kind, tall black egrets and even flamingoes wade in their never ending quest for food. Moses found himself there. He also found Kungwa lying beaten but alive in the warm water close to the bank.

Moses killed him. Exactly how it happened, why he did it, never became clear to him or was of interest to him. He was conscious that there had been a build-up of a great storm of rage within him from the moment he had seen the boy. It had seemed as though his head would burst with it. Kungwa was lying, propped up on his elbows, in the ankle-depth rock and sand shallows. Moses lifted a rock and clubbed it down on his rival's skull. There was no question of just wanting to hurt Kungwa, he wanted to kill him. There were eddies of blood in the water, more blood than he had ever seen before. That he could clearly recall later. The rest of it seemed to have become blurred in those swirling billowing red patterns and Kungwa, the rival, was suddenly no more.

The whole village turned out in a frenzy to search for the lost boy. For days they beat up and down the banks, scanning the waters and parting the reeds, no one working harder than young Moses. They never found him of course. There were many crocodiles in that part of the river. Kungwa was mourned and the Koper boy reprimanded. The whole incident was treated as an impetuous childish exploit that had gone tragically wrong. It was strange how the god *Kalunga* sometimes allowed the devil spirit *Shadipinyi* to work his evil . . . But that was the way of it. Together the boys had stolen the dug-out. It had broken up in the rapids. They could be grateful one boy had survived. The remorse the boy Moses was suffering was considered, and apart from a directive from Pater Wagner to study Lamentations 5, and some hard words from the tribal *Manduna*, no further official action was taken. Moses had surely learnt a fearsome lesson. It was enough.

Kungwa's parents did not get off so lightly. The *Manduna* instructed them to examine their consciences. Their ancestors were obviously unhappy. The spirits would have to receive a big sacrifice or more punishment would be imminent.

They were wrong, though, if they thought Moses was suffering. He felt no more remorse than does one who has wrung the neck of a table fowl. He suffered from his conscience not at all. He did not see why he should. Kungwa had caused him humiliation. As far as learning a lesson was concerned; he now understood just how easy it was for living people to become dead people. Concurrently, what became very apparent to him was that the consequence of any action depended little on the action itself. It depended on how much the wielders of discipline know of that action. Moses's 13-year-old mind had gained some extraordinarily dangerous logic.

The only thought that returned to haunt the youth was the memory of the smothering water closing on him as the dug-out broke its spine. There was pure terror in that: terror that months later still brought him gasping, lashing and screaming from a river of nightmares, terror that kept him awake long after the hot sheltering arm of his Hottentot mother had relaxed in sleep. The Kopers never stopped trying. With endless compassion and love they attempted to help their boy. Their boy, however, was then

34

beyond their reach. Kungwa's death had changed him. They could see that. What the simple folk could not perceive was the dimension and direction of that change. Even if someone had told them, they would never have been able to believe or accept that beloved Moses held them to be the direct cause of Kungwa's death. That would have been incomprehensible.

It was not that Moses blamed them for that. Blame did not come into it. Kungwa had been deprived of life because he did not deserve life. The long chain of events that had led to that judgment were hazy in the execution-er's mind, but they were there. If anyone had ever demanded of him, 'Why did you kill Kungwa?' he would probably have been able to string them together, but nobody ever asked him that. And so not even he himself really troubled to understand where the link was between the maintained lie of his parentage and Kungwa's death. It was there, that was all.

It lead Moses before daybreak one morning into the mission past the altar and the vestry into Pater's office, there to take a page of best cartridge paper and to write . . . 'Pater, my mother and father is not true. Today I am gone.' He signed the note with a bold flourish, 'Mazam-baan', then left the same way he had come. He did not go back to the Kopers still dark mission house, though. He was finished with them. As a new dawn was being welcomed by the quavering call of a sleepy nightjar, Mazambaan made his way to the trader's clearing. There was a truck there due to leave at daybreak; a truck that was at that moment being cranked into noisy shuddering life. He had no idea where it was going. That it was going was all that mattered. He hiked himself over the tailgate and found a comfortable enough spot on some bales of dyed fabric and there he slept, oblivious of the dust, the heat and the bucking of the merciless leaf suspension.

A day and thirty miles later the stowaway was discovered and thrown off at the border town of Rundu. Rundu was, however, a town with many more traders, and ivory hunters too, men from Portuguese Angola, big-bearded and strutting; others with ready sjamboks and oiled mauser rifles, who spoke a guttural language he had never heard before, Afrikaans. Mazambaan liked the look of them. He respected their strength and their hardness and tried to understand them. They were impatient men, quick to cuff an offending ear, but just as quick to feed a hungry mouth. He soon found employment.

A *kaffertjie* who could wield a hammer without bending the nail or use a saw or a chisel as they were meant to be used was an oddity. There were hide frames to be made and kegs to be repaired, crates to be assembled and a thousand other jobs for a carpenter at Rundu. Mazambaan did them. He did them until one day a trader he had seen before at Andara hauled him to one side and asked him if he was the runaway Hottentot from Pater Wagner's mission. 'You be careful, boy. They're going to come and get you here. They know you're here.' The man was drunk and had pushed Mazambaan around a bit .

'I might take you back there myself,' he warned. 'I'm going that way.' No one was going to take Mazambaan back. Two more days of stolen rides and he was well away from Rundu.

Otjisume the blacks called his next stop, mountain of green algae. Only the mountain was not green algae. It was green copper, more copper in one place than could be found anywhere else in the world. The trouble with Otjisume, or Tsumeb, was, though, that since the outbreak of Hitler's war no one was mining any longer. As the company was German-owned, the mine had been placed in the hands of the Custodian of Enemy Property, and embargoed.

Mazambaan from the Kavango knew nothing of the war but, for the first time that day, he felt its consequences. There was a drought in the area, too – no work, less food and the only water was stinking and green from lying in filthy cattle troughs at a strange and wonderful place where two ribbons of glinting steel stretched over the plains to the setting sun. It did not take him long to discover that this place was the railway terminal. He had been taught about railways at the mission school and if what he had learnt had any truth in it, then sooner or later a train would come along those steel tracks and sooner or later it would go back to where it had come from, and when it did . . . he would ride it. He would ride the train to the end of those metal tracks, no matter where that was.

The end of the tracks came up in the early hours of the second of two of the most uncomfortable nights he had ever known. The train clanked to what seemed like a conclusive halt, blew out unbelievable amounts of noisy steam, battered its coaches rearwards for a thankfully short distance, then after a bit more bullying, uncoupled itself and chuffed away into the distance. All alone in a row and mercifully still under the bright stars, Mazambaan climbed stiffly to the ground and left the coaches.

USAKOS – the name was painted on a big sooted white signboard. The boy gazed up, read it again, hoping it would suggest something to him. It did not. There was a happy sound there, though, the sound of running water. He soon traced that to a high wooden trestle with a big keg of water perched on top. Mazambaan drank until his swollen stomach revolted, then he started a hunt for food. Usakos was big, bigger than any place he had ever seen. Somewhere there would be something to eat.

In the morning Mazambaan discovered that the tracks did not in fact end there. The track he had travelled on ended there: from a kopje about 500 paces from the station he could see that. But there was another set of tracks and by comparison they were twice as heavy and twice as thick and as wide as those that trailed to far-off Tsumeb. The train standing on them in the cold morning air was a black monster that could have eaten up the other train and still been hungry. In fact at that moment it was doing almost precisely that. All the rock, the bags and everything else from the toy train was being shovelled or carried, or driven, or escorted from one train to the other. Mazambaan knew with certainty that that was where he had to be. Wherever that monster was going, there had to be a very big town indeed: that was common sense. That was where he wanted to be.

Stealing a train ride was not quite the same thing as climbing into the back of an unsuspecting trader's truck. The railwaymen, it seemed, expected to find people hiding in their coaches. They looked for them. On the Tsumeb train he had had to bury himself under a load of sharp, smelly black rock. There must be an easier way than that, but if there was it was not apparent to the boy on the kopje. If anything, the Usakos railwaymen seemed more vigilant than their narrow-gauge counterparts. There was a blue-uniformed man at the steps of each passenger coach, and if that wasn't enough a man in a khaki tunic and pith helmet was patrolling up and down the length of the train. Mazambaan was seeing his first policeman and no one had had to explain a thing. He knew instinctively that here was a man to be feared, a man of authority.

The engine was belching out steam and nearly everything that seemed as though it could go aboard the train was on board. One or two of the blue-clothed men had gone inside. The rest were standing smoking and chatting. The last few bales were being heaved up, the last of the goods trucks' sides slammed shut, and still khaki jacket was pacing. No cigarettes and no idle conversation for him. There was a war on and no miserable nazis were going to sabotage the Windhoek Flyer, not while he was on duty.

Then the miraculous happened. He went off duty. Another khaki individual, a plumper one, came from around the front of the hissing engine, tipped his finger to his pith helmet and beckoned to his thinner equivalent. He in turn touched his helmet, said a few words to his relief, then without so much as a backward glance, walked away. The new guard was far less enthusiastic about his

38

line of employment than the first one. He sauntered across to the railwaymen and joined them. There was a stuttering blast of steam, and at that the wheels spun. Mazambaan stood up. He had not eaten for three days and his legs were trembling. Khaki jacket, it seemed, was looking right at him and there were 500 paces between the kopje and the now moving train. He swallowed hard, choked down a breath and ran for it.

Even a starving but desperate thirteen-year-old can outpace a locomotive on the Grootberg mountain incline just outside Usakos. Fortunately for him the Windhoek line runs almost dead east; at that time of the morning straight into a rising sun. Sergeant de Beer of the South African Police at Usakos, saw Mazambaan but only for a split-second. The flitting silhouette could have been a chicken or a klipspringer or anything. There were plenty of buck in the hills. He squinted a while longer into the sun then returned to his conversation.

Mazambaan reached Windhoek, tired and hungry, on the bright cold afternoon of Tuesday, 7 June 1944, D-Day plus one . . . On the pounding shores of Normandy about 1200 Allied soldiers had shed their blood in the pre-ceeding 36 hours in an effort to tear down Hitler's Atlantic Wall, and on both sides good men were still being hurtled into the insanity with a 'Gott mit uns' or an 'Our Father which art in Heaven' ringing in their ears as they fell.

In Windhoek station a stinking, dirty black boy unsnap-ped the locked toilet door behind which he had travelled for the last 140 miles, flung it open – and dashed straight into the waiting embrace of the chief traffic inspector. 'I've heard of constipation!' the man quipped but Mazam-baan missed the joke. The vice-like grip on his neck was nothing to laugh about either.

They asked him where his home was and he said he did not know, which in his eyes was the exact truth. They asked him how far he had come and he answered, 'From far . . . too far,' which was not exactly a lie either. He had no idea, though, how far he had travelled. He felt as though he had gone from one end of South West Africa to the other, and in fact that was a surprisingly accurate speculation.

'Who are your parents?' they asked and when he told them he was an orphan things began to improve.

'Well, you must have a name.'

'My name is Mazambaan.'

'Well, Mazambaan, what the hell are we going to do with you?'

They washed him. One of the policemen brought him some clothes that were a little too small. They fed him. They asked him a few more questions, then they turned him over to old Father Ignatius who ran a boys' home-cum-preparatory school in the Windhoek location, the colourful but time-weary 'native' quarter. They could not have made a more thoughtful decision or a more disastrous one.

The school was a crumbling clay block and corrugated iron structure with no ceiling, a wooden door that would not close and about fifty pupils, ranging in size from wet-nosed puppies to big quick-fisted young roughs. They spoke a language which was nothing like Mazambaan had ever heard before – Herero. Another common denominator was their background. They were the rubbish-dump children, the by-product of backyard brew and careless semen. They were a human monument to the victory of urbanization over tribalism. It was all new to Mazambaan. The kid from the peaceful Kavango grew up quickly and often painfully. All he had to call his own that winter was a pair of shorts and a sleeveless jersey. He thought he would die of cold.

Old Father Ignatius did die. One week he started coughing, the next week he was dead. Two weeks later his replacement arrived. The new teacher was Mr Lazarus Nakwindi who had a BA degree from the University College of Fort Hare. Nakwindi was young and he was bright. He was a member of the recently formed African

Improvement Society and had some rather novel ideas about social reform. If anyone had called him a leftist he would not have minded. The term 'Marxist' might have raised an eyebrow, but in interest rather than reproval. He considered himself a revolutionary. He considered South West Africa ripe for revolution. He had a burning desire to set a torch to the hayrick of white racial supremacy. He set about changing old Father Ignatius's pupils into his incendiaries – torches for freedom, he called them.

They learned all about the just struggle being waged by the Communist Party of South Africa against the fascist Smuts Government. They learned about the UN and how the external political pressure being put on South Africa then had to be matched with internal action against the racist *boers*. They had to stand fast together, Nakwindi said, they had to reject all attempts by the Union Government to incorporate South West Africa as the fifth province of South Africa. Petitioners were beginning to make the voice of the people heard at the United Nations, Nakwindi told them. South Africa was under the whip.

On the seventh day of November of that year they celebrated the Bolshevik October revolution with readings from Comrade Lenin's 'State and Revolution', and that evening Nakwindi summoned his brighter torches, eight of them, to dine at his home. There was nothing memorable about a cross-legged meal of *osifima*, porridge with a strand of fatty meat, but Mazambaan never forgot that evening. It was not the meal, it was what happened afterwards.

When the last plate had been cleaned Nakwindi stretched up, switched off the dangling electric bulb there, then in the waxy glow of a little witches moon gathered the boys round him. Nakwindi certainly was a mysterious man. The chatter blurred to a whisper, slipped to silence. Still he waited until the boys there hardly dared breathe. Then, toning his voice to the hush of the night breeze, he spoke to them. 'There are things that you in this room

41

should know, comrades, should understand and think about constantly. Today is a special day. It is the day the Bolshevik forces seized power and freed Motherland Russia. Now I'm not saying that today is the day to free South West Africa, because it is not. But today let us think carefully where freedom comes from. It comes from inside a country, inside the nation, the people. If those Bolsheviks had waited for outside nations to come and free them, they would still be waiting. That is lesson number one.

'We have lived so long as third-class citizens in our own land that most blacks think they are exactly that. They have a slave mentality, believe what the white man wants them to believe; yes, that they are inferior, the sons of Ham, third-class citizens. They believe all that. They must be awakened, comrade pupils. That is your job for the future. That is your mission. It is not I who have chosen you, it is your country. Do you understand that?'

Mazambaan did not understand. It all sounded fine and brave and all around him heads were nodding and mouths were murmuring seriously. It did not concern him though, and he did not see why it should. Moreover, there was nothing he could foresee as happening that would alter his judgment. Comrade teacher was talking again.

'Don't you think it is strange that though I am a black South West African I haven't got a home? Oh! he's wrong, you say. Comrade teacher has got a home: where does he think we are sitting right now? Let me tell you how wrong you would be to think that. This is my land, my home in words only, and in words it can be taken from me, the words of the white administrator. Simply because he is white and you are black, he is the boss. Think of that!'

There were noises of approval again. As instructed, Mazambaan thought about it. The only whites he had ever known, however, had been rather good people. Maybe in Rundu there had been some rough men. He had not minded them though. He wondered if he was not suffering from the slave mentality. It could have been that.

Nakwindi had more to say on the subject. 'He can uproot

42

you like a poisonous weed. Yes, if he so desires he can change anything that concerns a native, and what are you expected to do? You are expected to say, "Thank you, baas!"'

That was true. There was an agitated rustle from his audience. They did not like being reminded of that.

'Yes! You are here now in the location, the old location. Look at our houses. Look at what they look like. Look at the houses of the *boers*, beautiful big houses all around us.

'One day some white people will get together and say, "Move them, they spoil the view. Get the *kaffertjies* out. They stink. We don't want them on our doorsteps any longer. We don't want our children soiled by playing with their shit-arsed brats . . ." Then what will happen? We will be moved, that is what will happen. By the word of the Administrator, by the stroke of a pen. The white people don't want to see our poverty so they'll shift us as far from Windhoek as they can without disrupting their precious labour force. We will be moved, we have no power to stop it.'

Nakwindi spoke for a long time, exactly how long Mazambaan was not sure. It was exciting stuff, a lot of it; a lot of it he did not understand, or care to understand. Some of it he did not really believe and wondered if he was the only one. He was the youngest there by far, perhaps the others had seen things he had never seen. Perhaps they had more experience.

If he had missed the finer points, though, Nakwindi's message became plain when he concluded crisply, 'I want to show you power!' That was the climax. There was not a boy there at that stage who did not want to see power.

'Real power.'

Yes, real power, they wanted to see real power. There was not a mouth there that did not drop when the object of Nakwindi's power was held out. A gun! Sweet Jesus, a real gun, still warm from the body heat of its hiding place. No wonder comrade teacher had turned off the lights.

43

Everyone knew that natives could not have, were forbidden to have guns. Mazambaan could not wait for his turn to handle the thing, could not wait to take it into his hands, could not believe the feeling of potency imparted by the big chequered handle, the heavy robust barrel. He pulled the heavy trigger slowly and deliberately until the hammer lifted and fell with a loud satisfying click. No one else had done that. Karunga! He felt strong.

If Mazambaan had known anything about guns at that stage in his life, he would have been able to recognize this one as a Webley .45 revolver from the Royal small arms factory at Enfield. But what thirteen-year-old would have known that? Power, though – he understood that. He had had one experience of power and that had been good. Power was the thing to have. If Mazambaan had failed to grasp a single other revolutionary dictum that night, the message in his hands then was abundant with clarity. Power was conferred by ownership. Let the others have the property, he wanted the gun. With a gun he could have all else. Yes, he believed that. That was a lesson he was prepared to accept.

He almost missed the rest of what comrade teacher had to say. 'There lived a Boer general, Christiaan de Wet, who told his countrymen as long ago back as 1914 that for them to invade German South West Africa on behalf of the British would bring a curse upon them. The South Africans of today, busy robbing us of our country, have long since forgotten those words. Perhaps you, my torches, will cause them to remember.'

It was all over. The gun was back in the comrade teacher's pocket and the comrade torches were trooping out. Nakwindi placed a restraining arm on Mazambaan's shoulder before he could leave.

'Wait,' he said, and when they were alone, 'Why did you pull the trigger of the gun?'

Mazambaan had no answer. He wanted to be gone now. He'd had enough for one night.

'You liked the gun. You held it longer than anyone.

44

I could see your face in the moonlight. You liked it, eh!'

What if he liked it and what if he had pulled the trigger? He answered the question hesitantly, 'Yes . . . yes, I like your gun. Where did you get such a gun, comrade teacher?'

The question remained unanswered but Nakwindi did say, 'There are black men who have guns,' and then, 'Did you hear what I had to say tonight, I mean really hear me and understand me? Did you hear me when I said the country will need you and your comrades to lead it?'

'Yes, I heard.'

'Mazambaan, I have watched you in the classroom. You are intelligent, comrade, but there is something inside you, something I do not understand and I wonder whether you do either. I tell you, boy, it is holding you back like a tethered beast. A teacher sees many things, comrade, when he sees his pupils, at work and at play. Many times when I watch you, Mazambaan, I think, "Here is a boy who will one day be a leader." Then I look again and see a coiled cobra ready to strike at anything that moves. Why is that, comrade?'

Where was the response? Nakwindi still had his hand bonded to his pupil's shoulder trying to stress each spoken word. Now he wanted to shake the body, passionately, until his stubborn unthinking head rocked in agreement. Puerile thoughts, he banished them; then, very conscious of the boy's movement of withdrawal, he removed his arm. It was so dark then he could hardly make out the silhouette of his own open doorway or the vague phantom shadow waiting impatiently to be dismissed. He could sense the boy's desire to go and suddenly that was what he wanted too. He was drained.

He needed to tell his pupil more. There was much more to tell. Instead he said, 'Good night, comrade,' and watched the phantom flit away. Then on an impulse he, too, stepped outside into the freshness of the night. Perhaps Mazambaan was still near. It was impossible to

45

see. His words then were as much for the soil beneath him and the glimmering sky as they were for the intractable ears of youth.

'Our country is like a young giant, Mazambaan – a sleeping giant. One day soon, though, it will awaken, like you, comrade, and gain a consciousness that will shake the world.'

He hoped he had been heard.

The giant did not awaken that year, though, nor the next, the year comrade Lazarus Nakwindi was arrested by the security police, the school closed and the torches scattered to every inflammable corner of South West Africa. The giant did not awaken until many years later; not until the hot wet summer of 1959. And when it did wake up, irritable, hungry and aggressive, and when it took its first lurching steps, white South West Africa stood back aghast, unable to believe that such a monster could have been slumbering in the woodshed. They tried to wall it up, trap it, bar it and ship it far away, anything; anything but feed its insatiable appetite. That was the tragedy. Berserk with hunger, it tore down the door and raged across the land.

It was huge now, God knows, but it had to be stopped. It had to be stopped because now it was a killer, now it had gone mad; now the beast did not want a political portion. It wanted the lot.

Chapter 3

It happened the way Nakwindi had predicted. The Administration gave notice that on the completion of a new bigger and better one-million pound township, three miles outside Windhoek, all native residents would within a prescribed period of time be expected to move; or be moved. They named the new township Katutura, which was rather a curious choice. The name in the Herero language meant 'Here we will not remain'. Perhaps the Administration had really meant to call it Katututurura meaning 'From here we do not move'.

Katutura's dwellings were an improvement on the shanty squalor of the old location. That was plain for anybody to see. It was also clear that the town planner who had blueprinted the place, who had been faced with the task of housing something like 16,000 souls with a bare million-pound purse, had been totally unable to afford a heart for his creation. Pulseless then, Katutura simply lay there in the South West African sun, a geometrical sprawl of endless boxes, tail to tail. The people did not much like it. Where were the shops? Where were the trees? Where were they going to find two pounds every month to pay the rent? The old 'hut tax' of three shillings and sixpence had been hard enough to scrape together some months. From Katutura it would no longer be possible to walk to work. Where was the money to come from to pay for transport? For that matter, where was the transport?

The black political renegades loved it. They had been waiting anxiously for this day, not because of any benefits or lack of them, nor for any reason other than that they knew administrative *kragdaadigheid*, the bull-

47

dozer mentality of the bureaucracy, would tolerate no opposition to the advertised move.

A confrontation would be a certainty. All they had to do was to ensure that the people acted as one, that their antagonism was not watered down by Administration promises of better things to come and that anger was maintained, developed and channelled against a target that had guaranteed international hate appeal: the South African Police, the guardians of white supremacy, the angels of apartheid.

Why not? Even the Hereros' conservative chief Kapuuo had declared his opposition to the move. The Herero Council, the South West African National Union and the Owamboland Peoples' Organization had linked arms. They all opposed it. The man in the street was swept along, if not unwillingly perhaps apprehensively. Certainly he was enjoying the excitement of defiance. There was no doubt that he was beginning to understand what white South Africans had understood for decades – 'Een-dragt maakt Mag', Unity is Strength. There was a new-found sense that was almost palpable among the workers as they made their way past the empty, boycotted buses and the empty, boycotted municipal beerhall – it was a feeling called power.

Smoke from the 'Uhuru' express that had rolled clear across Africa was visible on the horizon and there was not a black-skinned human in Windhoek who was not ready to climb aboard.

If the powers that were had not misread the gravity of the situation, they were not up to the mark in the translation of events either. They tried. A meeting was called and the advantages of the move spelled out by no lesser a personage than the Chief Bantu Commissioner. Three thousand people turned out to hear him, but three thousand people walked away resolved that there were no advantages, other than for the white man. Herero and Damara women tried to save the day. Singing, they marched to Government House and there in their quaint

Victorian dresses invaded the manicured terraces. They wanted to see the big man, the white man's Chief. They had come to talk. They asked to be allowed to put their grievances. The 'big man', however, was not available. The women were told to present their complaints in the proper manner; in writing to the right authorities. They were told that their presence there was unwelcome. They were told to go, and they went.

Who will ever know whether the voices of a crowd of washerwomen at that late stage would have done anything to palliate the fever that was burning in the location? However, to ask mere rustics who thought they had done the right thing (and who anyway would not have known one end of a pen from the other), to address their grievances in writing, did perhaps display a somewhat myopic vision. There were some who saw the event as a tragedy. There were a few who saw in the official posture a parallel to the utterances of a certain Marie Antoinette from the France of Louis the Sixteenth. The hotheads simply saw it as a chance to gain more ground, credence and support; to close in on the hayrick.

To those men the Administration's decision was welcomed with malevolent glee. The torches were burning.

The women went back to the location, but they were no longer singing. They went back to their homes and those men who were not already on the streets turned out then.

Mazambaan was already on the streets. He had been since early that morning. He did not yet have a gun but was doing good work on the picket lines outside the beerhalls with a heavy tyre lever he had 'borrowed' from the garage where he worked. His zeal and his patriotism were not going unnoticed.

Those were intoxicating hours, vibrant with the loud voices of men and handclapping, chanting of women. Everyone was an orator. Everyone was a warrior. There was not a man or woman who had not seen or heard something and who did not have a story to tell. It was said that a thousand policemen were converging on Windhoek from all over the country; that their homes were about to be bulldozed to the ground. Even the oldest of the old were there, warming to the deeds of the summers when the Hereros had been the proudest tribe in all Africa and Windhoek no more than a German fort, a funk-hole for the beleaguered Schutztruppe. Oh yes! when Samuel Maherero had taken on the might of von Leutwein's marines and fought them to a standstill! But no one was really listening to them much. They were old.

There were new strong men to hear, men who had fire in their bellies and ringing voices, who commanded crowds of cheering hundreds. Sam Nujoma was such a man, thickset and bearded beyond his years, an Ongandjera tribesman. An Owambo in the land of the Hereros, he was a symbol of the new unity of purpose. He had a tongue like a whiplash and for that whole week he had flayed them with it. He had them running.

On a Friday morning they picketed the streets of the location. The message was clear – no one to work! No one worked. They beat up the Uncle Toms, the Government stooges, the informers, the agents, and just about anybody else who looked half-hearted about the strike. They set fire to a few shanties and ripped up some flags, drank a lot of *mahangu* and then looked around. They had had a good day but surely there had to be more.

The whole thing was in danger of losing momentum. There was much speculation about what action the police would take, and when, and a lot of people were not happy about it. Moreover it was nearing evening and some of the less inspired and more thirsty were losing enthusiasm and eyeing the beerhalls far less antagonistically. The crowd bosses were doing their best but it was steamingly hot, and worst of all for them, the police seemed almost disinterested in what was going on. They had done nothing except observe them from a strategic, unobtrusive, and extremely safe distance.

Experienced mob manipulators were what was needed then. Such men would have realized that their crowd was either going to disperse or turn inwards upon itself in factional self-destructive violence. They would have exhorted them there and then to advance on the distant police lines. That would have been the approved Marxist course of action. They did not have such experienced men, though, and as fate would have it, they did not need them. Two things happened simultaneously that were to decide the direction of things to come.

A big group of Damara men defied the picket line outside the beerhall. The municipal police, ill trained and worse equipped, were sucked in to protect the drinkers' rights. Then a deputation from, of all places, the office of the Mayor of Windhoek, arrived, full of good intentions and trepidation.

If Nujoma had been at his ancestors' sacrificial altar all day, he could not have been better rewarded. That was the flash-point. The Damaras got into the beerhall, but only just. So did the municipal police. The problem was they could not get out. In addition, the place was put to the torch. The deputees were brought up short with an avalanche of rock, dragged from their official limousine, beaten up and chased around the shanties with sticks, while thick black smoke fouled the evening air. The crowd had become a venomous mob in the space of a minute.

Mazambaan was not aware of what was happening in the rest of the location. There was the sound of shooting, quite a lot of it. He saw a South African Police officer with a small confused squad of policemen, fighting a rearguard action, retreating into the location municipal offices. He saw a rioter, about to throw a brick, half tumble and fall in a fountain of blood almost at his feet. It did not excite him. He was not interested in dead men.

In the smoke and flickering firelight he thought he had seen two men dodge into a shanty. He was not sure . . . Then a man, a white man, emerged from a rear window and holding a pistol ahead of him, ran off limping towards the darkness of the adjacent town cemetery. It was not unreasonable to suppose that he had in fact seen two men.

It was also fairly certain that the remaining man, the man inside would have a gun too. That was interesting.

Mazambaan first peeped through the single old wooden sash window, the escape route. There was too much murk inside to see clearly. He eased open the door and slipped like a shadow into the shanty. It was not dark. The light from the burning location was unreal. There were only two rooms so there were not many places to hide. The man was under the bed. He was middle-aged, bald and sweating with the fear of death, but he did not pull the trigger. His face was a mess of blood and bruises but his eyes were fine as he looked up at Mazambaan, clear and white and supplicating. Perhaps he had some misguided thoughts of fair play. He had not done any harm. Indeed he had not fired the weapon. Perhaps he thought if he gave up, handed over the revolver, all would be well. That action would establish him as a bona fide good guy, one of the nice whites. Whatever reason he had for handing over the gun did not help. Mazambaan took it from his emasculated grip, as a man takes a naughty child's toy, then hit him with the tyre lever just once – not because of any sense of constraint, or mercy, or because the single blow had been enough to crush the man's skull. He hit him only once because there was not time for a second blow.

A Saracen armoured car, its engine and transmission revving to a high-pitched whine, had poked its angry pig nose into that very street. Behind it, with faces glowing like demons was a row of grim South African policemen holding Sten guns. Mazambaan fled.

He was not the only one fleeing. There were dozens of them, all heading north to Angola. There was international warmth in abundance for the freedom fighters, for the heroes of the battle of Windhoek . . . The South West African People's Organization was alive. SWAPO would take care of its own, and comrade Mazambaan would have all the guns his heart could desire.

52

Chapter 4

The little Bushman tracker, barefoot in faded khaki shorts and shirt looked woefully out of place among the tide of baggage-crazed passengers cramming the gleaming polished concourse of Windhoek's modernistic airport. A hand-painted placard he was holding up at full stretch was barely making eye level. It read – 'Bushmaster Photo Safaris'.

In attire just as faded, with polished calf-high boots somewhat upgrading his appearance, Matthew McGee looked down from the restaurant observation balcony, little hiccups of laughter shaking his wide shoulders. !Xai, his little tracker, would rather have been between a herd of thirsty buffalo and a water hole than where he was then. He noted that despite the lack of elevation of the sign and incredible language problems, !Xai already had two Bushmaster clients in tow, a man, middle aged and balding, his denim jacket worn tactically loose over a boardroom gut; and a raven-haired woman who could have been about twenty-five, and was at least three dominating inches the taller of the two. She had spent some time with the sunlamp and more with the hairdresser, and was, thought McGee, a little tarty, but nevertheless quite beautiful. He consulted his manifest:

Mr Sidney A Nielson USA

Colonel and Mrs W Baxter (Retired United States Marine Corps)

Miss Judy Pellew USA

and mentally ticked off Nielson and Pellew. Two more to come. McGee felt confident enough in the shepherding ability of !Xai to turn his back on the scrimmage below and slowly finish a scalding cup of coffee. His preparations were complete.

Bushmasters advertised themselves as the most professional in a most professional business, and they were. They undertook only small safaris and they went anywhere a four-wheel drive vehicle and a tent would go. Those four people, therefore, who had placed their trust (together with an extremely fat fee) in his safari would expect the best and he would deliver. There were, however, many, uncontrollable aspects to a tented safari. Aspects that were controllable had been carefully checked or overhauled during the previous week – tents, food, water, spare parts, fuel, utensils, tools, medicine, sleeping, lighting and cooking equipment, camp furniture, a thousand and one little items that clients would never notice unless they were not available. Vehicle tyres had all been taken off and checked for wear and cuts, the inner tubes replaced. The company mechanic had breathed on the four-litre Toyota engines. 'Good as new!' he had pronounced them. McGee judged himself satisfied and without a backward glance made off down the stairs leading on to the concourse below, his stride long, fluid and impatient.

His confidence in !Xai had not been misplaced. Colonel and Mrs Baxter were now in the fold with the others. McGee took advantage of his balcony reconnaissance and greeted them positively by name. 'Welcome to Namibia. My name is Matt McGee.' He extended his hand in greeting . . . 'Mrs Baxter.' She was caught somewhat off guard by the gambit. The colonel however was rock-solid, his handshake as regular as his American Legion crew-cut. No problem there. The Baxters would follow the tour guidelines with military precision.

'Mr Nielson.'

'Call me Butch.'

'OK, Butch, how was the flight?'

He pumped McGee's hand heavily. 'No sweat. You must be the tour leader?'

'Yes.'

McGee extricated his hand. Butch Nielson's handshake had been ingratiatingly overdone.

'Miss Pellew.'

'Hello.'

If she had smiled it was gone in a breath, leaving only cat-brown eyes to be read, and they looked as cool and stark as a desert cave.

'Well,' McGee observed, 'you've all passed through Johannesburg customs and emigration. There aren't any more formalities in Windhoek, so !Xai here' – He introduced the Bushman with a respectful gesture – 'will take you to the vehicles.'

It was mid-morning and the early winter weather had that quality that induces one to march out a bit, to swing one's arms and breathe in deeply. A crisp breeze licked down from the distant blue Ausberge, spinning the airport anemeter and punching out the airsock. Fifteen knots, plus, guessed McGee. 'Our vehicles are the dark-green jobs with white roofs.' McGee pointed out the two rugged land-cruisers, their high clearance chassis pushing them well proud of the clutter of lesser cars in the parking area.

'Help yourself to the left-hand vehicle. The other one carries the gear. I'll be with you in a minute.' He watched them cross to the Toyotas. If anything, the breeze was freshening and no one was dawdling. It was good tactics to let them settle down on their own for five minutes.

By the time he returned his passengers had arranged themselves in the comfortable outfacing seats bolted to the load area. Ondangs, his Owambo number two driver, was very much in charge, fitting big detachable plastic panes to the lashed canvas dropsides and spelling out the conditions of travel. 'They all come off maybe if when some time you hot.' The colonel was nodding his understanding of the arrangement. The others looked a little mystified so McGee explained: 'We'll keep the sides attached while we run fast on the tar. It's pretty cold this morning. We'll take them off as soon as it heats up a bit, OK?'

'And when do we reach whatsit's name, today's destination?'

The question was reasonable. It had come from Miss Pellew. The tone, however, had the blunt edge of affluent arrogance. Maybe, thought McGee, she was tired. He sidestepped her question and continued, 'We're going to be on the move for quite a few hours but once we're over the border into Botswana we're into game country, huge grassy plains, the best game country in the world. We make camp tonight in the Western Kalahari at Masetlheng pan, which . . .' he smiled at Judy Pellew '. . . we reach some time late this afternoon. It's wild country and that's what you all came for, right?'

Masetlheng: to articulate the name one required to tack tongue to palate and gently smile. There was no other way to capture the fugitive Tswana 'thleng' sound. Equally fugitive were the human inhabitants of the area. They were the Kung Bushmen, little people who could hide in the darkness of their own shadows. If you camped in one place for long enough they would appear and if you had tobacco they would come forth to greet you.

Atoning for its vocal intractability, Masetlheng provided the film-hungry cameras of the Americans with a first-day banquet of wildlife. Majestic, sleek kudu, wildebeest, eland . . . Thousand-strong herds of joyful springbok were there, it seemed, to perform an arching, gliding, spontaneous ballet of welcome, white bellies gleaming like trout over a water jump, black horns cutting the skyline like fine Spanish filigree. Near where they were to camp a herd of red hartebeest danced away like dry leaves in a wind, turning to cast long dragging shadows in the dust-filtered red rays of twilight.

McGee, who had seen it all so many times before knew that around that night's campfire would be sitting four tired but contented clients. And suddenly it was dark.

Ondangs, who had driven on ahead, had the tented camp laid out and operational by the time they reached his outspan. In the central clearing a biggish *mangwe* log was ablaze surrounded by an apron of raked cooking embers and steel pots, big and small, all giving off splendid aromas. Camp-stew, sudsa, boiled mealies and of course coffee. The drinks table was replete with white table cloth and ice. McGee did a flashlight tour of inspection with Ondangs. He had, as usual, done a good job.

'*Wa mana okulonga*?' Is everything finished? 'Everything is fix up, Boss Matt.'

'Don't forget keep the flame going till morning; it's their first night.'

'Yes, Boss Matt.'

It had been an unnecessary instruction: the Owambo had been with Bushmasters since the early days when McGee's father had kicked the business off with two army surplus jeeps and a tent after the Second World War, and he had been a camp boss for many years by then. McGee had been a child perched on !Xai's shoulders when he had first met Ondangs.

'Okay, Ondangs?'

'Okay, Boss Matt.'

It was becoming chilly. McGee moved through the darkness to his tent and felt for his quilted bush-jacket, laid out precisely where it was supposed to be. So was his heavy hunting rifle, loaded and ready as prescribed. He ran his hand over the bolt action. The metal was cold from the evening chill. He lowered it carefully back to its station on his metal trunk. McGee's camps were adapted to simplicity. Basic items were located in laid-down positions. It was Bushmaster's way and it was the only way. Where they were, dimension was no longer attainable at the flip of a switch, nor were there handrails and doorways or kerb signs and street lights at every corner, to show the way and purloin the senses.

But the night sky of the Namib was a great and potent catalyst in the chemistry of restoration.

There was a burst of laughter from the campfire. McGee tugged his jacket together, worked the zip up and made his way across. The clients had seated themselves within the defending circle of warmth and Ondangs had moved the well-stocked drinks table to within arm's reach.

One bottle of Jack Daniels was not going to see the evening through. For himself, no hard tack; just a beer.

The conversation wound down and they looked up at McGee expectantly. He said to no one in particular, 'Well so far so good, you must have got some pretty good shots with all that game running around.' It got the ball rolling.

'Gee!' Judy Pellew's voice had a new quality, appreciation. 'I never expected anything like it, you know, all those animals! What were those ones with striped faces and horns like big long V's?'

'Gemsbuck.' Nielson cut the word in quickly like a competitor in a game of snap. He just had to be noticed.

'Is it true that the gemsbuck is so aggressive? I read something about it in a brochure.' Mrs Baxter was careful to direct the question straight at McGee.

It was story time . . . 'About a hundred K's south of us here on the border of the Gemsbok National Park is the real home of the gemsbok. They roam in herds of up to two hundred there . . .' There was dead quiet as McGee opened a second beer and tossed the ring on to the coals – dead quiet except for a rumbling approval from Ondangs: 'Tonga amaxualombo'. He liked the destined story. It was his favourite. '. . . sometimes more than two hundred. You can get a permit to hunt one from the Botswanans for seventy five Pula, if that's your game but they're tricky, those gemsbuck, and you need to be on your toes. A game ranger I know, Francis Dippenaar, hunted a large buck, a real beaut, stalked it all day until he'd set it up in a dry river bed. Then somehow he missed the heart shot and wounded it in the lungs. The gemsbok dropped to its knees and Francis came up for the coup. But that buck charged him. He fired again and hit it in the chest, then the rifle jammed – but the buck kept coming. Well, he turned and ran but the trees were young driedorings, too small to hold a man and the buck caught Dippenaar before it fell again, gashed the game ranger from behind the knee right up to his spine. So there they lay in their blood looking at each other until it got dark. The next day a search party found them: both just alive. But there was a dead leopard there! That game gemsbuck had rammed its long horns right through the cat's body.'

But for the crackle of the burning log and the sharp rising giggle of spotted hyena there was no sound. Nielson broke the silence, 'No shit, that must have been some buck' and sloshed himself another bourbon. 'Saved that ranger's life. Man, what I really want to see is lion, though, maybe a kill. All these buck don't mean a thing to me.'

'There's plenty roaming around these parts, Butch, you'll see for yourself, maybe tomorrow. A kill, though, that's another thing. We'll try.' A tinkle of sound floated to them then, as gentle as the ripple of the windchime.

If man was capable of music that could give harmony to the keening grunt of the wildebeest, the whispering blink-blaar grass, the shattering roar of the lion, the dry rustling swarthaak thorn, that welded with the golden sunset and played in the shadows of the desert moon: that then was the music of the outi. As dry as winter river sand it was and as fluid as the running cheetah. !Xai struck its fine beaten brass keys into melody. He could hear all these sounds of his world and the little primal virtuoso felt close to God. He played as they ate camp-stew in hungry silence. He played as they settled awkwardly into sleeping bags. He did not stop until a reticent new moon had risen, and when he stopped the silence of the bushveld eased in and they slept, most of them.

McGee did not sleep because he wanted to write up his diary. Judy Pellew did not sleep because she was too excited. The transfusion of raw elements she had been given that day had exhilarated her beyond any measure of past experience. The wild vastness of the Kalahari sea of grass, the vitality of the abounding game . . . ah, and the man.

The man had more than a little to do with her insomnia. Faintly she could hear an intriguing ramble of conversation from the campfire and inched the canvas tent flap slowly to one side. The boss boy Ondangs and McGee were contentedly squatting at the edge of the wood coals. One could hardly say they were engaged in conversation. One of them would talk, then after a leisurely pause a reply would be offered. It was the most unhurried picture she had ever seen . . . 'Li mba tokerwa nawa'. Ondangs seemed to be saying goodnight. He stood up. McGee gave him a friendly salute and the black ambled away.

The man sat there alone then, cross-legged, writing thoughtfully in a book he had balanced on one knee, now and again lifting a coffee cup to his lips. Once she thought he had stared straight at her and the hand holding the tent flap wavered. He stood up but it was just to stretch lazily and splash more coffee into his cup from a pot on the coals. How easily he moved! She wondered what it could be that was exciting her. He had long muscular legs, narrow hips and wide confident shoulders. Yes, but she had seen all that many times before in the plush LA gym where she worked out and it had not quickened her the way he did. He squatted down once more and bent to the book. The man's face had clean sound character, nothing she could fault but nothing spectacular either. His eyes were good, acutely blue and, she was sure, acutely astute. 'Why,' she thought 'are you, Judy Pellew, coming on so bloody strong, then?'

He shrugged into a contented yawn, throwing back his head, his bared teeth picking up the coal glint. The movement had an animal quality that so belonged to the environment of that day, that place. She wanted in. He was harmony and she wanted part of it. Was that it?

Sleep for Judy Pellew was fitful; sometimes she was not sure whether she was awake or not. She relived the softness of the red Kalahari sand, she drew herself into the blond winter grass. It was total, and he was there too, sexually omnipresent. The dream remained excitingly with her when she awakened. They had mated like rutting animals, on and on and on and it had been glorious . . . Dreams. Ah! but now it was day.

On the canvas of her tent soft shadows of foliage were appearing; outside birds were chirping and singing in the newborn day and in the warm cocoon of her sleeping bag the metamorphosis of Judy Pellew was fast becoming complete.

She thought long and hard about all that was hers for the taking in Los Angeles – Cadillacs and jacuzzis . . . She could find nothing that was not totally dispensable. Moreover, she was a wealthy woman, very much so. There was safety in that, security, the ability to buy it all back any time she wished.

She thought about her movie-producer husband with his putty-soft belly and penis to match, his friends, their free and easy hands and fifty-dollar coiffures. It was time for a fundamental change. Judy Pellew shed her sleeping bag and stretched. Yes, she would take it. It was for her.

She smoothed her hands sensually up her thighs. They were good. Her buttocks, too, were hard and well formed. Somewhere in her suitcase was a pair of very tight satin joggers. It was still too cold to go without a woollen jumper but under it she wore a fine cotton vest that would show her nipples. It was a calculating, aware and highly predatory woman who emerged from the tent that glorious morning.

'Hi!'

Her partner of the dream looked up from a gas cylinder which he was tinkering with and returned her smile cheerfully. 'Hello, it's going to be cold for a while yet.' He gave the satin shorts a doubtful glance.

'Oh, I don't really feel the cold, Mr McGee, but I wouldn't say no if you poured me a cup of that coffee.'

'Sure.'

They walked to the fire, she grateful for its warmth. It certainly was cold, but there was no wind. Out of the corner of her eye she was certain he was taking in her legs. Good God, he had better be!

'What does your wife think of your life in the boondocks?' She cupped her hands around the coffee mug as he was doing, softly blowing the steam on to her face and regarded him watchfully.

'I don't have to worry about that.'

What a dumb answer, she thought. I still don't know. Another sortie was required. 'Well, if I had a husband with your job it wouldn't bother me. After all there's not much a man can do wrong hereabouts, is there?'

McGee wasn't listening. The gas cylinder valve was stuck. Ondangs had done it, he sometimes used a cylinder key like a monkey wrench.

'What was that?'

It was like pulling teeth. The boss boy who had the other gas stove going looked up and greeted her.

'*Wa lala po.*'

'He says how did you sleep, and how did you sleep?' McGee was looking right through her. Judy Pellew could not remember when last she had blushed but her cheeks were burning now. She squatted down at the fire, vexed with her emotions. Other clients were emerging from their tents, track-suited, unkempt, blunt-eyed with sleep. McGee greeted them happily.

She resented their presence that morning. She resented their claim to McGee's attention. She wanted the beauty of that flaming eastern horizon totally for herself, and if that was impossible, then there was something closer to hand, that, if she made right moves, she could possess. Judy moved quickly back into her stride. 'Can I sit up front with you today? Yesterday I thought I was going to lose my cookies when I couldn't see the road.'

'Lose your what?'

'My cookies, you know, vomit, hurl!'

'I'd rather you kept your cookies,' laughed McGee. 'Sure, you can sit in front. The roads are pretty bad. You should have said something yesterday.'

'I don't like making a fuss.'

It was breakfast time and satisfied with her gains Judy Pellew allowed the others to hold the field. It was going to be a glorious warm day she thought, T-shirt weather. She was not wrong.

To McGee it was a pleasure to have Judy Pellew sit beside him. He had misjudged her yesterday. Perhaps she had just been tired from the stress of the flight. An outside bend with a slight hump sent her bumping hard against him, her hair touching his cheek. Not an unpleasant experience.

'Sorry!' McGee lied.

He let her steer the land-cruiser across a dead flat salt pan. A herd of about eighty gemsbok broke and thundered past them, their hooves kicking up the powdery white dust.

'You know,' she said, 'I really envy you. Was this always your way of life?'

McGee shrugged. 'When I was a kid we had a farm in the Tsumeb district, nothing much there but thorn trees and kudu. !Xai our tracker was my guardian when my Dad was away on safari, which was most of the time. Now what can a Bushman teach you? Bushcraft, nothing much more than that.'

'You didn't go to school?'

'We had a mission school – one classroom and ten bright kids. When I was fourteen Dad packed me off to boarding school in South Africa.'

'And then you joined your Daddy in the safari business.'

'No, I joined the army. I was with them for a few years before I started with my Dad.'

He slowed down the land-cruiser. 'Look over there. Warthogs, a pair. Did you ever see anything more beautifully repulsive?'

The little beasts may have harboured similar thoughts regarding the dusty green land-cruisers, for, shooting up their spiky tails, they trotted briskly away, an oxpecker bird comically trying to maintain its perch on the male's rump. McGee swung the vehicle across their path and stationed them down-light. It was a movie photographer's dream shot: a oncer. The ugly little beasts turned and squinted at them, the oxpecker changed saddles, then they romped off into the grass. McGee climbed out of the land-cruiser cabin. 'Time for a leg stretch, folks.'

Baxter was smiling from ear to ear. 'What a sight! Bush pigs were they?'

'Warthog,' corrected McGee. 'The bush pig's a smaller fellow and much prettier – none around these parts, but we were pretty lucky there. Warthogs don't usually move down this far south, it's too dry for them.'

They clambered from the vehicle, Nielson looking unimpressed. He had not even removed the lens cap from his camera. 'How about lion, McGee, any this far south?' His tone was snide.

McGee let it be, but Judy Pellew had other ideas. 'Butch wouldn't know what to do if he saw one, would you Butch?'

'Ha! Ha! get that?'

Nielsen's laugh was brittle. The woman sensed it and waded in. 'Yes, get that. You've been nothing but a burst asshole since we arrived.' The American was not the most lovable creature the Kalahari had encountered but Judy Pellew's verbal onslaught was incredible.

'Lay off, Judy!' he hissed. The man was standing now, both fists balled, shaking with suppressed rage. 'Let's go easy on the insults, baby.'

Judy Pellew tossed her black mane, lasered him with a glance and stalked off to her seat. A long silence followed. It was not unheard of for clients to argue. In fact it happened quite often during the initial stages of adjustment. After that the worst antagonists usually became bosom friends. However, McGee could not recall when he had last witnessed so personal and intense a clash, and for what?

Nielson was totally fazed. He climbed slowly back on to the vehicle, sat down, lit a cigar and stared fixedly at the glowing tip.

'As a matter of fact !Xai found lion spoor this morning,'

McGee the peacemaker reported. 'Not much and not very fresh. We may see something today, with luck.' He walked thoughtfully to the land-cruiser. Women, he concluded, were an unpredictable breed.

Nielson cussed: 'Crissake!' and pitched his cigar into the sand.

They had luck all that day, glorious luck with every kilometre of their now north-eastwards trek through the central Kalahari. They saw in abundance, almost every type of game the Bushmen's hunting ground had to offer, but apart from a solitary cheetah disturbed from his midday slumbers, and a few scurrying wild dogs, no predators. They made camp late that afternoon in the sweet grass of Moreswe Pan and watched till sunset the wildebeest and eland herds nuzzling and licking the clay mineral-rich surface.

'Well,' Mrs Baxter sighed, 'it's even more beautiful than I could have imagined. It's Paradise.'

A nearby hyena whooped and giggled and was answered by another and another. They kept at it intermittently right through supper and McGee made a mental note to personally test that all the tent flaps in his camp were secure that night. After writing up the day's events and logging the fuel and water consumptions, he did so. First the Baxter's. No problems there. The colonel had done as requested. Nielson's gas lamp had just gone out but his tent flaps had not been lashed. McGee took the ropes and pulled them together.

'Hey, buster, I need the breeze. I'll close them later.'

'You'll fall asleep.'

'Crap.'

It was hard to keep a bad man down. In spite of his earlier humiliation Nielson had been a pain at the dinner table, had criticised everything, and drunk considerably more than he could cope with. Now McGee could hear the unmistakable chink of glass against glass from the gloom inside the tent. The bastard was still at it. 'You'll fall asleep,' McGee repeated. 'You're drunk.'

'Whadda you mean? You're not my bloody nursemaid. If I wanna drink I'll bloody well drink.'

'I don't give a damn about the liquor, Nielson, but this is dangerous country. You can't leave these flaps open at night.'

'Fuck'n thing's made out of tissue paper anyway. What difference does it make? Anyway, no bloody lions around here. I say it's bullshit.' The man was starting to raise his voice. It would be useless to talk to him. McGee walked away, Nielson's voice following him. 'Com'n have a drink, McGee, I wanna talk to you, buster. I wanna talk to you about my bloody wife.'

To commiserate with a belligerent drunk over a screwed-up marriage in the middle of the Kalahari night, however, was the last thing on McGee's agenda. He would close up the tent when Nielson flaked, which would not be long. Judy Pellew's tent was in darkness but the rope binding was sloppy and loose. Women! He squatted down to sort out the tangle.

'Matthew!' The voice was an urgent whisper and unmistakably hers. 'Matthew!'

'Yes,' McGee replied in a half tone, leaving the ropes.

'Matthew, what's going on?'

'Your tent doors. They're not tight.'

'Those hyenas scare me to death. I can't sleep.' Her voice was still a whisper but she sounded frightened.

'Don't worry about them, one of my boys will be standing watch all night. It's not a problem.'

'I'm sure it's okay, but I'm scared. I can't help it.'

McGee wondered what else he could say to reassure her. 'They won't come too close to a fire either, don't worry about them.'

'I wouldn't mind a cup of coffee.' She sounded more positive.

'I'll get you some.' He returned with the beverage and some more in a thermos flask, 'for later.'

'You're wonderful, Matthew. Those hyenas sound so

satanical, you know, so human, do you understand? Feel me, I'm shivering.'

And she was. She held herself to him and he could feel her trembling body, the heat of it seeping through. It did not seem wrong that he should stroke her neck, or that he should hold her for so long and comfort her. Her grip, though, had changed, firmed. Her hands were pulling and he responded. Her lips that had been gently touching moved more urgently. Somewhere in the forest of his emotion a breeze of tenderness still rippled, but a tempest was in authority as they kissed, then kneeled, then lay writhing on the rough canvas floor.

Old !Xai, whose senses were sharper than a bat eared fox, was playing a tune of great sadness, a lament for his son, whom he knew would not be hearing anything other than love sounds, mouthed to him like the seeds of the strangler fig, which, having taken root strengthened and twined, squeezed and sucked even the mightiest manketti tree to an embrace of sapless death. !Xai looked into the glow of the fire and set aside his thumb piano. There was something he had to do.

From a small leather pouch at his waist he shook four white worn antelope bones. Then cleaning a small patch of sand at his knees he cast them down. The 'chowe', the male knuckle, landed shamelessly on its spine – bad but expected. Far worse was the fact that 'dana', the young she bone, was belly up and almost touching. 'Hyena' had fallen some distance from the two, and 'Hyena' was upside down too. Sun was to the east . . . There was terrible misfortune close at hand – as close as the sounds of love he could hear.

'Oh Matt, I love you. Burn me. Give me. Love me, me. Oh Matt, me, me!'

When McGee left her tent the eastern horizon was pale and the air was icy. A slight breeze was flapping Nielson's unsecured tent flaps. McGee fingered the stubble of his beard pensively. There was no spoor, however, other than human prints in the cold early morning sand, and no problem therefore other than to shave, sponge off and get the gunk out of his eyes. It could so easily have been a mess, though.

The face that stared back from his shaving mirror displeased him. The eyes looked bloodshot and there was a trace of lipstick smeared on one cheek. The reflection also disclosed !Xai squinting reprovingly at him from behind.

'Okay!' he said to !Xai's reflection. 'Okay!'

'Dshauma wa oa ma.'

'That's enough, !Xai. When I need your advice about women I'll ask for it. Now bugger off. You've got work to do and so have I.' He spoke the words in English, a language !Xai didn't have the slightest grasp of, and !Xai who had watched over him as a boy, had seen his shoulders spread and his limbs thicken, and taught him everything a Bushman could, could not believe a son could be so stupid.

'A twa kxae tang.'

There were some roots a man could feed upon and some best left alone. Had his son learned nothing . . .? McGee ignored him as best he could and continued his morning ablutions. The Bushman, however, had one more comment to make.

'My son is a hunter, a man who understands the ways of the animals, a tracker of fame. Why then does he drink the !nara melon when sweet rainpools are to be found?'

McGee failed to see where all the water was !Xai was alluding to, but the little man was right. His behaviour had been unprofessional. In terms of the unwritten company code of ethics it was generally recognized among the tour leaders that 'Thou shalt not screw thy clients' was near the top of the list. But had he really done that? Had it not been two people who had found something good, something perhaps lasting? He would, however, not break the code again on the safari. After it was all over, he thought, who knows – maybe he would taste the !nara melon again. He looked over to the tent where he had spent the night.

A man had to drink. He made himself a vow, though. In fact he made it aloud: 'Not again, not on safari, and that, McGee, is a promise.'

The camp was coming to life and McGee felt he had to get away to be with himself for a while. It would be a full hour before the clients came for breakfast, and breakfast was Ondangs's department.

It was one of those desert mornings when one could believe the legend of the Kung Bushmen; that the sun was but a burning coal flung into the sky on an ostrich feather *zani* to hover there until the end of time. McGee walked unhurriedly, listening to the bubbling-cooing morning song of the Namaqua doves, and looking for their nests. About 500 metres from the camp, on a low termite mound, he rested. The sounds from the camp reached him clearly there. Ondangs was quietly and efficiently cursing out one of his camp boys for being a brainless half-wit. He could hear the ring of axe biting into bloodwood and the rattle of cooking pots. All was as it should be.

He would have sat there for a further ten or fifteen minutes but voices started to reach him that sounded less than friendly. At first it had come across as high-spirited banter. The drawling American accent was never clear to McGee even from a few feet. Then Judy Pellew's voice, sharp-edged with tension, jolted him to his feet. 'Butch!' There was a pause, then 'Don't!' The word was as close to a scream as mattered. If McGee had not already been running, that would have done it. He sprinted for the camp.

Butch Nielson had the hunting rifle, and he had it pointed dead centre of Judy Pellew's abdomen. He had his finger on the trigger and his hand was shaking. He was slurring his words and looked as though he had been drinking right through the night. Baxter, standing to one side, was trying to talk Nielson out of the weapon. With obvious relief he saw McGee. The strange thing was that Nielson also looked relieved when he turned and saw him.

'Ask the great White Hunter here what sort of a hole

thish baby could put in you, Judy. Gw'an, ask him. He knows the whole bloody thing.'

Judy Pellew, her eyes flickering between the rifle muzzle and Nielson's face, had yet to register anything but horrified immobility.

'Is jus' a joke,' Nielson slurred at McGee. 'Jus a fu'ing joke.'

'Butch . . .' from the tremble in Judy Pellew's voice she could see anything but humour in the situation, 'Butch . . . I will tell you again . . .'

'You tell me nothing. I've had enough of you. I've had enough of this stinking safari. You tell me nothing.'

What had seemed like a good idea to a drunken brain, a dash of bravado, had obviously slipped from his control. Nielson had no more intention of shooting the woman than he had of carrying out any of his other sad, alcohol-muddled threats.

The whole thing had gone sour on him and he did not know how to back off without losing face completely. McGee spoke to him quietly.

'Butch, if that rifle goes off now you're going to be in ten kinds of shit you never wanted. You'd never want to shoot Judy . . . Right?'

'S'right. Chrissake, I've had plenty chances to waste her already and I didn't, did I?'

'No, you didn't. So if you'll just put the rifle back in my tent then we'll all have breakfast and a good laugh.'

It was all over. Nielson replaced the weapon, then actually did come to breakfast. They ate in silence – no one laughed.

It was no good talking to Nielson then. He was too drunk and it was too soon. McGee resolved to cut back severely on the man's liquor availability. This was not company policy . . . Neither was unloading the cartridges from his rifle and placing them in the glove compartment of the land-cruiser. He did both of those things, though. Judy Pellew he left to recover on her own. He had made himself a promise and he would keep it.

He kept it for three whole days, three trouble-free, game-filled glorious days. Then they reached the paradise of Lake N'gami . . . Making love is English garden party language, not applicable to what it was that McGee and Judy Pellew conducted on those grassy shores. Rutting was the word that came to McGee's mind. God knew what she thought of it. It was endless and it was vicious. It was an attack of two people upon each other with hips and tongue, lips and teeth and more. It was orgasm for the sake of shuddering orgasm. McGee found there was inside him an appetite he had never known existed.

Early on the morning of the next day !Xai's bones fell in an even worse pattern. He threw them twice to be sure that they had not lied to him and twice they told the same story. At the very least the safari had to turn away from its present course to avoid God's frown. He would advise his son accordingly.

His son was not listening. His son had joyfully discovered the tracks of lion. 'It's a small pride, !Xai, four of them, certainly one male.'

'The bones have fallen very badly.'

'The bones often fall badly. The spoor is what counts right now and the spoor is good.'

'We must turn around.'

McGee looked into !Xai's grave eyes. He had too much bush sense to disregard a prediction made by !Xai. On the other hand the Bushman was displeased with him. He had shown it in a thousand ways over the past few days. It could just be his way of trying to punish McGee. To dispute outright the fall of the bones was unthinkable. There was another way though. He could petition a desert animal to appeal on his behalf.

'The fox!'

'You call upon the fox?' !Xai asked.

'Yes, yes.' McGee was impatient now. 'Do it!'

The bones were thrown again in the name of the fox. The fox, however, did nothing to modify the prediction. The hyena lay supine in the sand again, the male *chowe*,

71

his manhood exposed, ignominious. The female *gaichwe* of good things had distanced itself and the scorching sun lay too close, much too close. There was not a single redeeming prediction to be drawn.

'It is more than just your mounting of this witchwoman, my son. Surely you can see that there is a spirit of evil in the desert. I have felt it draw closer to us, my son, with every dawn.'

'So you think we should turn back, !Xai. You know I can't do that.'

'You must do what you must do. I must tell you what I see.'

Of course he could not abandon the safari. There was nothing to be seen that was not part of earth and sky, nothing except themselves, and the trail of lion spoor leading away. Finally it was Nielson who said, 'Well, are we going or aren't we, fella. Let's get the lead out.'

'We're going.'

'I thought you'd never say it.'

'How would you like to see a lion today, Mr Nielson?'

'Right on, McGee.'

'Lion?' said Mrs Baxter. 'Oh, really? Where?'

'There's a Mangetti-kiaat thicket about three kilometres over there,' McGee pointed to the distant tree line. 'That's where they are. Stay in the vehicles and I'll get you as close as I can. Keep your movements to a minimum, keep quiet and you'll get all the shots of Panthera Leo you could want.'

!Xai did not have to be told what to do. McGee steered the land-cruiser across the open veld, keeping about twenty paces behind the jogging tracker. For the Bushman it was an easy lope, something he could keep up all day if need be. The track was fresh, the ground soft and only McGee could sense the apprehension in !Xai.

Moving that way, they missed a nearby second set of lion tracks. The pug were huge and somewhat unusual in that the front right imprint dragged as though that beast was lame. The spoor was on a course convergent with theirs.

The feeling of excitement as they bumped and roared

over the treacherous slewing sand in pursuit of the tracker was palpable. They were about 500 metres from the tree line when !Xai stopped, cast around and went to ground. McGee brought the vehicle up short.

A single blue wildebeest in full gallop had broken from the cover, pursued by three young lionesses and a male. The buck would have outdistanced the novice hunters, who had timed their charge badly, but seeing the vehicle it hesitated then veered left. With a bound the front-running lioness gripped its haunches and down they went in a fury of dust and whipping tails. Then the others were there. The wildebeest struggled to its feet, a snarling lioness mauling its nostrils, clawing across its head and eyes, trying to gain leverage enough to break its neck and choke it. Another female clamped her claws to the buck's midriff, powerful jaws crunching into the thoracic spine. The wildebeest, trembling with shock, grunting and moaning, did nothing, took no evasive action, just stood there awaiting its fate. Then the male, a big youngster, sauntered around the stunned creature and with all the casualness of a domestic cat at a scratch board, leaned against the beast's rib cage and dragged its talons downwards. The wildebeest buckled rearwards then toppled. Even while it was suffering its death spasm the male lion clawed open the mouth, ripped out the tongue and ate.

'Ambitious two-year-olds,' commented McGee. 'Still a bit light to pull down a full grown wildebeest but ready to try anything . . . I'm moving forward.'

He engaged the vehicle's gearbox and careful to avoid wheel slip moved towards the kill, picking up !Xai. 'Something must have startled the wildebeest.' He mused: 'Lion can usually set up a competent ambush by that age. That lot hashed it up a bit.' He stopped as close to the kill as he dared in the shade of the kiaat trees. 'Okay, people, that's it. Shoot.'

There was no word of reply and no sound other than the whirring of the camera motors and the chawing of the pride at their feast. Away to the east the small wildebeest herd now reduced by one, had their heads turned towards them inquisitively. Some had begun grazing and two buck were sporting as though nothing had occurred. Was it a blessing, he wondered, the inability to mourn?

McGee felt smug. He reached for his thermos, took a pull of hot sweet coffee and relaxed. Later he would circle the kill in the land-cruiser to give his clients another angle. In the meantime film was being shot away at an incredible rate. Now, even in the impossible event of their not seeing another animal during the rest of the safari, all of them would still return home ecstatic.

The vehicle suspension rocked slightly as though someone had alighted. Without even glancing back McGee knew just who the hero would be. He threw open his door and yelled, 'Mr Nielson, come on, back in.' Butch Nielson, however, had ideas of his own. With one hand he waved McGee's demand down. With the other hand he held the movie camera to his eye, flanking the lion kill with little side steps. One of the lions, head covered in blood, observed him speculatively.

'He's been drinking from a hip flask all morning,' Judy Pellew shouted.

'The idiot's drunk!'

In a flash McGee's good humour had evaporated. He moved out after Nielson, covering the ground in quick agitated paces. He took twenty paces – twenty paces too far from his rifle. A lion, one of the biggest he had ever seen, hurtled from the scrub line. Where nothing had been a moment ago, half a ton of snarling pounding death materialized.

McGee screamed, 'Nielson!'

The ground was shaking from the ferocity of the charge. 'Nielson!' It would be himself or the American. They were that close. McGee had his bush knife drawn. He turned to face the charge, knowing he was a dead man. He lunged out. It was madness. The lion was past him like a brown thunderbolt. The blade was out of his hands and God knows where. Nielson's fuddled brain was reacting at last, too slowly, though and too late.

The man had bolted up an instant before the impact, swinging his movie camera in a defensive reflex. Then the beast hit him at full stretch, smashing him right off the ground in a splayed cartwheel, the camera whirling on its wrist strap. Flashing dagger-studded paws opened him up in a stroke.

The rifle! McGee spun for the land-cruiser and the rifle. Little !Xai had it. Running after him, arms extended, he all but threw it. McGee worked the bolt, aimed and pulled the trigger all in one swift movement, and even as he did it he knew the weapon was not going to fire. It could not. The cartridges, all of them, were still in the glove compartment.

Nielson was dead, and he had not even managed to exact retribution. By the time McGee had turned, got back to the truck and loaded, it was all over. There was not an animal to be seen. The lions had disappeared, the wildebeest, everything. It had been altogether his fault. Regardless of anything Nielson had done or his schoolboy antics, the protection of the safari was his responsibility. The rifle should have been loaded, should have been in his hands when he first left the land-cruiser, then Butch Nielson would still have been alive.

There was an incongruous whirring sound close to his head, McGee looked around and there she was – Judy Pellew, leaning comfortably against one of the stanchions on the back of the truck, with her super eight movie camera held calmly to her eyes. He watched her zoom slowly up to the bloody sprawled mess that had been Butch Nielson, then pan the instrument over the quiet bushveld around. When she swung the camera towards him he reached up and smacked it out of her hands.

'Bitch! You bloody bitch!' The words were out before he knew it.

Leaden limbs took McGee across to the corpse. There was no further need for hurry. The pungent taste of adrenalin was leaving his mouth and his breathing was slowing. He dropped to both knees next to the corpse but there was nothing to be done. He glanced around for his knife, but it was nowhere to be seen. Baxter and !Xai had come up. The colonel drew his breath in sharply at the sight. It was ugly.

Nielson's neck was ripped open at the larynx and broken like a slaughter goat. His head was twisted until it was almost under his body. 'Jesus Christ!' Baxter was whispering. 'What a damn awful thing! What in God's name happened with the rifle?'

McGee did not answer him for a while. He was thinking about that himself, cursing himself inwardly. Why had he not reloaded the rifle?

'I kept the shells out of it after Nielson's game with Judy Pellew. When we came out this morning I should have reloaded. I didn't, that's all.'

Baxter's opinion was that Nielson had brought the whole thing on himself. 'I saw men die in Nam for disobeying orders, or doing something Goddamn stupid. I never lost a minute's sleep over them. I hope you don't. Nielson had an incurable disease called perversity. He died of it, he was just lucky it was quick.'

!Xai was silent. There was something hiding somewhere deep in his mind that had to be found. It had to do with the drag-foot lion, but it had nothing to do with what his eyes had just seen. It went back a long way, further than that . . . No, what he had just seen had served to open a pathway leading to a place as yet too distant for even his vision.

He was sure of one thing. The big lion was no ordinary one, and the tracking of that lion would be something for the mind, not for the feet and eyes. Track it, he would. The lion had come to kill his son. It had failed and the fat man had tasted its anger. Next time the beast would have to be killed and perhaps that would end it. There would be a next time, for the beast had a will of its own and a mind. Now he understood the fall of the divining bones . . .

The lion was the evil. !Xai was a Kalahari Bushman hunter, as much a hunter as any lion. He was equal to the task that lay ahead.

The pathway in his mind would have to be travelled. The place too distant to see would have to be visited. !Xai could do it for deep in his belly vested the power his people called n/um, the power to exist beyond and above the ordinary level of existence. He would draw upon n/um when the time came. Then the god Gao !na would give him eyes to see beyond the sight of ordinary eyes.

The colonel was speaking. He wanted to know if there was some way he could help. There was, and McGee gave him the task of getting the women back to camp. 'The tyre marks will be clear. Keep moving and keep the revs up. Tell Ondangs to get out here with the other truck and a ground-sheet I can put the body into. Get your things packed and wait for me. I won't be long.'

'I drove a 4 x 4 in Nam,' said Baxter. 'Be seeing you.'

When they were gone McGee searched carefully for his knife. The sand was heavy, though, and short of a shovel party tilling an area of about ten square metres, the best he could do was look for it and sift through it with his fingers. He was lucky. He found it buried almost completely about fifteen paces from the kill, the long sharp blade tipped with dusty-red dry blood. It was a special knife, customized for him with nine inches of double-edged carbon steel, long and thin and honed like a razor.

He carried Nielson's corpse into the shade. The head was all but detached. He supported it on a pillow of sand. Then he closed the eyelids and the man appeared more comfortable.

High above, vultures were foregathering; little dots in the crystal blue sky. Soon they would become venturesome, brash. McGee opened his pocket diary. There would be official questions to answer: lots more than could be laid at the door of fortune or fate. He began to write.

Chapter 5

One whole wall of Danny McGee's office was taken up
with a composite one-in-five-hundred-thousand aero-
nautical map of South West Africa and Botswana, the
others by paintings and photographs. There was a glorious oil of a huge old elephant bull, titled *Konig*, in a
moulded frame that must have weighed a ton, and a few
lesser water colours, all of them exquisite in detail and
colour, and all of them autographed with the same
indecipherable signature. The photographs were mainly
black and white, or old sepia shots of the early days of
Bushmasters. There was a rare shot of Danny McGee
smiling under a surplus army great coat and an Aussie
slouch hat, his arm resting on the shoulders of a young
Bushman tracker-!Xai. They had all looked different in
those days. It was not just the pith helmets, baggy shorts
and young faces. The pictures seemed to be from another
world. His present resemblance to his father's faded
picture, though – that you couldn't miss. He was the twin
of the man there. A faded sepia burn-out in an oval
velvet mounting had always intrigued him. Hanging
below *Konig* you couldn't miss it. It was of a young,
plumpish, rather serious looking woman, with magnificent blond hair. His father had never told him who it
was. He had given up asking years ago.

On the desk top there was a picture of himself taken
by an official school photographer, pimples and all.
McGee looked at it, then crossed to the big map and
slowly traced the course of his last safari. His finger
halted at Lake Ngami, stabbing pensively at the little
blue spot. 'Damn! Damn! Damn!'

If he had ever looked forward to a meeting with his

father it was not that day. To say it was going to be unpleasant was an understatement. It was going to be hell.

The newspapers had made a meal of the incident. They had never liked the blunt old Australian. They had done a hatchet job on him, his company and his son, more or less in that order. McGee lowered himself into one of the studded leather visitors' chairs with a sigh. Danny McGee was already twenty minutes late. Damn! God knew he did not want a fight with his father. A few minutes later the door opened and Matthew McGee stood up.

'Hello, Matthew.'

'Hello, Dad.'

McGee extended his hand, which his father chose not to see as he strode around the big desk. The Australian nasalness he had never lost seemed broader than ever when he said, 'Sit down, boy!' He remained standing, though, looking straight at his son.

McGee had always been able to judge his father's emotions fairly accurately, both by voice and gesture. Now his accent was Aussie strine as broad as the Snowy River, his gestures as sharp as an outback axe. There was heavy weather ahead. McGee sat down as ordered.

'First,' said Danny McGee, 'I want you to know that because of the good operating record Bushmasters has in Botswana, the authorities there have closed their eyes to a lot of things. Nielson was a lush according to Baxter's testimony and he had been buggering around with your rifle so they've exonerated us. I've used up a lot of favours and a lot of hard currency in Botswana over the past few days, though. In short, no action is going to be taken against Bushmasters, no thanks to you.'

That was a relief, however there was a matter that concerned McGee far more than that. 'Has anyone had word from !Xai.'

'No.'

'Have any of the other Bushmen seen him?'

Danny McGee parried the question with another: 'Tell me, Matthew, what do *you* think happened to !Xai? When did you last see him after Nielson was killed?'

'I saw him when we made camp that night on the way back.'

'And that was the last time?'

'Yes. The next morning he was missing, gone.'

'Where were his tracks heading?'

McGee thought back to that morning . . . He had not slept at all the night before. In the first rays of light he had gone to look at Nielson's remains. He had gone because some idiot part of his brain was hoping that what had happened had not happened, that yesterday had not been yesterday and Nielson's remains were not wrapped in a canvas ground sheet in the land-cruiser. But Nielson had been there, of course, what was left of him, as repulsive in death as he had been in life. The camp site had looked so stark and empty that morning. Then he had sought out !Xai.

'I went to look for him at first light. He wasn't in his usual place so I hunted around for him. I found a dead campfire about two thousand paces off in a depression, but he wasn't there.'

'He couldn't have disappeared into thin air. Weren't there tracks leading off?'

'It gets rocky there. You know the Koanaka foothills. It would have taken me a month to track him. I waited until it was obvious that he wasn't coming back, then I returned to the trucks and drove back to Windhoek.'

'And that's the whole story?'

'Yes, unless *you've* got news.'

It wasn't really the whole story, not really. McGee had not mentioned the dance. Rather, he had not mentioned the track that he had seen there, worn into the ground around the fire, where a man had danced and danced and danced his way into a world of ghosts that night.

That's where !Xai had gone. McGee had seen the Bushman do it before: the primitive dance of !Kai that caused the magical super-heated rise of n/um from the gut into the spine and brain. The ritual at the dead campfire had been unmistakable.

The little tracker would come back from wherever he was when he had seen what he wanted to see in his state of !Kai. It would be futile trying to find him before then, futile and ignorant.

Danny McGee said, 'No I don't have any news of him. !Xai can take care of himself, which I believe is more than you can do, boy. I hear you need a full-time chaperone.'

'What the hell are you talking about?'

The elder McGee's hand hit the table hard. 'You know bloody well what I'm talking about. I'm talking about Judy Pellew, your client. I'm talking about your unwelcome attentions.'

'What?'

McGee half rose to his feet in astonishment.

'Sit down, shut up and listen. I'm going to give it to you straight. I don't need any bloody Lotharios as tour leaders. It's not the way it's done. You made a bloody fool of yourself and Bushmasters, trying to get her into the sack.'

'Bloody hell! Did she tell you that?'

'Yes, she did.'

'It was a bloody lie. It wasn't like that . . .'

'Well, what was it like then? Did you or did you not try to get something going with her out there? Tell me?'

McGee turned from his father, shaking his head. 'I can't believe it, that she'd say that.'

'You can't believe what? That she'd report you? Who the hell do you think you are? What did you think you were doing? That woman and Nielson were *married!* They went on this safari to try and stave off a divorce. To get it together again.'

McGee's face was a mask of astonishment.

'What! I didn't know that. She didn't say anything. They hated each other's guts, Nielson and Pellew. Anyway, why didn't you tell me before we set out?'

'I didn't tell you, Matthew, because I didn't know. They thought they'd have a better chance if no one knew that they were married. They might have too, if it hadn't been for you.'

'Bullshit! They fought like cat and dog from day one.'

'You're missing the point.'

'Tell me then, what *is* the point?'

'Okay. The point is, mister, that you still tried to screw one of the clients, and you know as well as I do that that is bloody taboo. Then when you couldn't get your way with her you started getting ugly.'

'That's what she told you . . .'

'I didn't suck it out of my thumb, boy. Of course she told me. She told me everything, all about it. The final straw was calling her a bitch and taking a swipe at her just after her husband had been killed.'

'She filmed the whole bloody thing. It was the most callous thing I've ever seen. All she could think of was making home movies while Nielson was getting mauled. I couldn't believe it . . . Her husband!'

'So you called her a bitch?'

'I did, but I never hit her. It was the movie camera.'

'God almighty, Matthew, is there any hope for you? You're going to have to apologize to her.'

'Is she still in Windhoek. I thought she'd gone back to Los Angeles.'

'No, she's in Windhoek. I want you to apologize to her.'

'I won't do that. Not again. That night after the killing I told her I was sorry about things. She must have forgotten to tell you that. I wonder if that incredible woman also forgot to tell you how turned on the killing had made her. She told me.'

'Listen to me, boy!'

'No, Dad, you listen to me . . . You've looked for a scrap with me ever since I can remember. Down on the farm in Tsumeb when I was a kid I was so shit-scared of you I used to run like a jack rabbit when you came home. !Xai used to walk with me miles into the bush to get away from you. It was !Xai who brought me up. You were never there unless you had a belt in one hand and a bottle in the other. I can't recall a single decent time that you and I spent together, not one. Judy Pellew is just an excuse to . . .'

Daniel McGee was white, his mouth open as though he couldn't believe any part of this. 'You bastard! You bugger up a lucrative safari, you lose a tracker, a man is dead because you left your bloody unloaded rifle in your truck – not just any man either, you have to pick a movie magnate. Nothing small about my boy. No, my boy does things in a big way. My boy . . . I wonder if you are my boy.'

'Shut up, Dad!' The words, not much louder than a whisper, shocked Danny McGee's mouth shut like a fist to the jaw. 'Now I'm going to tell you something, Dad. You see, sometimes I wonder, too, if I'm your boy. You said it, Dad, and you've said it before . . . I can't remember ever having had a mother. I haven't got the faintest recollection of one. You never ever talk about her. Where are the happy photographs of the marriage or the christening and all that . . . ? Tell me, Dad, what did she look like?'

'She died.'

'Yes, I believe that. Tell me about it.'

'There's nothing to tell. It's got nothing to do with this discussion either. The subject is closed.'

'What? Is everything closed, Dad – Judy Pellew, the buggered up safari . . . everything?'

'I don't like sarcasm, Matthew. Don't push me.'

'Why not, Dad? You've pushed me for years. I want to get one or two things straight. You say I buggered up a lucrative safari. Okay, I take the blame, but I didn't force my attentions on Judy Pellew and you bloody well know it. You also know that Nielson was a drunken idiot and that's really why he died. As for losing a tracker, that's rubbish . . . !Xai took off because he wrongly blamed himself for what had happened. He's gone to do what he feels he needs to do to put things right in his own mind.

Once that's done he'll be back . . . You know that too. I lost control of that safari because I lost my head over a woman and that's my fault, but that's not your beef, Dad. That's not what your anger is all about. Your anger goes a long way further back than that.'

'Bloody right it does.'

'Yes . . . I know. You never really wanted a son, did you? You never really wanted anybody hanging around you. You're a freebooter, Dad. You don't give a shit for anybody or anything.'

'And who are you to talk, boy? Where were you all the years? You were not dishing out all that much love either.'

McGee looked at his father. Danny McGee was pressed deeply into his brown padded chair, almost as though he was drawing himself away from the argument. He had not expected this reaction from his son. McGee wondered why he had said what he had. Father and son had always argued, sometimes bitterly, sometimes violently, but always with the brain and the limb, never with the soul. Today he was reaching for his father's soul. The acid of the bad years was spilling into his words and their relationship would never be the same.

'Maybe I didn't ask for you,' Danny McGee said. 'Maybe you're right, I didn't want you. Okay, let's say that's the truth. But I brought you up, didn't I?'

'No, you didn't. !Xai did, the schoolteachers did, the army did.'

'And Bushmasters?'

'Yes, Bushmasters.'

'Well?'

'Well what? Don't think you're Bushmasters, Dad. You don't even know what's going on out there any more or we wouldn't be having this argument. You haven't run Bushmasters since the old days; since the day you shifted the gun cabinet out and the booze cabinet in.'

Danny McGee's teeth were clamped tight together, his jaw bulging with anger. His words were clear, though, both in sound and meaning. 'Get out of here! Out! And don't come back, boy. Don't ever come back.'

McGee stood up, walked out – and wondered why his eyes were blurred with tears as he brushed past his father's secretary, past the big blow-ups of kudu and elephant that covered the reception walls. He pushed into the men's room, cold white and empty. There his fist exploded against the wall mirror shattering the glass, cutting knuckles to the bone. There he splashed his face and eyes with cold, blood-streaked water and said, 'So be it, Dad . . . you and I have had our last scrap . . . our last of anything.'

The public bar at the Namib Safari Hotel was already busy when McGee walked in at midday and ordered a draught beer. The beer was just right, slightly chilled and served in a tankard. It did not last long. Neither did the next few . . . It was the late afternoon crowd drifting in that reminded him of the passage of time, and the fact that he still had not in any way washed the bitterness that clung like mud to his mind.

'Jesus, it's Lieutenant McGee! How goes it, cobber?'

Another Aussie accent was all McGee needed. He focused on the lank, sombre-faced character addressing him. Andrew Patterson and he had served together in Buffalo Battalion. He searched his mind for the man's nickname.

'Gumtree, Sergeant Gumtree Patterson.'

'Sergeant-Major now. I've hit the big time, cobber.'

They both laughed. Now McGee was pleased to see the man.

'Barman!' roared Gumtree Patterson. 'Me and the Lieutenant's got a stinking great thirst on. Just keep 'em coming.'

The barman kept them coming, and it was good to sit and converse with such an unaffected man, to relive the ifs and buts of past fire-fights and to hear the recent deeds of Buffalo Battalion's fighting men.

'So what you into these days? Still with your old man?'

McGee glanced at the plaster on his knuckles. 'No, it didn't work out. We didn't see eye to eye on things.'

Patterson nodded his sympathy but frowned. 'I'm surprised. Seemed like a good set up, Matt.'

McGee was silent a while. A thought was forming in his mind. 'How're you off for officers in the battalion?'

'Usual shortage – there's plenty who'd like to get in but the commandant's a hard man, choosy.'

'He always was.'

'Yere,' Patterson took a huge swig of beer. 'Aah! What were we saying? Right, you have to be hard when you work with a mixed bunch of Angolan abo's. He's fair, though.'

'What's the morale like, Gumtree?'

Patterson cocked his head thoughtfully. 'You thinking what I think you're thinking, yere, they're happy as long as the skipper's happy and he's happy when the kill rate is up. Why don't you ask him yourself?'

'Maybe,' said McGee. 'How long are you still on leave?'

'On leave? What makes you think that? I'm not on leave and neither is the skipper. We're in town on business, but ask him yourself. He's right behind you, cobber.'

Commandant Nell had the build expected of some born under the zodiac sign of Taurus; bull-necked with the shoulder girth of a wrestler. There was nothing bullish about his eyes, though. They were dark blue and quick as an arrow as they fastened on McGee.

'My God, Sar-Major, look what the cat brought in.'

McGee got up from the bar stool. He wished he had had a little less beer that day.

'Good to see you again, Commandant.'

'You, too. What are you doing with yourself?'

'I'm busy,' said McGee, articulating with the greatest of care, 'joining the army.'

'Welcome back, Lieutenant,' said Nell . . .

'Cheers!' said Gumtree Patterson.

Chapter 6

In the neon-cold sepulchre that was aptly known as the Operations Room in the South African military cantonment at Ondongwa a young, rather drawn-looking corporal glanced up at the operational map. It was his task to update it. The map was so huge that a high scaffold on wheels was needed to reach the northern boundaries of South West Africa. If one stretched further upwards, one could reach such far-away places as Xangongo, Ongiva or Kassinga. By that time one's hand would have been well into Marxist Angola.

The corporal consulted a slip of paper he was holding, climbed the scaffold and shifted a bright red pin from one position to another. From the first position he crayoned a black dotted line to the new location. Then he clambered down, logged the message slip and relaxed. The electric clock on the wall read 04H31. Everything had been done precisely and exactly. The Ops Officer liked it that way.

The location of the pin was so exact, that could it have been magnified a thousand-fold and plunged into the Owamboland bushveld like some gigantic red beach umbrella, the circumference of its head would have been directly above the three-section South African patrol it was demarking.

The patrol was just ten kilometres short of the Angolan border and about fifteen kilometres south of the tiny village Oshikomi. More important, it was, according to the patrol leader's reckoning, about four kilometres behind its quarry. The patrol leader was Lieutenant Matthew McGee and the quarry was a People's Liberation army special assignments team, from 104 brigade, SWAPO first-team boys.

McGee was cold. He was uncomfortable, was glad the night was nearly over. He had slept badly, dreaming on and on about !Xai and the killer lion again. At one stage he had bolted upright in his sleeping bag, heart pounding. The beast had been at his feet, just standing there, watching him. That had been at about 0200. Since then he had lain awake watching the constellations steal across the sky. It was about an hour to first light, time to get moving. In a short while the Owambo woodland would strip off its cloak of black, the hyenas and jackals would slip peacefully back to their lairs and, in a highly organized way, men would start killing each other.

For Lieutenant McGee the issues were simple. The men he was pursuing were terrorists, not nationalists and not freedom fighters. They were plainly and simply thugs who would murder or maim anyone or anything, their targets depending on only expedience. They burnt and destroyed and lied about their political objectives: in short were evil and did not deserve breathing space. They were not even worth a shiny brass bullet, but he and the thirty men with him had never and would never begrudge them that. He shook himself out of his sleeping bag and heard the similar quiet rustle of nylon in the gloom around him. The horizon was yellowing, a new day was at hand.

McGee's men had always lived with war. They were black Angolans and they knew all about it. They could not remember a time when there had not been a war in Angola. First, it had been the Portuguese and after the Portuguese had been beaten they had still found themselves fighting – this time against their own countrymen, who wanted them dead because they came from the wrong tribe. That was Africa. It had taken the South Africans to see the potential of those men. They had recruited them, armed them and turned them loose against SWAPO in less time that it takes to say 'Kalashnikov!'

They'd been on the spoor the whole previous day, moving with the single-mindedness and speed of a pack of hunting dogs. They had their leader, but control had scarcely to be exercised. Like hunting dogs they responded as a pack to any change in pace or direction that was requested. Today they would make a kill. They knew it.

McGee waited just long enough for the soft orange lantern of the morning sun to give silhouette and substance to the sandy underfoot. He watched his men shrug into their webbing and check their weapons. It was cold. The metal of his rifle felt like ice as he ran his hand over the action and checked that the magazine was secure.

They were not the ordinary mine-laying squad, those boys ahead. They were a hit squad, no doubt with a death list. One name could be ticked off already – Mercy Shiwala, a schoolteacher. She was dead because she actively opposed SWAPO in the classroom. You did not do that on the Namibian border. That had been spelt out to everyone by means of a quick lecture and a long burst of AK fire into Mercy's body.

There would be others on that list. For instance, thought McGee, there was old Johannes Nanguguula. His tidy little kraal lay close to the village of Oshikomi, not far from Mercy's burnt-out school. Now Johannes was a born 'racist lackey' if ever there was one. On many an occasion McGee had shared a pot of *omalodu* with old Johannes.

As it was, Johannes was not on the list, a fact supported by his good health at that very instant. For one who was not a SWAPO sympathizer he was doing a fairly convincing turn for the hard men seated in the shade of his thatch, eating his fish mash and sipping cool water from his earthen pots. Of course it would have been stupid to deny those men anything. Food was a small enough price to pay to be left in peace, and the village head was anything but stupid. He had in fact anticipated the comrade commander's next demand, and had already seen to it before he was asked.

'Comrade Nanguguula?'

His guest had a lazy way of speaking. A big man and muscular, he held his assault rifle as though it were a twig, and pointed with it to the Mopani woodland from

89

whence he had come. He seemed quite relaxed, quite confident.

'Comrade,' he went on, 'the *boers* sooner or later are going to pick up the trail we've left, and sooner or later they're going to pay you a visit.'

Johannes nodded affirmatively. He agreed it was a certainty. 'Yes.'

'It would be wise, and being an old man you must be wise, to obliterate the tracks we have made.'

Johannes laughed. Indeed he was old, he agreed, and wise – in fact he had already seen to the matter.

'My herd boys have driven oxen already over your prints. There is no danger there.'

'You are a man among men, your wives appear happy, your crop looks to have been good. You are fortunate. May you grow as fat as a puffadder.' It was a compliment. Johannes regarded the stranger. The man's dialect he could not place. He was an Owambo, of that he was sure. His Kwanyama was perfect, and yet not spoken quite like anything he had heard before. He was not Ukwanjama and he was not Ondonga. The man was sitting quietly now, slapping the buzzing flies away from his face as he ate.

Then he caught Johannes staring stupidly, and as suddenly as a summer shower passes the easy mood was gone. He stood, and without a word the twelve men with him stood too. Johannes felt his stomach tighten, his mouth go dry. He wished they would hurry and go. The men were buckling on their rucksacks, their water bottles full. He had surely done all he could do. He did not understand the anger in the SWAPO commander's eyes nor the reason for it. He was no coward but the man terrified him.

'Old man!' The voice was like a cold plunge – but it was a relief that the commander was at least talking.

'It has happened before that headmen, even chiefs, have been stupid. Don't be stupid, eh!'

Johannes nodded his head. He would not be stupid.

'It would be stupid to inform on me when the *boers* come and drink beer with you again.'

'No!' It came like a gasp. God, how did the man know? He tried to pull himself together. 'No. Believe me, I am for the struggle.'

'Well!' The smile was back now, or was it? 'That's good thinking. I'm going now. Maybe I'll leave a man somewhere out there to watch your lovely kraal, maybe not. But if the *boers* come, and then, if they find our tracks, you and your eldest son are dead men. That is a promise.'

Old Johannes Nanguguula watched them go, then turned irritably on his principal wife. For some time every plodding ox he could summon up was employed.

McGee could see the dust pall while still more than a kilometre away. He had seen dust clouds like that before and he was not surprised therefore when he found the sharp imprint of cattle hooves all over the man tracks ahead. The Nanguguula kraal was as neat and tidy as ever.

Johannes was sullen. No, he had not seen any guns. What guns? Maddeningly, the man could not understand McGee's perfect Kwanyama any longer.

'Men with guns, Johannes – SWAPO. Now, how many?'

The toothy smile of old was gone, in its place an infuriating, puzzled, doltish look. 'I'm not a SWAPO.'

Johannes was giving him the runaround, or trying to. But McGee was too old a hand to be taken in by that bullshit and there was no time for games. He tried again.

'They came through here, Johannes, I know that. All I want to know is how many. How many were there, *omunongonu*; how many, wise man?'

Johannes was watching his feet, kicking at the dirt. He mumbled something about having been busy in the fields all morning.

'Doing a woman's work in the mahango fields?' McGee asked him. 'Since when did you become a woman? Will you be stamping the corn next?'

The old man said nothing. Downcast, he fidgeted his toes in the sand.

'If you do not answer me, I will burn down your kraal . . . Now.'

91

'You wouldn't do that!'

'Now you can hear me! No, I wouldn't do that because you were my friend, but you are no longer my friend. I am leaving now, sad because I have lost a great man as a friend.'

The emotional blackmail did not work either. Johannes turned away and squatted down. He had said all he was going to say. McGee instructed the men who had escorted him into the kraal to make a quick search. 'And take fresh water for us. Nothing will be given to us here, but lies.'

His troops had never understood the velvet-glove approach. Corporal Hosi regarded him with a look one might reserve for a close senile relative and in a stream of gutter Portuguese directed the men to do the white lieutenant's bidding. If he had his way the place would be a smouldering ash heap, and he would know exactly how many enemy were in the band ahead. But from then on he would never have been able to get another thing from old Johannes Nanguguula or his kin. McGee smiled. They were bloody savage, those Angolan blacks of his, no mistake, but he would not have swapped Hosi and his men just then, not for a full support company of the Grenadier Guards, not then, not any African day.

Fifteen minutes – that was all the time it took to shake the Nanguguula kraal down, but there was nothing there, nothing but an overlooked single SWAPO boot impression as unmistakable as a thumbprint.

McGee did not even bother to point it out to Johannes. It would not have helped. It was time to leave. They had lost thirty minutes by the time they picked up the spoor again three kilometres north of the kraal, heading for Angola.

Something else happened before they were away from old Johannes's land though. A young and very scared herd boy was brought to him by Teja, one of his machine gunners. 'He was trailing us, weren't you boy?' The question was in Portuguese and was accompanied by a cuff on the ear. The boy understood neither. Teja was one of his Kwanyama speakers. He should have known better.

'Leave him!' McGee snapped. 'Come here, omumati.'

The boy had something clasped in his clenched hand. He held the hand out and McGee found himself the owner of thirteen long sand acacia thorns. He counted them once more. Thirteen thorns for thirteen men. The cunning old fox had let them find the spoor on their own, waited in fact to see if they would find it at all, then placed his bets on the tall horse. Thirteen against thirty was fair odds – the old bastard! He gave the herd boy a message.

'Tell your father . . .' McGee thought about it for a moment. 'Tell him his beer is still sweet for me. I will see him soon.'

McGee did not know how wrong he was.

They reached the border at 09.35 hours. The South Africans had gashed the veld apart there the length of Owamboland. Straight as the eye could see from east to west, the gash ran like some abandoned gigantic freeway project. He watched his men cross over in three sticks of ten, hunched against the weight of their packs. They weren't dawdling. Nobody dawdled over the cut line. He crossed with the last stick together with his radio man, Baptista, the brothers Carlos and Felix, masters of the deadly rocket grenades – the RPG-and Oliviera, the medic. They regrouped in thick donkey-berry shrub and McGee used the radio. The signal was strong and his message was priority. He did not have much to say but in Ondangwa's operations nerve centre his little red pin was moved up the map and over the red line, and two Alouette gunship crews started in a crisp walk over the tarmac to their choppers.

The spoor was so fresh now that a urine patch they found was damp. The trodden finger grass was still buckled right down. McGee cut his patrol into open formation, set himself centrally where he could best control the action that had to come, and they moved off again at a cracking pace.

For an hour they moved thus well spread out. The ground became more wooded for a while, with heavy bush willow shrubs and tall syringas, rich with their early summer foliage. Here a man could find himself suddenly alone, the men on each flank gone, and only the sound of his own crashing progress for company until the woodland spat him out into the open.

The spoor was there, in single file, and fresher if anything by the minute. McGee pulled a machine gunner right to the centre of his patrol and right behind the tracks. It was not according to the manual, but he wanted it that way.

The People's Liberation Army of Namibia needed successes as much as it needed food and ammunition, and recently there had been more of the latter than the former. The execution of Mercy Shiwala had not been a crushing victory but it had demonstrated SWAPO's ability to reach out and hurt at will. A hundred children and double that number of parents would know that SWAPO was to be feared, its wishes respected, and above all that the South Africans could not be relied on to protect them.

Mazambaan had carried out death-list raids before, most of them successful, some of them acclaimed. He was not much motivated by politics and had used his compulsory copy of 'The Soviet Army is a Safeguard of Peace' as toilet paper but his job was killing and he enjoyed it.

All was well with him now – and they were back in Angola. There was a quimbo, a small village, about three kilometres ahead and slightly eastwards if he remembered rightly. It might be as well to see what they had to offer.

All the quimbo had to offer was shade, so Mazambaan took that. The people were pitifully poor. Their oxen looked diseased and their mahango was crawling, their children were withered and the place stank. The shade, however, was good. Dominating the central clearing a fine grey leadwood tree spread its boughs. Mazambaan sat at its base, waited for his body to cool, then drank some of his water. Leadwood trees were regarded by the tribal Hereros as the ancestors of their nation. He could not

94

imagine where they had got that from. *Omumborum-bonga*, they called them. The thought of being the descendant of a tree did not hold much appeal for him. But then neither did the idea of not knowing anything of his parents or his ancestry. He did not look like a Herero. They had different features. They were not anywhere near as big and broad as he was, but there were many exceptions. What, he wondered, if he were related to this very tree. Mazambaan laughed out loud.

'What is it?'

The question came from a small wiry little Owambo, Daniel Aluteni. If there had been room for a second in command in Mazambaan's platoon Daniel would have been it.

'Daniel,' Mazambaan asked, 'comrade Daniel, you know who your mother and father are. You know where your kraal is, who your brothers and sisters are, you know all that?'

'Yes, I do.'

'Does it make you feel as though you have a home, somewhere to go, a place for you when you die?'

Daniel shrugged. He wondered what his commander was getting at. Fireside talk in the heat of the day . . . He did not like the village, did not like the smell of the place or its proximity to the border and did not want to loiter there. Mazambaan was a good commander, but he took too many chances. He shrugged again, shook his head, and hoped it would discourage further talk. It did not.

'Daniel, do you know that the Hereros have a custom of taking their children and giving them to grandparents or relatives or friends to rear and they take other children in exchange and bring them up? Did you know that?'

'Not the Christian ones,' Daniel answered. 'The Christian ones don't do that any more.'

'Yes, they do. Not so much, but they do.' Mazambaan was adamant and annoyed. Daniel edged away from his leader. He was not in any way interested in the Hereros. All that he was interested in at that moment was getting going again. He tried to bring the subject round to his purpose.

'Do you wish me to change the guards I placed outside, or will we be moving on soon?' Daniel's job was sentries. He posted and positioned them. At that moment there were two men next to a big twin ant hill outside the southern palisade and another at the entrance to the kraal, but their vision was restricted to the bushline surrounding them. It wasn't all that good.

'We'll move soon, comrade. You worry too much.'

Daniel walked to the palisade and peered through a chink in the heavy poles. To the headman's credit he had made a good stockade. The stakes were well dug in and the wall was solid. His two sentries at the ant hill were staring boredly more or less in the right direction. They seemed as unconcerned as Mazambaan, but they were fools, and their commander certainly was not that.

Daniel had been with Mazambaan for many years. They had trained together at Fazenda, in Angola, and later in Dar-es-Salaam. Then Mazambaan had been selected for specialist leadership training at Prvolnye, in Russia, and a year later they had come together again. He thought he understood his commander. Mazambaan, constantly played a game of 'I dare you to', with himself. It could be that he had grown so used to it that he was not aware of it, but it was there. Often, over the years he had watched him in times of gut-twisting danger. Where most men would have fled, he had loitered, waded around the edge like a man who swims while the crocodile sleeps. It was not lack of concern. It was a love of the water.

Mazambaan was just as aware as he that they should be away from that place. There was something in him though, something that would not let him move until he had bathed in the danger just a little longer. One day the crocodile would get him. Mazambaan was looking at him thoughtfully. 'You think the *boers* are on our trail, don't you Daniel?'

'They could be . . . Yes, I think so.'

'Why do you think that, comrade?'

Mazambaan stood up and they walked at his pace to the outside of the kraal stockade.

'I don't know. I think we're taking a chance here, that's all.'

The guards at the twin ant hill saw Mazambaan coming and snapped up a little, but Mazambaan was not much interested in them. He stood for a moment studying the shrub line. Then he said: 'I agree with you Daniel. They are coming, and this is what we're going to do.'

McGee watched the kraal for a few minutes through his binoculars. There was not much to see. A sound mopani palisade about three metres high enclosed the living quarters with a live thorn hedge on the eastern perimeter holding some cattle. Centrally a spreading leadwood gave shade to those within, and patches of yellow reed thatch were visible here and there. That was it. He slowly swung his binoculars back across the settlement. But for the oxen, there was no life, not a piccanin, not a woman working the fields, nothing. The place was designated Quimbo 333 on his operational map. Quimbo 333 was poison.

McGee had not liked the way the tracks had suddenly cut eastwards a little while back. He had not liked the unhurried pace they had represented. And he did not now like the idea of having to cross 300 metres of open ground to reach the most off-key looking kraal in Angola. But he had no option. Either the thirteen SWAPO men were there, in which case they would have to take them out, or they were not, and the hunt would continue. Either way he had to get to the Quimbo 333 to find out.

They hit the field at a steady trot, Corporal Hosi's ten men with Felix's lethal RPG launcher to beef them up and, disregarding the manual for the second time that day, McGee moved with them. They jogged across the furrows, the stalk stumps of cropped millet scrunching underfoot, the sun warming their backs. At 200 metres one could pick out the individual poles of the palisade, gnarled into a fence as twisted as an old man's locked fingers.

A twin-shaped termite mound came into view. His men were closing formation now. He could hear their angry breathing and the rasp of webbing. Then, like a line of rugby three-quarters with the try line at their mercy, they rushed the Quimbo.

From fifty metres the enemy tore into them. A machine gun hammered, then an AK in support, then the air was alive with the crack of bullets. McGee felt his rifle kicking in his hands. It was all instinct now. There was a low ditch ahead and he dived for it, the earth around him erupting as it caught the venom.

The fire, most of it, was coming from the natural crenel between the ant hills. No bullet would penetrate there, but Felix's missile could. With a massive blast it did. The fury of it hurtled one cone skywards like a rocket ship, its twin smashed into a million pieces. The machine gunner there should have been killed. Mad with shock, he stood up and a dozen bullets took him.

The AK was still on to them, firing in short accurate bursts from the western side of the palisade. Hosi's men flayed the position, and from the bush line on his flank he was getting support as well, more than he needed. And suddenly it was over; the sound of firing was over, replaced now by the sound of crying. Someone, a woman, was crying desolately from inside an otherwise totally quiet kraal.

There was no escaping the sound. Keening, it rose and fell, fastened on to them and accused them. And of course they were guilty. That was fact. It was a fact, too, that there would be more shooting, regardless of the crossfire casualties. That was the way of it. Because according to McGee's arithmetic three or four subtracted from thirteen left a major fire fight still to come. But when?

He realized 'when' almost too late to avert the trap Hosi's stick was about to walk into. But he was in time.

The men they had fought and killed were decoys. They were also meant to give the impression of being the total SWAPO force, and they could have achieved just that but for old Johannes's acacia thorns. Had he snapped up the pawns, yelling victory and swarmed up the board with his main pieces, they would have been decimated. It had to be something of a black Attila they were up against.

The entrance gate to the kraal was on the northern run of the palisade, the far side. That was the key square, and that was precisely the square where Hosi's men were heading when he called quickly, 'Hosi! Stop!' and then, 'Bring the men back, not all at once, not too fast.'

Once they were back with him, McGee spelt out his fears, and as he spoke it became even clearer to him that he was right. 'They're on the other side, not in the kraal at all. They're in the bush over there, facing the kraal, waiting for us to wander around the gate so they can nail us in the open.'

'Or maybe,' put in Hosi, 'waiting for all the men to be brought into the Quimbo.'

He could have been right. McGee drew a little sketch in the sand of the kraal and the tree line where he thought the enemy position was and the direction of attack. Then he bent to his radio and had a short but obviously satisfactory conversation there, for when he again lifted his head he was smiling. He said, 'We haven't got much time, Hosi. Let's get into the Quimbo – but not through the front door.'

They blew a hole in the base of the palisade with a charge of RDX and crawled in like rats . . . Like most Kwanyama kraals, the place was a labyrinth of narrow passageways and openings arranged with high mopani fences in an order that no stranger would comprehend. The crying woman they found in the sleeping quarters, cradling the limp body of a young man. She did not even see them as they rushed past. Others did, though. An old man cowered in the shadow of a hut. A mother turned and ran wailing with her child, a skin and bone dog snarled and yapped.

'Over here, this way.' It was Hosi's voice. He had found

the key to the maze and the rats followed him to the central clearing under the leadwood tree. Chevroned SWAPO boot prints were everywhere there. The rest was straightforward. They re-grouped behind the northern palisade, spread out and searched for gaps that would make firing posts. Some of them leopard-crawled into the cattle kraal and scooped positions under the thorn hedge. McGee, ignoring the manure there, joined them and waited. The essence of his whole operation now was in the timing. It had to be perfect.

McGee's first action when he heard the choppers was to stand and hurl a red smoke grenade to the limit of his ability towards the tree line. Before it had even landed his men had opened up with everything they had. A fiery-tailed rocket from Felix's RPG flashed across the open, and then they were drawing fire. The People's Liberation Army were shooting back and shooting well.

They were shooting well until the Alouette gunships thundered across the battle front, each with a pair of .50 Brownings poking from the doors. They had had time to dig in, but it did not help much. The hail of half-inch slugs tore the ground apart, shredded the tree trunks and ripped into the human flesh. Not all of them were hit. Some of them were still shooting when Hosi's men stood up, yelling their battle cry 'Avance! Avance!' and charged across the open.

McGee was with them but they were not having it all their own way. The man next to him toppled as the gunships roared overhead, their blades thrashing the sand into a storm of stinging dust and grit. A white-hot searing explosion, just ahead of him, tore away McGee's hat and left him gasping in a grey haze, but still running. The next grenade seemed to punch him bodily. He jack-knifed into a mopani trunk with force enough to buckle the magazines in his chest webbing. His rifle flew heavenwards. The grass around him burst into flames and with the thought, 'Thank Christ we've reached the tree line!' he blacked out.

It was a good minute or two before McGee found his world shimmering back into focus. He felt no real pain, just a terrible inner numbness. His ears were ringing and his vision had neither depth nor dimension. A blind man, however, would have seen the danger there. Except for his enclave, the dry grass and bush were heavily ablaze and torches of fire were leaping for the timber. He could feel the acid heat of it in his eyes, roasting his skin. The whole woodland was about to go up. Shielding his face, he staggered upright and ran from it.

He could hear the ripping and hammering of gunpowder and he ran straight towards that, flailing his way through the thickets, anger pumping energy back into his limbs.

He passed a dead man, a terrorist wearing a Castro cap with a leather pouch slung like a bus conductor across his chest. The man's AK rifle was stretched out in his buckled arms like an offering. McGee took it, worked the breech mechanism and crashed on.

The next terrorist was not dead. He was very much alive and on the move. They did not see each other until they all but collided and then McGee was marginally better positioned to act. He dived sideways, drawing his rifle on to target and pulling the trigger. The AK did not fire. Mazambaan's did. A sledge hammer met with McGee's right shoulder, battered him down, overpowered him. For an instant there was nothing, a total absence of any sense. Then more vividly and more real than life should allow came a dusty sweat-streaked black face, a snarling set of perfect white teeth, a down-sweeping wooden rifle butt; impact, and wave upon wave upon wave of crashing, searing, bright red, mind-breaching pain.

Chapter 7

The comet of my mind is all I am, in hurtling endless flight through passages of colour as substanceless thoughts, as yet unthought. Abandoned, detached and more lost than vanished time. I am beyond alone. Do not call me, I cannot come . . .

The voice was calling again. For an eternity it had been touching him, sometimes so softly that it was lost in the clutter of colour, sometimes fastening on to him like a magnet. Then it was present, not strong but enduring, the words vague because of the distance. He was aware of the great distance, an eternity. He was aware, too, of the tone of the voice. It was of warmth, of the womb. He wanted to go to it, to turn from his endless outwards flight, to find the source of it, to go there, to stay there. And suddenly he was there for an instant of burnished clarity.

'You're alive!'

Then he was spinning away again. But he had been there and now there was a memory of not just tone but words with meaning and pain, savage pain.

'You're alive.'

With life there was pain. If he knew that, then he must know other things as well. The meaning: why was he here? And where was he? He was not flying any more at that frightening electric speed. He was travelling, but there was a major difference. He had substance. He had what seemed to be a disunited body accompanying him, and there was something else, something that had not travelled with him before; a confusion of constant pain.

It took time, a lot of time, for him to realize that it was

not just pain. It was *his* pain, and was not just going to go away. It seemed all around him at the same time, everywhere, all at once. It took still longer to locate it to his upper body, high and right. He tried to pull away from it but that increased the agony. There was a place beyond where everything could be lost. The pain too. It would be easy to let go. The womb voice reached him again. 'Fight for your life . . .'

'Matthew, you've got a reason to live.'

What stupid words! He was not dying. He wanted to let go now, to slip back to where he had been, for a while to rid himself of his tortured flesh. That was all.

'Matthew, you're alive, you're alive.'

With life there was pain. Did it have to be so monstrous? The voice would not let him be. It was leading him on and away and he followed it . . .

There was not that much sun that a man coming round after a five-day coma would notice. But it was there, trimmed into big warm benevolent squares by the west-facing recovery ward windows. McGee looked around or rather attempted to, but the lead weight that was his head would not co-operate. The best he could manage was a confused roll of his eyeballs slowly from one side of the ward to the other. The deduction this observation brought was that he was somewhere other than in familiar surroundings. He was somewhere where he had no desire to be. He moved to sit up, screamed in agony, and awoke again fourteen hours later.

With years of inured custom to guide it, McGee's internal hourglass had brought him from slumber just before dawn. He was dripping and soaked with sweat and with him was that lingering betwixt feeling that one suffers who has been jerked away from a terrible dream. A disjointed, ugly panoply of impressions was clamouring to be revived, but they would not come. All he could remember was a face – a snarling black face.

His head was throbbing and his comprehension wafting like a feather. His right shoulder area was scoured with pain and he was thirstier than a desert. But he knew where he was. He was in a hospital.

This time he managed to look around. The ward was in white. Even in the dull first light he could see that. The curtain rails squaring off the beds were white and all around him were high cot sides like prison bars. They were white too except where they had been chipped down to metal. There were a number of other beds in the ward. Some looked empty, some occupied. Those were difficult to see. When the ceiling lights came on, the neon brilliance was too much. A chair close to the left side of his head squeaked and a voice said, 'So you're awake, lieutenant, that's wonderful.'

It was a nice voice, but not *the* voice. It was not the voice he had most wanted to hear. The cot sides were dropped with a clank, and a cool hand felt for his wrist pulse. McGee dragged loose his tongue from the mire of his palate and implored, 'Water!'

She said, 'Not too much then' and a beaker materialized under his nose. It was water, that was all, but it was like rain in the dorstland. It filled him with optimism. He wanted more and said so. The beaker, however, was withheld.

The nurse came into view, a chubby little thing with freckles and a warm smile. She plumped up his pillows, busied herself with a manometer cuff, took his blood pressure, temperature, then went on to check something in an area where he had rather she did not.

'Catheter,' she said, but McGee did not register. Quite a few other nurses had stopped at his bed now. One said something about sleeping beauty, another queried his right to have had them all so worried. None of them, however, was the possessor of 'the voice'.

He was washed and cleaned and dried. His back was massaged and his hair was combed. His bed linen was changed and his pillows rearranged, and he detested it all. They were wonderful to him, gentle and kind – and all he wanted was to be left alone. Suddenly he *was* alone. The linen trolley was trundled out. The drapes suspended around his bed were swished closed, and that was it. The curtains on Act One had been drawn and he had never felt more isolated, dispirited and helpless. With those emotions as company he closed his eyes.

Act Two started in broad daylight with Major Kowalski's booming voice propelling McGee on to a quick slide to consciousness. 'How are you, young fella? You're in hospital. In Pretoria. Did they tell you that . . . No, well, that's where you are. You were lucky.'

The man had an RAF moustache and the personality to match it. He was, he announced to his patient, a surgeon, some kind of surgeon, McGee did not catch the first part. He had a torch which he beamed into McGee's unsuspecting eyes, and lots of strong fingers with which he prodded and poked his way around McGee's body. He seemed to know what he was doing and he fired rapid instructions at a splendidly aloof woman whom he addressed as Sister. 'Take him off IV, Plasmalyte B – yes, – good. Clear fluids only for the time being, eh. Physiotherapy from tomorrow, right.'

McGee was instructed to follow an index finger that was jabbed past his eyes like a benediction, then subjected to the indignity of having the soles of his feet and palms scratched with what felt like a kitchen fork.

'Can you feel it, fella?'

Yes, he could feel it. Sister was told, 'Get the cath out.'

McGee was told that everything would be fine, he was going to be given a few tablets and everything would be fine. He wanted to ask the major a few questions, the uppermost being what had happened to get him where he was, and what to do about getting out. He did not get a chance, though. Dr Kowalski had done a quick about-face and with Sister regally in tow, had plunged beyond the curtains.

During the rest of the day the doctor's instructions were carried out in detail. Like a red hot wire the catheter was extracted, a sign that read NIL BY MOUTH that had been suspended above his head rails was removed, as was the bottle of Plasmalyte B with its dangling plastic hose and bayonet of a needle. He drank some soup and some glucose cordial and later urinated shards of glass into what the nurse holding it referred to as the potty. But most important of all, he started to move his body.

First his toes. He wriggled them around, then began forcing his calves and thighs to contract. If the physio was coming tomorrow, that was fine. He was starting now. The fingers on his left hand were responding, the bicep and tricep too. He did some deep breathing, slow breaths in and out, then worked at his stomach muscles, sucking them in as a yoga teacher had once shown him. All that remained was his right shoulder and arm. He had left that until last, and now he could not procrastinate any longer. He drew in his breath and held on to it.

He had been expecting pain and that was what he got. It was raw and it ran into him like a sabre thrust. It crushed the breath from him and swamped his mind. He could not do it. He simply could not. But he did and he did it again. He worked his way into the pain, then pressed through it. He was covered in sweat, and when it was time to swallow Dr Kowalski's drugs no one had to force him. They pulled up his cot sides, smoothed him out and tucked him in like a baby. The voice was not among those present. He listened carefully but it was not there. He slept.

The voice was not there the next morning either. McGee was awake and alert long before the lights came on. He had even done his own workout. The night staff came in and did their thing with the bedpans and the bottles and the BPs and charts. Then he was delivered to the physiotherapists and spent an agonizing day with men taken apart by the rage of war: men without legs, men without arms; men without penises. He wondered if Kowalski had told them they were lucky too. 'Lucky to be alive, fella.' *Jesus Christ*, what barbarous things man did to man in the name of ideology!

That day he stopped thinking about the voice and came

to terms with his conscious mind, which had been telling him all along that it had been an illusion: a defence mechanism of a mind being prodded by the staff of death.

When he did his flexing exercises again that evening there was not so much pain and his mobility was greater. He was on the mend and went to sleep happy that he had done his best that day to advance his date of discharge from hospital.

So he continued, his shoulder wound dressing becoming lighter every day. He took delight in watching the bullet entry wound close and the livid scar tissue creep in. He had, according to Dr Kowalski, been lucky the bullet had entered just under his clavicle, leaving his shoulder joint mainly undamaged. It had tunnelled the upper pectoralis major and struck the scapula, mushroomed and tracked downwards tearing a gaping cavity in his teres muscles. As for his cranium, the concussion had fractured the parietal bone on the left of his skull but the underlying parietal lobe had taken only minor damage. McGee felt he was probably at odds with Kowalski as to the true meaning of the word luck. No one could tell him what had happened to shower him so liberally with such good fortune.

'It was not on your report. Can't you remember a thing?' Dr Kowalski had been asking him that same question for the last four days and McGee giving him the same answer.

'Not a bloody thing, I don't even remember getting up that morning.'

'You remember the previous night?'

McGee had answered that question before too. 'Yes, I remember going on patrol and following a spoor.'

'Does the name, Mungo, mean anything to you?'

'I know the place. It's a quimbo on the operational maps, just inside the Angolan border. It's Army designation is 333.'

'Yes, well, that's where your fire fight took place. I've been doing a bit of homework on you. Casualty reports are notoriously skimpy on detail. I've asked for a copy of

the patrol report but you know what the army's like . . .
You'll probably come up with the whole thing long before
they do. Something will jog your memory, maybe today,
maybe in a year, who knows? Retrograde amnesia isn't
pleasant but it isn't fatal either.' Kowalski enjoyed his
own humour.

'So when do I get out of here?'

'My dear Lieutenant, learn to be a little more patient. I
know it's hard. You're young and you've made marvellous
progress . . . really marvellous but I can't say when you'll
be discharged. There are still more tests to be done. I
want you to have a brain scan soon and if that's as good as
I expect it to be, you can start working out in the gym next
week. How's your walking coming on?'

Walking! He was all but sprinting, he told the surgeon.
'Good show . . . keep it up and who knows . . .' confided
Kowalski. 'You've done well, fella.'

'Very well indeed!' agreed a voice from just behind him.

So his conscious mind had lied to him. There it was
again. '*Very* well indeed.' McGee was almost afraid to
turn round in case it disappeared once more. He did,
though, twisting slowly as though any sharp movement
would startle.

'I beg your pardon.'

He addressed that comment to the owner of a pair of
kingfisher eyes that was all he saw for the moment. Then
the lips moved and said: 'I said you've done remarkably
well . . . since I last saw you.' The lips were beautiful, the
face the same. She had hair, gold like bundled cumulus on
a setting sun.

McGee completed his revolution, leaving Kowalski to
do as he wished, and sat with his legs dangling from the
bed. He found himself staring like an imbecile, behaving
like one too. She said, 'I'm Sister Christie' and extended a
hand which he took, hanging on to it then like a spaniel
with its first bird. Then, instead of saying anything
sensible, he continued: 'I've been looking for you.' It
sounded so stale. 'I mean, I heard your voice . . .'

108

For the first time he could remember McGee felt his cheeks flushing in the presence of a woman. He blustered on a bit about the voice but it all came out wrong. It sounded like a graceless and probably unoriginal pass so he ended it with 'I can't seem to say what I want to say. I really didn't mean . . .'

'Listen,' Sister Christie interrupted, 'I've got to do rounds with Dr Kowalski now. I'll pop back later and we'll talk. How does that sound?'

It sounded fine, McGee told her. Cursing inwardly he lay back on his pillows. More than ever he had to get out of there. He had two major projects to attend to now. The first, was to get out of hospital. The second – well that was to build upon the ashes of his first encounter with the girl who possessed the angel's voice.

Later, when rounds were finished, McGee waylaid Kowalski in an interward passageway. 'When am I going to get out of here? I'm sick of this bloody place . . . look at me, I can walk . . . I can talk . . . I can move my limbs . . . look . . . .' He flapped his arms like a bird. 'Just give me a date, doctor, so I know where I am.'

Dr Kowalski looked at him thoughtfully. He said, 'Walk with me to reception and we'll talk.'

Kowalski as usual did most of the talking. He could, he said, understand McGee's frustration. But McGee would get used to it. It really was not so bad.

'Give me a date,' McGee pleaded, 'something I can work towards, look forward to.'

Kowalski would not be pinned down. He asked McGee to raise his right arm. 'Go on lift it higher, higher. Ha! You see – you can't. When we've finished with you that won't be a problem. You need longer sessions in physiotherapy. Also, you could get dizzy spells, vertigo. I'm surprised you haven't had vertigo.' He turned earnestly to McGee. 'You haven't had vertigo, have you?' McGee said he had not and watched Dr Kowalski walk through the portals of freedom.

Sure enough, he had a dizzy spell. That evening, as

though cursed by the doctor's words, it came on. He was talking to a neighbour when a sparrow fluttered through the open window and into the ward. McGee looked up and the next moment found himself lurching across a drunkenly spinning room searching for a handhold. Five minutes later he was fine. It frightened him, but the thought of more tests and more Kowalski frightened him more.

Sister Christie kept her promise. Just before she went off duty at 19.30 she came and chatted with a few of them in the ward. When it was McGee's turn he deliberately kept the subject light and steered it away from anything to do with the hospital or his progress. She was from the wine valleys of Stellenbosch so he spoke about the beauty of the Cape. Her father was also in the services so he talked about the army as a career. Who was her father? Where was he stationed? Oh, he was Admiral Christie and he was stationed at the fleet base at Simonstown. An Admiral of the fleet! Christ! McGee was not sure but he might just have blinked. They spoke for a little longer, then it was time for her to go.

He set himself a deadline for getting out of hospital. Ten days it was to be. He vowed to himself that night that there would be no let up. He would meet his deadline. And he did, in nine days in fact. With his transient vertigo and his livid purple bullet brand as a memory of the darkest hours of his life, he walked through the front doors of Number One Military Hospital and into the bright Pretoria sun. He had a 30-day pass in his pocket — more than enough time to create a fairytale. 'There was once an Admiral's daughter . . .'

He was going. Sister Christie, standing well back from the window, watched the man ramble over the prissy grass verges bordering the old hospital and step towards the army duty bus idling in the avenue.

She was not in the habit of watching discharged patients for longer than it took for them to ambulate through the swing doors of the ward. She liked her goodbyes to be short and sweet, well, short, anyway.

The man turned once and looked intently back, then climbed aboard. A very special person, she thought. They were so damn hard to find, and then impossible to hold. The engine revved and the bus pulled slowly away. Not that she had wanted to hold him. It was not that. In fact the man had disturbed her, had interrupted the rhythm of a well resolved life, had upset her terribly, right from the start.

When *had* it really started? The afternoon he had been propelled into her ward, his fine body smelling of war flopped across the theatre trolley? Perhaps it had been then, she was not sure. More likely it had happened in the desperate days that followed.

Maybe it had started the night she first sat next to his body and spoke words of encouragement to a mind that was not fighting back. Talking through a coma was not a novel experience for her, nor for any nurse. To say she had simply spoken to the man, though, that would have been detracting from the truth.

She had willed strength into his body, consciously drawing upon her own reserves with a solicitude that debilitated her. She had talked to him as earnestly, closely and lovingly as one would address a stricken son . . . The days had passed, however, and the man had weakened.

Something else had occurred at the same time. The battle for life that should have been confined to the area behind the screens of Bed twenty two started to overflow its conventional boundaries. It became a thing that flooded in from the moment she opened her eyes to day's end.

She had not wanted it. Oh, no. It had just happened, and by the time she realized what *was* happening it was too late. Willy-nilly, she had found herself on an emotional slide at a breathtaking rate to God knew where.

She had told herself that it was strictly not sensible. That was the truth. Sternly she had warned herself that it

111

was not right, she had to stop. Emotions, however, once under way show notoriously little regard for prim good sense and righteousness. Sister Christie found out soon enough that in the breakers of human passion a life-raft packed with ethics gives scant support.

The afternoon McGee awakened she had been thrilled and frightened. She had been due to attend a course of High Care Technology . . . She had fled.

There, among the cardiac monitors in the High Care Unit, Sister Christie had rehabilitated her heart. Amid the life-support systems she had reclinicalized her soul. She was fine, she was cured. She ventured back into the Ward bursting with new knowledge and confidence . . .

That was until the man had turned to her and said: 'I've been looking for you . . . I heard your voice, you see.'

Now he was going. Sister Christie had taken a shade more trouble with her appearance that morning. She had treated her hair and dabbed on her most precious perfume. He had stood towering over her and said: 'I wanted to give you a present before I left. It was supposed to have been delivered here this morning.'

'A present?'

Yes, a present. He was really disappointed, he said, the present had not come and now he had to go. Could he contact her, would that be convenient.

'Oh, yes. That would be fine. Wonderful.'

Sister Christie watched the bus draw away, then turned back to the ward. Patients always said they would stay in contact. They never did, though. A trolley was being wheeled into the ward. There was work to be done.

McGee's first action after alighting from the duty bus in Pretoria's bustling heart was to look for an affordable motor car. It took patience and legwork but by mid-morning he had what he wanted – a VW beetle with a twice-around clock, a reconditioned engine and four good tyres.

More patience and he found what else he was seeking, a

not over-large wild life painting, a kudu at a waterhole. If he had commissioned the work it couldn't have been more to his taste. He loved it. The dealer loved it. It was a steal, according to the man. So he took it, and wondering what artists did with all their cash, he made his way back to the used car lot to see if the VW was ready. It was.

He found himself accommodation on the outskirts of town: a nice old-fashioned residential hotel with a nice old-fashioned proprietress who called him '*seun*' and meant it.

The sole telephone was in the hall. McGee was not one for lying, not if there was any other way out. 'I've got your present,' he told a delighted Sister Christie. 'They lost the address, can you beat that!' No she couldn't beat it. No, she was not doing anything that night. Yes, he could pick her up. Yes, nine would be fine.

At 21.00 – not a second before or after – he rang the little brass bell on her front door, which was opened by a girl in a full blue frock whose blonde hair tumbled loosely over her shoulders, who smelt warmly of bubble bath and shampoo and, was the twin of Sister Christie, only even more lovely. She was beautiful. She took his profferred arm and said her name was Patricia. McGee walked her to his car and waved open the door for her, for Sister Patricia Christie.

They decided on a restaurant that specialized in Swiss cuisine prepared by real Swiss chefs. While they waited for their order McGee handed her the painting and said, 'Don't open it. Before you do I want to tell you something. It's rather an unusual present, you see, not the sort of thing a patient usually gives to a ward sister on discharge. But then a patient doesn't usually go through the experiences this one did.'

He told her of his experience beyond ordinary consciousness. He told her how he could never have been able to return but for the voice that had somehow transcended eternity to reach him, to grasp the hurtling nothingness that had been him, and draw him back to life. He said, 'It was your voice, Patricia.'

The present, he said, was in appreciation for his life. He said she could open it, then he restrained her. There was something further he wanted to tell her. 'It's not just that, either. I bought that for you because I think you are very special person. There're no strings attached, believe me. It's just that I wanted to give you something that was meaningful . . . Please open it now.'

In the soft lights of the restaurant the painting looked different, a little less defined than he had remembered it. He watched her face anxiously, especially her eyes. They told him it was all right. She stood the painting on a chair under a wall light and looked at it for what seemed like an hour, then turned her face to him and spoke so softly he had to lean closer to hear. 'Matthew, thank you. This painting is one of the most beautiful things I've ever been given.'

The food came. They laughed a lot and talked about every subject under the sun – every subject except his father. McGee told her bluntly he did not want to talk about his parents absence from his sick bed. Other clients drifted across to admire the kudu which made McGee very proud and Patricia very happy.

She had been so stupid to run away from this man. He was perfect for her. Could any girl be as lucky? They finished with coffee and liqueur, and suddenly his hand was seeking hers. That changed everything. It was not just dinner out any more, things were not going to end with coffee and liqueurs.

Like strangers at a dance, their fingers met; lightly touching until the nervousness was gone, until they had discovered how exciting it was to press a little harder and weave the fingers deeper. If hands could mate, their hands were mating. That was how it was when they left the restaurant and, by the time they had reached the flat, nothing had changed but the intensity of what they were feeling.

They kissed, lightly at first, his lips gliding from hair to forehead to cheek and back again, until, as though by accident, their lips touched, and then joined until their tongues were hunting in the wetness of each other's mouths.

She had not left a light on and was glad of it. As far as bodies went, hers, she knew, was good, excepting for breasts that were too small.

There was a minute that was all zippers, buttons and anxious silent tugging. There was no dignity in that and the darkness was a friend. Then the hardness of him was behind her and hands were cupping her breasts and he was whispering, 'beautiful, beautiful, beautiful.'

She turned and he stretched his stance. They were groin to groin, nipple to nipple. Then, as though by some secret signal, for both of them, it was time.

Patricia was in love. How she had not known it before that night was a mystery to her. At six o'clock in the morning she ran herself a hot bath and together with the bed sheet that carried the memoir of virginity, and a cup of coffee, she sank into the torpid water.

He had been a wonderful lover. The fact that she had not been in bed with a man before could not obscure that certainty. He had done everything a man could do, unhurriedly and gently. Even so her vagina felt tender . . . She wondered how many women he had been with. There must have been many. How did he know to do those things with his tongue . . . ? She wiggled her toes and sank even deeper into the water and wanted him again.

She was in love. No matter how many women he had had; no matter what he had done all his life, she was in love. However, Matthew McGee had better watch out. His talent would have to be exclusively employed in future.

It was direct dialling to her father's farm in Stellenbosch and Admiral Christie picked up the phone after the first ring. 'Christie.'

'Daddy, it's me.'

'Trish, my darling, how are you?' She could almost hear the smile in his voice. 'What can I do for my lovely girl?'

'Daddy, I'm fine . . . I just phoned you up to say hello.'

'Oh, really,' his voice was disbelieving. 'Well, I'm always happy to say hello. Tell me what's happening in the capital city.'

'I met a super guy, Daddy, an army lieutenant. He was wounded, a casivac. He's got thirty days' leave, daddy, and I've got some leave due to me too. You know I haven't taken full leave for years. I was wondering . . .'

'Hold on. Hold on. Not so fast. An army lieutenant? Is Mr Wonderful a Permanent Force officer?'

'Yes.'

'You haven't even told me what his name is.'

'McGee. Matthew McGee.'

'McGee as in M-C-G-E-E?'

'Yes. He's a super guy, Daddy, a special person. I want to bring him down to the Cape to the farm. He needs the quiet. I think he . . .'

'What does McGee think? Have you asked him what he wants?'

'Not yet but . . .'

'Trish, don't. I just know my daughter. You go and ask McGee if *he* wants to come down to Stellenbosch. The farm life isn't for everyone you know. Goedehoop may bore him to death.'

'It won't, Daddy. He was brought up on a farm. He's going to love it there. Of course I'm going to ask him. I just wanted to check with you first.'

'Trish, if you like this McGee and you want to bring him down, that's fine by me. You're a good judge of character. He must be one of the good guys.'

'He is. Believe me he is.'

'Phone me if it works out then. Don't just pitch up or there won't be anyone to meet you.'

'I'll phone you tomorrow, Daddy.'

Patricia Christie walked back to her bathroom. 'Of course he'll want to go,' she said to herself. 'I love you!' – how many times hadn't he kissed those words into her mouth the previous night. Did 'I love you' have the same meaning for him as it did for her? Suddenly, damn it, she was not so sure.

116

Chapter 8

'Tell me a bit about yourself, McGee. I think I should know a bit more about you, don't you?'

McGee had been half expecting some such question since the previous afternoon, when, perhaps a little less self-assured than his bearing seemed to suggest, he had taken Patricia Christie's elbow and helped her from the warm cosseting Boeing belly of Flight SAA 301 into a belligerent 55-knot Cape south-east blow and Rear Admiral Christie's waiting, paternal and (in no small measure) protective arms.

In Christie's Range Rover they had driven from Cape Town to lovely Stellenbosch. To McGee, though he had not been there before, it had felt like coming home. Lining every street, grand old oak trees that must have seen three centuries of urban endeavour seemed to offer a special welcome in their shade. The south-easter, deflated by the guardian mountains girding the old town, had been no more than a cooling whisper there, dusting over the gables and thatch and kissing clean the grape vines on the slopes. It was a place, he thought, God could have looked down on and been proud to call his own.

McGee loved it. He'd have liked to stop there and just gaze at it, be a burger of that enchanting place. But Christie was driving and elected to drive on. There had been more magic, though, much more: a dappled dirt drive scored yesterday by steel rims and oxen leading to a mountain that rose up bursting with afternoon sun, corded with green vines at its feet, its massive shoulders folded in a cloak of golden kloofs and buttresses that lasted to the sky.

A voice had said, 'That's the Simonsberg.' Father or daughter, McGee did not recall. What he did remember

117

was that the mountain, Simonsberg, had beckoned to him as more than stone can call to flesh and blood. He was in the most beautiful valley in the world. He had sensed in Stellenbosch that he was nearing home. On the gentle sloping farmlands of Goedehoop he knew it.

Home had been there waiting for the road to dodge towards it. A Cape Dutch opstal wedged in the lap of the mountain, all Batavian elegance, limewashed gables with walls 'drie stene dik', and high grey thatch; more old oak trees, a yard full of curious soft-eyed Jersey cows, a growling tractor and the piquant smell of new grape must . . . They had arrived.

No questions had been asked over the table that night. There was just lighthearted, sometimes slightly tense conversation – almost all to do with the past. They had eaten tender beef and drunk some estate Cabernet 'as full and proud as any Bordeaux wine'. No, there had not been questions, but McGee had felt the Admiral's eyes probing him, like an awl testing material for signs of decay. They drank more wine and talked some more, before saying goodnight.

McGee's quarter was the loft beneath the great bare-adzed oak beams and thatch, the floor 'brand solder' clay and solid. There was a little window there that looked out on to the moonlit mountain that Simon van der Stel had claimed as being his. There, in a deep and old stuffed chair, he had surrendered himself to the night, gazing out at the black berg, slipping from reality to dream and back again until fantasy and truth were one and the same.

McGee's first night's sleep at Goedehoop was in marked contrast to his earlier sense of peace and home-coming. He was back on patrol with Hosi and Denga and the others. The mountain was there, bigger than life, and he climbed it all night long with leaden pack and rifle; waking with a bullet-impact jolt, sweating, disoriented and fending off something that held him in thrall until he threw wide the window and breathed in the valley mist.

It was just before first light and there was no sound from the house, no sound from below. He wondered if anyone else was awake.

He rummaged in his kit for shorts and his kudu skin boots, then went down the outside steps leading to the ground – and found he was not the only one awake. In the moonlight on the klinker brick stoep Christie was sitting, smoking. Had he been there all night? McGee smelt the aroma of his tobacco before he saw him. He felt somehow embarrassed, like a boy caught bunking from dormitory. 'I was going to climb the berg . . .'

Christie said, 'Ah,' as though he understood, and then, 'I thought you might want to do that. I wouldn't mind a climb myself. Do me more good than sitting here wrecking my lungs with this nonsense' – he tapped out his pipe, pocketed it and said, 'It's beautiful on the mountain now.'

They walked together, saying little. They climbed the early slopes and watched the first rays of dawn cut past the peaks and reach for the valley where shadows like big black oceans drew back and delivered up the land. Where the vines stopped and the gradient steepened in earnest, where the fynbos mountain heather began, they paused. All McGee could hear was the call of the guinea fowl and the sudden flutter of a startled pheasant, the distant grumble of cold tractor engines – and the footsteps of his companion.

Christie had been climbing a few paces ahead of him, leading the way. Now he stopped.

'It's beautiful, isn't it?' Christie said, and before McGee could reply, 'Tell me a bit about yourself, McGee? I think I should know a bit more about you . . . don't you?'

The air had a mellowness about it there, a subtle sweet warmth like the breath of a still slumbering lover. Was Christie aware of it too? McGee wondered.

He said, 'Yes, it is beautiful. South West has mountains just as big and majestic, but I don't think I've ever seen such a peaceful valley as this, not anywhere.'

And now there was a question to answer. It was yes – but not because he was ashamed of his background; far from it. He had been reared by a Bushman, had never known his mother, l.ad not felt leather under his soles until he was nine, was an old boy of a veld school that had been hard pressed to field one rugby team.

Christie was standing a little to one side of him, regarding him with his head cocked, waiting for the response he had every right to expect. Christie would not be impressed by what he had to offer, and Christie was the respected father of the girl he loved . . .

Rear Admiral Christie was not the sole key to his daughter: Patricia had a mind of her own, a very good mind, which she could make up herself. But that was not the point. McGee needed the Admiral's approval – and not for his sake only but for their sakes. And he was certainly not going to get that approval by standing gazing into the misty valley below or by apologizing for being in love with the girl down there. But where did you begin answering a question like that: 'Tell me a bit about yourself' – especially when you did not know all there was to know yourself?

So McGee began at the beginning. He began in the wide waterless amurumbas of the Western Kalahari, where, sometimes on foot, more often astride the copper-skinned shoulders of an ever-smiling little man who called you son, you fed from the product of bow arrow and digging stick. When you were there, you learned how to talk to the wind and hear the whispered answer; how to curl yourself so close to a night fire that the flames touched but never burnt; how to stalk like a shadow to hide, if there was nothing else, behind your own fingers or run like a cheetah. You found there was one great friend you never took for granted – water. You learned how to seek it, no matter if it was in tree trunk or tsama melon, bitter from the dead gemsbok belly or cool and sweet and sipable beneath the very sand. You learned all that and so much more and when you had learned it all you went to farm school with a dozen other bare-knuckled kids and beat them to a pulp for calling you a *bossie* and then . . .

McGee turned and regarded the man who had wanted

to know 'a bit more' about him. He knew a bit more, now.
If the man's wish had been to bring a qualified Bushman
into hearth and home, now was his chance. It did not
require a broker, however, to point out to McGee his
considerable deficit in marriage market currency.

It was daylight, wide and white by then, and McGee
was able to study Patricia's father, really study him for the
first time. If he looked a shade taller there than he had
first thought in the voorkamer of Goedehoop, that could
be accounted for by the up slope of the Simonsberg. The
man had an extremely erudite face. He did not look like
an Admiral in anybody's navy. He looked more like a
scientist or a professor. His eyes, however, had changed.
The gimlets were still there but there was an added
shrewdness behind them that McGee had missed the
previous night. He did not doubt for a moment that a
word or a gesture of his hand had gone unanalysed. He
was under the microscope all right, Christie was bisecting
him. He had had a bit to work on, now he wanted more.
'So you never knew your Ma?'

McGee gave an uncompromising 'No'.

'I suppose she was buried on your Dad's old farm?'

Jesus, did he have to! 'Yes, she was.' She was buried in
the silver mangrove thicket near the ever-wailing, labouring wind pump. That was where she was, under a simple
stone cross without so much as a letter chiselled into it,
that used to glow like a luminous thing in the full moon.

'She died of malaria three months after I was born.'

'Ah,' said the Admiral and it was almost a sigh. 'Patricia
didn't know her mother either. She died in childbirth . . .
Do you love my daughter, McGee?' The question was
sudden but not unexpected. He let it settle, let the
Admiral wait for his answer.

'Yes, I do.'

Both men stood there for a while, each with his own
thoughts, then Christie said, 'We can go down for breakfast if you feel hungry. I've got to get going now.' That
was all.

McGee did not feel hungry. He told the Admiral he was

going to continue the climb. He would go down later. Christie advised on the best route then took his leave.

'We'll talk again,' he said. McGee sincerely hoped they would. It was strange in a way, though, the direction in which Christie had delved, had left unsaid anything to do with his college education at boarding school, also his army career – all the things he should have shown an interest in. Perhaps he knew all about them already . . .

McGee watched the diminishing figure of Goedehoop's owner pass through the green vineyards. Stopping here and there to lift a vine and examine the fruit, Rear Admiral Christie moved with the confidence of a success-ful man. McGee watched him until he reached the *holbol* gables of the outbuildings then turned and began to climb. If he had wanted exercise, that was what he got.

Don Christie was in no way upset at having only his daughter's company across the breakfast table. In fact he was pleased they were alone. He had a lot on his mind but strangely for a man accustomed to the curtness of signal bunting and morse he was having extreme difficulty getting under way. It took three coffees and a brace of painstakingly prepared pipes – and by then Patricia could stand it no more. 'Well?' she wanted to know.

'Well what?'

'Oh, Daddy, don't fence with me! You've been sitting on the other side of the table like a smouldering bush fire. If there's something you want to tell me, go right ahead. I'm a big girl now.'

'Fair comment,' said the Admiral. 'Okay, I'll tell you. First let me say I like Matthew McGee, Trish. He's all man. He's got no pretensions and I think he's a straight shooter.'

'How do you mean, you think? Of course he's straight.'

'Yes, yes, yes. I've got no argument with you on that. Okay, he's as straight as you or me. How serious are you about this thing?'

'About Matthew? Dead serious.'

Christie puffed at his pipe reflectively for a moment then balanced it on an ashtray; it was beginning to taste raw after being smoked the better part of the previous night. Patricia's eyes were flashing in challenge across the table. His daughter, he thought, was a stunner. Half the boys in the Western Province were after her, good boys some of them. He smiled at her in an effort to ease the situation. The stunner was not having any of it.

'So?' she charged. 'If he's such a paragon, what's all this about?'

Christie held up his hand for patience. 'Bear with me, girl.' It was an appeal. 'I can see you love the man and I've already said I like him, haven't I? Just hold your horses, okay?'

'Okay.'

'Patricia, you know that it's standard operating procedure for Military Intelligence to run checks on people who . . . well, people who get close to us, to you. You know that?'

She knew, oh yes. She had lived with that with a pragmatic resentment for years.

'It's routine for birth certificates to be turned up, of course, drivers' licences, all that sort of thing. In McGee's case it was easy. All his documents are on file in Defence HQ in Grootfontein. That's standard.'

Christie leaned earnestly across the big yellowwood table separating them. He hoped his daughter would put her hands in his. She did not. She folded her arms and leaned as far back from the table as she could.

'Your young man,' Christie continued, 'had a sworn affidavit in place of a birth certificate. It stated that the original certificate had been lost and that application had been made for a copy document. As McGee was under twenty-one when he first joined the army, the whole thing had been sworn to by his father Daniel McGee and notarized by a Windhoek attorney.'

Christie busied his hands brushing away imaginary breadcrumbs. The pipe also came in for attention. When he looked straight at his daughter she did not waver.

'Yes?' She was responding now with the tranquillity of a plunging barometer. 'Yes, Daddy?'

'Trish, for God's sake why would anyone fake the birth of his own child?'

'The affidavit was a fake?'

'Yes.'

'There was no birth certificate at all?'

'No.'

'The birth had never been registered?'

'Never registered.'

Patricia stood up slowly from the table and walked slowly to the carved imbuia front door. She was frowning slightly, examining the polished brass escutcheon plate as though in its reflection were all the answers. Christie watched her eyes. He felt dirty. 'There's more,' he told his daughter. 'When that discrepancy showed up Military Intelligence went further into the matter.'

'Of course,' said Patricia. 'One has to be thorough.'

'Danny McGee was on record as having married a Susan Penrose, an Australian immigrant, just like himself. Susan Penrose, of course, then became Susan McGee, the mother's name which also appears on the bogus affidavit. Susan Penrose, however, could never have been Matthew McGee's mother because she left Danny McGee and re-emigrated to Australia a whole year before young Matthew was born.'

'Couldn't she have come back?'

'No, she never came back and there's no mistake with the dates either. For some reason or other McGee's father decided to falsify his son's records and never registered the birth. Why, I simply don't know.'

'Did you ask him?'

'Patricia, I don't think he knows. I think, I'm sure in fact he believes . . .'

'Daddy!' The interruption was imperious. Rear Admiral Christie did the unthinkable, he cut himself short.

'Daddy, I simply won't hear any more of this. You're right, I do love Matthew. I love him very much. If there has been some mix-up with documentation, I don't care. I know him. I know what sort of person he is. I love him and I intend to marry him and that's that.'

124

Christie clamped his jaws on his pipe stem and kept them clamped while his daughter was speaking. Having to pit his will against the girl was a new experience for him and there was no enjoyment in it. They had seldom disagreed in the past and to outsiders had always presented a united front. Now this. This outsider and this rift.

'I tell you, Daddy, I'm disgusted with all this cloak-and-dagger rubbish. It's unnecessary. I've found a man, a real man. Okay, he doesn't have a family tree worth a damn. So we'll start one for ourselves. He doesn't own the deeds to Constantia, or an ocean-going yacht, or have a Ph D but I don't care. He's a good man, Daddy, you said so yourself.'

Christie had not said that. What he had said was that McGee was all man, and that he was. His military record told that story adequately, a string of reports of contacts and hard-pressed battles. As to being a good man, that depended on what one meant by the phrase. McGee was a fighting man. Did that make him good enough for Patricia and big enough for Goedehoop?

Christie rose from the table and collected his daughter. With his arm over her shoulder they stepped on to the *voorstoep* then down the stairs to the lawn. The oak leaves, he noticed, were starting to fall. 'Come,' he said. 'Walk with me.' She tucked her arm into his waist and tilted her golden head on to his shoulder. Christie loved it. He loved his daughter. God, how he loved her! No one was going to hurt his girl, no one.

Together they walked to the end of the garden, to the old swimming pool. An armada of crisp brown leaves was scuttling before the wind ripples there. There was a promise of winter in the air. He held the girl to him and remembered his wife – the short season of joy that had been his and hers . . . If the spell of silence was broken by Patricia the charm of his memories lingered. How could she sever those when every word, every inflection, every little gesture of hers produced a mirror image of the woman who had conceived her. She said, 'Daddy,' and turned in his arms to face him. 'Oh, Daddy, I so much wanted everything to be good between Matt and yourself. Just give it a chance, please . . . please. I love him, Daddy.'

Christie knew he was at the crossroads, and the signboards were clear to see. If he did not take the path of compromise then everything could be lost. He did not like it but there was no other way. The man somewhere up there on the berg, his beloved berg, had etched a trail that was a lot more permanent than he would have cared for.

When he spoke again he was thinking as hard and as quickly as he had ever needed to. McGee was a fighting man. So was he. It was a good thing the woman at his side was not in a position to read his mind. What he said was, 'Trish, I've heard you out, lass, and I believe two things. One is that you are too deeply in love, too emotional to be thinking objectively. Marriage is for keeps, girl. That's what I always thought. You need to think with your head a little bit too. The second thing is that McGee, I believe, is himself not responsible for having organized the falsification in those documents. He probably doesn't even know about it.' Patricia tried to interject but he cut her short. 'No,' he insisted, 'listen to me. Give me credit for having brought you this far. You must know that all I care for is your happiness in this matter. I'm your father Trish . . . remember.'

He was on the right bearing. He could sense it and he pressed on. 'I want you to let me do your thinking for you for one whole week, just one week. For one week longer in your life. That's all. For one week I want you to make no decision regarding your future.'

'You mean, if Matt asks me to marry him, you'd like me to say no?'

'Not no. I want you to say, not yet.'

'For a week?'

'That's all, girl. It's not a lot to ask.'

'And then?'

'And then, if I've sorted this out, you'll have my blessing and a wedding the Cape will never forget.'

'And, if you haven't unravelled it by then?'

'Let's not talk about that, lass. One week is all I'm asking you for.'

'One week is the whole time that we've leave for, Daddy.'

'I know, but the world's not going to end then. There's a lot more time after that.'

'Yes,' Patricia said, but there was no happiness in her voice. 'All right, Daddy. I trust you.'

Christie almost sighed with relief. McGee was not the man for his daughter. He was simply nowhere near good enough. As he walked back to the house with Patricia it did not occur to the Admiral that in his eyes probably no man would ever measure up to his requirements for her husband. The Admiral had always taken on one opponent at a time. McGee was the man in his sights right then and that was all that mattered.

The next day was Sunday and even during the harvest nobody worked on Sunday. That was God's day. With the fickleness of the change of seasons it was warm again, hot in fact and humid. That, McGee learned, was not good for the vines. 'The grapes ripen too quickly and the acid level drops too low.' Rain, on the other hand, would bring about an equal calamity. Rain would cause the sugar level in the berries to drop dramatically. A high sugar level, he was told, was critical. 'Alcohol is produced by the action of fermentation on sugar and who wants a wine without alcohol?' he was asked.

The man passing on all this indispensable knowledge to McGee looked up from the mish-mash of grape pulp samples strewn across his laboratory desk and grinned. 'But we,' he boasted, 'have a vintage with just the right sugar-acid ratio. It's going to be a winner.' If he had added, 'thanks to me', McGee would not have been surprised, but he did not. McGee's tutor was Christie's farm manager. Aged by sun and soil, he had a face perpetually wrinkled by a smile that beamed light and warmth into the monasterial chill of the wine cellar. He was blatantly in love with the red loam and quarter million vines of Goedehoop. His name was Daniel Gerhardus

127

Jacobus du Plessis, but friend and foe alike called him Dup. McGee was invited to do so.

Dup knew all there was to know about vines, grapes and wine. Gangling, nut brown, sure and slow, he did not look too unlike one of his precious charges. He also seemed to know a fair amount about the character of his boss, *Die Admiraal*. When Patricia left the two of them alone to go and make Sunday breakfast he had some words of wisdom for McGee. '*Wie nie waag nie, wen nie*. Like everything else you bloody English have turned the expression inside out. You say, he who dares wins. Is that right?' McGee agreed that it was and Dup went on. 'I saw her grow up, that girl.' He lowered his words to a confidential undertone. 'Always headstrong, always knew exactly what she wanted and held on for that. Maybe because she never had a mother she grew up too quickly. I don't know, but that girl was the woman of this farm when her friends were still playing with dolls.'

There was silence for a while. Dup busied himself with a measuring flask and what looked like a specific gravity float. 'I don't know,' he continued, 'if that was a good thing or a bad thing. *Die Admiraal*, oh, he tried to keep her pretty and clean and away from it all. What a hope! She was happiest when she was sweating with *Volkies* in the vineyards. Digging, planting, pruning: she knows all about that. The vintage was a happy time with her singing in the old pressing vat, crushing the grapes with the *Volkies* until she was red with *mos en doppies*. *Die Admiraal* used to wave a finger at me and haul her out, but the next day she was always back. What could I do, man?'

'Not much, I suppose,' replied McGee. He wanted to hear more. 'They must have been good days, Dup.'

'They were. Oh yes, they were fine days. *Die Admiraal* was a captain then. He had his own ship, a corvette, when he was at sea, which was plenty of the time. I can tell you we had fun.'

'And when he was home?'

Daniel du Plessis turned from his work bench and wiped his hands on a cloth. He looked carefully at McGee, fingering pensively the stubble on his chin. 'Let me tell you something, *seun*. *Admiraal* Christie is the finest man in the valley and there's good men here, plenty. He's also the hardest man hereabouts. He believes that the man hasn't been born yet who's good enough for his girl and I don't think he's all that wrong. You just remember the first bit of advice I gave you.'

'He who dares wins?'

'Ja. *Wie nie waag nie, wen nie.* Now excuse me, I've been invited to breakfast with a very pretty girl and I want to clean up.' At the double doors at the end of the cellar he turned and offered his last word. 'He who hesitates is lost,' he warned. Dup could yet just be his 'friend in need'.

McGee lingered in the cool depths of the cellar laboratory for a while longer, not because of any viticultural inquisitiveness, for his eyes, though unwaveringly fixed on the clutter of lab paraphernalia there, were seeing something altogether different. Now and again his hand would trail to the outside of his trouser pocket and finger the ridge of the object cached there, then come back to drum silently on the bench.

If it was possible his reverie seemed to be deepening, then as though he'd made up his mind about something, he dipped into his pocket and with the greatest of care withdrew the article, a wrinkled little leather pouch not much bigger than a walnut, stitched at one end with the finest gut thread – it looked as though it could never have been new. The sewing had been done by hands that admired permanence. He did not even try to unpick it – a big clasp knife sliced summarily through the skin and as though rejoicing in its sudden liberation a gleaming gold and blue treasure rolled over and over on the bench. It was a ring.

The orange gold band fitted over the tip of McGee's little finger with a little to spare. He had remembered that. He had not forgotten how bold the setting was nor how rich was the azure of the gem it cradled. What time had dimmed in his memory was the brilliance of the bursting white asterisk hidden in the sapphire, waiting to match itself against the sun. God, how it came back to him as he walked into the autumn day: the blazoned crucifix that little !Xai in wonderment had named Sun-rival. Sun-rival – what memories the name recaptured, what memories! It seemed almost a sin that light should have been denied the gem for so long. Reluctantly he pocketed the Rival, and carefully buttoned down the flap, then he made his way towards the house. It was breakfast time and he was late.

Breakfast was served under the dappled shade of the garden oaks on the old klinker brick *voorstoep*. It was almost at an end when they heard the unmistakable beat of a horseman approaching at a quick canter. Whoever he was, the horseman was making a proud picture in the flicker of light and shade, rising well in the saddle and handling his chestnut thoroughbred like a huntsman. McGee glanced across to Christie to see if there was recognition on his features. The Admiral was beaming. He knew the man all right and was clearly delighted with the visit.

With the assurance of the well-bred the man approached the breakfast table. McGee noted that there was hardly a bead of sweat on his forehead and his Harris tweed hacking jacket had taken the ride equally well. McGee's big hand covered his easily, but there was iron in the other's grip. McGee was told that he was meeting Pierre du Bois. Pierre said he was delighted, and certainly was smiling warmly when he reached for Patricia's hand. 'Hello, Trish, how are you?' he asked.

Patricia was, judging by her face, a little more surprised than thrilled. 'I'm fine, Pierre, what brings you across . . . ?' There was a quick exchange between Christie and du Bois then, that McGee would have missed had he blinked an eye.

Du Bois answered: 'Heard the news you were home. I thought I'd come across and pay my respects.' Somehow it did not sound convincing and McGee felt he had a good notion of where the news had come from. The question was, why was the Admiral bussing in rival suitors? Why

130

the panic? He looked at Dup, but Dup was involved in an inspection of the toecaps of his Sunday boots. So much for friends in need. If the Admiral was against him, then why? And why had he agreed to his visit in the first place? McGee wondered what Patricia's father's next move would be and was not kept in the dark for long. 'You know . . .' Christie was speaking to no one and everyone. 'Trish's birthday is only a few weeks away. Wouldn't it be wonderful if we celebrated it while my girl was down here? It's years since we had a family party of any kind at Goedehoop.'

'Oh, Daddy,' his girl responded, 'you know you don't like parties. You never have.'

'I'll like this one,' the Admiral said with conviction and McGee believed he would.

'Oh, I don't know.' Patricia needed more pushing, so Christie pushed. 'It'll give an old man a lot of pleasure. If we have it next Friday night it will only be a week before the proper date. What's a week?'

'Where would we have it?' Patricia said, weakening.

'Not in the wine cellar.' Dup was adamant.

'The house would be a good place,' put in du Bois.

'Of course, the house!' thundered Christie. 'Where else?'

Pierre du Bois did not stay much longer than it took to finish two cups of coffee and a cigarette. His farm, he told McGee, was on the other side of the mountain and Patricia and he were more than welcome there. 'Trish knows exactly where it is. Why don't you two come over a little later and we can exercise the horses? How does that sound?'

McGee said it sounded fine, but they had other plans. They were going to the seaside at Noordhoekstrand to picnic. They walked with him to the thoroughbred and du Bois swung himself gracefully into the saddle, a Kieffer Barvaria, that had been polished until it dazzled. Patricia smoothed the horse's massive muzzle and made soothing noises as the beast snorted with pleasure. She even knew that the stallion's name was Prince. Du Bois had Prince execute a perfect dressage rein-back, then, breaking into a

131

grade A trot, horse and rider departed. To du Bois' credit he did not turn in the saddle and wave. The man was a gentleman to the tops of his hunting boots, but, try as he did, McGee could not bring himself to appreciate him. That was understandable, but there was something he did not understand.

Something was wrong. It was as indefinable as the ache that fades before the doctor's prodding hand. There was the pain of anger in him, but the cause eluded him. When Patricia said, 'Well come on, soldier, let's go get sand under our feet,' his response lacked his natural zest. The long scenic drive around the Cape to Noordhoekstrand did nothing to restore it, either. An Owambo expression that old Ondangs had been fond of quoting occurred to him. *Ngoka hali shaa shoka to lolo ota adike kuuvu Womela*. There was no real translation for it other than 'a man who feasts on all he tastes is a candidate for a stomach ache.' In other words, it was up to him. He could take things as they were or he could spit out the bitterness and select his own fare. McGee gave quiet thanks to old Ondangs, turned to Patricia, quite unexpectedly kissed her on the mouth, almost succeeded in running the Range Rover over the edge of a precipice, and completely succeeded in melting her.

Where Africa ends, where its last bastions of sandstone and granite slump like ancient battlements before the South Atlantic siege, beneath the southern keep of the Constantia mountains, lies a skirt of milk white sand called Noordhoekstrand.

Noordhoekstrand was a paradise for those who desired solitude. There were miles of it and it was empty. There were dunes to rival the Skeleton Coast and with hardly an exception they were smooth and clear of the print of man. No one swam there – no one besides penguins, blubber-fat seals from the polar cap and of course the rare health fiend from more adjacent Cape Town. There was not a soul there that day. McGee took to the waters and rallied still further in the numbing pounding surf with Patricia looking disbelievingly on.

When anaesthetized almost senseless by the cold he scrambled back to land and began to walk, she walked at his side. Then he jogged, the girl still keeping station – the zest of it all seeming to pour into him, filling him with it. Suddenly Patricia was far behind and he was running and leaping like a spring-borne gazelle, jumping the storm-strewn kelp heaps and careering up and over the sand hills until he was exhausted.

In the valley between two dunes she caught him, pounced on him in an ambush that sent them both toppling helter skelter into the valley, where the tussle continued. Strangely, the physically stronger of the two seemed unable to gain ascendancy, perhaps because of his laughter. When she demanded his surrender – 'Give up . . . Give up!' – he gave up. He said, 'Yes, I give up' and suddenly all the laughter was over and they were lying tense and silent next to each other. 'Come closer, Trish.'

She did not answer. Her body was saying it all for her. She moved unconditionally hip to hip across him.

She felt his masculinity and was heaved by it like a beached dinghy taken by an in-thrusting tide, tossed and heaved and driven by it until she surged free, riding the momentum of that sea, lifting and falling in the swell, spattered by its spray. A saturating deluge of ecstasy she would never have believed possible burst gloriously over her, leaving her exalted in his grasp. Then the tide drew out and they lay together on the sand.

Afterwards they sat close to each other contentedly eating from the lunch basket, and watched the cold green waves topple, then hiss up the beach. McGee knew there was something that, if it was to be done, had to be done right then before the sun had dimmed behind the clouds on the western horizon. He told Patricia to stay where she was. 'Don't move, I won't be a minute.'

It took less time than that and she did not move.

'Don't look,' he demanded. McGee's heart was pounding as it had not done since his baptism of fire. His mouth was dry and his hands were shaking so he almost dropped Sun-rival in the sand. He told her to hold out her hand and felt her fingers and arms go as stiff as wood. She was holding her eyes intensely shut, almost wincing. McGee slipped Sun-rival on to her finger and watched tears as fat as summer raindrops squeeze past the lids.

'Open your eyes now.' If his voice was steady it was only just. He had to ask her again. 'Open your eyes, my love.'

She threw her arms around him. Almost violently she pulled herself to him, big heaving sobs shaking her body. Her eyelids were still pressed closed as though she did not want to acknowledge what every other sense must have told her was reality, as though if she kept her eyes closed the whole scene would dissolve, time would reverse and they would be as they were before. That was unacceptable to the man with her. There was no going back. She had his ring on her finger. In a voice that was not much short of a command he said, 'Open your eyes, Trish, now,' and almost hypnotically she did. There were no more tears, not a trace. Her pupils were wide and black with challenge. 'Trish,' he said, 'there's a ring on your finger. Look at it.' She did more than that. She offered her extended arm and the star sapphire flashed back its acceptance. Sun-rival had never appeared more brilliant, more untamed, yet more reposed. She drew her breath in sharply. 'It's beautiful!' she whispered, 'beautiful.'

It was beautiful. It was a trick of the light, of course, but the crucifix deep in Sun-rival's cobalt heart seemed to be suspended in a blazing white aureola above the stone. McGee said, 'Trish, I've given you a ring. It's the most precious thing I've ever owned. Do you understand? I want you to marry me.' The reply was so soft McGee almost missed it in the sough of the breakers. 'Yes?' he queried.

'Yes!' This time it was loud and clear. 'Oh yes; yes; yes!' There was no doubt now. 'You mean we're engaged?'

'*Yes!*'

The solitary fisherman who witnessed the extravagance of joy that exploded then, the march-hare dance clean across the sand and well into the surf, could have been pardoned for the condescension of his smile. In that day and age crazy folk were everywhere. The only course was to humour them, then avoid them, pass them by with as much distance and speed as possible. He could not resist a backward glance as he trudged down the loneliest of beaches and so could not help but notice how unabashedly passionate they were. There was no excuse for behaviour like that in public! He humped back to his plodding boots and long fishing rod. It was not right, it really was not. He was not unhappy when he heard the Range Rover start and saw them drive away.

Patricia extracted a promise from McGee that the engagement would remain their secret until the end of the week, until the party. He promised also to observe etiquette and ask the Admiral for his daughter's hand. Everything was to take place on the evening of the party.

She made him tell her the whole history of Sun-rival.

'What a lovely name,' she said. 'It's so very appropriate.' McGee agreed with her. '!Xai called it that. He said that had always been its name. When I asked him where he got it he just said it was mine and it had always been meant to be mine. I carried it after that for years in a leather pouch which !Xai made for me, without ever looking at it.'

'What did your father say about it?'

'!Xai was my father – more than my father. If he said it was mine, then it was mine. He never told me a lie.'

'Didn't Danny McGee ever talk about it?'

McGee reflected on that. Certainly Danny McGee had spoken about it on many occasions but not once had he asked him where the ring was or if he knew about it. !Xai was the one he had always questioned and !Xai for reasons that he alone understood had lied. If McGee had ever admitted to his father that he had Sun-rival and !Xai had given it to him, it would have been the end for the little Bushman. So he had remained silent.

Xai's last words to him about the star sapphire had been, 'Your father wants Sun-rival but it is not mine to give him. It is yours. It belongs to no one else but you. Do not give it away until you know the day has come to give it up and the person has come who should receive it. You will know that in your head as the bee-eater knows when and where to make its nest.' And after this he had simply refused to talk about the matter. Patricia's question had still not received an answer, though. 'He never spoke to me about it.'

During the week that followed the albino-white shore at Noordhoek became a familiar place to McGee. Every morning he took the Range Rover down to the dunes, then ran until he ached from it, until his leg muscles were burning and pumped hard with new blood and he could go no further. But every morning he was rewarded by more distance and greater speed. It was all he wanted.

Some afternoons he spent in the autumn-leafed vineyards, filling huge baskets with tight bunches of smoky purple cinsau grapes, then bearing them shoulder high to the waiting tractor wagons. It was hard work. The wicker baskets, filled, weighed twenty kilos, but the sweat that flowed was unpolluted with the adrenaline of battle. It was purifying him. The days were cloudless and the grape juice in his throat warm and julep sweet. 'You eat more than you pick,' Dup complained. 'You'll never make a picker.' That was a pity in a way for there was a lot to be said for being a picker with the music of clicking shears and the laughter of the *volkies* in your ears and fifty shiny cents to be pocketed for every *ballas mandjie* over the target.

Some afternoons they climbed the berg and picnicked in secret shady kloofs known only to the fire lilies, the grysbokkies and daisies, and Patricia. They had more than enough to talk about. There was a lifetime, God willing, ahead. On those halcyon afternoons with the heather smell of *fynbos*, the sweet kisses of a lover under an unstained sky, God seemed more than willing. He seemed beneficent.

Friday came in a flurry of preparation for the premature birthday party. The guest list read like a Western Cape who's who. Patricia rationed McGee with an adequate if frugal breakfast then holed herself up with a whole platoon of the finest, fattest coloured cooks in van der Stel's valley.

McGee spent the morning in the wine cellar, observing a big spinning pneumatic monster crush the life blood from the grapes at one end and armies of dark bottles marching single file to the capping machine at the other. The mysterious years between the processes, the vat years – well, you could not stand and watch that happen, could you? Dup seemed to be avoiding him – either that or he was busier than usual. He had few words for McGee that day. '*In liefde en oorlog is enigiets geoorloof*,' he'd said but what on earth did he mean by it. 'In love and war . . .'

In the afternoon McGee cleaned himself and then Sunrival until both of them were shining. Then he lay down on his bed for a while. He had a lot of thinking to do. Maybe he dozed because the sound of Admiral Christie's official car did not reach him as it usually did.

Patricia had heard it. She left the kitchen and greeted her father in a reception hall now charged with the aroma of fine things mouth-wateringly cooked. He could not remember when the house had smelt as good and said so. He also told his daughter he would appreciate a word with her in the privacy of his study. 'Matthew McGee's promotion to Captain has just come through. You might like to tell him.'

'We could announce it at the party,' was her suggestion. 'That would be nice, Daddy.'

The Admiral's pipe needed filling. That was always a time-consuming exercise. He was a man who had something to say – that was obvious. 'I'm pleased for McGee. He deserves it, but I'd just as soon we stayed away from announcements at the party. Especially regarding Captain McGee.'

'No announcements?' she asked.

'If you don't mind, lass.'

'No engagement announcements . . . isn't that what you really mean, Daddy?'

The Admiral was wary. He was not going to make the

mistake of underestimating his daughter's will again. Nor was he prepared to backpedal in his reply. 'Let's not trifle with each other, Trish,' he said. 'You know exactly what's on my mind.'

She endorsed his sentiments. 'Let's not fence, Daddy, but let's be truthful too. Let's say exactly what's on our minds.'

'Very well,' Christie agreed, 'I will. First, let me say I have absolutely no objection to your getting engaged or married, provided the person is right for you.'

'And for you and for Goedehoop.'

Christie was unyielding. He considered the interjection, unruffled, and replied, 'For me, no. For Goedehoop, why not? It's not just a piece of real estate, Patricia. It's a home and an industry. There are over three hundred people dependent for their daily bread on the wise management of this estate. It needs a man here who understands the soil, who can make this place grow and prosper and progress and not make blunders. A man . . .'

'A man like Pierre du Bois,' she prompted.

'Yes, why not? Or any of half a dozen others I could name. Any of those boys would make a good match and make you very happy too. McGee's a bush fighter, girl, pure and simple. He wouldn't even like it here in the valley. He'd get tired of it, go wandering. Believe me, Trish, I know his type and thank God we've got men like that on our side on our borders, but not here, Trish, not in the valley, not as a husband, not as the owner of Goedehoop.'

A malaise of silence overtook father and daughter. Christie had said what he needed to. Patricia felt too troubled to speak. There was much to be said, but nothing to offer that would bridge the divide. Her father was a thousand miles away. He was on a different plane. Still, she tried. She pulled her lips into a smile and said, 'So he's a bush fighter! Is there any fundamental difference between that and a sea fighter? I've heard many tales about the man who owns Goedehoop right now. If only half of them are true he must have had skinned knuckles as a pretty ongoing injury.' She had drawn a smile. At least she had done that. Patricia pressed on.

'Still, those were the early days. Maybe he changed a little. Maybe he grew a bit old and settled down. There's nothing wrong with that. Still, I know his wife loved him as he was.'

Christie objected. 'That,' he said, 'is below the belt. I would rather this discussion took place without any reference to her.'

It was not to be. Patricia did not feel that she had referred to anyone with disrespect. It simply was not in her, nor was it in her to allow herself to be bulldozed. 'Mommy would have supported me,' she affirmed. 'She would have stood behind me. She married a wanderer. She married a fighter. She married a man whose total knowledge of land was that it was somewhere you went when you were not at sea. Did she do so badly? Did Goedehoop do so badly? No, it didn't, Daddy. It prospered. So I can't,' she concluded, 'see any merit in your . . . your objections. You're just being a stubborn old man!'

If Christie had been swayed by his daughter's argument he was not prepared to show it. Captain McGee's marriage to his daughter was simply not going to happen.

'You are quite wrong,' he said to his daughter. 'Your mother wanted the best for you. She's not here today to see that that happens, but by God I am, and I will not allow this, never!'

'Why?'

'Because you can do better, because there are things you don't understand and if you think that's just stubbornness, well, that's too bad.'

Patricia's smile was gone. If her father wanted the gloves off, and it seemed that he did, then she was happy to oblige. Christie was still speaking . . . 'Intelligence completed their investigation. Do you know what they found?'

'No.'

'McGee's father is a bloody drunk, that's what. He

139

spends his days trying to drink out the miserable profit he made when he sold – no, gave away – a damn fine little business. He's a soak. How would you like a drunken bum for a father-in-law?'

'Is that all?' Patricia asked.

'Is what all?'

'Is that all they managed to find out, with all their digging? Is that all your bloodhounds came up with, a drunken father? What about Matthew, didn't they manage to rake up some muck on him? I'm surprised. I'm sure they can do better than that. They weren't trying, Daddy.'

'They didn't have to try, my girl. Anyone in Windhoek can direct you to Danny McGee; if he's not in the first pub you'll find him in the second.'

'So what, Daddy?'

Admiral Christie's hand hit the table with a crack. 'So,' he declared, 'you are not marrying into a family with a mother who never was, and a father who sees the world through the bottom of a bottle. Not now, not ever!'

Patricia stood up then, so agitated that she actually found herself leaning across the desk top. 'I'm sorry, Daddy,' she said. 'You've told me a whole lot. Some things I knew. Some I didn't, but not a single thing have you actually been able to say against Matthew McGee. Not one.'

'He slept with a woman on his last safari, one of his precious clients. Did you know that? Her husband was the man killed by the lion, did you know that?'

Patricia stopped as though she had been slapped. She felt the blood drain from her head. The mere act of standing seemed to have become an onerous task. Her voice seemed to be coming from far off when she said, 'No, no he didn't tell me that. You didn't have to either.' The door to her father's study seemed such a distance away. She closed it quietly behind her.

Christie crossed to his antique drinks cabinet. He did not measure how much Scotch he tumbled into his glass, nor did he care. It did not help to wash the bitterness from his mouth, nor did the next splash. He wondered just how much difference there was then between himself and the other sorry man, the one in Windhoek.

Right above him was a splendid portrait, an oil painting in soft autumn shades of the woman he had married and loved, and who had died and left him. It could have been a painting of Patricia. She, too, wore the colours her mother had loved, her hair long and flowing. She, too, had eyes that flashed green fire when angered. The eyes in the portrait seemed to be gazing down now softly with under-standing, or was it sadness? How the temperament of paint on canvas could alter always surprised Christie.

It was becoming darker and the guests would be arriving soon. Christie reached for his desk lamp, committed the room to its soft yellow glow, then stood below the portrait again. He kissed his fingertips, then touched them to the tender Velazquez mouth on the canvas. 'I love you.' Did he say the words or did he think the words, and did it matter? 'Tell me,' he entreated, 'Was I right . . . was I?'

If by some inexplicable miracle of communication word had reached Christie in response to his question, it would have had to arrive with the speed of angel's wings, for he was still standing with his eyes fixed on the painting when there was a knock, a confident and masculine rap on his study door. He knew who it was and he knew exactly why the man had come. Had it been a call to battle stations he would have needed no more courage than he then sum-moned up. 'Come in,' he said – words that could not have been further from his heart. 'Come in.'

The Admiral looked as white as the uniform he was wearing. He invited McGee to be seated but the latter could no more have bent to a chair than a spring-steel man could have. It was an effort just to prevent himself from pacing back and forth.

'Sit down, Captain.' Captain? That was the first sur-prise.

'You've come, I think, to ask me for Patricia's hand.'

Christie had never been one to surrender the initiative or pull his punches. He did not then. 'I want you to hear me out, McGee. Frankly, I don't quite think you've any idea of what's involved here. You're not the right man for my daughter. I mean that and if it was for me alone to decide then I would say, No. My daughter has her own mind, however, and for that I suppose I should thank God. Whether she's using it right now, though, is a matter for conjecture. I'm inclined to think not, but be that as it may, her will must be respected. She's in her room at the moment, so if you wish to marry Patricia, then ask me. I will consult her, and if she agrees to this marriage, then so be it.'

McGee knew it was not the time for a fight. He was flaming with suppressed rage. He felt stung and insulted. He would dearly have loved to tell Christie that he was not ecstatic at the thought of him as his father-in-law; that he was damn right, his daughter did have a mind of her own, a mind that had been made up long before that day had dawned. It would have given him joy to take a pin to Christie's pompous hot-air balloon and watch the bastard plummet. Instead, carefully spacing each word, and without an outward trace of the anger consuming him, he began to speak. 'Admiral Christie . . . I would like your permission . . .'

Chapter 9

There was fire and heavy smoke everywhere and Mazambaan was glad of it. For while the smoke lay like a cloud upon the trees, the gunships screaming overhead like frenzied wasps could never find him. Through watering, smarting eyes he saw the Black South African soldiers running into the open mahango fields with the body of the big *boer* officer he had shot and clubbed. Near the burning Quimbo a helicopter was waiting to take him on. They had SWAPO wounded there too.

Mazambaan lifted his rifle and observed the scene for a moment over his sights. For an AK it was a long shot, too long. He lowered the weapon, lifted his forearms to cover his face, turned towards the terrible heat of the fire behind him, drew in his breath and started running.

For four days he tried to move northwards, and for four days he was beaten backwards by the *boers* with their dog teams, their Bushman trackers, and helicopters that appeared from nowhere, bringing fresh fast-moving troops always to cut him off, always driving him south. His best hope was to attempt to edge as far as possible to the east. If he kept side-stepping eastwards, ultimately his path would bring him to the fern forests of the Cubango and there they would never find him.

On the fifth day he came across bootprints of the same pattern as his. Someone else was in the same predicament. Like panicked beasts before a row of beaters, both men were being driven towards the hunters, the killer groups. Both men were in an ever-tightening dragnet. On the fifth day, too, some time during the morning, his big plastic water-bottle surrended its last warm mouthful, and by midday his tongue was groping over a palate as harsh as

143

the sand beneath him. If he did not find a well soon, he knew that the whole pattern of his flight would alter, without his being able to help it: as his body slowly drained, so one obsessive thought would consume him – bushcraft, stealth and all fear for the enemy bullet would disappear, as he stumbled through the *ombuua* plains in search of water. By mid-afternoon he could feel it happening. He knew the symptoms. He started muttering to himself, his legs began to shake and weaken, his body felt as though a fire was consuming it. That was when he threw away his assault rifle, all his webbing, excepting his dry water-bottle and his precious little Makarov pistol.

Some time later two helicopters landed fresh troops and dogs not more than 500 metres ahead of him. Mazambaan could only just stand by then. His shouted curses carried no further than his thick disobedient tongue. He was grunting like an animal. He knew it. He could hear it. Incredibly he could also hear a voice calling out his name. He turned to face the hallucination, but it was no hallucination – it was Daniel, wonderful Daniel.

'Mazambaan, over here quickly! They will see you in a minute. Come, comrade, I have water.'

'Water!' Water, precious water, warm and plastic-flavoured as it ran past his gullet and into his stomach . . . Water, and almost a full bottle of it! Mazambaan let it trickle into him, washing away the demon thirst.

Wiry little Daniel had supplemented his water supply before his flight by taking the water-bottle of a dead comrade. The extra supply saved them and kept them alive and running for one more day, the sixth day. And that day they reached the Cubango River and fell laughing into the cool clear stream. Now that they had the cover of the thick palm forests to conceal them they could make their way northwards without dehydration, without thirst.

'Not long, comrade, and we will be able to relax,' Mazambaan said.

The South Africans did not see it that way. They pressed on with their operation and the hunt for the

144

fugitives continued unabated. It seemed to the two men that for every northwards pace they took, they were conceding two to the south. Relentlessly they were being herded towards the Namibian border. On the morning of the seventh day it happened. After almost stumbling into an ambush, they finally fled back over the Angolan border and into Namibia and it became simply a matter of hour-by-hour survival.

They had crossed over near the little settlement of Tuguva with the *boers* not far behind, and just kept going. By afternoon they had reached the Omuramba Mpangu, where rain was falling. The whole wide river bed was awash with splashing drops, and not even a Bushman could track a man through that.

They walked the course of the Mpangu all afternoon without seeing a *boer* soldier or hearing a single helicopter. That night when they dragged themselves on to dry ground, Mazambaan knew they were safe for the moment.

It was just as well. Daniel was desperately sick. During the course of that day his urine had turned black as pitch and, in the afternoon, the terrible burning fever of the *oluidi* had started to shake his body. Now he lay whimpering in the hot night, shuddering as though his bed was made of ice, while the sweat flowed from him in rivulets.

A strange thing happened that night. For the first time in his life, Mazambaan actually felt the warmth of brotherliness towards another human being. The long sweltering night through, he sat close to Daniel, holding the water-bottle to his parched lips, wiping away the stinking vomit as it came; holding him, speaking to him words of tenderness he had not thought he knew. 'Come, little brother, the dawn is not far away.'

The man's fever-crazed mind was alive with swarming devil *boers*, chasing him no matter where he turned.

'I won't let them get you, my brother,' Mazambaan promised. 'They will never take you.' He meant every word. 'I will get you to safety. You will never be a *boer* prisoner.'

145

How he was going to carry out his promise, though, was a question the morning light would have to help him to answer.

When it came, it was beautiful: a kaross of silver clouds with sword beams of sunlight cutting clear of them. Mazambaan did not even notice it. Long before a single shadow had been cast he was on the move. Bundled in his arms, he carried the limp-limbed man as though he had no weight at all. Still holding to the course of the *amurumba*, he walked all morning until by midday his seeking eyes found what he was looking for: a small reed-walled kraal, the characteristic construction of the inland Kavango, the Kwangali people.

The first people to notice him were the women and girls, clubbing the mahango millet with pestles longer than their own bodies. Their steady thumping rhythm momentarily became erratic, then picked up again. They were conscious of the presence of the strangers, yet bound to the tribal conservatism that forbade any display of outright interest. There was no fear, no panic, just a curiosity that spread as quickly as a crackling winter bushfire through the kraal.

Mazambaan stood by the entrance with Daniel in his arms. He knew the Kwangali. He knew them well: they would not keep him waiting. They did not. Rukwangali was not a language he spoke well but they would understand Kuanyama.

'Wa lala po?' He greeted the blanketed elder who had come to meet him. 'Here I have a man, sick with fever. He needs help.'

The response he got more than surprised him. 'Ngoye lye? Ngoye oto zi pini?'

The man wanted to know who he was, where he came from. Mazambaan felt a flash of fury. The elder did not know how close he had come to death. He swallowed and started again.

'I bring no harm to your kraal,' he said. 'I have a sick man in my arms. Will you not help me?'

146

'You wear the clothes of SWAPO,' replied the elder. 'Why should I help the enemy of my friend? You may bring the sick man in and leave him. You yourself are not welcome in my house.'

Mazambaan could hardly believe the words he was hearing. He knew the Kavango people were not as involved in the struggle as the Owambos, but to encounter such outright antagonism shook him. He had no choice for the moment, though, but to step forward and do as he was bid. Three women relieved him of Daniel's languid frame, bearing him gently to a central reed hut. He asked, 'Have you the medicine of the omutiliana?'

'You want the white man's medicine for your friend?'

'Yes.'

'You want his malaria medicine, yet you fight against him, why?'

It was not an answer, and it was not meant to be. The elder turned away and disappeared into the village, leaving Mazambaan standing there, prohibited from going any closer.

It was a situation he would not tolerate. He had his Makarov and in his pocket a hand grenade Daniel had been carrying. He would do something to improve their attitude, and would do it immediately.

There were several girls gaping next to their mothers while they pounded their heavy pestles in the central clearing, which, unlike those of the Owambo kraals, extended right from the main access. He observed them for a while, making his selection. Then, once he had made up his mind, he struck with the speed of a snake. He strode up to the group, and before her mother could even turn, he had a child grasped, with his pistol to her head.

Immediately the women were crying. They were screaming, mothers' breasts were bouncing in haste as they plucked up their children and ran. But no blood was spilt. The Makarov remained unfired, and when it was all over and the central clearing held only himself, the infant

147

and the elder, Mazambaan was in total charge of a village known as Ruhodi.

'Now,' he said, 'we will start again. Do you have the medicine of the omutiliana?'

'I will send for it. The mission at Tondora is very close. They will have the medicine.'

'Send at once, old man, and don't forget to tell your messenger that if any *boer* soldier is included with the medicine, this girl for certain and anyone else I can find in your kraal, I will kill. Do you believe me?'

'I believe you.'

Pater Meinhof used to say she was as tough and whippy as old buffalo riem. This was not true. On a day when she did everything in the mission clinic the way he believed it should be done, he would claim her to be as sweet as bush honey. This was total fiction too.

Mostly what grieved the pastor was the fact that Dr Heidi Mueller, in her sixty-fourth year, was still probably as headstrong and impatient as she had been when he first knew her. And that, as he was fond of reminding her, was a good few years back. She was impatient with disease and the bad hygiene that generally accompanied it, impatient with the routine and dogma that made some people's working day so satisfying. She was headstrong in her opposition to sin. There was no subtle way to approach the devil's agents. You matched them thrust for thrust. She also could not abide Pater Meinhof's orderliness-at-all-costs attitude, his place-and-a-time-and-a-task-for-everyone methodology. She became irascible when criticized for rolling up her sleeves and getting the job done, but she was not as tough and whippy as buffalo riem, not at all.

She was simply a woman. She had a woman's heart and a woman's soul. She had observed her hair whiten, and her face crease as the years had swept by, with the consternation of a woman. Once during her solstice years, with a firm body and the passion of a woman, she had

148

given herself and loved like a woman. Ah! . . . but to a devil who had come in the night and taken all that she had given and more; a kidnapper and a thief, with a rangy Australian charm to hide his black heart.

She was simply a woman, and no longer a young woman. The long treks with her Bible, her medicine chest and her faithful Ezekiel, across the breadth of northern South West Africa, were just a memory now, mostly a lovely memory. She maintained it was the war that had stopped her, but in her heart she knew that was not the whole truth. Lately she had been feeling a lot weaker than in the past. And old Ezekiel, he was just a shadow of his former self. Sometimes during the stifling summer afternoons, she had had to clutch at her table to keep upright, to keep going, as the seemingly never-ending queues of the trusting, the hopeful, the downcast, presented their maladies to *ondoktola*.

She did not hesitate when news was brought to her of the sick man at Ruhodi. The messenger looked excited and was breathing heavily. She questioned him. 'You say the man has great heat and sweat?'

'Yes.'

'His eyes, they are yellow?'

'As yellow as the *edila tunga*.'

Eyes as yellow as a weaver bird sounded like blackwater fever, a result of chronic falciparum malarial infection. It was usually brought about by medication with raw quinine, instead of the up-to-date drugs. That alone was enough to bring Dr Mueller to a simmer.

'Why,' she demanded, 'was this man not brought for treatment long ago?' She turned to her helper. 'Disperse the clinic, the people now here will have to wait, or they can come back tomorrow. Tell them that. Now I am going to Ruhodi in the Land-Rover to attend to this foolish man, who it seems wants to die.'

The messenger from Ruhodi did not like the idea. 'Give me the medicine, *Ondoktola* There is no need for you to come.'

149

That was all that was needed to bring her to the boil. 'You stand there . . .' Her voice was quivering with indignation, '. . . and dare to try and tell me how to run my practice. Out of my way, *omunelai*.'

One might as well have tried to re-route a tornado. The messenger who had just been called a moron was not going to try. Heidi Mueller opened her old-fashioned Gladstone bag, threw in an assortment of drugs and instruments. Snapping it shut, she turned back to the Ruhodian. 'I am bringing this man back to the clinic. You should know blackwater fever cannot be treated in a kraal.'

Even old Ezekiel knew better than to try to hold her back. But something disturbed him. The messenger seemed so alarmed and he did not understand that. If *Ondoktola* wanted to bring the man back to Tondora for treatment, why should that bother the man? There were several things Ezekiel had assumed responsibility for over the years. He had to ensure that *Ondoktola*'s motor vehicle had fuel and water, that the big travelling medicine chest was loaded, and finally, that *Ondoktola's* precious paint brushes were beautifully clean, that her soft lead pencils were sharpened to a fine point, and that her paints and sketch block were always with them when they went out.

That day, though, as well as ensuring that all those things had been done, he packed his long spear into the rear of the Land-Rover. Had not the soldiers that had passed by that morning warned them that terrorists could be in the area?

'Are you ready, Ezekiel?' she called from the clinic.

'I am ready, *Ondoktola*.'

Pater Meinhof was at early vespers when he heard the roar of the Land-Rover engine starting up, the clunk of impatiently slammed doors. He listened to the fast receding engine. Only one person drove like that, and only one person always seemed to forget to tell him where she was going. When would she ever learn? He sighed and returned to his prayers. One of them was for the driver of

150

the vehicle. 'Blessed Virgin Mary, safeguard her in her impetuosity, steer her hand and bring her the wisdom that should be natural with age . . . you know I have tried.'

Mazambaan had the little girl's hands tied behind her back with a goat-skin thong. Around her neck he had attached a sort of choker with the leash he was holding.

'What do they call you, child?' he asked.

'Kaghonda.' It was the mother who choked the name out.

'Beautiful moon in the sky,' said Mazambaan. 'How lovely! Well, mother of Kaghonda, so that your daughter comes to no harm, you must tell her that anything I say is to be done, any command I give is to be obeyed. Do you understand?'

Her eyes said she understood. 'My daughter,' she implored, 'do not disobey this man.'

Mazambaan was satisfied. He would not be able to stay in the kraal. He knew that. He would make camp in the nearby bush land, and with him would go little Kaghonda, the lovely moon of Ruhodi. And while she was tethered to him, all would be well. Daniel would be nursed to health. He himself would be fed, and no *boer* patrol would know about it. In the circumstances, no one could have made a better plan, and Mazambaan felt a glow of self-satisfaction which lasted until he heard the sound of the approaching engine.

Raging at first, he thought he had been betrayed. In a flash Kaghonda was collared at his side, the Makarov at her head. Then he realized that there was only one engine to be heard. The *boers* would never come in a single vehicle. Not only that, but this engine did not have the familiar deep growl of the armoured *Buffel*. This was a lighter machine. It could have been the police, but that was not likely. They would also have come in one of their special anti-mine vehicles; their crazy waddling *Hippos*. He was less concerned than inquisitive when he

151

made his way to the kraal entrance, and watched the approach of the solitary white Land-Rover.

Bewilderment, his next reaction, knitted a furrow across his brow. Then, like the crocodile with the tooth bird, he was smiling. The messenger, whoever he had been, had served him like a king. For driving into the kraal was literally the vehicle of his salvation. A Land-Rover with, by the look of it, long-range tanks, and a built-in hostage.

He strode up to the doctor's door, jerked it open and had her gripped and off the seat before the engine had died. The old tribesman on the passenger seat reacted with surprising speed. The man was out of the cab and running for the rear of the vehicle before he could stop him. Mazambaan heard the clang of the tailgate falling, then he was fighting for his life against a demon with a poised two-metre spear and murder in his eyes.

He had the white woman kicking and twisting against his head-lock, Kaghonda like a dead weight pinioning his other wrist, and the mad spearman advancing. He would have to let the woman go in order to aim the pistol, and if he let her go, that long blade would skewer him in a stroke. There was only one thing to do and he did it. With the hand still holding the gun, he grasped the material of the woman's smock, and spun her, screaming, away from him towards the spearman.

Ezekiel's choice was to catch *Ondoktola*, or side step, let her fall and hurl the spear. He caught her, drew back his spear arm, and at that moment was young again; standing next to the Model A, facing the lion *Ongonga*. He saw the pistol flame and felt the death shock. What he heard was '*You are cursed*'. The pistol flamed again, crushing the air from him . . .

'*Mine will be the hand . . . In agony you will die . . . and your offspring*' . . .

No, Onosi the lion *Ongonga*, never will you find the offspring. He had had to do a deal with the devil to hide the offspring but *Ondoktola's* boy was safe. Now there was no strength left in his spear arm, there was no strength left in him at all, but the *Ongonga* had been wrong about one thing: he was not in agony, there was just a creeping numbness. Perhaps now he would see the great god of *Ondoktola*. Ezekiel looked up at his killer with certain recognition in his eyes. 'You took so long to come,' were his last words.

It was a pathetic victory, a victory Mazambaan would rather not have had. An old man was dead, an even older woman was keening over the body. It was no task at all to lift her into the back of the Land-Rover.

The closeness under the hot canopy bore her body smell of soap and cologne to him. She was still crying. He found this irritating and shook her until she stopped. 'Listen, *boervrou*!' He noticed that he had almost torn loose the lapels from her overalls. 'There is a man coming to share the back of the truck with you, a sick man. You are the doctor from Tondora, yes?'

Slowly she nodded in confirmation.

'Then you will cure him. You will make him better. If he dies, then you die, and you see this little girl here?'

She nodded her head in answer once more.

'Her name,' said Mazambaan, 'is Kaghonda. If you do anything stupid, anything, you will have caused this little moon never to shine again. Do you understand my meaning, doctor? The four of us are going for a very long drive, now, and all the time you will be sitting at the back, nursing my sick comrade, and little Kaghonda will be sitting up front with me. Please do not think for a moment that the *boers* will be along to rescue you. I am going to explain to the elders here what will happen to their little moon, if that should occur. You and your Land-Rover, doctor, will appear to have vanished into the *Mangetti* forests. Now what do you think of that?'

Ezekiel is dead, and his murderer must be punished, was what she thought. 'God, punish this evil man,' were the words in her throat. She was still thinking that when the sick man was laid down next to her, when the powerful

153

motor was thrown into gear, when the little village of Ruhodi disappeared in the dust. She thought it constantly with every turn of the wheels, with every hot day that passed. She thought it as she nursed Daniel, and questioned him in his fever, sifting his answers for reality. She thought it every waking minute along those endless tracks and side roads crossing the wide Mangetti and onwards, ever southwards through the rolling Otavi hills . . . 'God punish this evil man.'

The hope of retribution was constantly there as they journeyed. As she nursed Daniel back to strength, so she nurtured with the single-mindedness of a modern day Joan of Arc that single ideal, the vision of justice. It stayed with her all the way to a distant and deserted quarry near a road pointer that read, *Windhoek 25K*.

Katutura Bus Service the lettering on each side of a rather used, dull red silver-roofed bus proclaimed. It was rattling its way along as if in a hurry to be home and done for the day. The people it carried certainly had that thought in mind, as did the throngs of workers walking in the billowing dust thrown out by the bus's fat rubber tyres. No-one seemed unduly concerned by its noisy passage. With an almost suicidal casualness, they parted to let the transport pass, then reoccupied the road in its dusty wake.

They had not changed much, those people, Mazambaan thought from his seat at the back of the bus. The men wore their drab conservative shirts and slacks, the womanfolk their bold coloured traditional dresses and jutting turbans. There were mini-skirts, though, and skin-tight jeans on the young girls, that had not been there in earlier days. He tried to work out how many years it was since he had last been back – fifteen or sixteen or even more.

Katutura had been the place they had fought so hard and long against, that the leaders had vowed never to occupy. Now everyone was in a procession, nose to tail, to get to their houses there. 'The sheep!' He remembered Nakwindi's predictions. 'The white man will uproot us like a poisonous weed . . . and what will we be expected to say? "Thank you, baas."' What could have happened to Nakwindi? If the security cops had not croaked him he would be an old man. Where were all his 'Torches for freedom'? His old teacher's predictions had been so right.

The bus driver, in typical bus driver fashion, brought his vehicle to a staggering halt, obliging those standing to hold on to whatever was at hand. Someone had clutched his shoulder and Mazambaan's body jolted in alarm. It was just a young woman. She smiled an apology. He nodded and smiled acceptance. A dozen, maybe more, passengers disembarked at the stop, including a fat man who had occupied the better part of Mazambaan's seat. He invited the girl to take the space, and she did, her cotton skirt creeping up as she sat, exposing a plump pair of stockinged thighs.

Three rows ahead Daniel sat and beside him, her head just topping the seat back, Kaghonda. She had been surprisingly little trouble, that girl. Neither he nor Daniel had had experience in handling six-year-olds, either boys or girls, so they had no idea whether they had just been lucky to find a placid child, or whether their psychology of a smack for bad and a sweet for good was the answer to child guidance. Whatever the reason, Kaghonda hardly spoke a word, never cried and, since Daniel's recovery, had clung to him like a baby ape. They seemed to like each other.

The bus filled up until only standing room was left, then everyone was tossed towards the rear as they lurched off. Someone up front had brought a portable radio on board and a heavy guitar beat was filling the vehicle. Mazambaan felt his feet tapping, his tension ebbing. He was just another black face, just another tattily dressed worker going home, just another man. He was conscious of the warmth of the woman's thigh next to him. Her blouse was fashionably, he supposed, low-cut, and he could glimpse the top half of a lacy pink bra. Her breasts were rippling with the jolting of the bus, and the skirt had inched up

155

higher. Mazambaan felt himself harden, his breath quicken. It had been a long time.

Six more stops passed uneventfully and the bus was emptying. Regrettably, the woman went too, probably completely unaware of what she had done to him. Mazambaan moved forward to the vacant seat in front of Daniel and Kaghonda, sat there, and turned to his companion.

'Do you know where we are?' he asked.

Daniel looked out of the window. It was getting dark. That was how they had planned it, but now visibility was a problem.

'I think so,' he said. 'It's difficult to see, you know. We should get off at the next one, I think. Then it should be a short walk to her house.'

The 'her' being referred to was Daniel's sister and it was her house in Katutura that they were trying to find. Neither man knew the township well. Mazambaan had seen it as a raw sprawl of brick and tin. Daniel had attended school there. Neither had been back for many years. The bus drew up and they clambered off.

'Gabriel Street,' Daniel read from a hanging cornerpost. 'Yes, I think we got off at the right spot. Mary lives near Gabriel Street, I remember that.' Once on solid ground, he soon seemed to regain his sense of direction. 'This way.' He sounded more positive. 'Yes, it's this way.'

The three of them ambled together past the colourfully painted houses, Daniel and Mazambaan each holding one of Kaghonda's hands as she skipped along between them. At least she seemed to know where she was. Daniel did not seem so sure now. He was peering to the front, side and rear. They reached a corner and stopped to read the street names. 'This way.' Lights were appearing in a few windows and the smell of cooking meat was aromatic. Mazambaan's stomach stirred in hunger. He hoped they were close.

'This could be it.' Daniel sounded hopeful.

'It either is or it isn't,' Mazambaan snapped. 'Can't you remember the number? We can't walk around all night.'

'I think it is the one.'

156

'The number is sixty-three.'

'I think it is the one,' he repeated, leaning on the gate and peering intently into the open doorway a few paces ahead. Just then a light snapped on, throwing a young woman into silhouette.

'Mary?' Daniel called. 'Is that you, Mary?'

'Who is it? Who's there?' demanded the silhouette.

'Daniel. It's me, Daniel.'

The scene seemed to freeze with Daniel holding the half-opened gate, and the woman who Mazambaan hoped was his sister, Mary, staring into the gloom. 'Daniel?' There was total disbelief in the woman's tone. 'Daniel!' She was running down the short pathway. 'Daniel, my God, it *is* you.' The two of them were hugging each other. How they hugged each other. 'Come in. Oh my Daniel, but you've got so thin. Come in.'

Daniel was laughing. Mary was crying. Then they were both laughing. Then she saw Kaghonda. 'Oh my, a little girl. Is she your girl, Daniel?'

'Yes, she's mine, and this is my friend, my comrade.'

He turned his sister to face Mazambaan, who held out his hand.

'It's nice,' she said, 'to meet Daniel's friend,' and her hand was withdrawn almost before he had had a chance to touch the slim delicate fingers. She kept her eyes averted. 'Please come inside.'

Mazambaan sensed her disapproval of him: one of Daniel's bad friends. They moved into her comfortable living room, and, making a big fuss over Kaghonda, she invited them to be seated.

'Sit anywhere,' she said. 'Sakkie will be home soon. I'm busy in the kitchen and Kaghonda can come with me. I'm sure she's hungry.'

'Don't go yet,' Daniel said quickly, catching her. The woman was flustered. She regarded her brother with the eyes of a captured sparrow, ready to fly any second. 'I have something to ask you, my sister.' She looked even more alarmed, her eyes flitting from Daniel to Mazambaan as though she imagined one of them was about to attack her. Daniel spoke softly. 'We are running from the *boers*, Mary. We couldn't get back to Angola after an attack. We were forced south, so we ran to Windhoek. Now we need somewhere to stay.' If they had intended to hit her, it could not have been worse. Mary seemed to wilt in Daniel's grip. He continued. 'It won't be long, my sister, just a few days. There won't be any danger to you and Sakkie and soon we'll have regained contact with SWAPO. Please!'

Mazambaan could take no more. 'What's all this "please Mary" crap? Do you think,' he snapped, addressing the woman, 'that we want to be here? Do you think that? If you do, you're wrong. We would rather be in the bush, fighting the *boers*. We're here because every other man in my platoon is dead. We're here because we had nothing left to fight back with. Now, I'm not asking you, dear Mary, I'm telling you, we *will* stay here until we are ready to leave.' Mazambaan could feel a red haze of fury blurring his vision. He would have liked to grasp the woman's neck, smash his fist into her pretty face. It could have happened too, but little Daniel had shifted defensively in front of his sister. He knew the blind destructive power of Mazambaan's temper. Mary was standing behind him, both hands to her mouth, and Mazambaan was coming forward, when the sound of a car drawing up outside seized their attention, with one thought in both minds: Police!

But a friendly bleep or two on the hooter dispelled that possibility. Mary knew who it was. 'It's Sakkie!' she cried and fled through the front door, leaving the two men facing each other.

'Okay, okay,' Mazambaan threw up his hands. 'So I got a bit cross. So your sister annoyed me. Relax, comrade, it's all over.' Mazambaan smiled. 'Really, it's over. If they can't help us, we'll find somewhere else, that's all.'

His commander's range and mercurial shifts of emotions constantly amazed Daniel. It was over. He knew it

158

was over. He knew he could speak his mind then. 'She's only a kid,' he said. 'Let me speak to her. There's no problem with her or her husband, believe me.'

'I do believe you,' said Mazambaan. 'Don't worry.'

A shortish, thin man, his hair meticulously combed into a lofty Afro, entered the room. He took in the two men apprehensively and minced across to Daniel. 'How good to meet you, my brother,' he said. Then he extended his hand to Mazambaan. 'Welcome to my house. A friend of Daniel's is a friend of mine. You must stay for as long as you like.'

Mazambaan took in the platform shoes, the expensive safari suit, with the spreading underarm sweat stain, the slight whiff of cologne, and instantly hated the man. Was this, he thought, the type of buffoon they were fighting and dying for in the bush? Shit!

Isack Njoba, after seeing Mazambaan, was terrified. He was a completely non-physical person. The man standing in his lounge had an animal smell and presence. Isack Njoba felt his testicles draw up in apprehension, or was it just that? He felt excited too, stimulated by the maleness of his guest.

They had drinks while Mary worked in the kitchen to improve both the quality and quantity of the supper. Njoba knew all the right things to say, toasts to offer. 'The glorious struggle,' was followed by 'To our victorious fighters' and 'To the downfall of the racist *boers* and their running dogs.' Mazambaan had no objections as long as he kept the liquor flowing. He was starting to enjoy himself, spread himself and really relax for the first time in what seemed like months. Windhoek had been an excellent idea.

Mary came in with plates. She had put Kaghonda to bed, she said, and supper was nearly ready. She had put on a fresh dress and done her face for the occasion. Mazambaan was very aware of her. 'You haven't had a drink,' he said, and made it sound like a rebuke.

'Thank you, I don't drink.'

159

'Of course you do!' Mazambaan laughed.

'Of course,' Isack agreed heartily.

'But, Sakkie, you know I don't drink.'

'Rubbish!' roared Mazambaan. 'Here, listen to your husband like a good girl.' He passed her a brandy and cola that would have put down most men. 'Now,' he said, 'let's have a toast.'

'My turn for a toast.' It was Daniel, speaking thickly because Daniel, it seemed, had consumed the better part of a bottle of gin, and that, on an empty stomach. 'To Sakkie and Mary.'

'Yes. Yes, to Sakkie and Mary.' Mazambaan rose so quickly that he toppled his chair. One stride took him to Daniel's sister. One second and she was in a grip of iron. Big and comradely. That was how it was meant to appear. It looked that way to Daniel. Isack Njoba saw through it. Though both his wife and his guest were facing him, he knew where Mazambaan's hand was wandering, and there was not a damn thing he could do about it. He was mortified, shaken and frightened, too frightened to do anything but raise his glass in a humiliating salute, and hope that the evening would rapidly draw to a close. There was only a fraction of a bottle of gin and a few beers left and then they would eat. Then he and Mary could go through to the bedroom and leave her drunk brother and his loutish friend to do what they liked.

Mazambaan must have read his mind. 'Sakkie, my brother,' he said, 'we're nearly out of liquor. How about some more?'

'I haven't got any more.'

'I know that, but isn't there a *cuca* shop around where you can get some through the back door?'

'No,' sulked Isack, 'I don't know of one.'

'You're not trying to spoil the party, are you, brother? We're all having a good time, aren't we?'

'Oh, yes.'

'Then why don't you take your car and pick up some more liquor?'

160

Isack should have looked at Mazambaan's eyes then, instead of accepting those mild words at their face value. If he had, he would not have refused the request, not have said, 'Haven't we all had enough?' Nor would he have found himself suddenly off his chair and violently en route for his own front door. The end result would have been the same, though. He would have got into his car and driven the seven kilometres to the *cuca* shop, paid the black market price for another bottle of brandy and one of gin, then returned home . . . He would have found, as he did find upon his return, his brother-in-law Daniel in a drunken coma, spreadeagled across the couch, and his wife, blank-eyed and stupid with liquor, seated at their dining-room table, with Mazambaan right next to her.

Had he known what else was in store for him, he might not have returned that night at all. He did return though, with a bottle in each hand, to be enthusiastically greeted by the huge SWAPO man.

'What a man! What a bloody hero! Come on in, comrade, bring the booze. I'm just about dead with thirst.'

Isack complied. He deposited the two bottles among the clutter on the table and stood there looking at his wife. Pretty Mary did not look any better than a drunken whore in a backyard brothel. The fact that he was largely responsible for her predicament did not occur to him. She had brought it all about by attracting her brother and his terrible friend to their lovely home. If she paid the penalty, that was just too bad. If she suffered from a hangover the next morning, he would laugh in her face.

Isack Njoba was a babe in the woods. He had completely misread the situation. Once more he had ignored the danger signs. The penalty was to be a lot harsher than a morning's worth of headache. 'There's some more cola in the fridge,' he said to Mazambaan. 'Enjoy the brandy.' Then he bent over his wife to get her to her feet. 'Come on, Mary,' he said, 'bed time.'

Mazambaan was laughing. 'Bed time?' he said, 'Come on! The party is only just starting.'

'But Mary's drunk. She's not used to it.'

'Crap!' The cuff Isack Njoba received behind his head half stunned him. Mazambaan was still smiling, still mocking. 'You don't know your own wife, Sakkie,' he drawled. 'She's having a great time.' He placed a forearm as big as a girder across her shoulder, rocking her upper body. Her head was rolling and he spoke slowly to her as one would speak to an imbecile. 'You're having a great time, aren't you, pretty Mary?'

She couldn't even focus, let alone answer. It was then that, for Isack, the nightmare really began.

Mazambaan unscrewed the top from the brandy bottle and thrust it across. 'Now!' he commanded. 'It's your turn, comrade Isack. Drink!'

'I really . . .'

'Drink!'

'Oh, Jesus.' Isack took the full bottle and tilted it to his lips, almost choking on the liquid. He took a mouthful and with an effort, swallowed.

It was not enough for the other man. 'Drink!' he demanded. 'More.'

What was to be done? Isack looked around as though by some miracle a champion would suddenly appear to rescue him. There was no help however, so he turned back to the bottle. The man opposite nodded his head almost encouragingly, almost as if to say, Drink up, it's good for you.

The liquor was like molten lava flowing into him. He held the bottle to his lips until he could take no more. He could feel numbness creeping through him now. It had to be enough. But it was not. The man's voice seemed to be coming from a distance now.

'Drink. More. Drink more.'

It was not just a numbness any longer. Isack felt stupefied, concussed, paralysed. He put down the bottle and heard the hypnotic command, 'Drink'. He could not. He could not even reach the bottle, let alone hold it. But help was at hand. The man was holding him now like a baby to its bottle. A lot of it was spilling past his lips, but a lot was not. The funny thing was that it was not so terrible any more, and he could not really make up his mind whether what was happening was a good thing or a bad thing . . . His wife, for instance; should he condemn her or not for hanging on to the man, Mazambaan, as though she would probably fall over if she did not have something to hold on to? He had the table. She had the man. The way she lay on the couch, though, with her legs all open, he did not like that . . . Now that was wrong. And it was not right for her just to lie there while he hiked up her dress. She should not do that. Nor he. She was his wife . . . Not right . . . Mazambaan was smiling, 'Hello Sakkie, I thought you might like to watch.' Not right . . . Mary's pretty undies all white against her black body. Don't do it, Mazambaan. Please don't do it . . . See where his fingers reamed her, see her, stretched. Please don't do it. Please, no, Mazambaan, not to pretty Mary. Wrong, wrong, so so wrong . . .

In the days that followed, not once did Isack or Mary Njoba discuss the events of that night. He took to coming home late, mostly after midnight, and leaving before his guests had arisen in the morning. What his wife did while he was away, he dared not care. Possibly Mazambaan was enjoying her favours, possibly not. She had started wearing more make-up than usual, he had noticed. Also when he did finally climb into bed with her at night, she would feign sleep and keep her back turned to him. It did not matter. Sex was the last thing on his mind. Of primary concern to him was self-preservation. The rest, the retribution, that could wait. His time would come.

Mazambaan, he realized, was not just any soldier of the People's Liberation Army. The man was a psychopathic killer. During the few times he had sat at the table with him and Daniel he had come to realize that. Their conversation revolved constantly around the sublimity, the aesthetics of violent death. It was incredible. They could sit there over their drinks, and, using the same tone

163

of voice as, say, a piano-tuner might have used in discussing with a colleague the merits of a certain tuning technique, debate the most efficient, or quick, or painful, or whatever, way of terminating human life. God help them all, he thought, if ultimately such men were placed in positions of real authority.

In the meantime, he had to stay alive. They would go. They could not stay at his home for ever. He knew they had made contact with SWAPO agents. He had heard them speaking about leaving. One day soon, he hoped, that time would come. He had contemplated going to the police. One of the pupils at the school where he taught had a father who was a policeman. There would have been nothing easier than to have called the man in on a pretext then given him the information about the SWAPO men. He would probably even have received a reward.

It would have been satisfying to see Daniel and Mazambaan led away with a dozen guns pointing at them but he realized that the satisfaction would have been short-lived. He knew of a woman who had apparently been an informer. Installed now in a wheel-chair in the hospital in Stubel Strasse, minus eyes, ears, fingers and tongue, she was a living testimony to the length, the strength and the brutality of the arm of SWAPO. He had no wish to join her, so he bided his time.

One day it happened.

It was about three in the morning when a knock that turned his bowels to water came on his door. It all happened so quickly he hardly had time to wake up. Daniel was in the bedroom suddenly saying goodbye to his sister. There was not much other sound than the low voices of the few men, the soft closing of car doors, an engine being quietly accelerated – and they were gone.

Isack lay there for a few minutes, listening for the return of the car, then got up, slipped on his long trousers and padded through to the lounge. There was nothing left. They had even taken the little girl, Kaghonda, from her crib. They were gone. At last gone for good, and now there was something, something that would give him much pleasure, which had to be done. Mary would not be able to feign sleep any longer . . . But Mary was not even trying to. When Isack turned on the central light, she was sitting up in bed, her beautiful breasts exposed. And she held out her arms to her husband and smiled the smile that she felt sure would bring him eagerly to her. Come to her he did but not in the way she had expected. When he reached the bedside and she became aware of what it was he was concealing behind him, she drew in her breath and recoiled. But it was too late.

The first stroke of Isack's *makelani* branch had all the burning ferocity of the cuckold husband behind it. The cane caught Mary across the neck and shoulders and her scream was like soothing balm to his spirit. He needed to hear it again, but now there was no hurry. First he had something to say to her, words that had cried out to be spoken for two weeks.

'My darling, Mary,' he said. It was almost as though he was reciting lines from a letter. 'I can't begin to tell you just how much you hurt me. Perhaps the long *makelani* can make up for it all.' Then he hit her again and it was so exquisitely pleasurable that he did it again, and again, and listened to her screams. It was wonderful.

Dogs began to yap in the neighbourhood, and a few household lights were switched on. But soon the screams diminished to sobs and the sobs to whimpers. The lights flicked off, and the dogs became quiet, and Isack Njoba entered his wife's arms again.

Well out of earshot of all this a large American car was being driven at some speed. Its destination was Okahanja, a sleepy farming village – what the Afrikaners would call a *dorp*, some eighty kilometres north of Windhoek. Four very wide-awake men and a sleeping girl were the occupants. They did not seem to have much to say. Mazambaan, who occupied the back seat with Daniel, was about to break the silence with an enquiry as to their destination, when the man seated next to the driver spoke: 'Cigarette

. . . ? Anyone want a smoke?' Everyone wanted a smoke. His packet did the rounds, as did his lighter. He lit one for the driver.

'Call me Okawe,' the man said. Okawe was a Herero name. Mazambaan had already examined the man's features in the glow of the cigarette lighter. He had him figured as a Herero. Instinctively he did not trust him. His trust did not run to the other tribal groups at the best of times, and this was not the best of times. Okawe was young, sharp-featured and well-groomed, but that, as far as Mazambaan was concerned, did not constitute a plus either.

'So you're Okawe,' he said rudely. He did not emphasize it by saying 'so what!' He did not have to. The meaning was clear.

'Don't give me a hard time,' Okawe replied. 'I don't want to be here at this time of the morning any more than you do. You, comrade, are here in this car with us now because if either of you two had stayed in Katutura for another day, the *boers* would have picked you up.'

'Crap!'

'Not crap at all,' the man drew deeply on the cigarette. 'We got you out of there just in time. The *boers* have exact descriptions of both Daniel and yourself. Let me show you something that will shock you, Mazambaan . . . Here.' He took a copy of a newspaper from the front seat. 'News of Namibia,' he said. 'Only the largest morning circulation newspaper in Namibia. Have a good look at the centre page, next to the editor's column. I think you'll get a surprise.'

They did. Turning on the domelight, Mazambaan swiftly flicked through the pages. Awaiting them was more than a surprise. Under a six-column bold headline, 'HAVE YOU SEEN THESE MEN?' was a portrait of himself and next to that, one of Daniel. They were not just the usual police identikit monstrosities either. They were pictures that in different circumstances one would have been proud to call one's own. They were the work of an artist.

'Like it?' asked Okawe sarcastically. 'Tell me, did you

two heroes sit down and pose for the bloody woman, or what?'

'What woman?'

'The doctor. She drew the pictures – must have taken her time about them too.'

'I killed her.' It was Daniel. 'She couldn't have drawn them. I killed her.'

'Let me tell you something, comrade Daniel,' said Okawe. 'You didn't even get that right. Doctor Mueller, artist, missionary, beloved of the Kavango nation, is still alive. She's in hospital in Windhoek. What do you say to that?'

He did not say anything, because Mazambaan had struck him with the back of his hand, with all the force he could manage from his cramped position. There was the distinct sound of breaking bone, and Daniel buckled forward, his hands a mess of blood held to his face. Mazambaan would have hit him again, but powerful headlights from an oncoming vehicle flooded the interior of the car. He ducked below window level, as did Daniel and Okawe. The lights were from a military troop transporter which was followed by a further eight vehicles, then a Land-Rover with a blue spinning toplight. They kept their heads down until all the vehicles of the convoy had passed.

By the time he raised his head again, Mazambaan had regained some of his composure. The drawings had badly shaken him and he made no attempt to help Daniel. The man deserved what he got, and more. Their pictures were being circulated throughout Namibia. They were wanted for attempted murder. What else could go wrong?

'How did you get the newspaper before it even got on the streets?' he asked Okawe.

'Source at the printing plant.' It was the driver who answered the question. Mazambaan had almost forgotten the man's existence in his shock and fear.

'So, comrade Okawe, what next? What happens now?'

'Next,' said the man, 'we get you far away from

167

Katutura, and leave the *boers* and their informers running round in circles. I'm taking you to a cattle ranch called Bruchsaal. It's run by a tame German, a man with good reasons to co-operate with us. You two will be safe there. It's a massive farm about ten K's outside of town. Rest for a while. We'll be in touch when the heat's off, or we need you. The girl, Kaghonda, is being sent to Angola.'

But for the drone of the engine, and the tyres on the tarmac, there was silence as the car sped through the night. Mazambaan cranked down his window and let the fresh early morning air play across his face. Away to his right the power of the unrisen sun was working to bleach the easternmost stars from the fabric of the sky.

'Okahandja up ahead,' said the driver. 'You can see the lights.' Indeed you could, they were like a little cluster of diamonds in the neck of the mountains. Mazambaan settled back comfortably in his seat for the first time during the journey. His back was aching and his head was throbbing violently, but in spite of all that, he began to relax. Little Kaghonda was stirring. He placed his big hand on her forehead and gently stroked it. It was not so bad in Angola.

'You'll be safe at Bruchsaal,' Okawe said again, 'both of you.'

Chapter 10

The flight to the operational area was the usual well-organized sweaty crush of men, webbing and weapons. McGee found himself sharing the Hercules's copious belly with half a company of infantry-men: young keen-faced boys fresh from basics and ready for anything; and a tethered-down sewerage truck that was not brand new and smelt it.

With the engines revving with a violence that it seemed must tear fuselage from wing, they were moving. After that the journey, apart from the sight of one youngster, who curdled to an alarming green shade and threw up unbelievable volumes into relays of passed paper bags, was without event. They dropped on to Ondongwa with a gut-in-mouth plunge like a stone from the sky.

McGee had almost forgotten how hot the Namib late afternoon sun could be, even in the autumn. Ondongwa quickly revived his memory. The dropping tailgate of the Hercules was like an opening kiln door. He waited his turn, then stepped out and into the furnace that was to be his precinct once more for as long as it mattered. This time, though, something had changed and it was not Ondongwa. Ondongwa could not change. There was nothing left to change. Successive generations of unthinking exploitation by wood-hungry, meat-hungry, Owambos had seen to that. Ondongwa was white talcum sand, donkeys, goats, bicycles and people; people like ants. Ondongwa was modern-day black man's Dodge City. Everyone there seemed to have a submachine gun or an autorifle of some description and a brace of grenades. It was a place of contrasts where an ancient *Tate* in his skins and *omba* shells could alight from a taxi, accompanied by a son with a teased afro and platform shoes and more money in the back pocket of his Levi's than the old man had earned in a lifetime. Ondongwa was the worst of Africa old, and the worst of Africa new. It was a cancerous mole in the groin of war-sick Owamboland.

But there was another side to the place, excised and fenced off from the ailing countryside. That was where the whites, civilians and military, lived and went about their business – from the massive plane-a-minute airstrip, with its neatly parked camo-liveried 'copters and jets of every make, its dressed-to-the-inch tent town and shipshape homes on wheels, to the urban oasis where the leaven of sweat and ingenuity had rendered the desert into tree-lined streets and homely cottages where blond-haired children tumbled on the lawns. It was a miracle place, but it had not changed much either.

What had really changed was McGee himself. Before, it had all passed him by as just a stopping place on the way to the bush war. Now it marked a milestone on a road he was not quite sure he wished to take. There was a cleft now in the armour of his spirit and the sharp edge of discontent had found it. It did not make him a better soldier. For what before had been unnoticed was now intolerable. It did not make him anything but lonely.

He checked in with the logistics officer, a hairy, long-limbed individual with a pet monkey called Ertjies who could have been his twin.

'Captain McGee . . . Ah! yes. Here you are. I've got a place for you on the convoy to Fort Ompako. Leaves first light tomorrow. That right?'

'Ompako,' said McGee. 'Yes, that's right.'

'Nice little base,' ventured Ertjies' owner, 'It's Major de la Rey's base. You know de la Rey?'

'Not really. Not much, anyway.'

'He's a good man. Ombadje, that's what they call him. It means the jackal.'

That much McGee already knew about his new commanding officer. He also knew that de la Rey was considered by SWAPO to be one of the hard *boere*. De la Rey was a dirty fighter, or so he had heard. McGee was looking forward to meeting the Jackal.

'You going to be his 2 IC?' the man asked.

'Yes.'

'Good luck to you. There's a bed for you in the transit camp. See you tomorrow.'

The pub was open and crowded with brown-clad officers. There were a couple he knew quite well, but no one he wished to talk to. He drank until things did not hurt quite so much. That took some time. Then suddenly the pub and the people and the endless drink caught in his throat. He needed air.

Outside, a plump moon hung in the sky and the pale sand seemed to stretch to the horizon. Feeling as conspicuous as a bed bug on a starched sheet, he walked towards the eastern perimeter wire and stood there.

The bofors guns from the airstrip opened up: interdiction fire into no-man's land. In' the quiet night the noise was awesome. They spat out steel at such a volume and with such velocity, that it tricked the eye. The direction of the red streaking tracer seemed at times to have reversed, and be travelling towards the guns. No-man's-land was not the place to be just then.

When they ceased fire, not to be outdone the home guard from every kraal near and far, surrounding Ondongwa, had a turn. Hosing down the night sky with tracer had always been a local recreation. There was no military value to it, no reason for it. They did it for the sheer drunken hell of it, for the love of bedlam. They kept it up for the better part of the time McGee spent outside, and were still shooting sporadically when he made his way to the transit tent, where he stowed his gear. In spite of the lack of anything like peace, the captain slept well – too well: the convoy left soon after first light and it almost departed without one passenger.

They travelled at speed. No one could ever accuse South African military drivers of being dawdlers. They

171

hurtled their vehicles over Owambo's chalk powder corrugations as if tomorrow was of no interest. Perhaps that was true for some of them. McGee sat next to the convoy commander on top an open *Buffel* mine-proofed carrier and hunched against the biting slipstream, gratefully watched Ondongwa's goat-scoured countryside disappear. Tomorrow was certainly of interest to McGee, and the day after. He chatted with the convoy commander, a boy-faced lieutenant from Durban, but the strain of keeping his voice above the roar of the engine and the matching wind limited the conversation. There was nothing to do then but sit with the six other strapped-in soldiers, rock in unison to the dictates of an evil suspension, and think.

There was no shortage of subject matter. McGee thought about the days that had changed his life. There was no sequence to them, like a game of patience. One turned card brought up the face side of another. He thought about his last patrol, the attack, the vacuum that had been left in his memory.

'*Something will jog your memory, maybe today, maybe in a year, then you'll come up with the whole thing.*'

Who had said that? Kowalski, of course, dear Doctor Kowalski. Patricia had told him the same thing. God, how stunning she had looked that first day in the ward! He wondered about Goedehoop and Christie, the bastard. He had really dug up every bit of dirt he could lay his hands on. 'My daughter wants to see you, McGee. I think you should know that I told her a few things about your past history. She's a bit upset.'

A bit upset! The bastard had looked so smug when he said that. He had used the Pellew fiction to try to destroy him but Patricia had not let it happen.

The convoy moved into thicker woodlands. The Owamboland bush was closing in on the road. There would not be much difference in the topography from now on: fewer villages and kraals and more trees, kiaats, syringas, bush willows and everywhere, mopani. Five hours after leaving

172

Ondangwa, they reached the Ompako Omulonga. Fort Ompako lay just ahead.

The fort was a fair-sized encampment. It looked as though at a pinch it could have accommodated a battalion. Laid out on a rectangular basis, earthworks and dug-in machine gun emplacements at each corner served as a perimeter. All foliage had been laid low for hundreds of metres all around the place, giving it a raw, barbaric appearance. Only a man of war would have called Ompako a thing of beauty. As they rose up over the vehicle hump that breached the wall, McGee could see that Major de la Rey ran an orderly establishment. Ahead lay the parade ground, broad and well-swept; the tents divided into platoon units, demarked with little white-washed stones to indicate the pathways. Red, freshly filled fire-buckets, hanging on rough-hewn stands gave the place its only splash of colour.

A metal girder observation tower and a colony of aerials denoted the command area. It was there, looking more like a fugitive from a flourmill than Ompako's second in command-designate, that McGee debussed, thanked his driver, and with his equally dusty kit, made his way over to a board with the designation burned into it: 2 IC. Behind that was a tent with dropped flaps and inside that, watching him speculatively, was a captain about his age, with short-cropped hair and the name tag 'Richter' sewn above his shirt breast. 'You must be McGee,' he said.

Richter used only the left half of his mouth for talking. He aborted his words in a typically army clipped way of speaking. His handshake was cast-iron. The man was not taking any chances of being considered a sissy. He extracted a battered tin of Mills Extra, and McGee reckoned that was about as much of Richter as he was ever going to be offered, so he took one.

'The OC is on recce.' Richter had a remarkable talent, too, for combining speech with billowing tobacco smoke. 'He asked me to show you around. This will be your tent.

173

You and I will share for a few days while I hand over.' All that in one breath and with smoke still to spare, he concluded: 'You'll like it here.'

When soldiers shower, there is inevitably an air of festivity about the occasion. A patrol that had just come in was showering, and it was to that spree of gushing hot water that McGee, armed with soap and towel, made his way. The showers were housed in a corrugated iron shed on which someone had hung the sign: 'Abandon soap all ye who enter here.'

An exterior drainpit was fighting a losing battle against the overflow. He stepped into the section reserved for officers, pegged his clothing, and let the hot water wash him clean. The officers' section was completely private: it had a seven-foot partition and a separate entrance to keep it that way. The roof, however, was nine feet from the floor, leaving a two-foot gap, an unlimited acoustical freeway between officers and men. It was not the place for those with rank to discuss privileged information. Those without rank should have been equally wary but were not always so.

It did not take a smiling McGee long to hear that Richter, otherwise known as *die draak*, the dragon, was not going to be missed. The consensus was that his replacement could only be an improvement. Soldiers always grumbled. That was the way of it. McGee rinsed himself with cold water, dried his body and was about to leave when something was said that stopped him dead in his tracks:

'True as God, you can believe it or not. It just came in. We're going to get visitors, VIPs from Windhoek. *Groot Kokkedore*, politicians from Turnhalle.'

'What in hell's name do they want up here?' someone asked.

McGee wondered exactly the same thing. Ompako was not exactly a show base. It was too close to the border.

He spent the rest of the afternoon underground, with static frayed radio language in his ears and the smell of

174

sweat, gun oil and sandbagged earth in his nostrils. This was the place where Ombadje de la Rey's jackal schemes could be seen to come alive, where pencilled maps and messages told a tale of soft flesh and hard bullets.

By the time Richter and McGee emerged from the operations bunker daylight was fast fading. The entire western horizon was tinted with a combination of filmy bronze hues and Ompakos soldiers were moving quietly to their stand-to positions.

A neatly turned-out section of troops, having lowered and bedded the flag, was marching away from the now bare staff. Fine dust raised by the unisoned tread glowed like powdered gold around their ankles before resettling. Somewhere in the distance a lone hyena's 'wa hawa hawa' was breaking the stillness of the dusk. It was the time McGee loved best; for a moment he almost forgot Richter at his side and the men, the equipment and weapons of war all around. He was back in the serene valley of the Simonsberg with the girl he loved. But only for a moment . . . The growl of approaching engines jerked him back to the Ompako. The jackal was returning to his lair, there was war to be made.

De la Rey's tent was a delight. No hanging cable joint lights for him; he had standing lamps hewn from local timber. He had Kavango carved benches and game skin karosses scattered on the floor. The liquor was contained in lead crystal decanters, the glasses were best 'Waterford'.

The object was not to spend the evening there. De la Rey patronized the good pub at Ompako. What the major enjoyed was having one drink with his most senior personnel before dinner. Others there besides himself, Richter and McGee were a visiting Anglican padre and the base sergeant-major, a man by the name of Venter, a beery cheerful soul. De la Rey introduced McGee to the two of them.

'Well?' de la Rey asked McGee, 'what's your poison?'
'Scotch, if you've got it.'

'Ah!' the Major exclaimed with mock delight. 'A man after my own heart. Chivas Regal do you, Captain?'

The captain said, 'Yes, indeed.' It would do him.

'I'm surrounded by men who drink nothing but brandy, captain. Inferior stuff. I mean, you take Richter here, he drinks brandy and he's got an ulcer. Doesn't that say something?'

In the lamplight McGee had a better chance to study de la Rey. What he saw and heard, intrigued him. The man was somewhere in his late twenties and could have passed as handsome, but for a highly cynical, constantly flickering smile. The smile suited him, though. It suited his thistle-tongued dialogue. The man did not converse, he threw out challenges, and seemed disappointed when his verbal gambits were left to die.

'A patrol near Chana Hangadima picked up some good fresh spoor today.' The major was talking again. 'It looks as though they could be leading towards the Omudangila mission. Maybe we should think of an ambush somewhere down there. What do you think, Hans?'

What Hans thought was that the Omudangila area was too thick with locals. SWAPO would get wind of any operations.

'We've tried it before many times. All we've had is zilch.'

'Yes,' de la Rey mused, 'I thought you may think that. What do you think we should do, Captain McGee?'

It was a low shot, missed probably only by the padre. The sergeant-major glanced sympathetically at the new boy. Richter looked the other way. But if de la Rey had expected to catch his new captain with his pants down, he had miscalculated. McGee had not spent his hours in the Ops room just gawking. There were maps in the Ops room and on those maps the settlement of Omudangila and the mission were demarked, as was the dried-up pan Chana Hangadima where the spoor had been located. McGee wondered whether de la Rey would be pleased or disappointed with his answer.

'What sort of numbers were "*boy*" moving in? Did the patrol manage to read that?'

'About fourteen,' said the major. 'They split up into two equal groups.'

'Well,' said McGee, 'from the Chana to the mission, if my memory serves me, is about eight clicks south. From the mission to us, is about the same distance west. The actual ground, of course, I haven't seen, so I can only give you an opinion.'

'And what's your opinion?'

'Well, you can't just let SWAPO walk a dozen strong in and out in your own damn backyard, can you? That wouldn't be on, would it?'

'So?'

'So, I'd put in some ambushes tonight, then track the bastards down from first light.'

De la Rey appeared neither pleased nor disappointed. His expression was, if anything, more cynical than ever.

'And that's your opinion?' he enquired. 'That's it?'

'Yes.'

'Well, ten out of ten for doing your homework. I like your opinion. The trouble is, Hans is dead right. If we so much as break wind in the general direction of Omudangila, *boy* will hear about it. A straight forward ambush wouldn't stand a bloody chance.'

They went through to the mess tent and, joined by a few more officers, sat down to eat. There were seven of them at the table that night: de la Rey, Richter, McGee, the padre and three sun-bronzed and extremely athletic look-ing young second lieutenants. One of them had been the convoy commander of that morning. He had the incon-gruous surname of Ivanovitch. The other two bore, re-spectively, the distinguished Afrikaner names of Kruger and Fourie.

They could have been twins, that pair. They looked so alike. They were just kids who should have been kicking a rugby ball around some green field back in the Republic, not sitting there in that war-cursed land, waiting for the orders that would turn them loose on some equally homicidal black men. The padre said grace then and the meal was served. There was a bottle of rich red pinotage circulating. The label was strange to McGee, but recalled memories of the warm red loam of Stellenbosch, of the oaks and the cool wine cellar, and of course the woman.

He was not sorry when de la Rey nudged his elbow and announced quietly yet contentedly, 'I think I've got it.'

McGee noticed that the Major had hardly touched his food.

'I think,' he repeated, 'that this dumb *boertjie* has a plan that could, with more luck than good tactics, ancestorize a few more "*boy*". Listen to this.'

McGee listened and for the first time since his return to operations, he felt his interest in things military quicken. All Ombadje de la Rey had done was to rewrite the nursery adage, curiosity killed the cat, with a little hard realism added. Using his mind and the back of his cigarette box, he had worked out something that could result in a kill.

The lieutenants who were lingering over their coffee were told to have their platoons equipped for a night ambush, and ready to move out by 21.00. With hardly a change of expression, as though that sort of order was as normal as an after-dinner mint, they rose from the table.

They reached the sleepy village of Omudangila about an hour later. McGee climbed from his vehicle and joined in a search which was all torches, yapping dogs, confused inhabitants and more confused troops. They did not even find the haystack, let alone the needle. If SWAPO had ever been there, they were not there now.

At ten minutes to midnight they called off the search. The citizens of Omudangila watched gratefully as the South Africans climbed back aboard their great iron *Buffel* trucks standing so high above the ground, and growled away to the north . . . To the north, now that was strange! The soldiers had come from Ompako, which was to the east. So they were not going home at all: they were

178

going to lie out there on the track to the north and wait in the dark with their guns.

Half an hour later the *Buffels* rumbled back again, shaking the entire village with the roar of their engines. When the South Africans were not asleep, it seemed, they did not wish anyone to sleep. This time their big trucks were empty, any *Omuelai* fool could see that. So the soldiers were up the track to the north. How those men ever expected anyone to walk into such a blatant bumbling trap was a thing of wonder. *Ombadje* the jackal must have lost his senses . . .

Most of the villagers went back to their warm beds. But not all of them. One of them drew his blanket closer to his shoulders and slipped off into the cold bright night. Regardless of how clumsy the *boers* were or how untalented their ambush attempt, the Comrades were always hungry for information of the enemy. They would want to know exactly what *Ombadje's* heavy-handed lieutenants were up to.

The silver moon rose, and as was its destiny, it fell. Shadows of foliage lengthened into tangles of deep dark grey, that touched men where they lay shivering within the dragging irresistible web of fatigue.

The *boer* soldiers began shooting at 03H17 exactly. The blast of rifles, the shudder of the ground as the Claymore mines exploded, brought the villagers of Omudangila out again, brought them to the entrance gates, bobbing like inquisitive mongooses, with heads cocked and mouths agape as they watched the flashes and heard the thunder of fire that meant someone to the north was dying. How curious, because the *boers* had not been very clever that night! In fact they had been quite thick-headed. Then, when the firing stopped and they saw it was still so dark and cold that even the boss cock had not crowed, the villagers returned to their beds. They'd know all about it in due course.

But of course the South Africans had not finished. The trucks had to roar back to fetch the victors. This time it was dawn when they eventually left, when the smell of diesel smoke and dust had finally drifted from the village, and the last strident iron *Buffel* truck, crammed with those laughing, joking, black-smeared devil men, had mellowed into the distance.

The inhabitants would have been a great deal more curious had they known that not one single man among the 'victors' had fired a shot in anger that night. They had fired their weapons, it is true, most of them into the ground straight ahead, some of them into the trees. Their curiosity would have known no bounds had they known that the real *boer* ambush team was still in position, virtually at the same site, and certainly with exactly the same killing ground in their sights.

But the villagers did not know this, nor did the tribesman with the blanket over his shoulders, who came with the quick purposeful pace and darting, expectant eyes of a man seeking, a man who would not know exactly what he was looking for until he found it.

He found it at the ambush site: a dossier of death – pieces of flesh, flecks of thick blood on the sand, dappling the grass; the many boot-prints of the *boers* who had been there, who had fired their shots and then came forward to view the kill.

The tribesman stood for a while in thought, then walked slowly to the place where the South Africans had been dug in. He counted the positions there and seemed surprised. Had he moved ten paces further into the dense shrub and grass on the east side of the track, he would have been even more surprised, perhaps fatally so, for there was another line of *boer* positions and they were very much occupied.

But the villager did not walk further; there was no reason to. He picked up a few empty cartridge cases, scratched round a bit, then moved back to the butchery along the track. In light that was improving with every passing minute, he seemed to find more or less what he had been seeking: evidence that the bloody *boers* had not just hammered some poor cattle herder returning home late from a beer drink; evidence that they had indeed hit SWAPO – an empty curved bakelite magazine from an AKM rifle, lying half covered in sand. He pounced on it, took it and sniffed at its lip. The smell of gun-powder confirmed everything. With one last hurried glance around, wide-eyed now, as though perhaps aware of the dozen pairs of eyes upon him, he started to run back in the direction from where he had just come.

McGee, as far as was possible from his position under a stunted brandy bush, watched him go. The man had not seen them. One could be certain of that. They had taken a lot of care with their camouflage. The man had not been just an inquisitive tribesman, either; his approach had been too analytical to be anything other than '*boy*'. Now, if the shreds of fresh beef, and the medical whole blood, and the freshly fired magazine, had told the story the way the South Africans wanted it told, things could start happening.

In fact the eastern horizon was scarcely aglow, the earth around still orange with the promise of day, when things did start happening, though not altogether the way they were intended to happen. A herd boy, a little *Omafita* with a knobkierrie almost as big as himself, with an *ochia* charm and half a dozen plodding oxen in tow, came whistling up the track he probably traversed every morning and afternoon of his life. He stopped at the ambush site with the suddenness of the amazed, and began peering around. Eyes as sharp as tacks were taking in everything, and he was not looking at the bushes, but rather through the bushes he had known all his life. McGee willed him to walk on, but it was not to be. Knotting the headstraps of his charges, the boy followed much the same course of action as that of the man who had preceded him. The problem was that this youngster, this *Omunjasele*, had eyes twice as quick and a nose twice as keen as any man. If he did not see them, or indeed smell them, no one would.

He walked over to the vacated South African positions

just as the other man had done and he discovered not only the spent cartridge cases, but a very real and very live grenade that some fool had somehow left behind. Toying with the mechanism, his face a study of concentration, he began drifting further into the shrub towards the ambushers. He was not four paces from McGee, when he managed to get the grenade pin loose. McGee felt himself wince, felt his fingers dig into the earth. The boy, however, still held the safety handle. If he dropped the grenade, or even shifted it, they would have four and a half seconds to pray: any chance of jumping the little bugger was gone – and the grenade was not the only reason.

The blanket man was suddenly back on the scene. With him were seven men in the olive drab and Warsaw Pact webbing of the People's Liberation Army, SWAPO. They did not see the oxen at first, as the beasts had wandered happily into the longer grass to graze. They did not even see the little herd boy standing watching them from the shade of the trees, clutching his new-found toy. They posted a sentry, but he seemed more interested in watching what his own men were doing than performing his task.

What his own men were doing, was planting two big orange anti-tank mines in tandem on the track and salting the verges with black widow mines for good measure. They were too busy preparing a wonderful surprise for the *boers*, who undoubtedly would be along shortly to examine their night's handiwork, to worry about much else.

All might have been well for them. The South African ambush was a non-starter – the herd boy with his grenade had inadvertently ensured that. But the oxen, as oxen often do, had made a collective decision that the grass on the other side of the road looked greener and juicier. Together they started plodding towards the track, the mine layers and the mines.

The SWAPO men should not have reacted the way they did. The cattle were calm and their passage over the mined area could easily have been averted. But the SWAPO men were standing next to many kilograms of pressure-sensitive TNT, with half a ton of beef bearing down on them. What happened was that the lead oxen, the pride of the herd, received an energetic rifle butt across the snout. It reared back, bellowing with fright and pain, and started a stampede. The herd boy, still clutching the grenade, let out a scream of rage and took off in pursuit.

They shot him out of instinct, reflex, whatever sense it is that men acquire when trained for the split-second kill. Whatever it was, they swung their guns on him and brought him tumbling down just short of where they were working. They saw what they had done to the boy, but did not spot the grenade. They had four and a half seconds to look sheepish, then shrapnel tore them apart.

Four men went down with the blast; four were left to fight it out. McGee shot comrade blanket while the man's Tokarev pistol was still half drawn. The rest Ivanovitch's crew blew away with a single sustained volley. It was all over in less than ten seconds.

They tried to win the life of the little *Omunjasele*. They tried everything they knew. He was still alive when they ran with him through the dust and chaff of the helicopter rotor wash. McGee had heard of worse injured casivacs surviving, but somehow he did not think that brave little herd boy would ever whistle to his oxen again.

Chapter 11

Detachment Commander Maduro took the news of the deaths of seven members of his team and the agent at Omudangila stoically. He had no real friends among those killed. Even if he'd had any, no amount of grief had ever brought back a dead comrade. That he had learned long ago. So half his force was gone. It was not a novel situation for him. He had often operated at half strength in the past and would, no doubt, be called upon to do so many times again.

Msimba Maduro's war was not really motivated by patriotism. He had never been a gun-waver or slogan-chanter and was not even a true Namibian. His tribal ties lay in a little kraal outside what had once been the prosperous Portuguese settlement of Vila Pereira de Eca which the MPLA government had renamed Ongiva and which was now so much exploded rubble. Maduro had no illusions about SWAPO. SWAPO would never beat the South Africans on the field of battle, and all the propaganda to the contrary was just so much crap. They were not up to it and no amount of Russian AKMs and SAM 7s or mines or RPG 7s would change that. As he saw it, there was no way in which the People's Liberation Army would ever be able to deliver the conventional clout required to blast the *boers* from Owamboland, not while truculent Impala jets blasted everything on wheels on the wrong side of the border, and gunships buzzed the treetops like spiteful hornets; not as long as *boer* soldiers ranged far, wide and hostile from laagers as durable as bushveld ant hills.

The *boers* would not be chased from Namibia; they would be talked out of it. One day when they imagined they had built up a local territorial force big enough to take on the Liberation Army in the field, and a puppet political structure to take on Sam Nujoma at the ballot box, they would haul down the South African flag, and dust the sand of the Namib gratefully from their boots. In the meantime, their army was buying them time – that was all.

The truth was that when the *boers* departed, win or lose at the polls, the People's Liberation Army would march from Ruacana to the Orange River and nothing would stop them. The blue, red and green flag of SWAPO would fly over Windhoek and he, Msimba Maduro, would have his place in the sun. No, not just a place, rather a throne, because he was ambitious, and that was why he was a SWAPO man. Nujoma would reward his faithful fighters when the struggle was over. Hell! Was there anyone more faithful than Msimba Maduro?

In the meantime, the struggle was far from over. He dismissed the courier who had brought the bad tidings, and returned his gaze to the open map he had spread on the soft ground at his knees. At face value it was a thorough map, drawn to scale, and not covering much more ground than the immediate vicinity of the Ompako Omulonga. The heading on the sheet read, *Encampments Ompako*, which meant that it had been produced by Cuban Intelligence. That annoyed Maduro. Anything Cuban rankled with him. The Cubans thought they were the liberators of all Africa, whereas the truth was that any time the *boers* looked as though they were going to get serious, the comrades from Havana dropped their cigars and soiled their shorts. They would not even take on Jonas Savimbi's home grown army, unless they found themselves balls-to-the-wall at the wrong end of an ambush. He peered at the map again; studied the fortification drawing and wondered just how much of the detail was from a thumbsuck and how much from hard intelligence.

His orders were to attack Fort Ompako: 'To press home the attack with all the valour of the victorious People's Liberation Army of Namibia. To inflict casualties on the *boer* oppressors and their running dogs. To return trium-phant.' They had been issued by David Kalenga, Chief of the Victorious Armed Forces of the Northern Front. What precisely they meant was that he was to drop a few mortar bombs into the Fort to remind the *boers* that their day would come, plant a few TM 46s and then scoot for the border. Comrade Kalenga had an admirable way of putting things, though.

How he put in the attack was his business. The map showed the fort's layout in some detail; the breastworks with the machine-gun positions marked in, the command area, the accommodation, and – what interested him considerably – a position designated 'petrol storage'; the fuel dump. As for the rest there were the usual mortar pits and a dug-in magazine.

It would be useless to try to do any damage there. The petrol dump was the thing to go for. He pulled a red pencil stub from his shirt pocket, licked the tip and made a little red cross dead centre of that area. Then he called across to a man who seemed to be lying dreaming under a bush. 'Hinuanye . . . Comrade Hinuanye!' Comrade Hinuanye was not asleep, though. At the mention of his name, he lifted his bush hat from his face and craned his neck like a wrong-side-up tortoise. 'Yes, Comrade Commander?'

Maduro beckoned to the man impatiently. Hinuanye always seemed half asleep, which was a totally false impression. The fact was that Hinuanye was probably the best mortar man on the Northern Front, who had with him a crew of mortar men who could feed their pieces at twenty-five rounds a minute and still remain accurate. You had to be pretty alert to be able to handle that kind of shooting. The man ambled across.

'Have a look at this,' said Maduro. 'It's a detailed map of the target.'

Hinuanye looked doubtful. He said, 'It looks okay. I hope it's accurate.'

He ran his fingers to the point Maduro had marked. 'This is where you want to place the bombs?'

'Yes.'

'I can't promise anything, comrade.' Maduro wondered if the man was always so negative. Sure, he could not promise anything. Sure, the map could be the figment of some Cuban Intelligence officer's imagination, but it was all they had. They could not very well go up to the Fort in broad daylight and start pacing it off. He sympathized with the mortar commander, but the man would have to show a better face. Hinuanye must have read his mind. He said, 'We'll have to go in quite close for accuracy. If we can find a tree to climb and observe from, we can be much more accurate.'

That was better. 'Fine,' Maduro agreed. 'We can go as close as you wish. We can select a site later on today and find your tree too.'

'When do you plan to attack?'

'Tomorrow,' Maduro told him. 'We attack tomorrow at last light.'

'We'll make the *boers* pay, Comrade Commander.'

'Yes,' said Maduro, 'we *will* make them pay.'

They had, he thought, built up quite an outstanding debt, de la Rey and his *boers*.

Rifleman James Michael Simms was in the fifteenth month, third week and fourth day of his two-year National Service stint. If anyone had asked him to be more accurate, he could probably have included hours and minutes in the calculation.

James Michael hated the army with more than average hate. The strange thing was that none of his officers and few of the NCOs ever realized it. To most he was the good soldier Simms, a quiet humble man who had agreed to forego the glory of battlefield for the sake of his brothers in arms. Simms, to all in authority, was the original *vasbyt troepie*; an example to all men. In truth James Michael was a natural and gifted malingerer who, apart from a few excruciating months during basic training, had managed to side-step by various means, any activity that could vaguely be categorized as hard work, in fact any work at all.

Perhaps the fault was that he simply thought differently to most men. He could not see the sense in it all. He did not want to be killed, so why train for it? There were more than enough men around him whose sole mission in life seemed to be the pursuit of hero status. He was happy to let them get on with it, if only they would leave him out of it. Unfortunately they would not.

B Company, 14 South African Infantry Battalion, had arrived at Ompako that previous summer, a summer that even by Owambo standards had been considered hot: one in which, if the sun had not been flaming out of a merciless sky, then rain had been pouring from it. One hundred percent humidity means simply that the air around is saturated: it cannot hold more moisture. It also means that any movement more strenuous than feebly flicking at flies is liable to cause a man to all but drown in his own sweat. It was in the middle of such a summer that the crusaders of B Company arrived, more than willing to close with the enemy; fresh and keen and determined to a man, to bear whatever hardship had to be borne *vir volk en vaderland*, but mighty pleased, just the same, to discover that Ompako had within its walls a quartet of old but apparently serviceable refrigerators. A frothy beer, even if it was not as damn cold as it could have been, went a long way to restoring a soldier's morale; especially if that soldier had just watched the mail sack empty out for the umpteenth time without so much as a postcard from home; especially if that *troepie* had just dragged himself in from a six-day slog across the summer swamps of Owamboland; especially if a good buddy had just left for home in a body bag.

Rifleman Simms was the exception. *Volk en vaderland* meant to him two old-timers who still called him Jimsey, and a seven-acre small holding just outside the little town of Mafeking.

He did not drink and if he had any buddies, he did not advertise them. One thing he did possess was an uncanny ability to coax into life things mechanical. When others who were better qualified failed, Simms's kiss of life often

188

did the job. So when during that first sweltering summer one of the precious refrigerators gave a geriatric cough and rattled to a pulseless death, and a state of emergency was declared, the name of Jimmy Simms was brought up at the highest levels as a man who might be able to do something. Of course the man would have to be detached from his platoon for a day or two. 'No problem,' Richter said. 'Get him.'

They got him, and James, after hours of dedicated labour, mainly supine on the relatively cool floor of the main mess, breathed back life into that indispensable piece of equipment The hierarchy had been overjoyed. They could now drink their beer cold without a conscience. The men were overjoyed. The beer was colder than ever before.

Simms was more pleased than anyone. He had discovered, he thought, the pathway to salvation. He asked Richter if the captain had ever heard the word maintenance . . . The fridges needed regular maintenance; apparently very regular maintenance, to avert any further catastrophe.

Again the matter was brought up at top level. 'If they need maintenance, Hans, damn it, maintain them,' de la Rey demanded. 'Ask Simms's platoon leader. No, tell him to release the man, that's all. Can't have that happening again.'

Simms protested that his only wish was to patrol and shoot his rifle, but in the end good sense prevailed. As Richter put it: 'It's as important a job as any to keep the vital services on the go, is it not?' The rifleman agreed reluctantly that it was, laid down his gun and accepted a spanner in lieu of it. The ice man and the four refrigerators lived happily ever after . . . Well, if not for ever after, then certainly for some considerable time.

No mortal thing lives happily ever after and Simms was not exempt from that natural law. Seasons change and men with them. The long hot summer rained into a mild tolerable winter and Captain Richter received the news that he was going to move on to greater things. A brand

189

new man arrived at Ompako, Captain Matthew McGee, who, it appeared, liked night ambushes and Gung Ho fire-fights. Captain McGee had a bullet scar as big as a fist. Captain McGee had shoulders wide enough to do considerable boat-rocking.

Flinty-eyed Captain McGee . . . Simms was apprehensive. Had he been a fly on the wall of de la Rey's tent right then perhaps he would have been a damn sight more apprehensive. Perhaps, too, he would not have made his fatal blunder. 'We,' Major de la Rey was saying to his new 2 IC, 'are getting visitors. Don't ask me why, but a contingent of politicians is visiting some operational bases. Ompako is on the route. We can expect them tomorrow afternoon – as yet I'm not sure of the time, but they're going to eat and spend the night here.'

McGee did not mention that the news had already been leaked in the showers. He would turn off that source in his own time and in his own way. What he said was, 'We'll have to tighten up base security even more. I suppose you want to give them some kind of reception?'

De la Rey said he would like to give them a rocket up the arse and aim them for Windhoek. That was what he would like to give them.

'Bugger it, man. As if we haven't got enough on our plates without those twats coming out here for a jolly! This bloody place is thick with "*boy*" right now. The General must be out of his bloody mind to allow it.'

McGee, who privately agreed, said nothing. Every good soldier knew that Generals never made mistakes. How could they – they communicated directly with God.

'Matt' – so it was Matt now, de la Rey was bringing him in from the cold – 'Matt, I want you to get on to Ondangwa, see if you can get us a troop of armoured cars to beef us up a bit. I want you to check that every mortar pit commander is on the ball with his fire plan. The buggers get rusty! Don't we all? I'm not pulling any men out of the field. The war can't come to a stop, Matt, so every available man in the camp will have to be used in your defence plan.'

Richter came in. He had been packing in preparation for his departure the following morning. Already he bore that unsettled look that seems to descend on a man on the eve of a big move. He no longer looked at home in de la Rey's tent.

'Well, I'm packed,' he announced. 'And ready to go.'

'I was just saying,' de la Rey continued, 'that I'm not going to pull any man out of the field for the benefit of the Turnhalle types coming in tomorrow. What we must do is patrol the boundary of the base and do it well with base personnel.'

They spoke about other things; the Omundangila ambush. It was the first time the major had spoken about the events of the previous night. He was distressed about the herd boy. He was going to meet the youth's parents, he said. 'It's a bloody shame, a crying bloody shame. When the kids get wiped out, it makes you wonder what it's all about. I know how I'd feel if it was my kid. All the money in the world wouldn't compensate me.' He had nothing to say about the eight terrs they had taken out. It was as though the little boy's death had negated the success. Richter said, 'Anyway we hit SWAPO hard, gave them a thrashing. They'll feel it.' That summed it up. SWAPO would feel it. A youngster had gone in addition but there was no time for tears in that bloody land.

McGee had work to do. Leaving de la Rey and Richter still conversing, he went in search of Sergeant-Major Venter. They had a defence plan to draw up and rehearse. It was tea-time, so the first place he checked was the mess. That was where he saw Simms, in fact almost tripped over the man. The rifleman was lying flat on the floor with his head and shoulders wedged into the works of the refrigerator.

'What the hell, are you doing?' demanded McGee.

It was just the opportunity Jimmy Simms had been hoping for. He had, in fact, been lying under various fridges, on and off, for the better part of the past twenty-four hours, waiting for the new 2 IC to literally stumble upon him. He jumped snappily to his feet, slammed to attention and presented himself.

'Rifleman Simms, *captain*! These refrigerators are very old *captain*! They are in constant need of maintenance, *captain*!'

'And you repair them . . . all the time?'

'*Captain*!'

McGee was amazed. The little soldier was too good to be true, like a Barry Cornwall character, only more so. *Courage! – nothing e'er withstood. Freemen fighting for their good.*

Perhaps he should not be so sceptical. 'What else do you do?' he asked.

'What else, captain?'

'Yes, four bloody fridges can't keep you busy all day, can they?'

'They break down constantly, captain. Captain Richter will tell captain, if captain asks him. Captain Richter knows all about it.'

McGee made a mental note to check with Venter on the activities of Rifleman Simms. In the meantime he had pressing matters to attend to – like the defence of Ompako. 'Have you seen Sarmajor Venter around?' he asked the rifleman. 'I'm looking for him.'

There was an unseasonal winter rain shower the next morning. The only other uncharacteristic occurrence was that Rifleman Simms was jerked from the peace of his slumbers at a most unusually early hour, well before first light. He first thought he was in the clutches of a nightmare. A white blinding light was shining into his eyes and from behind it a growling voice was addressing him. But the light became a torch, and the gravelly voice became undoubtedly that owned by one Corporal Kreuzer, the Ogre of Ompako. Rifleman Simms cringed.

Kreuzer had information for him. Sarmajor Venter would appreciate his, Simms's, company on the wall that morning at stand-to. It was, Simms was informed, Simms's lucky day. Did he understand that it was his lucky day? Simms said he did not understand, but he had an awful feeling that he was going to.

'Simms, ol' buddy, we know how badly you've missed all the patrolling and all that. Well, you don't have to worry any more, you're back in it, you're with my section. How about that?'

Simms said, 'Corporal, could you please turn your torch away, I can't see anything?'

'Oh! . . . oh! Dear me . . . Yes, can't have one of my men blinded.' Kreuzer flicked the torch off, leaving Simms with a floating purple patch where his vision should have been. 'That better, ol' buddy?'

'Yes . . . thank you, Corporal.'

He heard rather than saw Corporal Kreuzer lift his tent flap, but the man had not gone. He had one final piece of advice for his new rifleman: 'Simms, ol' buddy. It wasn't my idea to have you back in the section. I know you, fella. You're a fucking useless prick. You've been up Richter's arse far too long now. Your goofing off days are now over, and unless you believe that, I, me, Corporal Kreuzer, will kick your backside until you do. I'm stuck with you. I don't like it any more than you do. Now get out of the sack, pick up your feet and get to the wall. Then be on company parade sharp and shiny. Do that and we'll get on fine but give me one bit of shit, just one little bit, fella, and so help me, I'll screw you.' Kreuzer had finished. He walked out.

Simms could not believe it. He had gone to bed patting himself on the back over the job he had done on McGee, and in the night his world had fallen in. He sat up and reached for his smokes. For the first time he noticed it was raining. There was a steady drumming on the roof canvas and the seams were leaking. He slid the zip of his sleeping bag down and sat up. Shit, it was freezing! He lit his cigarette, and the stub of the candle next to his bed, then stood up. The luminous clock on his metal service trunk showed 05.15. The almanac gummed to his metal cupboard showed he had eight months and six days of National Service remaining, and he had an awful feeling that he would not survive it. He made his way to the tent side, pulled back the canvas, tilted his pelvis and urinated into the downpour. 'Fuck you, Kreuzer,' he said, but he said it to himself.

It rained all morning. At midday it was still coming down; not heavily like in the summer, this was not much more than a drizzle: a cold, miserable soaker, just enough to seep through your shirt and trickle in little streams down your spine. Kreuzer's section completed one full sweep of the perimeter of Ompako, then came in at midday. They were scheduled for the same operation that afternoon. Simms had a cigarette for lunch. From his seat in the main mess hall he could observe much of the base. He watched Richter's departure, watched de la Rey and McGee and a few of the lieutenants shake the man's hand. Oh God, he despised them, the whole stinking power-clutching clique! The convoy departed and almost simultaneously, three armoured cars, with their big masculine cannon poking well ahead, came in, splashed across the parade ground and parked. He watched Captain McGee, huge in his poncho, walk to them, greet one of the men emerging from the glistening beasts, then escort him to the Ops Room. They were joking, seemed to know each other. Didn't all officers? The cars had Ondongwa insignia upon them.

At 17.30 he found himself back on the base line patrol of Ompako's perimeter. Kreuzer, the bastard, had put him on the extreme outside of the sweep, which meant simply that on each of the four corners the inside men could practically mark time, while he had all the added distance to walk. The corporal, in his wisdom, had also saddled him with a radio with which to report when he was back on the straight and the patrol could continue in one copybook line. In theory, it was great, especially if the outside man was experienced and motivated. Simms was neither. In fact, he considered the whole exercise a complete waste of time and energy; so much so that apart from one half-full magazine in his rifle, he carried not another round. The magazines filling his chest webbing were conveniently light, they were empty. It was his second hike around that day and he was tired, wet, peeved and becoming with every step more and more resentful. The whole thing was a bloody joke. A bunch of dum-dum black politicians, fresh from the tree-tops, was coming to pay them a visit. The conceit of it – a bushveld admiration society, and he had to slog his way 300 bloody miles around the base to look after their worthless skins. Shit!

He picked up his pace in anger with only one thought in his mind, to get the fucking patrol over with. He would wait for them at the last corner and enjoy a smoke there. At least it would be a dry smoke. It had stopped raining. The radio reports he would ad-bloody-lib. He pressed on, happy with his decision.

When Simms heard the familiar whop-whop sound of helicopter blades cutting the air he was moving fast, much too fast. 'Early,' he muttered to himself. When, seconds later, like two giant locusts the puma choppers swept over the bush line barely thirty metres ahead, Simms looked at his wristwatch and realized that they were not early, they were dead on time. He should have been somewhere on the north-eastern corner of Ompako right then. Instead, he was within the blade wash of the chopper and right on the western boundary. He had realized he was ahead but he had not thought he was that far ahead. He looked back to see if he could possibly locate his point man. No one was visible. Simms did not realize it then, but the nearest other member of his patrol was almost 300 metres to his rear. He watched the chopper hover for an instant then swoop down out of sight of the base. Then he lit a cigarette.

Chapter 12

It was almost an hour before dusk by the time Commander Maduro had his mortar sited to his own and Hinuanye's satisfaction. They had found their tree, an autumn-garbed bloodwood that topped the surrounding bush by at least 5 metres; it was almost ideally situated some 800 metres from Ompako's west-facing wall, with probably 100 metres beyond the wall to the target: the petrol dump. If Maduro could have wished for anything more, it would have been more foliage, just a few more leaves. From his position in the fork of a high limb he had a perfect view of de la Rey's fort. But it also seemed to him that any serious observer from the camp would spot him, Maduro. It was an illusion, though – there was foliage, sapless, thin, and drooping under the rain, but the colour of it matched perfectly the pattern of his winter drab camouflage and there was enough to mask him.

Maduro watched Hinuanye and his men digging their big-barrelled weapon in almost just below him. An 82mm M37 mortar was an ugly weapon in every sense of the word. At 900 metres, in good hands, it was deadly accurate. Its projectile carried 4kg of high explosive that burst its heavy steel casing into a thousand deadly shards.

Their mortar was in good hands. They were assembling it now, bedding down the big base-plate and slotting in the barrel and bipod. It was all done quietly, proficiently and quickly. Hinuanye personally secured the sight and attended to the business of selecting his aiming points; cross-levelling and doing all the other things mortar men did.

The rain was easing now to a light drizzle. In places big blotches of late sunlight were highlighting the surrounding tree-tops. He welcomed it, and congratulated himself on his choice of the western flank. His attack would come directly out of the blinding setting sun.

Now that he had his mortar set up, Maduro had four men to spare: two teams of two. It was fewer than he should have had, but more than enough. Their intention was not to take Ompako, just to shake it up. Each team had an RPG launcher, and an RPD machine gun. He watched them slither forward towards the fort until they were out of sight. Their job was to keep the western wall's machine-gun posts busy and he was confident that they had the clout to do that.

There was nothing more to do but wait until the sun had but a few minutes of life left to offer the day; then to attack. Maduro went through a mental check list to see if anything had been forgotten. The *boers* had patrolled the area earlier that day so there was really nothing to worry about, for the moment. He picket up his powerful binoculars and Fort Ompako in every detail was an arm's length away.

It had stopped raining and a few officers on the earth parapet were engaged in some relaxed pistol practice, smoke from their gun barrels visible seconds before the pop-pop of the shots could be heard. On the parade-ground a squad of troops was drilling, and three armoured cars, their turrets glinting from the shower, had just crewed up. He watched them with interest. A lot of brown-clad troops seemed to be lounging around with rifles and webbing, probably waiting to go to their last light positions. He wondered if he should hit them now while they were all standing in the open. But it would be suicide to allow the *boers* too much daytime to get after him. No, he would wait, but not much longer. Maduro glanced at his watch then craned his neck back to watch the setting sun . . . Certainly not much longer.

As with all South African camps, the *boers* had erected a massive girder watchtower. Maduro, even from his lofty perch, had to look up to see the sentry in it. A new man was climbing to replace the guard, climbing slowly and

197

methodically. Maduro watched him. He could count every rivet on that structure with his binoculars. Then he swept back to the fuel dump. It was well sand-bagged but even so red drums of dieseline were clearly visible. An armoured personnel carrier was filling up at that moment. Stay there, just a little longer, he said to the driver; just a little longer.

The new guard was, it seemed, just as bored with life as his counterpart had been. Perhaps not quite so bored . . . Maduro watched him sweep the horizon then the tree-line to the west in one casual movement, then back again. The man's body was suddenly keyed with interest and his binoculars were locked right on to the big bloodwood tree. Maduro froze. He could not be seen. The tree trunk was shading him perfectly. What then? A flash from the mortar barrel? Even more impossible. A movement? No. It was all wrong. The sentry was looking right at him. Maduro felt the knife blade of fear twist in his gut, his heart pounding. If the man so much as reached for the field telephone at his elbow, Maduro vowed to begin the attack. But the sentry did nothing of the sort. Leaving his binoculars hanging from his neck strap, he cupped his hands to his mouth. Elevation lent his shout incredible clarity – even at that distance Maduro gleaned the words of his yell: '*Chopper! Chopper!*'

Then he could hear it himself, the whining turbine, the basting blades. At first he thought the *boers* had trapped him, that gunships were coming in to blast him. Then he realized that gunships would have made their pass over the fort towards him, and not from behind him and on to Ompako. So they were not gunships, but they had certainly been expected. The officers had sheathed their pistols and were jogging to the centre of the base. Troops were running everywhere and the armoured cars were rolling into hull-down position behind the wall.

Then the chopper was overhead and it was not just one of them. There were two of them – and the noise was incredible. Maduro could almost have reached up and touched their big camouflaged bellies, and the bloodwood writhed into a frenzied tempest of lashing branches.

The luck of it, the unbelievable once-in-a-lifetime luck of it. If things happened now the way it looked as though they were going to happen, he was about to be presented with two of the fattest, most sought-after targets in the world of war – two of the most valuable pieces of equipment in the South African arsenal! His voice sounded to him like a stranger's it quavered so much, when, as loud as he dared, he shouted: 'Stand by! Stand by!'

He could see Hinuanye below him, head up, gaping into the tree like an imbecile. God, if the man messed it up he would personally shoot him! In front, on the landing strip of the fort, the doors of the helicopters were sliding open. Men in bright shirts, wielding cameras, spilled out of one of them. From the belly of the other, with the studied dignity of very important people. well-dressed civilians were emerging. Politicians or tribal chiefs, or both; it did not matter. Either way, they were prime targets. The officers, one of them undoubtedly *Ombadje* de la Rey, were also prime targets. The helicopters were the icing on the top. He was not even faced with the dilemma of a choice – they were all in the killing ground together. All the mortar needed was a quick adjustment.

It did not matter about last light any more. It did not matter if the South African retaliation was wicked. 'Now!' Maduro screamed, 'Fire, Hinuanye! Fire!'

The first bomb landed some eighty metres to the west of Ompako and rent McGee's ears like a thunderclap. The second and corrected shot hit the eastern parapet with a bang that seemed to fill the sky with smoke and falling earth. In the safe seconds they were allowed, between the fall of the first two missiles, a lot of things happened. The chopper crews, finding themselves in their worst possible nightmare, reacted to get airborne. They started their turbines and started them quickly. The civilians seemed divided into two categories: those rooted to the spot, and those in nimble motion in every direction. They shared one thing only. All of them were yelling. De la Rey shouted: 'Fetch 'em!' almost as though he was turning his dogs loose, and the soldiers of the honour guard sprang off their bellies and obeyed. They fetched them, they tackled them and pulled them down, into trenches, into bunkers and behind walls.

By then every gun in Ompako seemed to be firing and the bombs were coming in again. Shrapnel was scything through the entire camp, cutting guy ropes, spanging off armour plate, tearing through the skin and perspex of the desperate helicopters, and men were falling.

De la Rey fell. He and McGee were running for the Ops room to co-ordinate the retaliation, moving in a sprint, with the deadly rhythm of the Russian 82s to keep them keen. There was the crescending wail of an incoming shell, and down they went; the terrible double crack-crump of a close one, then McGee was up and going. De la Rey was still on the ground.

It was a scalp wound, the splinter must have stunned him cold but *Ombadje* would survive. In the meantime the command of Fort Ompako was in the second-in-command's hands, a second-in-command who was practically brand new. It was obvious that things were bad, bloody bad. McGee did not realize just how bad until he clambered down the bunker steps and into the Ops room.

A stream of messages was coming in. The western wall was under attack by rockets and machine-gun fire that was not having much effect. They were returning fire. Good . . . no problem. The civilians had mostly been accounted for; certainly all the VIPs were safe . . . That was the last of the good news . . . The choppers were grounded . . . both had taken shrapnel . . .

'We're sitting ducks out here!'

'Leave the Pumas and take cover. There's trenches at the side of the strip.' That was all the advice McGee could give them for the present. As he knew they would, they ignored it. 'Negative. We're standing by inside with fire-fighting gear.' 'Neutralize that bloody mortar, for Chris-sakes.'

It was easier said than done. The defence mortars were bombarding the veld, but it was a hit-or-miss situation. The sentry in the girder tower thought the bombs were coming from the west, but there was a hell of a lot of ground to the west: the 82s could shoot from 3000 metres; three whole kilometres on a wide front; and if they were dug in, it would need a direct hit to take them out. To complicate things, there was Corporal Kreuzer's patrol somewhere out there. In the meantime a projectile was shaking Ompako just about every two seconds.

An almighty explosion rocked the Ops room bunker and the acrid smell of Amatol lanced McGee's throat. Then a breathless voice came over the radio: 'I've got a contact . . . zero. I've got . . . bloody contact.'

It was unprofessional. The voice procedure was poor, but to the acting Officer Commanding it was the loveliest message he had ever heard. He grabbed the hand mike himself and instructed. 'Send! Man with contact, send.'

'It's Jimmy Simms,' someone said.

'Simms,' McGee repeated. 'Send.'

There was a crackle and a hiss of static. Everyone was watching the receiver as though it was alive. Another blast shook the ground, but McGee hardly noticed it. 'I've got 'em.' Simms's voice was high-pitched with excitement. 'They've got machine guns close in. Their mortar, it's next to the big bloodwood tree to the west. You know the one?'

'I know it!' rapped Sergeant Major Venter.

'We know it!' McGee told Simms. 'Keep your bum down, Jimmy. We're going to give it to them right on the nose, so stay down.'

McGee reached for the field telephones, connecting him with his mortars. At the same time he opened the channel to the armoured cars.

'Okay,' he said. 'Here's your target . . .'

201

He wondered why the enemy bombardment had slackened off.

Msimba Maduro was high on adrenalin. His mortar ranging had been true and Hinuanye's men were lobbing bombs into Ompako at such a devastating rate it was hard to see the place for the black smoke and dust. A burning tent threw great sheets of orange flames skywards.

In the minute or so they had been in action, all that had been thrown back at them in anger was a fair volume of machine-gun fire, from which they were fairly well covered, and some shots from the cannon on the armoured cars. That had been uncomfortable. Maduro raised his binoculars and swept them over the parapet of Ompako. An RPG rocket exploded on the crest of a dug-out, heaving up splintered logs and sand. Through the firing post an uninterrupted stream of tracer continued to pour. If the idea was to get out with their skins intact then now was the time to make a move while the *boers* were still shooting blind. The first South African mortar bombs were screaming over.

But that was not the plan any more. Maduro was certain he had damaged the two big helicopters or they would have been airborne by now. Two damaged helicopters would go a long way towards the big promotion. Two burned-out helicopters and he would be able to write his own ticket. There would have to be sacrifices made, chances taken. Only a direct hit was going to do it. He had to get a hit. Now was the time to slow things down, let the smoke clear, assess the situation, then hit the *boers* with every last thing that they had. That was what a true commander would do, and that was what he planned to do.

There were five 82mm projectiles primed and lying in the mortar pit: five more chances. He took the most careful calculations and called them down to Hinuanye. There they were, the two Pumas, looming from the smoke now as clumsy and useless on the ground as they were formidable in the air. He had to have them.

202

'Are you ready?' he called to his mortar men. 'Each shot will be corrected. Fire only on my orders.'

'Yes.'

The first shot was on the verge of the airstrip. They must have hit the avgas bunker or something. It sent up a black-tinged column of writhing flame. He called down his corrections. The next one would be dead on . . . But there was to be no next one. There was instead the staccato, throaty roar of a machine gun firing really close – the sound perhaps every infantryman dreads hearing most; the point-blank shock of a gun emptying itself right at you. Hinuanye's crew were probably dead before the sound even registered. Hinuanye himself was probably saved by the splintering flesh and bone of a man shielding him. He went down – but in an instant he was up again with his rifle and shooting. Shooting at a *boer*, a typical every-day South African soldier, only this one did not have a typical South African weapon, he had a Soviet RPD in his hands and that was the weapon that had done all the damage.

From his perch in the bloodwood Maduro aimed his pistol. He shot the man. He saw the puff of dust on the chest of the brown shirt. The man's gut was a mess of blood from Hinuanye's shots. Still he was coming on. He was on his knees and he must have been dead, but his finger was tugging the trigger. Then the RPD ran dry.

There were still the helicopters and there was still the mortar in the pit, aimed and upright. Maduro cast one last glance towards Ompako, before he swung himself to the ground. The entire western wall was alive with troops, the armoured cars, like enraged bull elephants, had breasted the earthworks, ripped up the perimeter fence, poles and all, and were charging. He reached the ground and the world around him seemed to erupt as though a hundred volcanoes had broken loose. The South African mortars had found him, and there was nothing to be done.

Maduro knew he was dying. He was sure of it. The explosions couldn't be counted now: there was just one never-ending concussion. He had no idea whether he was on his face or his back, upright or upside down. From every side his every sense was being pulverized. He knew he was screaming because he could hear that now, and he could hear it because suddenly that was the only sound around him. The South Africans had stopped shooting and he was still alive. They had stopped shooting and that meant their troops were almost upon him. Maduro's ears were hissing so loudly he could hardly hear his own movements as he heaved himself from the blood-bath of the mortar pit. It was like a silent dream, a very bad dream, the one when your legs won't move and you've got to get away.

His limbs did begin to function after a while – so well, in fact, that at one stage he thought he might make it. That was until the armoured car latched on to him. Maduro sensed rather than heard the thing behind him, then when he looked back he knew he did not have a chance. He jerked to the left and ran on, then to the right, but the vehicle stuck to him as though he was tied to it. They were so close he could see the grin on the commander's face. The man was going to try and run him down, squash him like a jack rabbit. He knew he had him. The man was shouting something.

'Hey, boy, *kalojika*. Stop, *jong*.'

The words, far from stopping him, gave him strength. He felt a bullet chase past his neck, then heard the crack. The man had a pistol, held in both hands, his whole upper body above the armour. 'Hey, boy.'

The panzer man was whooping and yelling in pursuit, his car was a short pace away when Maduro knew it must end. He had nothing left. He spun round and threw up his hands, but it was too late. Like a giant mailed fist, the Eland struck him. Maduro remembered spinning free of the ground for an age, and there he had the strangest thought. He hoped the pumas at Ompako were still sound enough to do a casivac. Then all was black.

Darkness is not a sudden thing in the Owambo lowlands. There is a special time that the Kwanyama tribesmen call *Etango otali ningini paife*, settling time, when the day's labours are done. When the purple sky still smoulders along its western edge and good men peer into a dying sun and whisper, 'Lord help me through the coming night . . . I pray. Then favour me with one more splendid day.'

They found Jimmy Simms then. Someone yelled, 'Stretcher!' and pounding feet converged, but there was no need for hurry. The little ice man was there in body only, holding the enemy machine gun he had won so tightly they had to prize his fingers loose.

'Easy with him boys,' Kreuzer's voice sounded tight. 'Bloody little hero.'

Chapter 13

One week and a bit later Jimmy Simms's remains were buried back in his home town in the Republic. It was a freezing day and not many people had turned out. But then Jimmy had been a quiet boy – even the padre had said that; a good boy. Those who had not come missed a fine occasion, grand stuff; maybe not full military honours, but enough to warm the hearts of two sad parents. There was talk of a posthumous decoration too.

The politicians had left Ompako with quite a different angle on the war. It was a subdued party of men the Air Force lifted from the fort in two brand-new Pumas. The damaged craft had taken two more days to patch up and by the time they had left, all the other mortar damage had also been cleared up. Ombajde de la Rey was back on his feet and so were the other hurt men. It was amazing but in spite of all the high explosive thrown at them, the South Africans had come to little harm. Perhaps they had just sited their trenches well. Perhaps the 82mm Soviet mortar was not such a capable annihilator in the soft going of Northern Owambo. Perhaps they had just been damn lucky.

A lot of men had much thinking to do on that subject, McGee no less than the others. He had the bloodwood levelled and any other tree that could serve as an observation post within three kilometres of Ompako. He improved the trenches and the communications. For days he roamed the environs of the base, putting himself in the place of the enemy. Retaliation in future would be swifter, more accurate and more telling . . . He hoped . . . And when all was said and done, Ompako's second-in-command had to admit that he sided with those men who believed that they had all been very lucky soldiers indeed.

McGee became the perfect admin. officer, a dream second-in-command. Major de la Rey was removed from things mundane and allowed to concentrate on the job of sowing death, dismay and destruction among the enemy who were unfortunate enough to have been assigned to his battle sector. His kill rate was astonishing. His reputation continued to rise. All was as it should be.

As the Ekanjo rain diviners would have it, the cold dry hungry months passed by and the sky once more responded to their calls. Black, fat rain clouds surged in with the summer wind and emptied their bloated bellies on to the land. The vast flat *oshanas* soaked up the storms for days. Puddles became pools and pools lakes. The rivers filled, then failed to hold the spate and as the plump fingers of water reached out and intertwined fully three-fifths of Owambo lived under muddy, warm, knee-deep water.

It was a time for rejoicing. The lands were planted and the cattle grew fat but more important, suddenly, almost as though they had sprung from the very ground, the fish were there. Where before there had been sand and grass, shoals of bream now swam and Owambo women with their *shikuku* fishing baskets reaped that harvest from morning to night.

The powdery dirt tracks that passed as roads during the dry months could obviously not stand up to it. Almost overnight, certainly after the first few convoys had waddled through, they became nothing more than slippery axle-deep sludge trails that changed the character of driving and transformed normally surefooted four-by-four vehicles into treacherous, wheel-spinning, mulish dead weights; the drivers into demented men.

It was no way to fight a war, not from the South African side anyway, but fight it they did. Patrols went out hunched up against the rain and in spite of wet weather gear were drenched in minutes.

For SWAPO, however, it could not have been better. No longer was a man restricted to the distances his water-bottle would take him. He could range far and wide, have his spoor washed out behind him, then sleep soundly in the lush new green forests all around. Mines were easier to lay and harder to detect. It was not uncommon for a car-load of locals to have their destination violently rear-ranged. But then it did not take long for the crater to seep full, nor for the survivors to continue the feast of the *Egomboto*. Life in Owambo went on.

As for McGee, he got out of Ompako as frequently as his duties would allow. It was not the clever thing to do. The clever thing was to thank heaven for your desk and the chair on which you were entitled to glue your bum, then wait for the sun to shine and the mud to go away. Any admin. officer worth his name knew that. McGee's problem was that he was a sham. He was no more an admin. officer than Gengis Khan had been a minstrel. He knew it, but what he also realized was that as a career soldier he was expected to get all his toetsies in line and solidly upon the square on which he stood before he would be given the chance to 'advance to Pall Mall' – and he was now a career soldier, pure and simple.

Sometimes, like right now, there were genuine reasons for getting out. Headman Shelongo of the kraal *Oshamdada* had sent a message to Ompako that he had matters to discuss, which probably meant that the old man was going to ask for more ammo to blow away than the army was currently allocating to him. Then someone at Brigade wanted an evaluation of an aspect of the civic action programme, which probably meant that someone at Brigade did not have enough to do. What it added up to, however, was the assemblage of a two-vehicle convoy and a gratified captain. The doctor requested permission to come along. They had a new medical officer now with a totally unpronounceable surname and a burning Living-stonian zeal. McGee called him Schmal. 'Sure you can come, Lieutenant Schmal. My pleasure.'

He and Lieutenant Schmal rode in the lead truck with a section of riflemen riding shotgun to the rear. As a bonus it was not raining. They had a tarpaulin rigged just in case, but the deep dark grey clouds that morning had drifted reluctantly back to the horizon and McGee hoped they would stay there. 'We're going to Oshamdada, the kraal of Headman Shelongo. That's near the Odila river, over on our eastern boundary. That's where we'll start, then we'll work our way back to Ompako, taking in the smaller kraals on the way.'

'Fine,' said Schmal. 'Anything you say.'

'It's a round trip of some seventy five, eighty K's so we're going to have to plan our stops quite carefully or we won't manage it all in one day.'

'Fine,' the doctor repeated, 'No problem. I really don't know how much there will be for me to do. You're the boss, anyway.'

They reached their first port of call at 10.00 on schedule, debussed, then McGee waited under a kiaat tree, its boughs on fire with sprays of yellow orange and humming with bees. He squatted down patiently. The headman would summon him soon enough. He enjoyed his visits to Luke Shelongo's kraal. The headman was a dignified old *elenga*, an old school traditionalist. He and McGee got on well. His fields were always in good condition, his cattle sleek, his beer of the best. He had many healthy children and grandchildren. What else was there for a man to concern himself with? Well, there was SWAPO . . .

Shelongo's *omupopili*, his adviser, had come from the kraal entrance and was advancing on the tree. McGee greeted him. '*Ua penduka?*'

'*Eh! na ovewa penduka.*' Yes, he said, meaning one was indeed wide-eyed and awake.

'I am as strong as a lion.'

'The wise and industrious Headman Shelongo, does such a busy man have time to see me?'

'Indeed he awaits you.'

'I come when he is ready.'

'He is ready.'

McGee rose slowly, careful not to give any appearance of one in a hurry. That would mark him as petty person, a

209

man of little stature. There was nothing more to be said to the *omupopili* and anyway it would be shocking behaviour to talk to him while the man had his back turned. He followed him through the labyrinth of Shelongo's *Eumbo* to the headman's reception area, a sandy circular clearing with an open-sided hut, for inclement conditions, to one side. Shelongo was there waiting for him, seated on a curved log. A lesser but similar log had been placed nearby for McGee. The headman was seated, so he was expected to sit too. He did so with a show of appreciation, then waited for the senior man to address him.

Shelongo was an adept at the dignity of delay. One by one his advisers, including the man who had escorted McGee, came in and seated themselves to each side and slightly to the rear of Shelongo. Then, with a smile that bared a whole stockade of roots, he acknowledged McGee.

'You bring us honour,' he said.

'Indeed,' McGee replied. 'It is I who am the honoured one.'

'Did you travel well? The roads are like rivers. Perhaps a boat would be the best thing to use now.'

'Ah, yes,' agreed McGee. 'But the rains bring the fish and that is good. But they also bring the terrorists and that is not good.' There wasn't a single Kuanyama word for terrorist so McGee used the word *omukolokosi* which literally meant the man who had the law against him. His intention had been to frame an opening that would allow Shelongo easy access to the subject matter of his topic.

It did not work. The old man was not yet ready. He said, 'But now the crops can be planted and that is good.'

Everyone was nodding in agreement with that statement. 'And the mosquito and the bad blood of *oluidi*.' McGee had reason for throwing in malaria. 'I have with me today a new doctor, a man of much experience. It would be a good thing if while we talk he could go about his work.'

That made sense to everyone too. Headman Shelongo

despatched one of his bodyguard to organize a bush clinic for Schmal under the kiaat tree while the conversation pottered around every subject under the hot Owambo sun; every subject other than the *real politic* of the instant, the survival of the best armed. McGee laughed inwardly as his precious time-table tottered to irretrievable collapse. He should have known better than to plan a day that included a visit to old Shelongo. 'And you, *ondjai*, are you well?' Shelongo enquired of McGee. 'You always appear very well.'

McGee did not like being addressed as warlord, but he answered politely. 'I am well, Headman.'

'The people of my tribe speak highly of you.'

'The people of your tribe are good people, industrious and law-abiding.'

'Yes,' Shelongo agreed thoughtfully. 'They are good people. There are few enough good people today and they become less in number. You must know that . . . Good people must be protected.'

They had cut through to the heart wood. It was not for McGee to talk now. It was for him to listen. He settled on his log and did just that. 'I had a visitor,' the old man said. 'Not more than ten days back. A man from far across the Angolan side of the border, the son of a son of a brother of mine. He was hungry so we gave him food and beer. He told me he had a message from my brother. He told me to be warned, to be on my guard. He said that in the camp of SWAPO my name is spoken of as one who is close to the *boers*. He told me that I am judged by those men as being a traitor to my own people.' But for the everyday sounds of the kraal there was silence for a while. McGee let it be. He wanted Shelongo to get closer to the point before he responded. 'When have I ever been a traitor to my people? Do they not draw grain from my storage? Do they not get justice from the tribal court? There is no better place to live in all the land than my *omikunda*, from here to the Odila river. Now they will come for me in the night. Like jackals they always come in the night. Now what must I do?'

McGee answered his question with a question. 'Have you not got men with guns to face SWAPO? You have your Home Guard men. Are they not ready to protect you?'

'The danger has increased,' the headman replied. 'I and my loyal followers are in much greater danger now than ever before. It is our friendship with your people that has put us in such a position. Were I to feed and hide the SWAPO fighters as others do and run my oxen over their spoor as others do, would I have this trouble?'

'Would you feed and hide a snake and if you did would it still not come from its hole and strike your ankle as you walked one night?' McGee countered . . . Shelongo was justified in his stand and as far as McGee was concerned he would recommend that his fire power was upgraded. The trick was not to accede to the request too readily, though, or the wily old headman would be back knocking on Ompako's door before they had even taken the grease from their new weapons. 'Well,' McGee repeated his question. 'Would you feed a snake?'

Shelongo said he would not feed the snake, no, but if a good neighbour was troubled by such a serpent the least he would do would be to offer the neighbour a *kierie* with which to defend himself.

'Remember, *ondjai*,' he warned McGee. 'Once your neighbour has been overcome by the snake the next one may be you.'

McGee took the point. He said he would propose the matter of more weapons and ammunition and a training programme for the home guard to his commander. He did not foresee any difficulties, he said.

'You must do it quickly. There is no time to waste.'

'Yes,' McGee promised. 'I will do as you ask, Headman, but tell me one more thing. If the matter is now so urgent why did you wait for so many days before sending your message to me?'

Shelongo shifted his position, but it was not the log making him uncomfortable. He turned enquiringly to his advisers, then back to McGee.

'You,' he said, 'are a man who speaks our language as a tribesman, you seem to understand matters, too, that your brothers have no knowledge of, so I will tell you – but you must be thirsty now after all the talking.'

It would have been an act of patent rudeness for McGee not to accept the gourd of *omalodu* offered him. He did not have to read his watch to know that he was so far behind schedule that time no longer mattered. From Oshamdada they might now have to head straight back to Ompako. He reached out and accepted the gourd, conscious that every eye was on him. Fortunately McGee did not have to pretend his approval. He had developed a taste for the tribal beer many years before. He wrinkled his nose, sniffed at it, then ran the thick tart brew around his mouth as one would the finest Cape Cabernet. 'Good,' he said. 'No one can match your brewmaster.' Dup might not have agreed with that statement, but then Dup was not there. McGee had not eaten breakfast that morning so he took things slowly, but having just pronounced the beer good, he could not drink only one gourd.

They drank quietly and appreciatively for a while, then Shelongo beckoned him closer. The man seemed depressed and that was strange. His tone was unnaturally subdued. McGee wondered whether he was about to have his question answered. Apparently he was, and more than that. 'You are a strange man,' he told the captain. 'There are very many things that bother your mind, I think.'

'Haamba?' McGee was slightly rankled by Shelongo's presumption. He said, 'Perhaps you would like to tell me all about myself.' The slight edge of sarcasm was wasted on the headman. Like all older generation Owambos, words to him were accepted at their face value. To him McGee had just expressed a genuine wish to be enlightened.

'It is not for me to tell you,' he said. 'There are others here, though . . . But let it rest my friend, sometimes knowledge does not bring happiness. Now, you asked me why I did not call you straight away after my brother's

213

son's son had given me that message. Walk with me and I will tell you. Come.'

They left the *olupale* and took to the passageways of the kraal, this time in an anti-clockwise arc that brought them to the southern gate and the cattle-enclosure with its green dolf hedge. Three oxen were standing there, flicking their tails and chewing the cud. McGee could see from where he stood, too, that Lieutenant Doctor Schmal still had a long queue of mothers waiting in the shade of the blossoming kiaat with their suckling infants comfortably hip-slung, the toddlers scurrying playfully in the sand and the older boys and girls in tow. You would have searched long to find a more peaceful scene in all South West, McGee thought. He could not understand therefore why Headman Shelongo appeared so apprehensive. 'Look,' said the older man. 'See what happens when I walk among my oxen . . . Watch.'

McGee was intrigued. The old man shed his goat-skin kaross, rolled the sleeves up on his torn khaki shirt and stepped into the clearing. 'Watch!' he called unnecessarily once more. McGee could not imagine what the headman had in mind.

Shelongo walked to the centre of the enclosure and there he stood. He did nothing else, just stood glowering at the beasts, which just stood there in turn, gazing back, still whipping their tails at the flies, still chewing with that mechanical tireless rhythm cattle the world over possess. It was bizarre. McGee found his mouth hanging open in puzzlement and snapped it shut. Then the damndest thing happened. The ox in the middle, the biggest, blackest fellow of them all, slowly advanced on the old headman, stopping but a pace in front of him. It stood there for what could have been a minute, then slowly lowered its big head until its neck was bent to almost between its legs, gouging its horns deeply into the soil in front of its owner. McGee understood then.

If it had been a circus act that had just been performed, it would have been worthy of applause. There was, however, nothing funny about it. McGee had heard of this omen before, but had never witnessed it. The message would be totally clear to the headman: as the ox had turned over the soil of his cattle kraal, so his own grave would presently be dug in that same kraal. He probably knew, too, exactly the way his death would be enacted. The *Elenga* turned away from the beast and shuffled the distance back to where McGee was standing. He suddenly did look really old, as though the coldness of the grave had already reached out for him. 'You see,' he said to McGee, 'there is no hurry for me, I am already a dead man. Tell me now, warrior, would you like to step next into the enclosure. There is a message for you, too, there, I know it.'

They left Oshamdada five hours later than they had originally planned, but still in good time, McGee reckoned, to take in another little kraal near the Odila river, barter some fresh bream and be back in time for supper. It was not to be, however. They reached the Odila but the *shikuku* fisherwomen were not to be found, and from that moment on things began to go badly awry. It started with rifleman Wilson. Never the most dexterous of soldiers, he slipped while manhandling the doctor's medicine trunk on to the back of the truck. The heavy metal case went with him, landing on his leg and snapping it like a chicken bone.

Dark clouds were closing in and McGee decided to call it a day. 'Patch up Wilson,' he said to Schmal. 'We're heading for home.'

That should have been simple enough. The injured rifleman had his leg set into an inflatable splint and gentle hands hoisted him on to his transport. 'The doctor will be back soon,' McGee announced to a gaggle of disappointed patients. 'Maybe tomorrow.' Everyone was smiling and nodding again. 'Let's go,' he shouted and the first truck, the one with the doctor, the injured Wilson and half the rifle section on board, started up and drove off. The truck that held McGee and the rest of the rifle section did not start at all.

What should have happened was that those in troop transporter number one, when they saw they were not being followed, should have returned with a tow for the less mobile counterpart. That was what was laid down in standing orders for all drivers. The problem was that those in the first troop truck did not notice that the second vehicle was not in convoy on their tail, for with the violent rudeness that only an African tropical storm can display, a driving cold grey, almost solid sheet of rainwater lashed down on them all. Visibility was hosed away to nothing in spite of the efforts of a flapping wiper blade. In truck number two McGee and his men were left cursing, wet and static.

The downpour lasted until it was almost dark, when, as abruptly as it had come, it was gone. They worked on the motor then and probably with a combination of good advice and good luck, the driver got the beast to growl into life. McGee could not recall when last he had heard six thumping cylinders sound so sweet.

It was always a pleasure to be on the move. The cool wind of the passage was like a tonic and the flies that infested every kraal were swept away. McGee drew himself upright against the machine-gun mounting, unbuttoned his shirt to the waist, and sucked in deeply. In many places the track was under water for short stretches and fine muddy spray swept right up and over all of them. Nobody seemed to mind. There would be hot showers and hot food, too, at Ompako. A massive, aged and lightening-scarred baobab, its giant limbs like big groping arms, reached out for them from the side of the track, the fingers of its branches grappling along the armour plate. McGee did not remember having passed such a tree on the way to Odila but in truth he had not been paying much attention then. His mind had been on a big black ox that could divine the fate of man.

Soon they had to switch on headlights which were no match for the conditions, the mud spray cutting the beams to nothing and forcing them to no more than a crawl.

What McGee could see of the landscape did not look familiar to him and he was beginning to feel uneasy. The driver should have known the area like the back of his hand, so he dismissed the feeling, and had no sooner done so than, without warning, they were in serious trouble.

The engine was over-revving, the wheels slewing. The vehicle was labouring and spinning up great gouts of mud. They were shuddering, sinking deeper with every wheel revolution until they were stuck. McGee thumped on the driver's armoured box and called for him to switch off. Instead the driver tried to reverse them out and any chance they may have had was lost as, four-square, they delved themselves into the mire. 'Cut the bloody engine!' McGee yelled into the hatch. 'You've screwed it up, you prick.'

McGee, the officer, usually felt sorry some time after speaking to a troopie in that fashion. It was not his usual style. This time he had no such reservations. The noise of the engine stopped at last and as it did so the occupants of the vehicle became aware of the orchestrated symphony of a thousand swamp frogs calling out for love, and not just to the left of the vehicle, where the Oshana was supposed to be, but from all sides. McGee could hardly believe it. The bloody driver must have wandered right off the main track. He stepped gingerly over the steel side gate and climbed to the ground, which was a lot closer than it should have been. It took his weight but it was sodden and spongy. A flashlight revealed what he knew it must reveal – the heavy truck was stuck like a beached whale, all four wheels firmly embedded into the oozing Owambo swamp.

There was only one way out of it, but that would require the services of another four-wheel drive vehicle, a tow cable or two and a considerable amount of digging. The essential ingredient, the other four-by-four, was missing.

'It looks,' said wise corporal driver Mentz who had joined him on the turf, 'as though we could be stuck . . . really stuck. I'm sorry, captain, I've travelled this road a hundred times, night and day. I really don't know where I went wrong.'

Corporal Fourie, the rifle section leader, was on the ground now too. McGee ignored the driver and spoke to him. 'You've got the section radio, haven't you?' he enquired. McGee was losing faith in all corporals. Corporal Fourie did have the radio. 'Good,' said McGee. 'Now get hold of Ompako Ops and tell them what's happened. Tell them there's no chance of getting us out until tomorrow morning; they had better bring out spades and tree trunks when they come. Tell them there's absolutely no way we'll get this bastard loose tonight and that we'll give them a pinpoint grid reference at first light. Say we're staying put. That's it. Okay?'

'Okay, captain.'

De la Rey must have been in the Ops room at the time for at the end of Fourie's message his unmistakable voice advised them to 'Watch out for crocks, Ha! Ha!' McGee could not think of any rejoinder so he left it at that.

The division of five prone adult soldiers into the square footage available in the back of an armoured troop carrier obviously had not been a consideration of the designers of that fine vehicle. You were supposed to fight from it, not sleep in it. What McGee did finally was to take the tent floor they had brought as a rain shroud, lay it on the wet turf beneath the vehicle and crawl on to that. Fourie worked out a guard roster, giving the driver the worst possible deal, and they settled down.

The others may have settled down, but McGee simply could not. It was not the conditions – he had slept, and soundly too, in situations a lot worse than this one. There was a restlessness within him that had nothing to do with the damp canvas under his body, the unrelenting attack of the mosquitoes or anything else around him: a sort of gut-feeling anticipating something hostile. His mind's gallery of pictures of the girl with eyes the colour of kingfisher wings and flaxen hair did nothing to dispel it.

Does a sleeper ever know when he has reached that fine

point when his final conscious thought becomes displaced by the unbounded potential of dream? There must be that incipient stage, by all the laws of nature, but who in truth can ever claim to have been there, to have realized it, to have by his own will transcended it? McGee had given up all thoughts of sleep when suddenly he found himself plunging, twisting like a falling cat to meet the shock of an impact that never came.

He was awake again, his senses in chaos, pulses pounding, lungs drawing like a marathon man. He composed himself, glanced at the luminous face of his watch and was surprised to discover that he had in fact been sleeping for a few hours. He tried to recall the nightmare, to place the ragged ends and fragments into some meaningful form or relationship, but there was nothing left that would fit, no matter how he juggled the pieces. There would be no more sleep for him that night; he did not want it. He edged his body away from his impromptu shelter with the least sound possible, then drew his cramped frame upright.

God, it was dark. A new moon, the phase the Owambos called *okahani kovalodi*, the little moon of witches, swung like a Moslem pendant. Enlaced in a fabric of scudding silver clouds, it could have been a comet in the midnight sky. McGee, looking up, felt unbalanced by the slipping movement of it and compelled to turn away. The vertigo, however, possessed him unpleasantly for a spell, long enough to disturb him, long enough for him to be glad of the solid metal side of the vehicle, but not long enough to prevent him from seeing a tiny point of flame where there should have been nothing but darkness.

There it was again. He could not believe it at first. It must be a transient defect of vision, something to do with the dizziness – but it was not. Away to the south west somebody had a camp fire going, just a small one, not any more compelling than the blush of a glowworm, but a fire just the same. He was more intrigued than concerned. Somewhere in his pack was a pair of good binoculars. He dug for them then returned to the flame. It was nothing more than that, a solitary fire and, highlighted delicately as though brushed in by an artist's hand, the outstretched lower boughs of an adjacent tree, a biggish tree.

Who would chance a camp fire, even one as small as that, isolated in the middle of the night in the middle of war-torn Owambo? A tribesman? The kuanyama were not nomads. They spent the dark hours well inside their kraals. The enemy? No SWAPO commander would ever have tolerated such lunatic luxury. Who then?

There was a way to find out. Behind and above him, sitting high on the vehicle, McGee could see the vague silhouette of the sentry from Fourie's section. If he recalled the guard roster correctly, it would be Fourie himself. McGee had already formed his lips to whisper the man's name, when on an impulse he stopped. Waking up the soldiers and then getting them mobile would be a noisy affair. He did not know Fourie, his team or their capabilities. Some South Africans patrolled like men in a three-legged race. That would not do, not at all. If there was anything out there, and there had to be, he would reconnoitre it alone. If it required back-up he could return for Fourie and his boys.

McGee took a last glance through the binoculars. Someone had tended to the blaze or raked it. Minute sparks were dancing like fireflies in the heat. No-one was visible, though. He found a marker star fore and aft of him and lay down his binoculars. Then, drawn like a solitary moth towards a candle, and just as quietly, he set off to find the keeper of the fire.

It was just an old man, a lonely traveller perhaps who with the optimism of memories as his guide had misjudged the distance of a journey, then settled his ancient limbs beneath the tree to see through the night. To call the little yellow glow at his feet a camp fire was being kind. He had a crucifix of four little logs arranged to kindle a tongue of flame no larger than a tented handkerchief.

So that was it. There was nothing more to be seen than an old *omukulunu*, resting under the limbs of what seemed in that flickering half-light to be an even more ancient tambotie tree. There was nothing more to do, no action need be taken. McGee could turn his back on the scene and go back to the vehicle as quietly as he had left it, maybe even get some sleep. Sleep seemed suddenly like a very attractive idea. The sky was still sprinkled with stars. The moon still had a long path to travel. There was still time for sleep. He cast a final backwards glance towards the *omukulunu* . . .

The scene had changed. No longer was the old traveller seated benignly by the fire. He was kneeling now, his forearms outstretched, the whiteness of his palms visible, almost as though he were warming his bony hands. Something was trickling from his open hands into the flame, something that looked to be powder. The fire seemed to have changed its character too. What had been nothing more than an overblown candle was now swirling up in a dancing deep purple veil.

McGee knew he had to leave that place. Sound was of no consequence any longer. He half-turned and that was as far as he got. He was no more able to run than a darted cheetah would have been. The effort of it was drawing little crying gasps from him. He had been trapped, caught by the terrible power of an *Ongonga*. He was being paralysed, brought to his knees and sucked numb by it. As though a great physical pressure was upon him, McGee felt himself being drawn relentlessly towards the leaping flame. His strength was waning, his will, too. He was no match for it, had no power or knowledge to oppose such a thing. All the time there was a voice, a bold whisper in his ears, telling him, 'Come, Warrior. I mean you no harm.' Over and over again the message came to him. It was a lie, a lie. If he believed it, if he gave up, he was dead. 'Come Warrior! *Uja omukuaita*! . . . Come . . .' So imperative it was. He was tiring.

And now, just in front of his eyes there was a face: a twisted, snarling, ghastly face; a mask, carved by a demon in the workshops of Hell. Warped, gaping leadwood lips, cold with the rigor mortis of half a century, touched his mouth. He twisted away but the kiss was persistent . . . There was nothing more he could do. Smoke from the fire was smarting his eyes, eroding his vision.

Then, surprisingly, he did not need his eyes to see. He was floating and gently tumbling. He was an embryo in the amnion of space. He could see the high vault of the night sky, could almost touch it. His breathing was easy and he was alive. It troubled him not at all that he could neither see nor feel his limbs. He was intact, he knew it. He seemed to be gathering speed, suddenly accelerating, as though about to be propelled from one cosmic phase to another.

He was not surprised to find that he was in the smoky interior of a *kuanyama* hut, nor that there were others there; a woman, and judging by her *omba* shell finery and the styling of her hair, a royal woman. It was quite pleasant, would have been more so if he could have remained. She looked up and saw him and her pretty face creased in pain for a moment. She said something to him but he could neither hear her nor answer. At the rear end of the hut was that which he had come for, her *epasa* offspring. He gathered them. They were his, his to kill, for it was right for them to die . . . and one died.

Then, as though a whirlwind had struck, the other was snatched away, torn from him and he was chasing, searching, darting here then there in houses, huts, missions and schools, in rivers and reeds under the very rocks, always seeking and always too late. There was a grave on an arid farm near a wailing, screeching, barely turning wind pump, a small white cross that he knew so well among the silver mangwe trees. It was empty, black cold and empty.

He was tiring now. His limbs felt stiff, his skin parchment-dry and cold, and he had found nothing, neither the whirlwind nor the offspring, either together or separately. There was nothing to do but continue. He wanted to rest so badly, but there was no rest. The comfort of it all was that he knew he would succeed – and he did.

By the time he found that which he was seeking, the

infant had become a man, clothed in the drab tiger stripes of a soldier. There was no mistaking him, though. He knew him at once to be the surviving twin. There was the turmoil of battle, flames leaping up from every side. Then he faced him. As strong as a warlord he was, the royal blood giving him the strength of ten men. Too much time had passed. The infant was now a giant, a giant with the eyes of the hungry leopard. There was the crash of a gun, no pain . . . no pain, he was a drifting thing again; in a desert this time, a desert of blood-red sand. A rock shaped as a huge upright finger was beckoning. Someone was shaking him. He still had to search . . . He had to reach the rock now . . . God, he had to find him . . .

'Captain!' a voice was calling him, 'Captain . . .' It was Corporal Fourie, and it was daytime. McGee woke up shivering but not from the cold. It was dawn. 'We've brewed some coffee, Captain.'

The coffee was hot, sweet and sobering. McGee sat up on the canvas and took in little appreciative sips, reflecting at the same time on the nocturnal antics of his mind. The vividness of his recall astonished him. He tossed away the grounds and pulled himself from under the mine-proof steel into the open. God, it had been so real!. He looked up to the back of the bogged-down armoured transporter. He had to know.

'Corporal Fourie, what time were you standing beat last night?'

'Midnight, until two . . . just after. Anything wrong, Captain?'

'No,' McGee replied. 'Nothing at all. You didn't notice anything wrong, anything out of the ordinary?'

The corporal did not hesitate. 'No, Captain,' he said. 'It was as quiet as the grave.'

They plotted their position and sent the co-ordinates to Ompako. There was nothing to do then but wait: no hurry, for the others, that was. Captain McGee however still had a lot he wanted to do. 'I'm taking a walk,' he

223

told Fourie. 'In the meantime, get your men to start digging. I won't be long.'

Fourie nodded in what he believed to be complete understanding. Riflemen and corporals did it where they stood and liked it too. Majors and captains, even some less robust lieutenants, found distant trees. One day one of them would get a bullet for his modesty, right up to his naked arse. He said, 'Right, Captain,' then watched as the officer made his way to the south west. The man seemed to be seeking something. 'Funny buggers, officers,' he said to no one in particular.

The tree was precisely where McGee knew he would find it, on a small spit of high ground above the marsh. There was a dearth of large trees thereabouts and not a single other tambotie, so it was an easy task to locate it. For a moment he stood and observed the spot where part of him must have stood or been or existed the previous night. A word materialized, arose in his mind. It was difficult to find an ugly tree, he thought. Almost all trees had some grace to them, but this one was revolting. It was in bloom with little flowers that hung like rats' tails from the boughs, giving it an obscene, infested look: as he was observing it, it seemed to be aware of him.

Something told him to let it be, to turn about and get away from there. But it was out of the question. This time there was nothing stronger than his own pressing need for sanity that was drawing him on: a hunger for any knowledge that would help him to dispossess himself of the phantom interred in the subsoil of his mind. If such knowledge was not to be found beneath the tree then it was to be found nowhere. If there were no secrets for him there, then there were simply no secrets at all.

He found something, and if he had looked up just then and stirred the branches just above his head, instead of just scratching around in the thatching grass at his knees, he would certainly have found more. What he did find hidden on the ground was an ancient *oshimbe*, an *Ongonga's* ceremonial dagger, its carved ivory handle almost

224

perfectly preserved, its once keen blade rusted and flaked to not much more than a stub. McGee had seen them too many times to have been mistaken: it was an *oshimbe* all right, a really old one. He felt his gut contract with excitement. With a breath of triumph he seized it and held it to the light and willed it to yield its secrets.

It did not however, and as his search had still failed to include the heart of the tambotie, there was nothing further to be found, not on the surface anyway. He took the dagger to the marsh water and tried in vain to wash out the dirt embedded in the ivory carving. Later he would take soap and scrubbing brush to it and perhaps it would then deliver its story. For the moment he was delighted with his find. He thought he was winning.

There was nothing further to be found around the tambotie, no camp-fire ashes, no spoor other than those he had just made; nothing, providing you were prepared to discount the sensation of enmity emanating from that poisoned tree, to disregard that second sight that warned of hidden eyes. McGee had lived too long, too close to his senses, to do that. Something was there all right, something frighteningly hostile.

McGee steeled himself. He was not prepared to be terrorized by the inhabitants of that place, no matter what darkness they could work. He returned to the shade beneath the tambotie, reached up and rested his arm on a lower limb. Rewarded by what he had so far found, he was more determined than ever to oppose, hunt down and destroy whatever it was that was trying to destroy him. At times his head spun with the force of concentration.

He did not know where to look, that was the problem – or how to look or even what it was that he was looking for. How did you go about such a search? What colour, size and shape would the thing be? Would he know it if he saw it? What logic, if any, was there for him to bring to bear? All McGee knew was that there *was* something there. He shifted his position and became aware for the first time of the rough warty bark under his hand. That was when he realized how lacking in dimension his search had been. His eyes flicked upwards. His heart almost stopped.

A deadly mamba poised to strike his bare hand could not have caused him to recoil faster than he did. The rapture of sudden shock expanded through him like an explosion. He was superheated. He was rampant, exhilarated and ready to fight – but there was no need to fight.

He had won. It was over. All he had to do was reach up into the foliage again and seize the *Ongonga's* mask pinioned there, remove it, destroy it. Those were the rules of *lodi*. It could harm him no longer.

He took his time about it. With his long knife he cut through the branches until the mask was clear of foliage so that all that still held it was a thickish branch growing through the left eye socket and the fork on which the snarling jaw rested. McGee was smiling when he stood back and contemplated it. He had put his Medusa to the sword. All that remained was for him to lift the head from the body and incinerate it, there and then . . .

But it was not to be. No sooner had he cut the mask loose than he heard the rumble of distant engines. The tow vehicle had arrived. McGee took off his bush-jacket, wrapped his prize carefully in it and hurried back to his vehicle. He would do away with the mask when they got back to Ompako.

They were home for lunch, which suited everyone. It was Sunday, and on the Lord's Day the cooks extended themselves. They had roast beef and an Owambo version of Yorkshire pudding which tasted all the sweeter to McGee, for stowed safely under the bed in his tent was the *osipala lelodi*, the face that bewitches, that had caused him such terrible trauma; and in his breast pocket there were two letters from his beloved Patricia. One didn't *read* letters from loved ones: one crept away to a private spot and digested them, and there one laughed or cried, depending on the content, or one's mood, or both. McGee's private place was a shady unmanned firing pit

226

near the perimeter gate. Once he had instructed the gate sentry to keep clear, he was on his own there.

The first letter was her usual breathless mish-mash of gossip: everyone at the hospital was fine, everyone sent regards; one of her friends, a colleague who she was sure he would remember, if only because of her long brown hair and superb body, had become married. 'It was lovely, Matt. I cried all the time.' The blue taffeta dress she had worn, however, had not looked right. 'It's *got* to be white when we get married! Don't you think so my darling?' There was not much else. Prices were going up and up; and Transvaal had been thrashed by Western Province on the rugby field. Dup and the Admiral were well and sent love. McGee had a quiet laugh over that line. She concluded with the usual tons and tons of love and kisses with various sized X's at the bottom of the page. There was a postscript: 'My sweetheart, I may have some super news by my next letter.'

McGee opened the other letter wondering if it was the 'super news' one. It was. 'Matt! Matt! Matt! STOP PRESS! You won't believe it! I've got myself a posting at Windhoek Hospital. A super job, Senior Sister in the High Care Unit. Isn't that wonderful? I'm sure you will be able to get down to Windhoek easier than all the way to Pretoria so we can see each other more often (on long weekends and things). Isn't that just the bestest news? I take up the position at the end of next month. I'm so excited I can't tell you.'

McGee bleakly finished reading the letter. The fact was that, yes, Windhoek was closer to him than Pretoria but no, he certainly would not be able to see her more frequently than in the past. It was not just distance that counted, it was the availability of transport. And there was probably a lot more air traffic between Pretoria and the Operational Area than there was between Windhoek and this area.

McGee re-read the jubilant lines several times, wondering how he was going to respond to her STOP PRESS without ruining the whole loving, dumb, beautiful thing she was trying to do for them. He took the letters to his tent, opened his writing pad and laboured through: 'My darling Trish. It was great to get your incredible STOP PRESS news. Hey! There wasn't a more surprised man in South West than me when I read that letter . . .' Then he tore off the sheet, screwed it into a ball and tossed it into his waste bin. What the hell was he going to say to her? It was not a matter of thinking through a solution to the problem: there wasn't one. His dilemma was simply how to tell her that the plan she had conceived, and put into operation was a failure. She should have known better, she should have asked someone's advice. But she was headstrong. She had wanted to present him with a surprise that would knock him off his feet. She had done that all right!

The pub was open and a brace of cold beers seemed indicated. McGee laid down his uninspired pen, lifted his big frame from his chair and set it in motion in the direction of the mess. The beer was icy. McGee bought two, claimed one of the camp-made 'easy chairs' and sat down. The only easy thing about the chairs was the way they pitched with their occupants to port or starboard. He settled himself warily, stretched out and opened one of his beers. On the floor next to the chair lay open a fairly recent copy of a Windhoek daily newspaper. He picked it up, popped a spine into it and set it up between himself and the rest of the world. He never did finish the second beer. Staring at him from the centre page was a nightmare in pen and ink, a head and shoulders sketch of a face: a face he had seen only once in reality, but which had been interned by his subconscious and paroled upon him almost nightly since the contact at Quimbo 333. There was no mistaking it. The police artist had captured the features brilliantly – the predatory smile, the heavy handsome face. It was all there. There was another sketch of a face he did not recognize, and above them both, in bold Gothic capitals, the words, 'HAVE YOU SEEN THESE MEN?'

He certainly had. There was a brief caption beginning 'Wanted for Attempted Murder.' He read it with fascinated interest, then read it again.

It was incredible that the man was wanted by the Windhoek police! For some reason, instead of running for his base camp in Angola after the fight at Quimbo 333, he had taken off in the opposite direction, then made the long journey all the way to Windhoek. McGee folded the centre page, carefully placing it in his breast pocket with Patricia's two letters. Then he went off in search of his officer commanding.

De la Rey was in his tent. He listened attentively to what McGee had to say, made a note or two. 'Are you sure,' he asked tapping the newspaper clipping McGee had presented to him, 'absolutely certain that this is the selfsame character you came up against at the contact at 333?'

'I'm one hundred percent positive. There's no doubt in my mind.'

'Do you think you could recognize the bastard if you saw him again?'

'No question! I'd know him anywhere.'

'Well,' said de la Rey, 'I suppose I'd better inform Brigade about this. What they do about it is their business.'

What Brigade did about it, was to inform Major de la Rey that the services of his 2 IC were temporarily required by the South African Police, Windhoek, that a chopper would be sent to pick the captain up the following morning, and that the reason for Captain McGee's attachment to the SAP was to be considered privileged information. De la Rey's comment was, 'They must be pretty anxious to pick this guy up, that's all I can say.'

McGee was stunned. It usually took weeks to get a reaction from Brigade for any matter other than routine, but what he found really astounding was the fact that less than three hours previously he had been trying to compose a letter to Patricia to tell her that Windhoek for him would be as difficult to reach as the moon. Now the count down had begun. 'Anyway,' de la Rey concluded. 'If you don't find police work too agreeable, maybe we'll see you again.'

'I'll be back,' said McGee, but somehow he doubted his prediction. The Major may have had the same feelings.

'Don't hold your breath,' *Ombadje* de la Rey said. 'It sounds like anything could happen. It was good having you, McGee.'

Chapter 14

Captain Matthew McGee, dressed in casual slacks, sports-jacket and suede shoes, his sandy hair curling over his ears, looked quite different from the infantry officer who had arrived at Windhoek a month previously. It was not that he was untidy – he just did not look like an army man any longer.

Seated as comfortably as one can sit on a straight-backed Government-issue chair, he was at that moment giving nothing less than all his attention to the man opposite him behind a broad expanse of Government-issue desk top. The man was a major in the security police, McGee's co-ordinating officer and his name was Zietsman, Zacharias Zietsman. Major Zietsman had a Clark Gable moustache, pomaded hair and smoked through an onyx cigarette holder. He was known to his field agents as Z, or Major Z, and that was where the levity ended. For the rest, Zietsman was as heavy and as hard as a teak truncheon and just as ruthless. 'Tell me, McGee,' he said, 'what do we have to go on so far in this case?' The question was rhetorical. Tabulating with his fingers, the major summarized: 'One: we have everything Dr Mueller left us hidden in her medical chest, her drawings, her descriptions. We have, thanks to her, the names of the two killers, their dress, their peculiarities. We know just about everything there is to know about them from their bowel habits to their respiratory rates. Two: we have a person who can do a positive ID. You.'

'And Dr Mueller,' put in McGee. 'Ondoktola they call her.'

'Dr Mueller is a dying woman. She's in a nursing home on a ventilating machine. She's not going to be with us

231

much longer, I'm afraid.' Major Z folded back his ring finger . . . 'Three: the ballistics boys have at last been able to match the cartridge case found where Mueller was attacked as being from the same pistol as used in several political assassinations in Owamboland over the past few years – a Makarov apparently.'

Z leaned back in his more comfortable chair, lit a cigarette and puffed at it distastefully. It was obvious that he hated himself for the indulgence. Then he stared at his fourth finger as though willing it to give up its clue. 'Four,' he said at last: 'there is a little Kavango girl they nicked from her parents. She has not surfaced yet, so she's either lying dead somewhere or she's still with them. That's worth remembering, isn't it?'

McGee said it was and waited for the emergence of point five. As far as he could be certain, Major Z had covered all the positive ground. He had a gut-feeling, however, that there was more to come. Zietsman had not invited him to his office just for afternoon tea. He looked smug; a man with a secret. He pressed his intercom and an electronic voice responded. 'Yes, Major.'

'Is Adam with you yet?'

'Yes, Major.'

'Send him up then.'

'Yes, Major.'

Sergeant Adam was a dapper little coloured, a member of the half-caste race that had resulted from interbreeding between whites and blacks. McGee had seen him before at one of Z's briefings. The man had the presence of a bantam cock. He strutted into the room and stood by the window, haughtily observing both McGee and the Major. Z had him summed up. 'Breathe out,' he said to the man. 'Come over here and sit down.' Adam came over and sat down. Zietsman stubbed out the rest of his cigarette and said, 'You two know each other, right? . . . We've had a break in the hunt for comrade Mazambaan.' Point number five was about to be revealed.

'Yesterday I received a phone call from an informer.

I've got it on tape; listen carefully.' He popped a cassette into a desk top recorder, tapped down a button and said again, 'Listen carefully.' There was the hiss of blank tape then a man's cautious voice came on. 'This is Kulu.'

'Hello, Kulu.' It was the major's voice. 'What have you got for me?'

'Well, I don't know how good this is . . . A teacher . . .' There was heavy traffic noise then. 'Did you get that . . . Hello, you still there?'

'I'm still here, Kulu, you were talking about this teacher . . . go on.'

'Yes, his name is Isack Njoba. Well, this guy Njoba got pretty smashed with a girl friend, one of the PTA members, can you believe it? He told her that his wife had been screwing around with some guy who'd rocked up at his house together with her brother.'

'Yes.'

'Yes, well it seems that Njoba is dead-scared because this guy is a SWAPO killer. He thinks the guy may come for him.'

The major's voice sounded quicker now, more interested. 'What else, Kulu?'

'Nothing.'

'Where does this Njoba teach?'

'Saint Dominic's . . . Is that okay?'

'It could be, Kulu. Is that all you've got?'

'Yes, is there anything else I can do?'

'No . . . Drop it. I'll handle it now.'

'Seems like quite a lively PTA they've got going, doesn't it?' There was the sound of Kulu chuckling, then the tape went dead.

They played it again, then the Major put both tape and recorder into a drawer and gave a rare smile. Obviously Z felt he had something to be cheerful about and the men seated before him fitted somewhere into the happy scheme of things. The Major did not keep them guessing. 'I think Njoba's visitors were our boys,' he said. 'I think SWAPO has taken the comrade fighters underground. If

233

that's the case and they run true to form, then they'll be surfacing soon with brand-new identities, to be filtered into the local scene. They're always trying to get their hit men into Windhoek.'

Almost simultaneously both phones on Z's desk began to ring, giving McGee a chance to think about what had just happened. He and Adam were obviously going to be operating as a team. What kind of team, he wondered? He could identify Mazambaan. What was Sergeant Adam's speciality? McGee had been employed covering railway stations and observing at road-blocks until then: dry, tedious, uninteresting work, but if a change in his function was on the cards, then the last thing he wanted was for that change to occur at the moment. For on the Cape Town-Windhoek flight that very evening a VIP was due to arrive, a girl by the name of Patricia Christie. He had not seen her, it seemed, for years and had an evening planned that she would never, never forget.

The axe fell. Major Zietsman looked up from his muted telephones. The smile had gone. 'Gentlemen,' he said, 'I'm putting you on a twenty-four hour surveillance of the Njoba house. I personally am taking you to your observation point. Gentlemen, if you haven't already understood this yourselves, then let me tell you. We have had presented to us the best opportunity in years to crack SWAPO's urban underground wing. When comrades Mazambaan and Daniel come out from hibernation then SWAPO will have to look after them, liaise with them. When that happens we will be watching and listening . . . We'll peg every last one of them. First, however, we've got to locate them. Njoba's wife Mary is our best chance.'

'You think he'll come back to her?' Adam asked.

'Why not? Wherever he is lying up now you can be damn sure that sex isn't on the menu. She's young, she's pretty, wears a bit of make-up. Can you imagine what's been going through our boy's mind over the last few months. I think there's a better than average chance that he'll come trotting up for more. What do you think, Captain McGee?'

The major was right. McGee could only agree with him. Anyway there were no alternatives. He had only one question. 'When does the surveillance begin?'

'Tomorrow morning at 04.00 hours. I will be picking both of you up personally, then I'll take you to the site. Sergeant Adams is a surveillance expert so you don't have anything to worry about other than being there.'

The interview was over. They all stood up and walked to the door. Adam left them there while McGee went with the major to the courtyard where the cars were parked. Z had one last bit of advice to offer. 'What I always tell new men is that security work is like doing a jigsaw puzzle by torchlight. Every piece has to be held up to the light to see if it's the one you want. Now and then you get a lucky break: a piece just yells to you: pick me up, I'm the one you want.' He swung himself into his car, rolled down the window and looked up at McGee. 'Do you know what I mean, Captain?'

McGee didn't. Was he supposed to be the torch, the little talking segment or was he either? He said, 'Yes, Major,' and watched Z drive off. A glance at his watch and he was scurrying for his own car. Patricia's flight was due within the hour. Zietsman's jigsaw could wait.

Patricia was first into the concourse, peering this way and that, anxious to find the one face among the many. McGee, using his height, did not have to push to the front. He waved and she saw him.

The passage of time had pressed and thinned the material of her image. He had had photographs to reinforce the memories, but they did not give the quickness of smile, the whirl of hair. They did not surge upon you in a cyclone of hand-luggage and jasmine scent and say, 'My Matt, my darling, Matt. Oh Matt . . .'

High on love, they drove to the two-roomed flat McGee called home. No one could accuse him of lack of forethought. Three candles provided the only light. A rugged bowl of proteas centred a dining room table crisply laid for

235

two. Best Simonskelder cabinet stood open. But there was a desert thirst burning the two of them that no amount of wine would satiate, that needed first to be slaked.

Later, in whispered conversation, circled in each other's limbs, they talked and talked into the early hours. He told her of Ompako, the newspaper sketches; of Z and his assignment. He told her about his bizarre experiences over the past months. He spoke to her about the satanic dream that somehow had not been a dream: the old man, the traveller under the tamboetie. 'I swear I've seen that wrinkled face before.' The *oshimbe* and the snarling mask . . . 'What on earth could it all have meant, Trish . . . It seemed then as though I'd been sucked into a whirlpool of *oulodi* magic.'

She lay still listening quietly and when he had finished talking she said, 'Show me the mask.'

'Come on! Not now, Trish.'

'Please, Matt, I want to see it now.'

'I have to get up in a minute, anyway.'

'Now . . .'

There was not much left of the candles, just little runny stubs that were barely spluttering. McGee took the chandelier and raised it from the side of the bed to the wall at the headboard.

There, within a stretched arm of where they lay, it hung. Tortured and heinous, uglier than McGee could ever have described it, it gazed hollowly down on her nakedness. Patricia could not believe it – that it had been so close to them; such malevolence and she had not even known it. She kneeled then on the mattress and, trying to be objective, examined it. McGee seemed hardly interested in its presence. He sat up, leaning against the wall, his head almost touching the mask and said, 'Do you like it?'

Did she like it? She hated it, loathed it. It was evil. He slipped, self-conscious in his nudity, from the bed, found his shorts and padded off to the bathroom, then to the kitchen. There was the rattle of cups and the hiss of a kettle. Did she like it? Patricia drew herself away from the mask to the very bottom of the bed. What was the man thinking? After all that had happened, there the hollow-eyed demon skull hung right above their pillows. 'Matt!' she called to the kitchen. 'Please come here . . . *Matt*!'

McGee appeared, a cup in each hand, a picture of domesticity. 'You'll get cold there,' he said. 'Climb back into bed.'

'Not while that . . . that thing is there. It's evil.'

'You're quite wrong. It could have been evil once, Trish, in fact there's no doubt about it. If it's as old as I think it is then it probably goes further back than the first chief, Mandume. His *Ongongas* used to make prisoners of war roast their own hands over a fire. How do you like that? If someone was convicted of a crime in his time they had their hands and feet, lips, tongue and nose, penis, ears – the lot – lopped slowly off. But I own it now. I found it and it's mine. It's just a chunk of wood now, a very valuable chunk of wood, I've been told.'

'Matt, you're crazy . . . Get rid of the thing. If it's valuable then give it to a museum. There's an aura of violence about it. Look at it, look at the way it's carved like a . . . like a torture victim. How can you let it hang above your bed?'

'Honestly, Trish, I haven't had a single bad dream, nothing, since I took it from the tamboetie tree. It's harmless now. But if you like I'll take it down.'

'Please, darling.'

'Here drink your coffee.'

He put down his cup, unhooked the *Ongonga's* mask and carried it across to his cupboard, opened the door and looked at her enquiringly. 'Can I keep it in here?' he asked. 'I'm not going to give it away. It's a valuable artefact, you know.'

What could she say? It was 2 am, and the candles had burnt away when they sat down at the table McGee had prepared. The talk turned to Goedehoop and the Admiral. 'He accepts our engagement now,' she told him.

237

'Does he know I'm in Windhoek?' McGee asked her. 'Does he know you're going to be sharing my flat?'

'He knows neither, but if you ask me to share your flat and if I accept, then I'll write and tell him both.'

'Will you, Trish? I mean, would you like to make your home here?'

'If it's what you really want, Matt, then it would make me very happy. My Daddy must know, though. I respect him too much to hold back the truth from him.'

'Well then, that's settled.'

By ten minutes to four McGee was dressed. He had packed a change of clothing, toiletries and also a big black pistol which she had not seen before. It disquieted her, and the words of intended reassurance – 'Just in case' – did not help either. In the dead quiet just before dawn, a car hummed to a stop in the street below. They kissed goodbye – and suddenly she could not let him go.

'What happens if I need you for something, an emergency or something?'

'Major Zietsman – ask for him at the police station. He knows about you. But nothing will go wrong. I'll see you in a few days. You'll be fine here. I'll be back before you know it. Get some sleep now.'

That was an impossibility, however. She listened to his footsteps, heard a car door slam and an engine fade away, then turned on all the lights in the flat and had a look round. One side of the bedroom cupboard was empty, probably meant for her. She unpacked her suitcases and transferred her belongings, selecting which places in the flat she could rightly annexe. The bathroom of necessity required a his-and-hers stamp to be put upon it.

She could not resist a look into his cupboards, and forced herself not to slam and lock the door against the dreadful mask. She could not help but notice the old ivory dagger lying there too. How strange to wish to have such a monstrosity within your bedroom walls, on the wall above the bed in fact! He had spoken of the mask in the past tense as though its evil had been conquered . . . 'It seemed then as though I'd been sucked into a whirlpool of *oulodi* magic.' It seemed then . . . Patricia did not believe the mask was half as benign as McGee obviously did. The *oulodi*, the wizardry of the *Ongongos*, was very much alive in it.

There was a letter to be written. It was no good procrastinating. The Admiral would have to know. She was a big girl now, able and willing to make her own decisions. She had shown him that on the night of the party at Goedehoop.

'You would be proud of Matthew, Daddy,' she would write. 'He's helping the police search for a terrorist, a man who shot a mission doctor near Windhoek whom he can identify, someone he came up against face-to-face in the operational area.' What then? 'Daddy, Matthew and I are going to live together.' *That* would never do. 'Daddy, Matthew and I are going to share a flat.' Was that any better? 'Daddy, we are more in love than ever, we want to be together all the time.' Perhaps that would soften the blow. 'I can't stay at the hostel knowing he's just a few blocks away. I'm not a hypocrite. I refuse to be false to myself.' What the hell was she going to say? 'Birds do it, bees do it'?

She finished writing the letter at 7.30. At 8 o'clock she was due at the hospital for her first day in the High Care Unit. McGee's Volkswagen was parked where he had said it would be. It started first time and his directions to the Windhoek Hospital were easily followed. She parked the car in the staff bays as the pips for 08.00 came over the radio, then stood waiting for nearly an hour before she was introduced to matron. A while later her day began, but not before she had given her letter to an outbound nurse with a request to post it and money to cover the stamps.

Nurse Florence Nitengo read the name and address on the envelope she was holding and her eyes widened.

Perhaps the letter would reach its destination, Simons-town Naval Headquarters – but not before it had been passed on to a SWAPO informant. A pat on the back would be the least she could expect: an Owambo pat on her Herero back was more than one could ask for.

Soon the whites would be booted out of Namibia. They would leave as ignominiously as they had in Angola, Mozambique and Zimbabwe, then the witch-hunt would be on. One could not accumulate too many favours from the rulers-to-be, especially when you came from the wrong tribe.

About the same time that Florence Nitengo was entrusted with the letter and Patricia Christie went on duty, on the farm Bruchsaal some seventy kilometres north-west of Windhoek, Mazambaan sat up from his rush mat bed and stretched with the indolent lethargy of a man completely at ease.

Life on Bruchsaal certainly had its advantages. He had been eating well and had put on a lot of weight. In fact he had been asked to put on weight for disguise purposes. 'Grow a beard, too,' he had been told. Both Daniel and he had been given clothes, not new but respectable, and in his case, a pair of heavy-rimmed spectacles had been provided. He put them on then and examined the new, more prosperous Mazambaan in a cracked wall mirror. Short of surgery there was not much more he could do. He smiled and the split-image crookedly smiled back. The added weight, he thought, suited him. The beard, he noticed, showed a flare of silver over the chin.

Daniel was still asleep, snoring faintly, when Mazam-baan stood up, levered open the wooden shutter from the sole window of the wooden hut and looked out at the rolling acacia-studded ranch that was their sanctuary. He slipped into his trousers, buckled his belt and with the familiarity that comes with habit, slipped his prized 'Makarov' pistol into his waist band. The inactivity was beginning to irk.

Outside *onuti* doves were cooing from the blackthorn trees. The air had an early stillness that could not have provided more peace; if he had wanted peace. The morning held all the promise of being as long, lazy, hot and tedious as any of the previous Bruchsaal days – that was until he saw the rider approaching down the valley.

It was not hard to recognize the horseman from his panama hat and khaki drill garb as Herr Moltke, the owner of the cattle ranch. Now Moltke never came near their kraal so in itself the visit was an event. But he had a feeling, just a feeling, that something was about to break. Their days at Bruchsaal, he thought, could be drawing to a close. Moltke was as welcome as the rain prophets.

He watched the rider draw down the valley to the dry river bed. The man rode well with his body erect. From that distance one would never have thought him small. He passed the wind pump with the circular cement reservoir from which Daniel drew their water every day, then kneeing his nugget-coloured horse expertly through the thorn scrub, he began the ascent to the kraal. Now Mazambaan could hear the thud of hooves on the dry soil. Moltke looked up, saw someone waiting, and waved uncertainly. He never seemed sure of himself, that German.

The rancher lived with his plump wife and child about two hours' walk from the kraal. He was apparently a fervent SWAPO supporter, especially, Okawe had said, since the day the comrades had shown Herr Moltke some artistic colour shots of himself doing *verboten* things with a pair of very naked, very ample Nama bar whores.

Moltke rode into the kraal with great circumspection. As usual he was twitchy and nervous. The horse beneath him, probably sensing his rider's apprehension, was skittish too. He greeted them in German-flavoured Herero: 'Wa penduku?' That was a mistake.

'Speak English,' Mazambaan said. 'Herero is not our language.'

'I have a message from comrade Okawe for you.'

'Yes?'

241

'Yes . . . Okawe asks you to meet him at my house this evening at 19.00.'

'I hear you.'

'Yes.' The horse was suddenly wheeling and prancing and generally giving its rider a hard time. Daniel had thrown back the door of the hut with a bang and was now standing there blinking in the sunlight, quite unaware of the trouble he had just caused. Moltke managed to get out the last part of his despatch. 'Take all your things. You will not be returning.' And that was it. Mazambaan found himself almost liking the messenger. At last something was happening. 'I hear you,' he said, smiling at the German. 'We will be there.' 'Gut, gut!' Having got his story out the man worked his bridle violently and rode away at a face-saving canter.

Mazambaan watched the departing horseman and smiled. Whatever was in store for them, it suited him. He'd long since had his fill of Bruchsaal. 'Daniel,' he said. 'Comrade Daniel, I have a feeling we are going back into business. What do you say to that?'

'When will we know?'

'Tonight at Moltke's farmhouse,' Mazambaan replied – but he was wrong.

There had been a change in plan, Moltke explained when the two men arrived that evening. 'Okawe couldn't come out. There are too many road-blocks at the moment. The police and the army are very active. What will happen is that tomorrow morning I'll be taking some cattle to the abattoirs in Windhoek. I have made a special crate to house you and Daniel. When the cattle are loaded it cannot be seen at all. I have done it before. It is quite safe.'

It did not look safe and it did not feel safe, either. In fact as Moltke's truck lurched southwards to Windhoek early the next morning, it seemed to the two men inside the creaking wooden cage that the army and the police road-blocks were the least of their problems. What was going to happen at any second was that with twenty-two

242

huge demented slaughter oxen heaving against them, the straining planks were going to give in, splinter into matchwood and crash inwards upon them. But it did not happen. Somehow Moltke's cage held.

They passed through a road-block about ten kilometres from the outskirts of Windhoek, hardly slowing. There was no problem. Then there was the rising buzz of early morning suburban traffic around them and Mazambaan's spirits rose with the sound.

Moltke dropped them at the Katutura turn off. He seemed to be a good deal more cheerful. Perhaps he had had the last laugh. Perhaps he was simply pleased to see the back of them. He actually chuckled as he said, 'You see, there was no danger, just as I said. Now . . . there is a police control point on the road into Katutura. You can by-pass it easily through the veld. Once you have passed it, walk back to the road and keep on walking towards Katutura. You will be picked up. Do you remember the recognition signals? The passwords?'

'Yes.'

'You have everything, comrades?'

'Yes.'

If everything was the clothes on their backs, one hand grenade, R100 each and a Makarov pistol, then they had everything. The false identity documents Okawe was supposed to have brought out to Bruchsaal together with a replacement pistol for Daniel they would receive later.

'Good luck then,' said Moltke and in spite of his cocky new smile, the hand he offered to them was damp with apprehensive sweat. Without a backward glance he revved up the huge diesel engine and drove off.

The police control point was where Moltke had said it would be, and it was by-passed, just as the German had said it could be, with ease. They rejoined the road and had not gone two kilometres when a white Valiant, a late Seventies model, passed them and drew to a quiet halt. The driver could have been older than Mazambaan but was remarkably similar in looks and build. He climbed from the car and opened the bonnet.

'Such a fine car,' said Mazambaan, joining him over the engine, 'should never break down.'

'Only a minor adjustment is required.' They had both been word-perfect.

The two men shook hands quickly. The ignition key was swopped, they closed the bonnet and Mazambaan took the wheel. The engine started at the first turn and accelerated sweetly. 'A good car,' he commented.

'Yes, it is a very good car,' said the ex-driver. 'It is my own and I look after it very well. Now my instructions are to give you these.'

Perfect sets of identity documents were handed to both men – though they were brand new they had the worn and buckled, back-pocket look that was vital. Mazambaan glanced at a time-yellowed photograph of himself that had been taken hardly two weeks previously at Bruchsaal. The name that appeared beneath it was Elias Kaluenja. SWAPO had gone to considerable pains to resurrect him safely, and SWAPO did not do anything without good reason. 'Do you know your way round Katutura?' the man asked.

'Daniel does.'

'Good, I will show you the house where you are to meet with Okawe. Then you can drop me at the bus terminal and go back there.'

'No problem,' Mazambaan said. They dropped the Valiant owner, then turned the car round. Mazambaan, however, was enjoying his freedom. He had no intention of driving straight to the meeting with Okawe. The Herero could wait. 'I'm hungry,' he said to Daniel. 'Let's go and get something to eat first. There must be a store around here somewhere.'

A small grocery store, dwarfed by a massive cigarette bill-board, caught Mazambaan's eye. 'There's a shop,' he said – and what a shop it was! It was a pleasure just to stand inside the place and gaze at the shelves and display cabinets bursting with bright packets, jars and tins. But he could not just stand and stare indefinitely.

'Can I help you?' A young and very pretty coloured assistant and he were the only two people present there at that moment. 'Yes,' he said – and then realized that he had not the faintest idea of what could be bought. He wanted food, certainly, but you could not just say, 'Give me food'. You had to know what you wanted. There were endless varieties of everything. What should have been a simple transaction was dragging him out of his depth. It had been such a long time.

'Cheese,' he said. 'Yes, and bread . . . and cool drinks.'

She wanted to know what kind. She wanted to know how much. The bread was on a self-service counter, round rolls, square loaves, brown, white and wholewheat, fresh and crusty. The smell of it, of the whole shop, was incredible, so that juice was pouring into his mouth. A shop like that in central Luanda would have caused a riot.

He left the supermarket weighed down with enough groceries to feed an army. They took the car to the outskirts of the township where streets of smart new houses were being built and there they ate. There were workmen on the building sites. There were passers-by. No one stared, no one pointed fingers at them and said, 'There they are!' They hardly rated a second glance, it seemed. So, encouraged by their anonymity and sated with fresh bread and cheese and sour milk, they cruised the streets with the windows down and the radio up high, in the direction that would bring them ultimately to the safe house and Okawe. It was a lazy drive that took them in a wide loop past Sakkie and Mary's home. Quite naturally, no one was there at the time.

Okawe, when they reached him, was far from happy. He had been waiting, so he said, for over an hour. 'Over an hour. What the hell were you two doing?'

'No one fixed a time for us to be here.' Mazambaan was quick to rise. 'Nobody told me a bloody thing, except to get here. If you wanted us here at a definite time you should have said so. It's your fault, comrade, not mine.'

'You should have come straight here, that's what Moltke told you, didn't he?'

'No.'

'He should have.'

'Maybe,' said Mazambaan. 'On the other hand, maybe you just forgot to tell him. I really couldn't care less, but this I would like to tell you, comrade Okawe. I know your type. I know where you fit in. You're just a messenger boy in the Organization. You get your orders and you pass them on, but you would probably wet your pants if a gun was put in your hand and you were told to do a job. So, dear comrade, don't give me any of your big tough talk about what this one should have done or what that one should have done, or what I must do. If you've got a message for me from higher command, cough it up, that's all. Stay off my back in future. Now what have you been told to tell me?'

It was all over. A much quieter Okawe did have a message for them, from higher command, of course. Daniel was to be filtered back into the system. 'A job has been arranged for you, comrade Aluteni, at the Namib Safari Hotel. It's the biggest hotel in Windhoek, six storeys. You'll be absorbed there without too much notice. The personnel manager is with the Organization. Her name is Dolly Etembako. There won't be any problems.'

'What will my job be?' Daniel asked.

'They are in need of a driver for their mini-bus. Mostly your duties will be to fetch and return guests from the airport. Do you know your way around Windhoek?'

'I used to; not so much any more.'

'That is the reason,' said Okawe, 'why I . . . why it would have been better for you to have met me earlier. We have established a routine for the Valiant, you see. To avoid suspicion and searches, we only move it through the police check-point on the Katutura-Windhoek road at peak traffic periods, in the morning between seven and eight, then back with the home-going traffic at around

246

17.00. Today I'm afraid has been wasted.' Okawe, with that mild admonishment, had regained some of his lost face. He looked cooler now, more his old self. He wooed Mazambaan with a cigarette, which the big man accepted. Some of the tenseness had left the air, some remained.

He was very careful with his words when he spoke again. 'Comrade fighters,' he said, 'as you know, in Windhoek there is a building called Turnhalle, an old gymnasium hall built by the Germans many years ago. You also know, I am sure, that the *boers* took over the building and spent a lot of money converting it into a venue for their so-called Constitutional Conference. It is at that hall that the racist Pretoria regime have brought together their political puppets and where they hatch their futile plots.'

Mazambaan shifted uncomfortably on his chair. Okawe was starting to sound like a political commissar, and political commissars were something he did not need in his life. The man was going on about puppets and racists. Next he would be on to imperialist running dogs and lackeys and the rest of it. He held up his hand. 'Okawe,' he snapped, 'do not try to indoctrinate me. I was fighting for SWAPO when you were sucking tit. I do it for a lot of reasons. Maybe I like it, maybe there's a future in it. If you've got something to say, then say it but stop talking like Radio Havana. That kind of speech gives me a loose stool.'

Daniel did not think Okawe was going to recover this time. He sat there with his jaw in motion, forming words that would not come. Unperturbed, Mazambaan tried to move things along. 'Okay, so we've got this Turnhalle where the *boers* and their tame blacks and the Bushmen and all the rest of them get together and talk, is that it, is that the problem?'

Okawe did not answer immediately. He did not seem to know how to pick up the pieces again. Perhaps he thought he had had enough verbal manhandling for one day. But then out of the blue, as though it was the most important

247

question on his mind, he said, 'Is it true, comrade Mazambaan, that you enjoy killing? Does it really give you pleasure?'

'Is that what they say about me?'

'Yes, yes, it is.'

'Do you believe it?'

Okawe had both feet in the quicksand of his curiosity. It was obvious that right then he would rather have been anywhere but where he was. What made things even more disquieting was that opposite him the man was chuckling, if you could call it that. His whole huge frame was shaking in soundless and it seemed, mirthless, laughter. 'Well, do you?' he persisted, 'Do you believe it?'

'I don't know. It's what I heard.'

'I'll think about it next time,' said Mazambaan, 'and let you know. Is the next time going to be at Turnhalle?'

248

Chapter 15

The next time was going to be at Turnhalle. That was what Supreme Command wanted and Okawe did not waste a word in delivering his message. 'You have been tasked with the assignment of eliminating a traitor of the Namibian people . . .' The assassination was to take place in the main hall; it was to be timed for the opening address. Everything had to be done to achieve maximum impact. 'I have been told to tell you, comrade Mazambaan, that the people of Namibia must clearly perceive that the shield of white protection is a myth; that SWAPO can reach out and do what it likes, when it likes, that all traitors will be crushed.'

'And who is this traitor?'

'Comrade Mazambaan, there are many traitors who sit at Turnhalle. I was not told who was the target so I can't tell you anything other than that he will be seated alongside the chairman. Tomorrow evening we meet here again. Perhaps I will have that information for you then.'

Okawe walked to the door, stood there hesitantly for a moment then turned back. He had something else on his mind. 'You've had a lot to say this morning, comrade Mazambaan. You've given me a hard time, but that's okay. Now it's up to you, you've got to make the plan and you've got to execute it. Let's hope you're up to it. In the next few days you and I will have to work quite closely together. It will not be my fault if co-operation breaks down.'

'Nor mine,' said Mazambaan thoughtfully. 'I will do my best.'

'Yes . . . If that is the case then we stand a better chance. Do not forget from now on to have your new identity documents with you at all times. Your name is now Elias Kaluenja. He is the man who handed your car over to you this morning. Did you notice that he even resembles you?'

Mazambaan wondered whether he resembled him sufficiently to fool the police and voiced his concern.

'Don't worry about that,' said Okawe. 'As long as your face matches your ID photograph, and your name and description aren't on their wanted lists, there's no problem. Elias Kaluenja has been tucked away at Bruchsaal for a while. You are now Elias Kaluenja. There's no reason why the police should show any special interest in you. We will meet again tomorrow afternoon at fourteen hundred in the Kuchen Restaurant on Leutwein Strasse. I will have more information for you then. Don't worry about being identified . . . you're clean, Elias Kaluenja.'

He was right. Moving in the stream of Windhoek-bound traffic the next morning, Mazambaan was waved through the control point with no more trouble than having his number plate recorded. It was raining quite hard and the police on duty in their slicks looked anything but keen to hunt terrorists. They did not give him a second glance. Okawe's directions to the old tournament hall, too, were faultless. It was little things like that, that made you feel you could trust a man, even a Herero. He drove the Valiant slowly past the big building.

Not even to Mazambaan's uncritical eye did Turnhalle's lumpy unmatched gables and heavy Germanic lines appear as anything other than functional. It was neat enough, with high cream-coloured walls and a red roof. All the windows and doors were barred and grenade-screened, he noticed. That was interesting. Beneath the entrance gable that displayed the bas-relief numerals 1913, an old uniformed coloured man was standing jangling a bunch of keys and staring into the clouds. Mazambaan watched him while he waited. The time was 09.55, and if Okawe was not mistaken, the tourist bus he was waiting for would arrive at any moment.

Okawe, it seemed, was never wrong. Ten metres of air-conditioned, encapsulated luxury on wheels splashed to a stop and smoothly passed its passengers to the pavement. It was the easiest thing in the world for Mazambaan to link up. The common denominator was the camera to the eye, and Mazambaan had come equipped. They clicked their way past the portals into the foyer and onwards . . . 'The main conference hall,' announced the guide. It was the old man with the keys. They were shepherded through double doors into a place that once must have echoed with the thud of medicine balls and indian clubs and smelt of sweat and 'Wintergreen'. Now it was all painted, panelled, carpeted and curtained in delicate shades of sand and terracotta. There was a central chandelier descending in an angel glow of oblong crystals. A long sweeping table circled the entire hall, leaving a massive carpeted circular oval across which the delegates could glare at each other. The guide rapped on a central podium beneath the closed curtained stage like a furniture salesman. 'The chairman's dais,' he said, proud to be part of so solid a thing. 'It has an electronic console which connects him to each delegate and the interpreters.'

'Interpreters?' someone asked. 'Why interpreters?'

'Ah! You see there are seven different languages spoken at Turnhalle – Herero, Lozi, Kwanyama, Damara, Afrikaans, Nama and Kuangali.' He indicated a series of booths in an overhanging gallery above the entrance doors. 'That's where the interpreters sit. As you can see, the booths overlook the entire hall so that they can see proceedings and translate those languages for the Chairman and the delegates. Each and every delegate can tune into the language of his home.'

The man had more to say about the electronic wizardry that had been fitted in the building, but Mazambaan was not listening. He was working out the angle between the door and the Chairman's dais. To get a clear shot he would have to advance right into the hall. Even if that was possible, with the security arrangements that would be in force, it would be suicide. There had to be another way . . .

'All that can be seen of the original construction are the ceiling beams.' The guide pointed upwards and twenty-six heads obediently tilted to observe the heavy arched timbers. The twenty-seventh head did not. It was looking in the direction of the staircase from the foyer leading to the interpreters' booths. An American-accented voice said, 'I'm going to get a pic from where the translators sit. You can shoot the whole goddamn thing from there.'

And so you could. The cubicles, there were eight of them, were small and stuffy, but from a standing position a clean shot was possible at any person on the floor. Mazambaan aimed an imaginary rifle at the Chairman's dais. It was almost dead ahead just below him, not more than twenty metres away.

Already a plan was starting to tumble around in his mind. There was still a lot to be worked out: how to breach the security arrangements, what to do with the interpreter who would be seated in the booth. Then, of course, a fail-safe escape plan. At least now he had a starting point. The rest would come.

The tour meandered through the rest of the building, the lounges and innumerable committee rooms. Finally it was over. Mazambaan left with the tourists and stood outside for a while. The rain had cleared. An interesting fact about the location of Turnhalle was that right opposite the old building lay the headquarters of the South African Police, Windhoek. That could present a problem, a big problem.

He drove into Windhoek proper, parked the Valiant, and sought out the 'Restaurant Kuchen'. He wanted to sit down and think, and there was quite a lot to think about. A newspaper headline caught his eye, so he bought a copy of the paper and read:

'MASSIVE BLOW TO SWAPO. TOP MAN NAKWINDI
SWAPS SIDES IN STUNNING MOVE.'
'SAM NUJOMA'S RIGHT HAND MAN TO ADDRESS
TURNHALLE.
RENEGADE OR HERO? ....'

Lazarus Nakwindi had swapped sides, gone over to the *boers*! Comrade Nakwindi, the original son of SWAPO, had decided to walk away from the household.

Mazambaan did not know how to take the news. Eventually the irony of the situation became clear. His schoolmaster, his comrade teacher, the man who had set him in his tracks and had first put a pistol in his hands, had now become his target. He, a flaming torch, was about to be assigned the job of extinguishing the source. Nakwindi was going to be incinerated by a fire of his own making . . .

Mazambaan had a theory that life was simply a progression of mistakes; that man's fate was to err. Like tweaking a bull's tail, he often tested his theory, but he had never found it wanting. Mankind could do absolutely nothing right. If you tried to do a thing well, your mistake would be compounded by the effort.

Nakwindi thought he had made the right move. Why should he not? Nakwindi did not know the rules. He did not know that man was cause and mistake was effect. Nakwindi had made a blunder. How could he help it?

Now SWAPO had decided that Nakwindi was Enemy Number One. Mistake. The man had to go. Mazambaan should do it. Mistake . . . The possibilities were endless, but basically one point had to emerge: whether he shot Nakwindi or not, either way it would be a mistake.

Victory was a mistake as much as defeat and any judgment as to which side had achieved what would be a mistake. It was a universal doublecross from birth to death that no one could escape . . .

Mazambaan began to chuckle. He ordered himself a substantial lunch and was still in wonderful humour by the time it had gone. It would be good once more to tweak the bull's rump and see what became of it. Nakwindi! My god, Nakwindi!

Another reason he was happy was because Okawe would be able to tell him nothing he did not already know. Some good ideas on how to set up the interpreter's booth

253

for the assassination were beginning to assemble. The problem of the rifle, for instance. He would have to use a rifle to be sure of a kill, but how did you get a weapon that size past heavy security? Answer: you did not. You took it in before such security was mounted, a day or two before. He could have carried a bazooka in with him that morning and the old coloured guide would not have noticed a thing. Yes, he would be the one to spring the surprises at the meeting after lunch.

It did not work out quite that way. Nakwindi was to be the target. He had been right there, but something else had occurred that shook Mazambaan. 'There has been what my superiors consider to be a serious setback,' Okawe said solemnly. 'There is a man in Windhoek, an officer in the South African Army, who it's believed, has been brought here, especially to identify you.'

'Impossible! How can that be?'

'I'm a messenger, comrade. Isn't that what you called me, a messenger boy? How should I know? I'll tell you this, though, there was a letter intercepted.'

'I can't believe it. Who the hell would know me?'

'Didn't you ever come face to face with a *boer* officer when you were fighting in Owamboland?'

'No!'

'Think back.'

'I am thinking . . . There was one man, but whether he was an officer or not I don't know. The *boers* don't wear rank in battle.'

'What did he look like?'

'God, how do I know? They smear themselves with black paint . . . He was a big guy . . . very strong . . .' His thoughts went back to that savage day when so many of his men had died. He recalled the man who had come at him, wild-eyed and daubed with battle paint, his hair almost singed away.

'I shot him in the shoulder, then my rifle jammed. His rifle wouldn't work either. Strange, that.'

'Strange?'

254

'Yes, AK's hardly ever jam. We fought for a while longer, but he was bleeding badly. I clubbed him across the head as hard as I could. I can't believe he lived . . . and even if he did, how would he ever be able to recognize me again? You can laugh it off, Okawe. It's all nonsense.'

'It does not matter what I think, Mazambaan, you know that. My superiors . . . your superiors believe he can identify you. They think he will have to be killed.'

'How?'

'The letter they intercepted was apparently from his girl-friend to her father, a *boer* Admiral, believe it or not. She gave the address. A bomb should be fine. I believe you're an expert with explosives.'

'I haven't got the materials for a bomb.'

'I have,' said Okawe. 'Right here, everything you could need.'

'When do they want it done?'

'The flat's empty at the moment. How about now?'

McGee had taken something of an instant dislike to the place Z had laid on for surveillance. It was nothing more than a dirty asbestos broken-walled shack, the type you could erect or take down in a day. Perched on the flat roof of a karakul pelt-processing plant it could have been a work-cum-store-room, but did not appear to be used now. Behind the door, dust-covered mechanical spare parts were stacked and against one wall there was a work bench with some old Playboy centre-spreads taped above it.

The hut had one great merit: a west-facing window which, once it had been forced open, provided an open-ended view of Gabriel Street, Katutura. Half way down Gabriel Street was the home of Mary Njoba, pretty Mary Njoba and her cuckold husband Sakkie. In real terms the house lay about a kilometre away, and one kilometre to the type of optical gadgetry that was now cramming that window aperture was about from your nose to your thumb. They had an infra-red telescope yoked to a Zeiss

SLR that could have photographed an ant on the Njoba's bedroom wall day or night. They had a self-illuminating dark hours snooper with a barrel as long as a baseball bat. They had binoculars; they had everything a peeping Tom could have ever wished for, and more.

Zietsman had left them at about five on the first morning. It seemed as though a lifetime had passed since then. How long had it been . . . ? forty eight hours . . . ? A bit more. How long did he think he was going to keep them there? A hard man, Major Z. 'Remember,' Z's last words had been, 'I want twenty-four hours' surveillance, nothing less.'

Twenty-four hours' surveillance was what they had given him. McGee squinted down the pre-focused Zeiss system and the Njoba's lace-covered bedroom window jumped towards him with astonishing clarity. It was getting light as he tracked the scope across the yard. Njoba, in his own way, was a gardener. He had a nice little patch of pumpkins and beans growing around a postage-stamp lawn. A pathway led to an outside toilet with a long rusty damp stain down the whitewash. Sakkie was not into plumbing. There was some junk and an old car tyre against the back fence, nothing else.

He swung back to the bedroom window. The panes were glistening with dew. The curtains stirred faintly for a moment then were quickly flung apart. Mary Njoba, her brown skin in sharp contrast to the whiteness of her slip, stood there for a moment; she seemed to look straight at him, then rolled her head back and yawned. McGee felt disconcertingly guilty, like a schoolboy caught at a keyhole. He did not like this business. It was humiliating. He swung the scope into the street and let the Njobas be. Head and shoulders, the advancing workers trudged up the telescope. The treadmill of life . . .

'Coffee,' Adam said from behind him. 'You give me the scope now. I've already had coffee.' The sergeant's vision, it was apparent, was not clouded by threads of moral gossamer. He sprang the scope straight back to Sakkie's

256

place. 'I'll be damned!' he said. 'Why didn't you say something?' His trigger finger was occupied for some time after that. 'Let's go.' Click. 'Cheeky.' Click. 'Nice angle.' Click. 'More to the right . . . Oh boy!' Click.

An outsider could have been forgiven had he taken Adam to be nothing short of a legalized, and well-contented voyeur. According to Z, however, he was the surveillance supremo. McGee drank his coffee hot and listened to the camera eye commentary of events as Mary Njoba prepared for the day ahead. He was not sure if he was cut out for the job.

Isack Njoba was a creature of routine, as was his pretty little wife. He left home, briefcase in hand, every morning at seven-thirty on the dot and returned between 18.00 and 18.30. She left half an hour later and returned half an hour earlier. McGee and Adam had been given a portfolio chronologizing the Njobas' movements. Of course, it did not include what was happening right then – right then, according to Adam, the back door had just swung open and Sakkie was picking his way across the pumpkins for his appointment with the leaky cistern. 'It's good when you're regular like that,' Adam said. 'You can't fool around with nature.'

Indeed you could not. McGee eyed the little caravan lavatory they had been issued with and hoped it was more efficient than it looked. Just then the radio on the workbench stuttered into life. A phantom voice by the name of Control wanted a word with Oscar Pappa. They were Oscar Pappa.

'Come in, Control,' McGee invited, and in they came.

'Oscar Pappa, good morning . . . Radio check, how do you read me today?'

'Read you loud and clear, Control.'

'What's news, Oscar Pappa?'

McGee thought the easy-going police radio procedure was a refreshing change. Adam said he had some news for them. His news was that he was sick of Njobas, that the neighbour had bigger tits, and he was doing surveillance there instead. McGee pressed the transmitter button and said, 'Nothing to report.'

'Okay . . . test your signals with Tango Tango and report back . . . Out.' Tango Tango was the tailing team; a squad of police radio cars that looked like anything but radio cars. Their job in the operation was to latch on to any suspect persons or vehicles. McGee had no idea how many units Tango Tango had operational, he reported only to the command vehicle. He tested his clarity as requested and reported back to Control that all was well.

Rain began to drum softly against the asbestos roof, a lulling sound that McGee enjoyed. He picked up his binoculars and casually perused the street with its monotonous corrugated iron wet-roofed houses. Sakkie's car was gone and apart from a few piccanins kicking at the mud pools there was nothing much to see. A long leaky day lay ahead before the Njobas once more occupied their dwelling, and they watched them sit down to eat, watched them switch off the lights and go to bed, watched them . . . McGee glanced at his watch. During the whole time they had been there not a thing had happened, not a hint had been given that anything could happen that would divest pretty Mary of her mantle of marital fidelity. Z, he thought, had underestimated comrade Mazambaan. It began to pour then and he wondered whether it was raining in Windhoek proper. He hoped Patricia had parked the Beetle under cover. It wouldn't get her to work if the ignition got wet.

Patricia, was not on her way to work. She had in fact just returned from a full night's duty in the High Care Unit. While McGee was away she had decided that it would be a good time to get a night shift behind her. Tired, heavy-headed but not quite ready for sleep, she had but a few minutes previously walked through the front door, drawn off her blue cape and shaken off the raindrops, closed the curtains tightly and undressed. Some yoga was indicated, she thought, to chase the dragons from her temple. It was remarkable what yoga could do. She opened the balcony door a few inches for air, then settled down behind the curtains to do her *asanas*: the diamond seal with some relaxed breathing would be fine and calming. It was. Hardly ten minutes passed before bed began to beckon her. It was not twenty minutes before she was snuggled beneath the duvet, asleep.

When Patricia opened her eyes again she guessed it was late afternoon. A sword blade of sunlight was playing across the wall near her head, and . . . that was stupid because when she had gone to sleep she had closed the heavy curtains tightly! She was about to stretch when intuition insisted that she stop, *stop dead!*

She did not know what sense it was that had warned her. For a few moments she lay still, then her head cleared and she wrinkled her nose, sniffing softly like a cat. An alien smell that should never have been there was tinging her nostrils. It was the acid-sour malodour of stale sweat. She lay absolutely quiet, feigning sleep, every nerve ending in her body ringing its warning.

There was someone behind her, someone within touching distance, and whoever it was, was observing her quietly and carefully. She tried to keep her breathing evenly spaced and sleep-toned. Her mind tautened with the concentration of it. A scream impelled itself into her throat and tightly clenched teeth locked on to it, smothered it. Whoever it was, was doing her no harm at that moment. If she did not present a threat perhaps he would leave it that way, and go.

She listened. One of her fellow night sisters had promised to call, if she could, that very afternoon. She strained her ears to hear the friendly squeak of heels on the polished hallway, the friendly tap-tap on the door. But the only sounds came from a buzz-fly trapped between the curtain and the window panes, and the occasional car as it droned by outside.

Then for reasons of its own, the fly gave up trying to make a hole through the glass, found an escape route through the curtains and flew into the room. It zoomed around, settling here and there, then attracted by the fissure of sunlight now touching Patricia's hair it landed on her cheek and crawled towards her slightly parted lips.

Mazambaan held his breath, aimed his Makarov at the base of her skull and waited. She did not move. He had observed people day-slumbering many times. Inevitably, if an insect tracked across eyes or mouth, there was some drowsy dissenting flicker or twitch. The girl in the bed had not budged. The fly was actually crawling into her parted lips, yet she did not move. If that had not given her away her hands would have. Though her body was sprawled and her breathing was even, the hands that were drawn up beneath her chin were clenched with knuckle-whitening intensity. She was awake and knew he was there. It had to be that.

Mazambaan sat slowly on the bedside stool, mouth breathing as softly as he could. There was no need, really. He knew she was aware of his presence; also she knew that he knew she was awake. A bizzare sham truce was being observed. She would not break it, if he did not make it impossible for her not to do so. Well, he would see . . .

It was an intriguing situation. He had been startled to find the sleeping girl in the first-floor flat. It was Okawe's first bad slip. But she had been out cold, then. Of that he was certain. It had not taken him long to discover the perfect place for the booby trap, and only minutes to wire up and pack the half–kilogram of plastique. All that time she had been sleeping. The problem now was what to do about her now that she was no longer asleep.

He could kill her. That was a thought, a not altogether unjustifiable thought. Okawe was wrong if he imagined there was pleasure in the simple act of execution. But the anticipation of it – that was different! The knowledge that you and you alone for a period of time held a life in the balance – now there was power! Did anyone on earth ever possess more power than at that instant? Once it was all over, once the life had been taken, you had nothing, you were anybody. Mazambaan aligned the sights of his Makarov on the flowing blonde hair scalp on the pillow and considered. He could feel the ecstasy of that power, from his head to his loins it stormed within him.

He did not shoot her, however. If he did pull the trigger, if he did leave a corpse in the bed, then the *boer* officer would probably survive the bomb. Some prying homicide cop would end his life in the flat. That was not what he wanted. He wanted that *boer*. He wanted him so badly that he let the girl be. There was too much at stake. A plan had occurred to him. Perhaps he could salvage the situation.

There was not much more time. Mazambaan knew that the pressure on the woman had been built up to flash-point. Sporadically an irrepressible tremor was shaking her whole body. He made his decision and acted. It had to be a burglary, straight and simple. That way his bomb would lie preserved, intact and waiting. Into the gym bag that had held the explosives went a gold coin on a chain, a breast watch, a little portable radio and a purse. What else was there? There had to be more. The shaft of sunlight touched the pedestal by her face. There was a ring on it with the biggest, bluest stone he had ever seen. That was what he wanted. If she kept the truce a moment longer he would have it and be away.

Patricia broke the truce. As his hand reached for the prize, she coiled up in her nakedness and struck out at him with the venom of a cornered cobra. Mazambaan was unprepared for the ferocity of the attack. He had made up his mind not to kill her. Perhaps that was the reason why it was so difficult for him. He had set himself on a course of action and now he had a hitting, clawing, kicking *enuengu*, a mad thing, in his path. Strangely, she did not scream. That was a life-saver for her. That was why he kept his resolve and was so careful not to snap her chicken-thin neck as he twisted her helplessly face-first into the pillow. That was certainly why she was still alive to watch him with wide horrified eyes as he crossed to the balcony, flung back the curtains and jumped.

Then the scream came, as hard as the ground it hit him. He rolled like a paratrooper, stood up and sprinted. The scream pursued him as he ran through the parking bays, it followed him into the street where he strode quickly away. Only when he reached the Valiant, slammed shut the door and started the engine did his ears seem to be free of it.

Mazambaan drove from Windhoek as fast as was legally possible. He did not stop driving until he reached central Katutura. There he parked, sat in the car and brooded. Okawe had not been so damn smart that time. He had said the flat would be empty and it had not been empty. He opened the gym bag and contemplated his loot. The ring, he was sure, was worth a lot of money. He thought about the blonde in the bed. He remembered very clearly the naked blonde, pinned down and powerless. How long he sat there thinking he did not know, but it was dark when he reached for the ignition key once more, and the Valiant seemed almost to steer itself through the lightless Katutura streets: its direction, 63 Gabriel Street, the house of Mary Njoba. Mazambaan was smiling, Mazambaan was laughing – an extremely deep need was going to be fulfilled, and soon.

Chapter 16

There were no fingerprints to be found. That was what Captain Wells of the uniform branch said. 'He must have been careful. You'd be surprised how quickly they learn, Miss Christie. Once they've been collared before on the evidence of prints only the idiots get caught that way again.'

A plainclothes man who had been frosting the balcony doors and cupboard edges with fine silver dust stood back from his work, and shook his head. 'Not a thing, Captain,' he confirmed with a shake of his head. 'I'll check out the balcony railings but I can tell you now . . .' The sentence did not need completion. Wells sat down on the bed, opened a brown cardboard folder, took out a pen and began to write. 'I'll need a statement from you,' he said to Patricia. 'Right. Now what time did you get home?'

She went over it again, from the time she had closed the curtains and curled up to sleep to the horrible moment of realization that she was not alone.

'You feigned sleep?' Wells looked up from his folder. 'That was the best thing you could have done. I don't understand why you didn't keep it that way. He'd have just taken the things and gone. By making a fight of it you could have been killed.'

'He could have taken anything he wanted, Captain, anything except my ring, my special ring.'

'Wasn't it insured?'

'You don't understand. That ring was given to me by my man. It was precious beyond money. No amount of insurance could have covered it.'

'Captain McGee gave it to you?'

'Yes.'

'So when the man reached across the bed for the ring you did not pretend to be asleep any more, you went for him?'

'Of course. He was right over me. I held on to his arm and hit out as hard as I could.'

Wells started writing again. 'I held on to his arm . . .' It had been many a year since he had been called on to write up a burglary statement and he hoped it would be an equally long time before he was again asked to do so. It was not a captain's job. His mind went back to the orders he had received that afternoon from his boss, the Divisional Commissioner and Major Zietsman from Security. Put a lid on it, Captain, he had been told. Get out there and sort the thing out personally. The woman's fiancé is on a vitally important job. There's no way, just no way he can be released. Hold her hand. Do whatever has to be done and do it with kid gloves. Her father is Rear Admiral Christie. One phone call to him and the shit will hit the fan. We don't want that to happen, do we?

Captain Wells looked up from the docket and smiled his most reassuring smile at the girl standing there. 'Well,' he said, 'don't worry about a thing now, everything will be taken care of. I'm just very happy that you weren't badly hurt. That's the main thing, isn't it?'

Was it the main thing? Patricia Christie put her hand to her neck and felt the bruises hidden beneath the cheerful chiffon scarf she wore. No . . . the main thing was that the precious and irreplaceable Sun-rival had been stolen. Had she been raped, she could hardly have felt more violated, more bereft. The police officer was trying to be kind, she realized that, but she knew he was lying to her when he stood up, folded the docket and said, 'We'll get him and we'll get back the ring and everything else, I promise you. If there's anything you need you can phone me. I'll leave you my number.'

'There is something you can do,' Patricia said. 'I want to speak to my fiancé urgently.'

'Captain McGee?'

'Yes, Captain McGee.'

'I'll arrange that as soon as possible.'

'And when will that be?'

Wells side-stepped the question by walking to the balcony. 'You don't need to be an acrobat to get into the flat this way.' He demonstrated by reaching sideways along the wall, just how close the fire escape was. 'I'll have a man watching the flat for you from now on, but keep this door locked, anyway.'

'Captain McGee,' she persisted. 'I have to speak to him.'

'That could be tricky.'

'Why?'

Wells found the woman disconcerting. He had come to the flat with orders to carry out a Kleenex and nappies job. Instead of which he had been confronted by a very quiet and determined young woman. He had tried to beguile her. He had tried to side-track her . . . He tried the truth. 'Captain McGee,' he said, 'is involved in a very sensitive operation. Even if I knew what it was, and I promise you I don't, I would not be at liberty to disclose it to you. The fact is that he cannot be called away, believe me. You'll just have to rely on me until he gets back. It won't be long. Please be patient.'

Sincerity at last, and Patricia responded to it. She told Wells that she wished to speak to McGee as soon as it was humanly possible. She would be patient, she said, but she would not be messed around. Messing around, the police captain vowed in return, was something his department never did. They wound up with a clear mutual understanding.

'You're not even going to inform Captain McGee about this, are you? You've no intention of telling him a thing?'

He did not lie. 'I doubt it,' he replied. 'It depends on his Control Officer, Major Zietsman, but, as you say, I don't think he'll be told a thing until the operation is over. It's better that way, Miss Christie, there's nothing he could do now anyway. We've got it all in hand.'

'I understand, but I want to make a request.'

'Sure.'

'I want to be the one to tell him about what happened here. No one else. I can't begin to tell you how much that ring meant to both of us. I don't want the news reaching him third-hand.'

Wells wondered whether his sigh of relief had been audible. There certainly would not be any objections to that condition. He said, 'I understand. That's a deal then.'

'I have to go on duty now,' Patricia Christie said. 'Please keep me informed.'

She let him out of the flat and together they walked to the bottom of the stairs. Then he watched her as she stepped towards her VW. The girl had guts, he thought, and a lot more. He could not see the tears filling her eyes, or the teeth biting her lower lip. Even if he had, he would not have thought less of her. What he could, and did observe, was the proud bearing of her head and shoulders, and a long, extremely good pair of legs. 'McGee, wherever you are,' he whispered to himself, 'you're still one lucky bastard.'

The lucky bastard was still in the shack on top of the karakul pelt factory. He was watching a day-worn Mary Njoba preparing a meal over her kitchen stove. It was gloomy enough at that time of the evening for inside lights to be on, and still too warm for curtains to be drawn. In other words, it was ideal surveillance weather.

The woman was quick and birdlike in her movements. There was a sort of tension in all her actions that was obvious. Njoba's car drew up outside. The man must have hooted or something, for she left her cooking and disappeared towards the front door. Two men left the vehicle and McGee swung his attention to them. One of them was Sakkie, the other was of similar stature. No luck there. They made their way into the house and went to the kitchen. He could see them better now. Both had that harassed petty expression that schoolmasters seem to cultivate, both had on identical safari suits, both had afro hairstyles and carried briefcases. Tweedledum and Tweedledee, mused McGee, and returned to the roadway.

There were still many people slouching homewards tired and hungry. Mostly they were moving in little groups. Now and then one would break away to kick open a front gate or hoist a scampering piccanin joyfully skywards. Nothing else.

In the Njoba's house supper was proceeding. Both men were in earnest conversation and Mary was serving them. 'It's their evening for the PTA meeting,' Adam said. 'They should be on their way pretty soon now.'

The sergeant had just joined McGee at the window and had picked up the binoculars. 'Meat and osifima mash,' he commented. 'Yeagh! I'm sure we can do better than that.' McGee heard him rummaging in the big cardboard box, their pantry. 'What do you feel like tonight?' Adam asked. 'Choice fresh garden peas with tender sausages made from the finest prime pork with added cereal, or solid pack light meat tuna, quality controlled? Maybe you'd go for ze chef's surprise?'

'Chef's surprise sounds okay,' said McGee, watching Njoba and his mirror image rise from the table as one, go to the front door, climb in the car and depart.

'They're on their way,' he said simply. 'They never bloody well miss, do they?' Adam did not answer. There was an aroma of bully beef being fried with onions in the shack now, the chef's special. McGee had no appetite for food. God, he thought, I'm a patient man, I really am, but let the bastard come tonight. If he remembered correctly the schedule gave them Sakkie returning from the PTA usually about midnight, never before 23.00. The chef's surprise was ready, Adam announced, 'Come and get it.'

McGee would have done that. He would have handed the scope to his companion, then forced some of the muck down his gullet. He had in fact already drawn back from the cushioned eye-piece, when with his naked eye he spotted the red glow of tail lights moving down Gabriel Street. With more curiosity than hope he lowered his head back to the lens and was rewarded by seeing the cruising car's brake lights blink as it passed Sakkie's house, and then come on again a little further down the road. The car, a pale coloured Valiant, had stopped.

'Your special's getting cold,' the chef complained, but McGee hardly heard him. The car door opened and a man stepped out. 'Adam,' McGee said in a voice that was all too calm, 'get over here – we've got a visitor.'

He was a huge man, with a belly running to fat. He had on a pair of heavy spectacles with a snap-brimmed hat pulled low that made his face difficult to see, but the body was not the body of the lithe bush fighter of his memory. McGee did not think it was him. 'He's too fat, much too fat. It doesn't look like Mazambaan at all.'

Whether it was their man or not did not matter. For the eventuality now occurring they had a standing operating procedure. Adam depressed the transmit button on their set and said slowly, precisely and twice over, 'Oscar Pappa to all stations . . . Status Yellow.' Then they waited and watched. Yes, and prayed. The man, whoever he was, had carefully closed the car door and was making his way up the pavement towards the house. McGee's breath escaped in a disappointed hiss. He had walked right past, had not even looked the place over. The status would have to return to zero . . . No it *would not*. The man had stopped. McGee could see the wisp of a beard under a heavy chin. He stood there for a moment peering around, then turned and with quick purposeful steps walked back down the road and into the Njoba's yard. The radio crackled into life then. It was Control – which had been surprisingly slow in responding to the new status.

'Control to Oscar Pappa,' came the voice. 'We have you on Yellow. What does it look like?'

Adam told them what it looked like. 'A Valiant car, and one black male now in the subject's garden. No positive ID at this stage.'

268

'Right, we're standing by on Status Yellow.'

For all his bulk the intruder was easy on his feet. He stood at the front door for a moment as though listening, then jumped lightly off the step, and keeping close to the wall moved round to the side of the house to the lighted window. McGee watched him intently. Mary was at the table, still leisurely finishing her meal, sipping what looked like a glass of milk. She was being carefully observed by the man at the window who was now casting quick uneasy glances to each side: the scent of danger on a down-wind breeze of intuition perhaps. The man should not have disregarded it. Another stronger instinct, however, seemed to be pounding him off balance: Mary had just eased out of her chair, squirming, her arms upward in a fabric-tightening stretch.

'Oscar Pappa . . . Still no positive ID from you?' Control was getting anxious. So was McGee as he strained his eyes into the nightscope.

'I can't be positive,' he said to Adam. 'This guy is at least fifteen kilos heavier than is Mazambaan.'

'Keep on him,' came the reply. 'Changing weight is the oldest, easiest disguise in the book.' Control wanted to know in which direction the car was pointed. They told them. Constantly now they were prompting for progress reports.

There was progress. 'He's moved to the bedroom window,' McGee said. 'I think he is going to climb in.' He did climb in. He hiked himself up the wall and through the open bedroom window with the sure professional movements of a man who had done it all before.

'He's in the house,' McGee told Adam.

'He's in the house,' Adam said to all stations.

'We've got it,' Tango Tango responded. 'Keep on it, boys, keep it coming.' The voice was new to the net, but not to any of the listeners there that night. It belonged to Z who had taken personal control of the mission.

Mary had finished eating. She cleared her plates and returned to the table with what looked like a paperback, sat down and began to read. A full ten minutes passed before McGee saw the man again. He had removed his spectacles, coat and hat, and was advancing on the girl at the table with the concentration of a stalking cat. And with every inch that he narrowed the gap, his smile expanded. It was a smile that defied duplication. It *was* Mazambaan!

'Behind you!' McGee found he had actually whispered the words out loud. But Mary, of course, like the classic horror movie heroine remained oblivious of her peril. Adam's urgent voice broke through his concentration.

'Is it him?' He was demanding. 'Is it him?'

'It's him!'

It was Status Red.

It was Mazambaan and now, after all those nightmare months, McGee was impotent to do more than call in the hunting dogs. Revenge, the demand for bloody revenge flooded every channel of his conscious thought, and all he could do was sit there as a spectator, an observer. Sweat poured from his forehead, blurring his eye-piece as he watched.

Mazambaan came right up behind the girl, reached out slowly with both hands, then suddenly he hoisted her like a convulsing wrung-neck fowl. He turned her towards him, and the whole picture changed. From a frightened cringing woman she became an animal on heat. Her arms gartered his neck and she writhed into sexual hardness.

It was sheer bad luck that Isack Njoba decided to return home early from his PTA meeting. There must have been a reason for that astonishing break in routine, but that did not concern the observers. What did concern them was that Sakkie had parked his car and was now walking up his short pathway. In a minute he would open his front door, walk in and discover his wife all but copulating on the kitchen floor with a SWAPO hit man. It was likely to be the death of him.

'Njoba has arrived home.' Adam's voice was way above its normal pitch as he transmitted. 'He's home early.'

Major Zietsman had got the message. 'Roger,' he said, 'keep it coming.'

'He's letting himself in . . . He's in the house.'

'Roger, Oscar Pappa, no problem.' No problem! Maybe the Major didn't have a problem, but if someone did not help poor little Njoba he was going to have one hell of a problem.

To his credit, Njoba did not hesitate. He hurtled into the room, picked up a kitchen chair and swung it down upon his tormentor. It was his last attacking blow. Mazambaan stood up, shaking off the effect of the jolt, and Isack took a pace backwards, staring at the chair in his hands as though he could not believe what he had done. Njoba was no fighter.

'He's going to kill Njoba,' predicted Adam who now had the microphone jack fully extended so he could both observe and transmit.

'He's going to kill him now,' he repeated. Mary must have come to the same conclusion. She scampered for the sanctuary of the bedroom.

Control said, 'We read you, Oscar Pappa. There's nothing we can do about it. Just tell us the moment he leaves the house.' As though sensing that it was now open season Mazambaan advanced on Isack Njoba, who was retreating like a scared lion tamer behind his chair. It was not much of a defence, but it kept Mazambaan at bay for a few paces, just a few. Then the big man lunged out and, chair and all, Sakkie went flying against the dresser. Mazambaan hit him hard twice.

All that was missing from the horror movie they were watching was the sound track. It was unreal. A man was being killed in front of the eyes of two law men, and all they were going to do was watch. Isack was lurching from the punishment he was taking. His safari suit was covered in his blood, yet still he was resisting in his feeble unco-ordinated way. He was probably in his first fight. It was certainly going to be his last.

A crashing head blow slammed him against the dresser

again, and plates came spinning silently down. He propped himself against the piece of furniture as his persecutor came forward. Suddenly Isack had a carving knife in his fist. It flashed downwards but not nearly fast enough. Mazambaan blocked it and McGee knew that the end was near. The two bodies were locked together for an instant, elbows working, then the killer broke away, and Isack crumpled to his knees. It was futile trying to pluck out the blade, it was in up to the hilt.

'Right in the heart,' McGee said softly. 'The poor little bugger had no chance.' He took the mike from Adam's hand, inhaled deeply several times and said. 'Njoba's dead. He killed him.'

'We read you,' came a subdued reply. 'We're standing by.'

'You know, he's probably going to kill the girl!' McGee had addressed the words to Adam, then realized he still had the transmit button depressed. He did not care. There was no reply from man nor radio.

The lights in number 63 were being switched off. Then the front door opened, and McGee transmitted the last operational message from call sign Oscar Pappa.

'He's leaving.' His voice sounded weary and flat. 'He's on his way, Tango Tango. He's all yours.'

If bother was the right word, then the slaying of Sakkie Njoba and his wife had bothered Mazambaan most of that evening – but not because he was suffering from remorse or regrets. What concerned him was that it had been a messy and unprofessional affair, while Mazambaan generally prided himself on being neat and professional.

The next morning he bought the papers and looked for two items. One would concern a bomb blast in a Windhoek flat; the other, the double slaying of a Katutura schoolmaster and his wife. Neither item was anywhere to be found. The papers were full of speculation regarding the Turnhalle Conference that was due to begin the next day, the possibility of elections that included SWAPO and

272

the defection of Nakwindi. The puerile deliberations of the Western Five contact group were also covered fairly extensively. Mazambaan's activities did not rate a mention. But all that would change soon; the following morning at Turnhalle in fact.

He had a leisurely breakfast, and while he ate, toyed with the jewellery on the table in front of him, wondering what he should do with it. It would be a shame simply to throw it away. The ring especially, with the big blue stone – that was something worth keeping. It did not remotely fit any of his fingers but it would certainly look good on a thong round his neck. He dropped it into his trouser pocket. Everything else he dumped during his trip to the outside toilet that morning.

There was no rush. In fact there was only one thing he had to do that day: to meet comrade Okawe once more, just after lunch. He drove into town, whisked through the police control point, parked centrally and spent the rest of the morning strolling among the shoppers.

The site Okawe had selected for their final meeting was a pub just off Kaiserstrasse, Windhoek's bustling main street.

Das Keller was not marked on the upper-class tourist maps of the city, the reason probably being that it was somewhat nasty. It was dank with the corrosive odour of yesterday's sweat, spilt brew and burnt tobacco that no amount of airconditioning would expel. But it had its advantages, for Mazambaan, anyway – it was dark and perpetually thronged with noisy people. As far as the management of *Das Keller* were concerned, as long as you had a beer in your hand, you were welcome to a seat for as long as you liked. Okawe was late by half an hour. It was nothing to get wound up about, but sufficiently troubling to ensure that Mazambaan's head snapped up and his eyes were looking each time the bar doors swung to admit a blaze of daylight and yet another customer.

It was too late for the hard-core lunchtime drinkers and too early for the hookers and their after-work Johnnies.

Still, there were plenty of people flopped around the bar room, losers with bodies and minds softened by alcohol. Mazambaan sipped his drink and watched a bald pot-bellied boozer who had just entered. The man stood unsteadily for a few seconds blinking out the noon-day glare, then tottered over to the bar.

Okawe was wearing dark glasses, which he removed once inside. He saw Mazambaan, came quickly across, sat down on the opposite bench and ordered the mandatory beer. Soon settled, he leaned over the table, and, with the clipped speech used by those who count the day in minutes, told Mazambaan that all was arranged.

'The rifle . . . folding stock AK and full magazine, is where you wanted it.' The beer was brought and sloppily put before them. Okawe paused until the waiter had departed, then continued rattling it off: 'The uniform is there . . . everything is there . . . This afternoon at fifteen hours thirty . . . Outside the Namib Safari Hotel you join the tourist party. The bus will be crowded. Keep to the back, board early. They don't count heads so no one will miss you when you don't return with them. Once at Turnhalle, go to the main kitchen. The staff will have left by then. Stay there.'

Okawe pushed his glass around, marshalling his thoughts. Then he looked up decisively. 'That's it, then,' he said. 'Proceedings begin a bit after zero nine hundred tomorrow. Soon after that you'll hear the diversion. Hit Nakwindi then. Get him comrade! With Nakwindi on the side of the *boers* our people are confused. He *has* to go, Mazambaan.'

'Nakwindi,' was all Mazambaan said in reply, but there was no mistaking the crushing hand-to-fist gesture that went with the word. Nakwindi was as good as swatted. Mazambaan meant it. Okawe nodded his head.

'Do you have any questions?' he asked Mazambaan. 'There isn't much time left before you board the bus.'

He did have a question. He wanted to know if the diversion was exactly as he had planned it. Okawe said it

274

was. 'Exactly. That is why I was a bit late. I had arrangements to make.'

He had no other questions and said so. He thought the meeting was over, but it was not. Okawe had questions of his own that he wanted answers to. The first one nearly caught Mazambaan off guard. 'Have you been back to the Njoba's house since your return to Katutura?'

'I drove past once but no one was home. Why?'

'Something very strange happened there,' Okawe said, 'very strange. Yesterday Njoba was at school, his wife at work. Today neither of them showed up. People went to their house to check up. It's empty . . . They've disappeared.'

'Disappeared!' Mazambaan interjected in astonishment. 'What do you mean?'

'I mean,' said Okawe, 'disappeared. They searched their house. Their clothing was gone. The rest of the house was normal. The bed had been made up, the floors swept, the crockery washed. Now why would a respectable couple like the Njoba's do a duck like that?'

'How should I know?'

'You didn't see him at all, Mazambaan? Perhaps just frighten him or his wife?'

'Why should I?'

Okawe looked at his fellow-comrade thoughtfully. 'We know,' he said, 'a little bit more than you think about what went on in that house when you were staying there before. As long as you kept away since you've been back, there's nothing to worry about.'

'I'm as surprised as you are,' said Mazambaan truthfully. He was wise enough, however, to let the subject rest. But buzzing like a bothered hornet in his mind were questions that would not let him be: Who on God's earth would have wanted to launder the Gabriel Street killings? Who had anything to gain by it?

Okawe had been talking for a while and he had missed it. Mazambaan pulled himself back to Das Keller.

'The *boer* officer?'

275

'Yes, how many more times . . . ? You were supposed to eliminate him. What happened?'

'Yes.' He had been waiting for that opportunity to tear into Okawe regarding the information he had received from him, and now he was fumbling. 'The *boer* has been taken care of, believe me . . .' Then it came to him in mid-sentence. He had the solution to the Njoba riddle, and Mazambaan felt his bowels turn to water . . . As a bushbuck carcass is left hanging in the Mungwa tree, so he had been baited with Mary Njoba, and like the leopard he had come snarling with hunger to be netted. He was in the net. Okawe was in the net. The security police had seen to the trap at the Njoba's house. The security police! He almost said the words aloud.

'I must go now, there is not much time.' Okawe started to ease his way from the booth. 'Good luck, Comrade Mazambaan.'

'Wait!' The edge of alarm in Mazambaan's voice was easy to detect. Unfortunately it was misinterpreted.

'Cold feet, comrade?'

'No.'

'It's too late now. You've less than an hour to board that bus. You know, I want to tell you something, Mazambaan. I always thought my superiors had made a mistake in choosing you for such an important job. Now I'm sure of it. I think you're going to fail, Comrade big mouth. You haven't got what it takes for this job.'

Okawe could go to hell. Mazambaan sat back in cold fury. 'I can do the job,' he said, 'and I promise you I will . . . One day, too, I might have the pleasure of being your executioner, Okawe. I hope so. Then I assure you there will be pleasure in killing.'

It was hardly the way for two men on the same assignment to part company, but as he watched the Herero leave the bar room, Mazambaan felt totally vindicated. He had tried.

No more than a few seconds passed, then the bald-headed boozer, leaving the drink he had been sipping, stood up, and, looking considerably more sure-gaited than he had when he had come in, also left. So that was it! Mazambaan sipped what remained of his beer and pondered the situation. Not one of the customers in Das Keller looked like a *boer* agent, but then, what did a *boer* agent look like? He thought he would find out.

The entrance to the men's toilet was clearly marked with a little blue man on a square of white plastic. He dawdled over to it, pushed, and hydraulically the door hissed closed behind. The smell of urine and washed camphor blocks was almost more than he could stand. He did not have to bear the affliction for long, however. The door opened again and a rather nondescript man with the features of a *Baster* or coloured, poked his head round the edge. Mazambaan smiled at him. 'It's not the cleanest, but come on in.'

Committed, the man entered. He recognized him as one of the boozers who had entered the bar just after he himself had. Mazambaan turned from the hand basins and observed him as he made a great play of relief. All the right sounds were there. The man was a born actor. The trouble was, there was no stream. Either the man was nervous, or his bladder was already empty. Either way, he now knew what a *boer* agent looked like.

The two-fisted rabbit punch had all the fury of the netted leopard behind it. It thudded accurately into the agent's third cervical vertebra, which collapsed like a papier-mâché mock-up. He went down pole-axed and paralysed.

It was not the easiest thing in the world to prop him on to a toilet bowl. The limp form kept flopping to one side, but Mazambaan managed it in the end, pulled shut the cubicle door and left.

He had fifteen minutes to catch the bus and only one more thing to do. A phone call had to be made, a phone call to the Chief of the Security Police in Windhoek.

Working carefully at daybreak, it took McGee and Adam two hours to take down the delicate equipment in the shack, pack it and carry it to the ground floor. At 06.00 an unmarked police car picked them up and drove them to the station. It was not till nearly midday that the two men, working together, had developed and printed their last film.

McGee wanted to see the job done to the end. It would be, he reckoned, his last day with the police. He declined an offer by Adam of a black and white blow-up of Mazambaan as a souvenir. He did not need any reminders of the past few days. 'Thanks a lot,' he said. 'No offence, but it really wasn't the kind of operation one brags about to one's kids was it?'

'Suit yourself,' the little agent laughed. 'We did a job and did it well. If Tango Tango are on the ball, they'll bust SWAPO's internal terrorist wing wide open now. It was worth it.'

It probably was. McGee prepared a report while everything was still fresh in his mind, and, by 14.00 was ready for his final interview with Major Zietsman. Zietsman was not ready for him. He kept McGee waiting for more than an hour and when at last the summons came the news was not good; not all of it, certainly not the part concerning Mazambaan.

'I'm really sorry to have kept you, Captain.' You had to forgive a man when he started out like that. 'Sit down, I've sent for some coffee . . .' It was not just the regulation muck either, the two big steaming cups that arrived. Z knew his way into a man's heart. He allowed McGee one sip then ruefully said, 'Mazambaan, I'm afraid, has managed to give us the slip.'

McGee could not believe it. After all that, after all those days, the hard slogging grind at Oscar Pappa!

'He killed the man I had tailing him,' the Major was saying. 'Dumped him in a toilet cubicle and walked away.'

'Walked away,' McGee mimed senselessly. 'Surely he couldn't just walk away and disappear.'

'I didn't say he disappeared,' said Z. 'In fact, he hasn't. We think we know exactly where he is.'

'You *think* so . . . where?'

278

'Listen to this.' Z scowled. 'Listen carefully.'

It was the old tape-recorder routine again. How many years ago had it been since he had heard those exact words. McGee had the feeling that he was sinking helplessly back into a bad dream. Zietsman's voice on the tape said, 'Hello,' and again, 'Hello.' It was not Kulu who responded this time. It was a new voice. The man's tone was deep, his vowels well rounded. He seemed to be rationing each syllable, gauging each pause as one who had weighed, measured and balanced each word. They would get their portion and not a jot more from that voice. 'Is that the Security Police Chief?'

'Yes.'

'I have information that you want.'

'Yes . . . who is speaking?'

'Call me Jola.'

'Okay, Jola, what have you got for me?'

'The man who killed the Njobas, you would like to locate him, would you not?'

'Certainly. Do you know where he is, Jola?'

'I have never been there, but I can tell you . . . There is a farm called Bruchsaal just outside Okahanja. It is owned by a German called Moltke. Do you know it?'

'I'm sure I could find it. Is he there?'

'Yes, there is a kraal a few kilometres from the farm house. Moltke lets SWAPO use it.'

'He's in this kraal?'

'Yes . . . I must go now.'

'Just one more thing, Jola. When did he leave for Bruchsaal?'

'When? You know when he left. He left after he'd killed the agent you had following him.'

'Have you anything else for me, Jola?'

'No . . . I must go now.'

'If your information is good, there will be a reward for you.'

'Reward . . . Just get the man who killed Mary Njoba. That will be my reward.' .

'You knew her?'

'Judge for yourself.' There was a click as the line went dead.

Z switched off the machine. 'What do you think, Captain?' he enquired. 'How did it sound to you?'

McGee knew what was coming. They wanted him to go to Okahanja and, if Mazambaan was there, to take him. Zietsman was not really concerned with what he did or did not think. There was only one way to check out Jola's story, and that was to go to Bruchsaal, find Herr Moltke and persuade him to guide them to the kraal. He crossed to the window and looked out. The afternoon was grey and sultry. It was too late to start a manhunt at that late hour.

'It's going to have to wait until tomorrow morning,' he said. 'There's going to be a shortage of daylight soon.'

'You're the boss,' lied Z. 'I've got two choppers and a stick of counter-insurgency cops waiting at the strip for you. What do you want to do?' There was only one thing to do. To start the operation the following morning at first light, they would need to get to Okahanja right then before the weather closed in.

'I'll leave now,' McGee said. Z seemed to breathe a sigh of relief. 'Before you fall over your feet to get to the choppers, though, I want to make one point clear. You are going for Mazambaan and Mazambaan alone. I want to let Moltke stew in his own juice for a while. Don't take him in. I want to see in which direction he jumps.'

McGee did not have a problem with that. He said, 'What about Mazambaan, though? He's not going to come out smiling with a posy for us. More than likely he'll be keen on a spot of action.'

'Then give him action,' was Zietsman's response. 'Mazambaan has outlived his usefulness to us. The man's a terrorist in the true sense of the word. He's a murderer. Treat him like one. If he starts something, nail him.'

That certainly was a change in policy. McGee may have looked a bit surprised, and Z feeling it fair to divulge a little more went on, 'You know, McGee, you and Adam did a bloody good job. I know how you feel about Mazambaan giving us the slip, but we couldn't follow him with a whole army of agents. We had to take a chance and were lost out, but not entirely . . . Mazambaan led us on to some very important people. That's all I can tell you.'

The Major eased himself from his comfortable swivel chair and crossed to a big grey office cabinet. 'Security police don't usually carry rifles,' he said, 'but I suppose you're not really a cop in the true sense of the word.' McGee accepted the weapon handed to him, an early model FN with a mounted scope. The metal work and wooden stock were in fine condition. Someone had cared for that rifle. 'Shoots like a dream,' Z assured him. 'I know you wouldn't mind trying it tomorrow.' McGee lifted his cup for his second sip. The coffee was cold.

They came in low and they came in fast: two Alouette helicopters, eight camouflaged policemen with alsatians, one very frightened German farmer in pyjamas and not much more; and McGee.

Elias Kaluenja, to give him his due, tried to make a go of it. As the police were scrambling from their hovering choppers he appeared at the doorway of his hut with a Scorpion sub machine gun and shook everyone up with a long criss-crossing burst. Then he took to his heels, bounding down into the thorn-tree-studded valley like a startled rock rabbit.

They took their time with him. In theory a Scorpion is not much with its piddling .32 calibre capability. In practice, you treat the man on the other end of any weapon with a great deal of respect. They tracked him through the gullies and over the rocky ridges. With two helicopters and two tracker dogs it was not a great feat. Several times they saw him and bullets clipped the stony ground at his heels. Not once did he manage to throw off the pursuit.

By 09.00 they had driven him out of the bush willow and

thorn thickets, and on to the ridge of a hump-backed mountain. Ten minutes later he was in a dead-end gulley with the option of surrendering or dying. He chose the former and came out with his hands held high. He was not the man they had come for. McGee had guessed it earlier. Comrade fighter Mazambaan was elsewhere. Comrade fighter Mazambaan had set them up.

Chapter 17

Under the lacy summer foliage of Buanhoff Street's old jacaranda trees a small multiracial crowd had rallied to witness the arrival of the delegates to the Turnhalle conference. There were no placard-wavers or demonstrators around. South Westers, to the general despair of most of the political columnists, took their politics rather like their schnaps: chased with a beer it was digestible. Politics was for the pubs not the pavements. Their *einer kleiner* approach did not mean they were totally uninterested. It just meant there were not going to be throngs of fervent citizens waiting outside Turnhalle at that hour of the morning to adore the arriving delegates. The arriving delegates, however, were accustomed to that kind of treatment. They still came. They still waved to the faithful, then went inside to talk about a finer country; a new Namibia; a new future for all races, all colours.

No officials having arrived as yet, the crowd was being pleasantly distracted by the efforts of the army to remove a locked three-quarter ton truck loaded with old tyre casings that had been forsaken by its owner right in front of the main entrance to the Turnhalle. Six good men in army brown were heaving and snorting and getting nowhere. A sergeant appeared and, as sergeants will, summoned up a swarm of reinforcements so that soon the truck, tyre casings and all, was bounced about twenty metres down the street and deposited in front of the police station. The crowd applauded and the soldiers, somewhat sweatier than they should have been, trooped back and took up their honour guard postings.

Comrade Daniel Aluteni did not take part in the ovation, but not because he wasn't appreciative of the army's efforts. The truck could not have been better positioned had he personally directed the move. He was simply too damned nervous to do anything other than emit a faint sigh of relief. He crossed Buanhoff Strasse and shuffled as unobtrusively and as closely as he could to the rear of the truck. He had to be near the truck, because in the rear of the vehicle, wedged beneath the tyre casings, were two phosphorus incendiary grenades, their safety pins loosened and knotted to a measure of tough nylon gut. The nylon would allow him a short walk before it tautened, then a sharp tug and the truck would literally go up in mountains of smoke. Daniel stretched down casually and felt for the gut. Both ends of the street had just been closed to civilian traffic. It was almost time.

Peter Efilu sat in the kitchen at Turnhalle chatting with his colleague the Lozi interpreter. Another sitting was due to begin soon, another day totally alone in his stuffy little sound-proof box, waiting to practise his linguistic talents for the benefit of the men seated round the huge wheel of the table beneath him. It was usually a boring job but that day things could be different. With Nakwindi due to address the assembly there could be some fireworks. There were those who believed that the ex-SWAPO man had only converted to democracy and returned to Namibia because he could not hold down his position with Sam Nujoma's Organization. There were those who muttered under their breaths 'Once a comrade . . .' Peter believed that Nakwindi had seen the light, had become tired of the blood-letting. He was convinced that a new force was about to enter the South West political arena, a unifying force. God knows, they needed it, didn't they? They needed Nakwindi.

He finished his tea. It was time to go. Someone discovered a pair of trousers and a shirt stuffed behind the microwave oven. 'Not mine,' he laughed. Now who on earth would do a thing like that? He walked from the kitchen to the foyer and was about to climb the stairs when Nakwindi arrived. Flanked by two bodyguards with pistols, the man had a presence that was electrifying, a charisma that radiated all around as he stepped quickly through the double doors and into the hall. Peter was thrilled. He took the stairs two and three at a time, a thing he never did. Booth number three was his. He flung open the heavy twin doors and was surprised to find someone already there: a huge man in the blue uniform of the South African Police was occupying a seat next to his.

'Come in,' smiled Mazambaan. 'It's going to be a bit of a squash with the new security arrangements but it's only for today, I believe.'

'Security arrangements?'

'Yes. You were told, weren't you?'

'You must be joking,' Peter Efilu said. 'Who tells anybody about anything around here?'

The interpreter took his seat at the console desk, clamped on a pair of headphones, then threw a few switches. The lights on his monitor began to glow.

'Ready to roll,' he said, smiling at his guest with all the aplomb of an airline pilot. 'It's going to be quite pleasant to have some company. My name is Peter. What did you say your name was?'

'Call me Jola.'

Below them most of the delegates had either taken their seats and were delving into their briefcases and files or were standing near their chairs, chatting. The Chairman was at his dais with one disapproving hand raised to his spectacles as he watched a three-man television crew attempting a *coup d'etat* of the centre floor. Nakwindi was making a slow passage past the dozens of hands outstretched in solidarity. At last he reached the dais. The Chairman raised his gavel. 'They're starting,' said Peter Efilu. 'Would you like to hear the proceedings, Jola?' Without waiting for an answer he activated a roof-mounted speaker and the words 'Honoured delegates, ladies and gentlemen, let us pray,' filled the booth.

There he was, Nakwindi. If anything, age had creased his features into more hawkish lines than ever. Hands folded, brows furrowed, steadfastly regarding the assembly, almost contemptuously it seemed – had he not stood before Mazambaan a thousand times just so! God, the memories . . . The day in the old tumble-down school when the security cops had bust in – he had stood there just like that then, daring them to attack him, hoping they would, the better to illustrate to his 'torches' the full meaning of the word *boer*. He had had his wish fulfilled that day.

Perhaps that was his wish now. Perhaps assassination would speak for him of the true meaning of SWAPO more forcefully than any living words. There could be eloquence in blood Nakwindi had often claimed.

Mazambaan felt the fist of battle twist his gut. The prayer on the loudspeaker was winding down. 'In the name of our Lord . . .'

Nakwindi was looking around. He was looking up, looking straight at his ex-pupil.

'Then I look at you again, Mazambaan, and I see a coiled cobra ready to strike . . .'

'Amen.' The speaker ended the prayer.

Almost immediately the Chairman introduced Lazarus Nakwindi. 'A man of vision, a hero in the true sense of the word . . . Swords to plowshares . . .' Peter Efilu the interpreter, the whole assembly was bent forward in concentration. Nakwindi took the dais to an applause that rocked old Turnhalle. Holding his arms wide, his head high, he waited for silence. He waited in vain.

A muffled thump, a shock wave beneath the feet and Mazambaan was moving. Maybe over the headphones it sounded louder because the interpreter started to rise in alarm. A hammer fist, however, smashed him straight down again. One heave and he was out of the chair, sprawled against the door.

The AK fixed under the console came away with one quick tug. A slap and the stock was locked in place with the handle cocked back and the safety lever off. Nakwindi was still at the dais. No coward, he had not liked the sound of the explosion, had not written it off as something outside and therefore no danger to those within Turnhalle's castle-thick walls. His bodyguard were closing in. Mazambaan was tempted to shoot him there and then, but there was still the double layer of soundproof-glass to shank the bullet between himself and his target. He chopped at the barrier with a steel chair. The first pane shattered and he lunged again.

The breach was stubbornly still too high to aim through. People were looking up. Nakwindi was looking up. A bodyguard was reaching for his holster. There was no more time. Mazambaan threw the chair clean through the remaining glass, brought up his rifle and opened fire.

He had taken too long. He was not the only one shooting. Bullets were punching through the wooden-fronted booth, shards of glass flying everywhere. He had the satisfaction of seeing Nakwindi topple, then had to dive for his life. It was time to get out, but he had taken too long. They were closing on him.

The door was being shaken by massive blows that neither locks nor hinges nor Efilu's obstructing body were going to withstand for long. There was no exit that way. A murderous fusillade was splintering the front of the booth. He had seconds left, time to use the smoke grenades that Okawe had cached for him. The firing from the hall below became sporadic; then, as the choking blanket rose solidly above eye level, it ceased altogether. Mazambaan clambered through the shattered glass on to the pelmet ledge and looked below. The smoke generators had been different shades, one red, one yellow. The effect was a witch's cauldron, a bizarre rising multi-colour scream-torn mush. Behind him the door burst off its hinges, pitching into the booth. Mazambaan jumped.

It was worse than anything he had ever known. The chemical smoke had wrung all the oxygen from the air. There was a stampede for the door and Mazambaan, for all his strength, had no choice but be part of it. Pressed with agonizing slowness in the grip of the brutal maul which he had created, his power meant nothing. His legs became ensnared, he buckled and the mob lumbered over him and on.

Somewhere ambulance sirens were wailing. Somehow he was looking into a smoke-smudged sky. Someone was carrying him, there were voices in Afrikaans, slamming doors, then the fluid swaying of a vehicle at speed. Now the siren was filling his ears it went on and on. A mask was over his face, breathing new life into his lungs, smoothing the numbness from his limbs. The concerned face and the concerned voice of a nurse hovered in and out of focus. 'Don't worry, constable, you're going to be fine. You're on your way to hospital . . . you're going to be fine.' There were others there, floating with him. A young girl was lying opposite. Her lips looked so blue, her eyes so staring. The siren was fading.

They were stopping, doors were opening. He was gliding through white passageways into a room with chrome and dials and tubes and bustling people.

He tried to raise himself and an appalling pain knifed up his arm. The wrist was puffed and cocked into a ridiculous zigzag. A hypodermic stung his biceps and the lights blurred into soft blue pools. As the comfort of pethidine kissed him into a carefree haven of warmth he heard again, 'Don't worry, constable, you're going to be fine. Fine . . . Fine . . . Fine . . .'

When Mazambaan skidded from languid oblivion back into the bedrock world of reality he was no longer drifting in warm waters, but sheathed between stiff starched sheets. The first thing that came to him was a realization of time. Not of the passage of it – he had no way of knowing how long he had been lying there; it was the lack of it that suddenly loomed so large in his consciousness. He knew with the absolute certainty of a bush-born intuition that he had moments left in which to get out of a trap.

The second thing he realized was that he was badly

hurt; there was not an inch of him that did not pain. The two realizations were, of course, totally opposed in purpose. His mind demanded that he get out, go quickly. His body screamed that it was impossible. He managed to reach a compromise. Slowly, cradling his plaster-cast arm, he rolled on to his side and surveyed the ward. It was bright-white and clinical, and, but for the other patients lying in their beds, empty.

If the journey to the floor was short in length, agony gave it distance. A head that knew the room was not really turning gave it improbability. He made it though, and for a reward found that he could, if he carefully shuffled, even breathe while he moved. At the bedside cabinet he found his policeman's uniform neatly folded. Even his polished pistol belt and shoes were there. It did not take longer than a hundred agonizing years to effect the exchange from his surgical robe.

A man, deathly white but still curious, was watching him from a neighbouring bed. Mazambaan mumbled something to him and with steps that he hoped looked purposeful, made his way towards a pair of swing doors. They had two big glass insets, and that was fortunate, because on looking through, he discovered that there was a cop, a real cop, sitting on a stool just on the other side, staring down the long empty passageway that led to freedom.

If he had had his pistol with him he would simply have shot the man right through the door. Unfortunately whoever had so kindly left him his holster had decided to remove his firearm, his deadly Makarov. What else could he do? Mazambaan was pleased to find that his mind was drawing out of its lethargy. It was not, however, turning up any acceptable answers.

A thought occurred to him and he crept to a window – only to discover that he was two storeys up. Back at the door, though, a solution seemed to be at the production stage. The policeman was no longer seated but standing. He had an unlit cigarette in his hands and was looking anxiously and plaintively around. He wanted a smoke. The silent comedy went on, with a plump little nurse miming that if he did what he wanted to do inside the nurses' station, no-one would be any the wiser.

The nurses' station had a big glass window pane that allowed whoever was inside to see clearly anyone who walked past it along the passage. It was an acceptable post for a man on duty, especially if he disregarded one minor drawback: it did not afford a view of anyone who kept his body below the level of the sill. A man crawling, if he moved close to the window, would be able to get past without being observed.

Everyone in the ward seemed to be interested by then, observing the black constable as he got down on his good hand and knees, butted the doors slowly open, then grovelled through. No one said a word, though, or rang an alarm bell. If duty demanded he leave in that unusual way . . . well, he was a policeman, wasn't he?

That was something Mazambaan had to keep telling himself. It was not easy. In the first place, had he been a policeman, he would not have been stumbling around clutching banister rails and sweating with pain. Not even tough cops were expected to leave hospital in that state. Secondly, a policeman would have known exactly where the exit was. He did not. All he knew about the layout of Windhoek Hospital was that somewhere on a floor above him was a ward, with a guard on it, and a bed that should not have been empty – and that the quicker and further he got away from ward and guard, the better. The reception hall came up unexpectedly at a right-angle bend in the passageway. People were no longer speaking in hospital tones. Voices were raised, phones were clamouring, men and women were coming and going. Mazambaan braced himself, took a few paces back like a man preparing to overcome an obstacle, then with as purposeful a stride as he could muster, stepped into the foyer, past the reception desks, through the massive glass doors and onwards into the midday sun. He was out, out into a spiral sweep of bright sky, undulating waves of grey asphalt and shiny parked cars. Like a beaten boxer he found himself at odds with his surroundings. Everything was too distant or close, or not present at all when you reached for it.

Panic was a novel emotion for Mazambaan. It hit him then as he had never felt it before. Perhaps that was what kept him going. Perhaps that was why when he felt strong hands, supporting arms across his shoulders, he tried to tear them off. The voice he recognized in an instant, though: 'Just a few more steps, comrade. This way,' it said, and it belonged to Daniel Aluteni. 'I have brought the hotel bus. Here it is, comrade.'

It was one single big step into the minibus and Mazambaan managed it alone. There were pairs of seats for sixteen passengers and a long soft bench across the back on which he stretched out. He read a sign that said 'THE NAMIB SAFARI WELCOMES *YOU*', and allowed soft ripples of painful laughter to, bubble up within him. 'Daniel,' he whispered, 'I did it. I did it.'

Had he not been so obsessed by his search for men in blue uniform, had he been capable of giving more than a vertiginous glance through the rear window, he would probably have bitten back those triumphant words. For he could not have failed to spot the pretty blonde woman with sister's epaulettes standing wide-eyed in startled realization in the parking area. He would have recognized her too; he would have seen her dash for an old VW beetle parked there, swing into the traffic, and come after the Namib Safari Hotel bus.

Had either of the men in the bus subsequently been observing counter-surveillance traffic discipline, they would quickly have spotted the little car as it latched right on to their tail and followed every inch of the way down busy Kaiserstrasse and onwards. They would certainly not have driven in such a direct and tearing rush all the way to the Namib Safari Hotel. But they were not observing, and that was because just after having left the hospital grounds, the man stretched across the rear seat had blacked out. The driver had only one thought on his mind: get him somewhere safe, and get him there quickly.

Major Zietsman slammed shut an office window in a room that still reeked of burned rubber. Beneath him in the street, as an ugly reminder of an ugly morning, reposed the carcass of the burnt-out truck, buckled and melted. Where white hot phosphorus had seared through the coach work even the tarmac had been ablaze.

His mind returned to the blind confusion in the street that morning. He had been at work when the truck had gone up, throwing chunks of burning phosphorus everywhere. Personnel from the police station had stormed into the street, only to be blinded by billowing black smoke from the tyres. He had thought for a moment that the police station was under attack. Then he had heard the shooting from the Turnhalle and realized that a far greater emergency existed . . .

'Good God!' he said, turning to the man seated in the office. 'You can't believe it. You couldn't get near that truck to put it out.'

McGee nodded. He had seen the burnt-out wreck. He believed it. 'You could see the haze from the chopper even when we came in,' he said. 'Windhoek looked like a smoked hornets' nest.'

'You couldn't see your hand in front of your face for about fifteen minutes, before we started picking up the pieces. You know what phosphorus is like, McGee. Once it touches you it burns through like a laser. The street was littered with hurt people and there were more casualties at Turnhalle.'

'So they were after Nakwindi?'

'Yes,' Zietsman sounded bitter, 'and they got him. Last I heard he was still in the theatre with his condition said to be deteriorating. Christ, I hope he makes it. SWAPO will be doing handsprings if Nakwindi croaks. That's all we need.'

McGee was thinking about the attack. 'How the hell did

292

they get past security?' he asked, 'with that bloody great big rifle? Don't we have the place pretty well sewn up?'

'Sure we do!' Z was stung by the question. 'I even had Adam outside in the crowd on surveillance. He was one of the cops who got hurt. He got burned by phosphorus but I believe he's okay. There's four wards full of casualties, McGee, men, women and kids too. Other people were treated at Out Patients and we tried to do what we could too. It was a bloody mess, I can tell you.'

McGee had not meant to get the Major's back up. It had been a question more of interest than criticism. As a tactician he really would have liked to know how the hitman had pulled it off, that was all. He said he was really sorry to hear about Adam.

'He's going to be okay,' Z said again. 'Why don't you go down and see him? While you're about it, take a quick run through the casualty wards. We're not sure what we've got there yet. Uniform are handling statements and screening, but it's all pretty chaotic still. Just have a sniff around. Tell Adam I'll be down later, as soon as I can get away. Give him my best wishes, you hear?'

McGee promised that he would do that. 'My fiancé works at the hospital. Did I tell you that?' he asked Z.

'I don't think you did.'

'Yes . . . She's in charge of the High Care Unit.'

'That's nice.' Zietsman's mind seemed to be elsewhere for a moment. He stood up and walked with McGee to the door. 'Why don't you give her a surprise and go and see her while you're there.'

It was fifteen minutes' drive to the hospital. McGee made it in eleven traffic violations and about the same number of minutes. Even so he missed Patricia.

'She came in for the emergency and then left about 30 minutes ago,' another nurse told him. 'She's on night shift, so the double shifts must have whacked her.'

McGee thanked her, then went in search of Adam. He did not reach him. A young, out-of-breath plainclothes detective caught up with him as he was leaving the High

Care Unit. He had a message, an incredible message from Z. 'I've been looking for you everywhere, Captain. You're to get down to the Namib Safari Hotel. Major Z says it's a Red Alert, sir, a positive Red Alert.'

McGee was running before the man had finished speaking.

Patricia stuck with her quarry as the bus turned from the mainstream traffic and entered what was not much more than a service lane for the hotel it skirted: a narrow, one-way lane that led, if you followed it, back into another major road, and if you did not, to the part of the hotel that was not featured on the colour brochures; an up-ramp with a double entrance that was designated PUBLIC and HOTEL GUESTS PARKING and a dark and precipitous-looking hole that plunged into the bowels of the building. It was into the second entrance that the minibus dived. The sign above it read GOODS DELIVERY and STRICTLY NO ENTRY TO UNAUTHORIZED VEHICLES.

She tried to make herself look like an authorized vehicle – and failed. A comfortably fat watchman, all peak cap and *kierie*, with an equally substantial boom gate backing him, stopped her. He had the burdened look that comes with great responsibility, and a practised tired gesture, that without a word having to be uttered told Patricia that it had been a nice try but would she now move on.

There followed an argument which she lost, so she left the Beetle as it stood, blocking the gangway, and ran past the gate-keeper and down the steep ramp into the first basement.

The minibus was not there. There was a further down-ramp that led into a darker, dirtier, deeper basement which she took at a run. The second basement held crates and refuse bins as big as a room. It also held the Namib Safari minibus. The bus was empty. She had to get right up to it to make sure. Even then it was so gloomy down there that there was no question of a casual glance around. She began to search. There were a lot of hiding places, the crates for a start, and when you had cleared those there were some recesses so dark that you could not see the end of them. There was a metal door that led to a steep twisting stairway, corkscrewing straight down into a damp-smelling chamber where some kind of big engine was whining in solitude. She climbed back to the basement. There was one more metal door but that one was locked – and it was at this stage that she stopped dead; at this stage that she realized how foolhardy she was being. What would she do, she asked herself, were she to open some door, or reach into some black recess and find the man there? What would she do? Yell at him, 'Give me my ring or I'll call the police?' He *was* the police, and a criminal too. 'A bent cop' – she didn't know why the cliche kept going through her mind. No, it was not the way to go about the recovery of Sun-rival. It was the way to get oneself killed, and what would that help? She had to get out. The way out was up.

Patricia had not taken two paces towards the ramp when from behind her she heard a familiar sound. She turned and stared. In what had been a solid umber wall, double doors slid magically back. Where there had been gloom and danger, there now stood a warmly lit and invitingly empty lift cab. She was inside in a flash. There was the usual row of buttons. She chose 'G'. The entrance to her haven closed on command, and when she breathed again she was but a few short steps from the thronged foyer of the Namib Safari Hotel, the reception counter, and right next to that a panelled door with tasteful gold lettering painted on it: 'Assistant Manager/Stellvertretender Geschaftsfuhrer'. She had hardly knocked when he opened the door.

He was young, had an indoor skin and a wispy blond moustache, and when the girl facing him mentioned the word 'police' he was horrified. They possessed an internal security system that would be able to cope with her small problem with the greatest of ease. 'We are geared for anything like this, my dear. There is absolutely no need for the heavy hand of the law, believe me . . . *believe* me. Policemen rushing all over the hotel would simply wreck our chances of apprehending this man. Now you just sit there and let me organize everything . . . He's dressed as a policeman, you say, now that should make it easy.'

Organizing everything consisted of three internal phone calls and a conversation with a squat black walkie-talkie lying on his desk that answered when prodded to the name of '*Sicherheit*'. When he had done all that he looked up brightly at Patricia. 'There,' he said with practised reassurance, 'what did I tell you!'

Indeed what had he told her? Only that if he could help her without upsetting a single precious guest, then he would do so. If it came to a choice, though, between putting the clip on a man for a crime that had nothing to do with them, and the rocking of the Namib Safari pleasure boat, then they would opt for a stable deck. That was what he had told her. It was not half good enough. She had a call to make that the Stellvertretender Geschaftsfuhrer would not approve of.

She was to be escorted to lunch – 'At the expense of the Namib Safari, of course. By the time you have finished, I assure you, everything will have been sorted out.'

'How nice!' She smiled her most gratified smile and accepted. It would give her a chance to wait inside the hotel until the police came. In the meantime she had a number to dial. 'Of course!' she smiled again. 'I must go to the powder room first. Where shall I meet you?'

'Wunderbar!' the man clapped his hands together. 'It's settled then . . . I'll be waiting for you in the Bismark Room.'

Herr Schneider was genuinely delighted. Even if you did not like girls, it could not do your reputation any harm to be observed over lunch with one like this.

Chapter 18

All the more noisy for being squeezed between four cramped walls, the intercom continued with its buzzing for several minutes before its sound plumbed the abyss of the man's unconscious mind. Disoriented, he jerked up, still heavy with pain and drugs and peered around. There was nothing to see because the room was totally without light. Then the phone stopped in mid-buzz and in the sudden silence it all came back. He realized what it was that had disturbed him. Someone had been trying to reach Daniel, or Daniel perhaps had been trying to reach him. Either way the thing had stopped. There was nothing he could do about it.

Mazambaan stretched slowly into the darkness, unsure of his surroundings, taking time to feel what sort of shape his body was in. Then he stood up and fumbled against the wall for the light switch that should be there.

There was not much to recommend the room he was in if you valued peace and quiet. Entombed between the goods ramp and the lift shafts of a 12-storey hotel, the whole place seemed to be constantly atremble. If, however, bedrock privacy was what you craved, if you wanted a steel door and night latch between yourself and the world, then here was home. He found the light switch and worked it.

It was a workshop with a grease-stained floor. There was a cupboard against a wall holding spanners and screwdrivers and beneath it a workbench which supported an array of motor parts old and new. More important than anything however was a suitcase which he knew contained his change of clothing. Against one wall hung Daniel's chauffeur's cap and dust-coat, next to it the intercom housing. Near the mattress at his feet a little feast had been laid out; a litre bottle of cola, bread and a tin of meat. Had it been a smorgasbord it could not have tasted better. Mazambaan finished it all.

It was what he had needed. He could stand without feeling stupid, and walk without tottering. He began to prowl about the room, feeling baulked by the four walls around him, frustrated that he was dependent on someone else. Then something familiar on the workbench caught his eye. Apple-green paint, scratched and bush-worn from long carrying, the RGD 5 grenade that he had carried all the way from Angola. He hefted his old friend a few times, then slipped it into his trouser pocket, where it stuck out like a baseball. He did not mind that; all he wanted then was to get out and away. He did not want to see Windhoek again until the SWAPO colours flew over the state buildings.

The vibration of the lifts caused the metal door of the room to rattle momentarily – or that was what it seemed like at first. Then it happened again, and he knew it was not the lifts or anything else mechanical. Fingers were drumming against his door, quick and insistent fingers. It was not Daniel's hand. Daniel would have a key, anyway, and it was not the way an army or police team would have gone about things either. He would have ignored the sound but he could not ignore the words. 'Daniel! Daniel! Open up for God's sake.' It was a woman's voice, so close to the door that her cheek must have been pressed against it. It was high-pitched and staccato in panic, and Mazambaan had a good idea who he would see when he turned the lock.

The name tag told him he was right, she was Daniel's boss, Dolly Elumbako, and if she had not looked so wide-eyed and drawn in panic she would have been a most attractive woman. Once she was inside there was not a moment wasted. She took in the room and its occupant. 'You're Mazambaan,' she said. 'You must get out of here and away at once. You were identified by some woman, comrade. She's with the assistant manager, or she was. Hotel security have been notified to watch out for you. I'm sure they will have called the police.'

'When was this?'

'How long she was with Herr Schneider I don't know, but security were called in about ten minutes ago. I tried to reach you over the intercom for a long time.'

He had wanted to get out of there but he had not wanted to do it that way, not with the *boer* dogs baying at his heels. Now he did not have a choice. Even as he was pulling on his shirt he imagined he could hear the whining of distant sirens. He had hardly slammed the steel door behind them when the first police Land-Rover lurched down the ramp and skidded into the basement; blue lights flashing angry authority. Doors were slamming, men were running.

'Follow me,' hissed Dolly Elumbako, and Mazambaan did not need a second bidding.

She knew her way through the building. Like a pair of conditioned rats they took to a stair-well then a series of service passages. There was no hesitation, she walked ahead of him with her skirts billowing, her long booted legs confidently stepping out. Mazambaan was pressed to stay with her. There was a big kitchen, all stainless steel and tiles, clanking plates and hissing steam, where sweating men with long white hats and baked faces coddled the food. Aproned women, some of them laughing, all of them with bold active eyes, followed their passage to the swing doors.

The dining-room had wood panelling to the ceiling, subdued lighting and a grand piano that was being softly played to quiet, politely eating, guests – and one not so polite who stood up, pointed a finger and shouted, 'That's him!' *Stop him*!' and then, when nobody did stop him, came after him herself like a terrier.

He would have made it. The police were still running to close the noose. They were everywhere but they had not yet shaken out of their confusion. There was still a flow of people, porters and baggage moving through the lobby. The bitch, however, would not let go. Twice he hurled her away and twice she fell stumbling and sprawling into furniture and diners or anything else that was in the way. The place was in an uproar and all the time she was screaming, 'It's him! Stop him!' The third time she came at him she was not alone. Her cries had drawn a knot of policemen. Pistols drawn, they were closing at the run.

This time he did not hurl her away. This time he welcomed her to him in a rock-hard embrace. He had a hand grenade with the pin drawn, he had the ring; and he had the girl, the daughter of a war chief, no less. Either both of them would die, or he was as good as home. The *boers* could have it any way they chose. It was the best deal they could get. It was also the best deal he could get.

Mazambaan willed the policemen closer but they would not join the game. The action was suddenly frozen . . . almost frozen. There was one man who looked like being a competitor. Big and tall, his face a mask of undisguised hatred, he pushed through to the front rank, but there he stopped. Mazambaan knew he had seen that big *boer* before and knew where. He knew, too, that in a way he had won, and in a way he had lost. There would be no consummation for him that day, that would have to wait. He began instead to speak to those around, to tell them all about the new rules: his rules. Mazambaan was going home, 'Listen to me,' he said, and they listened.

'What he said,' McGee was telling Admiral Christie, 'was that his life and Patricia's life were entirely in our hands. Either we did exactly as he ordered, followed his instructions and his time schedule to the minute, or he would happily take both of their lives.'

'And you believed him?'

McGee answered with absolute conviction. 'Yes,' he said, 'Yes, I believed him, Admiral, and so did everyone else who was there. He was not fooling, would not have minded going up with that grenade, and there was no way

Patricia could have got loose. He had that plaster cast of his clamped under her neck till she could hardly breathe. He had the grenade in his other hand right against her stomach.'

'Christ, McGee, wasn't there anything you could have done, shot him and rushed her away . . . something. You were on the spot, damn it, man!'

'Admiral, a RGD 5 has a three-second delay . . . One and Two and Three . . . How far could you have moved in that time I just counted? It contains 110 grams of TNT. It's deadly over fifteen metres or more. What would you have done?'

'I don't know, McGee, I don't know.' Christie shook his head bitterly. 'You did what you did and you did it in Patricia's best interests. I'll accept that.'

'We had exactly one hour to meet his requirements, Admiral, one hour. There was no negotiating. He wasn't interested. After sixty minutes he'd have let that safety lever fly if every requirement hadn't been met. I had no doubt about that then, and I still believe it. I had a team of young cops, volunteers I can tell you, shadowing them all the way, keeping as close as they could. If Mazambaan had made one slip we would have had him. If he'd let that safety lever go they were ready to hurl themselves bodily over Trish to try to save her. Thank God that never happened because you can take it from me, Admiral, they'd never have made it. We had precisely sixty minutes to lay our hands on a suitable aircraft, get it fuelled and find a pilot who was prepared to fly to anywhere in Angola with a live grenade at his back. We did it. Patricia is still alive . . . if the Angolans had kept their part of the bargain she'd have come back in that Dakota, and you, sir, would be telling me what a bloody smart operation it was. Well . . .'

'Well, she didn't come back, McGee, so it wasn't so bloody smart was it?' Christie held up his hand to stop the younger man from speaking. 'Listen to me. I didn't get you all the way back to the Cape to scrap with you. I've already said that I believed you acted in good faith, okay, well, that's the truth. Had I been on the spot I probably would have done exactly as you did. Well, I wasn't there. You were, and you carried the can. Let's take it from there.'

Don Christie looked into the troubled eyes of the soldier standing on the other side of his desk. Not so long ago the man had stood there exactly as he was standing now. They had fought then, too, and no good had come of it. He could not help but wonder how things would have turned out then had he not been so heavy-handed. They could have been very different. He could have struck an entirely different bargain with his daughter. He could have . . . Admiral Christie tore himself away from that line of conjecture. His daughter was now locked in an Angolan prison, being used as a political football. That was fact.

The Angolans could have had her out in five minutes if they had wanted to, but they did not. It suited them to humble the *boers* into negotiations with SWAPO and it suited SWAPO to drag their heels. He could not honestly blame McGee for that. It was time for a truce between the two of them. In fact it was overdue. 'What would you say, Captain,' he asked, 'if I told you I knew exactly where Patricia was being held?'

'Let's go get her out – that's what I'd say. You know that.'

Christie stood up, crossed to his drinks cabinet and made a big thing of pouring two glasses full of liquor. 'Rum,' he announced. 'I don't know if you like it and I certainly don't, but in the Navy there's a wardroom tradition that when two officers from the same vessel have exchanged words they settle with a noggin together. It's traditional for the junior officer to propose a toast. How about it Captain McGee?'

'Do you really know where she is Admiral?'

'Yes, I do.'

'My toast, then, is to Operation Perseus.'

302

'Perseus, son of Zeus, rescuer of the beautiful Andromeda . . . Yes,' said Christie, 'I'll drink to that.'

McGee's next question was, 'Where do we go from here?' The answer to that was to a map, a British Admiralty Chart, to which had been pinned a traced, detailed overlay. It was headed BAIA DE MOCAMEDES (Little Fish Bay).

'Mocamedes?'

'Yes,' Christie said. 'What do you know about the place?'

'I know it's about two hundred kilometres north of the Namibian border. I know it's used by SWAPO and is their key logistical port.' He thought a while then shrugged. 'Not much more,' he admitted. 'So where is Trish exactly being held?'

'Right here.' The Admiral's finger stubbed a square marked CAMERA POLICIA. 'It's the old police station. SWAPO use it now as a detention barracks. She's there.' Both men looked at the little inked illustration of the Camera Policia. Then Christie went on talking; and talked until fully an hour had passed.

Mocamedes, he told McGee, was a tough nut, a base for Cubans, Russians and MPLA troops. 'SWAPO have a detachment – what we call a battalion – undergoing desert training close by the town, and there's a battalion of FAPLA militia with supporting armour at the harbour.' That was not all. The bay was studded with anti-tank and anti-aircraft cannon of all kinds.

'The People's Navy have a pair of Bellatrix patrol boats there that are hardly ever operational. As for the rest of their Navy, apparently it also works in fits and starts. They've got four useful Argus-class large patrol craft, but they keep them further up the coast at Lobito and Luanda, too far away to give you a hassle.'

The old man had mentioned that Mocamedes was a tough nut and it sounded just like that. But if you squeezed nuts the right way, they cracked open without too much fuss or mess . . . McGee was listening, and thinking. It had to be a clandestine Op, a quick raid by a small group of highly trained daring men.

'Specialists' was the word the Admiral used – 'men with guts'. McGee agreed: that was the only way to do it.

'You can't just come straight overland,' Christie said. 'It's 225 kilometres of impossible territory, high mountains and soft sand. We'd be detected before we got half way. A raid straight in from the sea would be equally disastrous. They've got radar at Mocamedes and would blow us out of the water with their Seventy-sixes without even using their navy.'

'What about choppers?' McGee asked. 'The place is well within range. They could lift us there and back.'

'You don't know that part of the world!' the Admiral said. 'The fog whips in there as fast as a giant squid tentacle. One minute the skies are clear, then within seconds visibility is down to zero. It's unbelievable! If there was a fog the pilot wouldn't even find the place, and if he did you'd never find where you left him when you wanted to get back. The whole Skeleton Coast is the same. More importantly, choppers are noisy. They'd alert the defences unless you landed far into the desert. And then what would you use for transport?'

McGee stared down at the map on the desk for a while. There had to be a way. No defence situation was ever totally unassailable. There was always an approach that was best, a tactic that was superior.

The Admiral, of course, had probably worked it out days ago. Now he was testing the bright young Captain. If you could not go overland, and you certainly could not; if coming in by air was for lunatics only, and he would take the Admiral's word for that; that left only one other element available, the sea. If sailing straight into Mocamedes bay meant instant suicide at the business end of a Seventy-six, then what you had to do was to find a beachhead as close as possible south of the place, and land your forces there. McGee's finger stabbed the map and the Admiral exclaimed, 'On the head!'

'Porto Alexandre is where we go in. It's a sleepy fishing village, where seaward defence comprises a pistol in the harbourmaster's drawer. The place is less than eighty kilometres from Mocamedes across a desert road that any car could handle. It makes Operation Perseus a one-night job; in and out.'

Christie did not go into explanations as to how he had figured on getting the raiding-party up the west coast to Porto Alexandre. He just said, 'I've got it in hand. There's an old service friend of mine who's promised to help. I can tell you this, however. We won't be getting any help from the Navy, not a thing.'

'They want to keep their hands clean?'

Christie shook his head. 'Negative. *I* want to keep their hands clean. The authorities are turning a blind eye where they can. That's all I want. It's better that way, believe me. Now we can fight dirtier. Do you know where we can find men like that, dirty fighters?'

'The dirtiest.'

It was good to hear Christie laugh, even though it had a nervous timbre to it. 'You know,' the Admiral said, 'I haven't even asked you if you'll command the operation. I've just taken it for granted that you'll do the job.'

'That goes without saying.' There were some questions, though, that McGee needed answers to, questions like, 'How blind does the Defence Force intend to become in the matter of recruiting?'

'Very blind,' Christie was adamant. 'I don't want anything more South African than a Free State accent on board when we sail though and not a single item of South African equipment.'

McGee knew where to find the men needed for that operation and they would not be from the Orange Free State. They would not be from South Africa's provinces at all. The hardy black faces answering to this mental roll call at that moment were Angolan, men from his old battalion. Big Corporal Hosi would want to come. Denga the 'machine-gun' and the terrible twins, Carlos and Felix, he would not be able to keep out. Oliviera, the medic, Felix, the RPG artist and many more . . . Recruiting was going to be the easiest task. There was something else bothering McGee, however.

An inside man: they needed a man or a woman who knew the where and the when from the other side of the fence, an agent. Did Christie have such a person? If not there was one last black face in McGee's mind's eye: a SWAPO prisoner he had come to know well.

'Do you think you can trust him?' Christie did not like it. 'We know exactly where Patricia is, don't we? Our intelligence is good enough. Do we need this man?'

'Oh yes,' McGee said. 'We need him. Not for our sakes, but for Patricia's.'

Chapter 19

In 1487 a gentleman of the Court of John II of Portugal, lord of all African possessions, sailed into a small inhospitable harbour on the African West Coast. His name was Bartholomeu Diaz, and he called the bay Angra das Voltas, Bay of Tacks, having found the sailing conditions formidable.

After five days of foul weather the gentleman entered into his log that the bay was not worth owning. It lacked everything they needed – water, slaughter stock, firewood, indeed any vegetation. Moreover, there was a total absence of potential slaves. He therefore slipped away. It was not until 1882 that Adolf Luderitz, a stubborn German merchant and visionary, persuaded his government to colonize the bay and, coincidentally, protect his trading interests. They built a town, called it Luderitzbucht, and never left. The South Africans, when they came, shortened it to Luderitz. They did not have, however, the teutonic stubborness of their fellow colonialists, and most of them left for the greener pastures of the interior.

Admiral Don Christie had read the history of the bay, and the salty western gale tearing at him as he climbed from his car at the customs harbour post that morning served to confirm his opinion of Bartholomeu Diaz as a truthful sailor indeed. He glanced around as though expecting someone, checked his wristwatch, then slammed the car door and bowing his head to the gale, hands tunnelled into the pockets of his duffle coat, pushed his way on to the jetty – a robust construction of spaced heavy timber planking, with choppy little waves visible beneath. Christie fished a piece of paper from his pocket.

It was a telegram which even by naval standards was stark. It read,

'BLUEFISH YOURS. GOODLUCK. STEINER.'

Ex-Commodore Rudolph Steiner was still as short on words as he was large on generosity. 'Bluefish yours,' meant just that. The fishing vessel Bluefish was his, no questions and no strings attached. There was something to be said for having old service friends.

'Bluefish.'

Twelve sturdy fishing vessels were tied up there, hoisted high by the tide, gunwales rising well clear of the jetty; and they were big, a lot bigger than he had imagined they would be. He strode along the jetty, pacing them out, ten metres, twenty metres. Thick rope hawsers were put to it to keep them moored against the roguish wind and sea. They reminded him of ageing prizefighters, somehow, used and bruised, but game for another bout.

'Bluefish', berthed right at the tip of the jetty, moored against a sister trawler, looked neither better nor worse for wear than the rest of Steiner's fleet: crusted, thick with generations of paint and rusty nail streaks, her hull was sea-bleached grey, the superstructure white, and the metal work more rusty than black. Other than a solitary policeman to whom Christie had nodded at the harbour entrance, there was no one to be seen on jetty or ship. It was not surprising. The season was over; it was mid-May and the last possible crayfish had long since been snatched from those cold West Coast waters. The boats were there, tied-up and waiting. The crews from skipper to deckhand had migrated to fish the southern waters off the Cape of Good Hope.

Christie climbed aboard and discovered that Bluefish was not as deserted as it looked. A shivering and very small spotted mongrel lying inside a coil of pitted chain stood up, stretched, sniffed and followed him along the deck and up the steps of the superstructure.

At first he thought the sliding wooden door to the wheelhouse was locked but there was no padlock on the hasp and a good heave sent it rasping back. Christie looked around guiltily. Where was the bloody man? There was not much inside, an eight-spoke teak wheel, a central binnacle and compass, a lever protruding from an E-shaped brass gate marked FNR – forward, neutral, reverse. That much was easy to figure.

Set into a compact teak console were four gauges; water temperature, oil pressure, revs per minute and an amp meter with a smashed glass face. On the right of the structure a Furuno aqua sounder and radar screen were secured. They looked as though they had recently been installed and were in good shape. The instrumentation could not have been more basic. Five tightly wedged sash windows allowed good forward vision, past the heavy steel mast and derrick. He tried the wheel. The cables moved in their system smoothly.

Behind him was another sliding door. It led down a short companion-way into the wheelhouse quarters, the skipper's cabin – and there he was, exactly where he *should* have looked for him, comfortably seated examining the short-wave radio transmitter: the skipper.

'You're Skipper Almeida.'

It was more a statement than a question. The man stood up and Christie liked what he saw. Brown, 55 years, young eyes wrinkled into a smile of genuine pleasure, and the hand he extended looked big enough to double as a windlass.

'Almeida,' he confirmed. 'I arrive yesterday. The boat she look fine, inspect everything, when the engineer is come we can do trials on the engine and electronics.' The accent was pure Madeira.

'The engineer,' Christie said, 'was supposed to come with you from Cape Town. That's what Steiner said.'

The man looked genuinely troubled. 'No engineer, no allowed to leave harbour, that is law.'

Admiral Christie seldom showed emotion. Now his mouth tightened and he spoke deliberately so there would be no misunderstanding. 'Skipper Almeida, we will be going to sea. We will be travelling to a destination off the Angolan Coast, and we will be coming back, breaking the law every sea mile of the way. Steiner told you that, didn't he?'

'He tell me just like that.'

'You were chosen for this job because you owe Mr Steiner a rather big favour, something about citizenship for your entire family in South Africa. Is that right.'

'Is right.' The man's eyes hardened. 'I do it for Herr Steiner, anyway. He's a good man.'

'Yes, he's a good man,' Christie agreed. 'What he didn't tell you was that you'll be getting ten thousand rands for a few days' work. Now let's not hear any more talk about what is law and what's not law.'

The smile was back. It had a whimsical slant to it now though. 'Okay, you say we sail without engineer.' The skipper shrugged. 'So we sail without engineer. Bluefish is good vessel; good engine. Six-cylinder caterpillar never let you down.'

'I'm sure the man will be here by tomorrow,' said Christie. But the man was not there the next day.

McGee was. He arrived in the late afternoon with two nondescript trucks, a crew of hard-faced blacks in jeans and T-shirts and some crates that needed a lot of muscle to get on board. Muscle was one thing they were not short of; engine-room skills – there lay their deficiency.

'No engineer?' McGee repeated. 'How bad is that?'

'You're involved in a round trip of some eight hundred sea miles, give or take a few. These trawlers were made to take anything nature can throw at them. Bluefish's engine is a 20,4 six-cylinder cat. They don't come more reliable. If the engineer isn't here by tonight, we'll have to sail without one . . . Now tell me,' he asked McGee, 'how has your side been going. Are the men up to it?'

The men, McGee told the Admiral, were indeed up to it. 'Don't forget, they've been living and fighting together for many years. I personally have worked with each and every one of these men before. There's not one I wouldn't trust with my life. Does that answer your question?'

'How much have you told them?'

'They know they're going to do a job up the Angolan coastline. They know it's not a military mission, that they're going to get paid and how much. The exact briefing I'm going to give them just before we go in so it's fresh in their minds . . . How much does Almeida know?'

At that moment the skipper's head and shoulders appeared at the engine-room hatch. Christie called to him. 'Meet Captain McGee . . . Captain McGee, Skipper Almeida.' It was all a little formal until Christie mentioned a bottle of brandy he had brought aboard. The time, he said, had arrived to crack it.

Almeida apparently knew all there was to know about Operation Perseus. There was just room enough for the three of them in the wheelhouse quarters. The skipper spread open an Admiralty chart of the Angolan coastline headed Plans of the West Coast of Africa. 'I know Porto Alexandre from the old days.' The brandy was excellent. Almeida swished it through his teeth in appreciation, then went on. 'Porto Alexandre, I fished from there. Alexandre has natural sand breakwater, see here.' There was a sand spit long and thin, curving at its end towards the port. 'There is a big bank of sand and mud there. In old days to keep harbour mouth clean every month Portuguese send dredger from Mocamedes. Who does it now, not Cubans, not Russians? We get into harbour for sure at high tide. At low tide . . .' He shrugged. 'Maybe, maybe not. There is channel somewhere. Local fishermen use it, but their boats smaller than Bluefish. Bluefish draws twelve feet . . . I do what you want, I take you to Alexandre, but must be at high tide.'

'Well, there you are,' said Christie. 'I wanted the skipper to tell you in his own words. What it boils down to is the fact that in order to meet the high tide Almeida needs at Alexandre, and the moon you require for the operation, you'll have to sail dead on schedule, engineer or no engineer.'

McGee did not have any problems with that. So Alexandre was not going to be as easy as he had first thought. A lot of things would not turn out to be as he first thought . . .

'One more thing,' Almeida said. 'There has been much talk of money. Okay, ten thousand rands is much money, but while we are together I tell you is not enough to make me go. I go because I want to go. I lose friends and family in Angola. You understand this?'

Christie said he understood and for a while the three of them stood in silence, each with his own thoughts. Almeida was going because he wanted to go. McGee knew why he himself was going and could guess at what must be on Christie's mind.

For Christie was not going. Christie was staying to mount the rearguard. Someone had to do it. He had the clout to get things done, to pick up the pieces if things went tragically wrong. And that could so easily happen. No matter how ready he was to step in and beard the lion, it was not for him. That had been a bitter pill to swallow, but a sensible one. Christie was back up. God knows, they had little enough of that.

A fog was closing in on Luderitz. Somewhere a foghorn started its monotonous throbbing warning. At least the wind had dropped. In the wheelhouse they drank a last toast. What the hell else, Christie thought, was there left to say? Not a thing he had not said already. 'Good luck, skipper . . . Good luck, Matthew.'

The Admiral turned towards the companion-way, then stopped. Without turning he said, 'Just get her back here, Matt. For God's sake get her back for me.' The man's back was too upright, his neck too rigid, he was dying inside.

'I'll do that, Admiral, for us both.'

'Yes, Matthew, for us both.'

312

They could hear the clip, clip of his heels on the deck planking, then without actually seeing it, both men knew that Admiral Christie was ashore. He was away. Almeida turned to McGee. 'Okay,' he said. 'I hear you are one bloody fine soldier. Let's see whether you make good sailor. I give you extra quick training. Show you around a bit. Tell you what to do. Then we sail, okay?'

'Okay.'

On deck the breeze had freshened again from the north west, giving more authority to the bay waves. Almeida talked and McGee listened . . . There was the harsh metallic clash of the starter gears and six diesel cylinders thumped into life.

'You know now what to do, Capitao,' Almeida called down to the jetty where McGee stood. 'You ready now?'

'I'm ready.'

Either the skipper had been a good teacher or the Capitao an astute learner. Either way, what mattered was that Bluefish, with the aid of a spring rope aft to take the strain, and a breast rope forward which McGee paid out, started to swing away from the jetty.

Almeida kept the revs up, the massive asbestos-bound exhausts drummed to the beat, and on a shout from the wheelhouse McGee let go. The rope fell into the widening gap with a splash and McGee sprang for the deck. So did someone else; out of the darkening fog: a very heavy man.

Had McGee been rugby-tackled right then he could not have gone down with more of a crash or greater astonishment. A canvas sea bag spun across the deck and a voice said, 'So sorry.' Then removing his bulk from McGee's chest, the man, straightening a battered nautical cap, apologized again, 'Desconsolado. Thought you move quicker. Nearly miss the boat.' The accent was grossiero Portuguese, the figure was that which a gents' tailor would have described as 'portly short'. The surprise of it all gave him a further moment of grace, before McGee roared, 'Throw the bastard off,' and sprang for the fat man, who

313

jumped away. He was too slow by far. They had him
before he had taken a second pace. Four of McGee's men
ran him to the side.

'No, pliz!'

The man was terrified. He had been sweating when he
jumped on board, now he was streaming. They held him
squirming, half overboard, toppling. Sink or swim he was
about to go when he said the magic word: 'Steiner.'

'Hold him!'

Reluctantly the soldiers did just that, they had him by
the shoulder straps of his overalls, no more. The nautical
cap was just a memory.

'What about Steiner?'

'Mary, mother of Jesus, no throw me, senhor! Steiner
sent me from Walvis Bay. Help me. I don't swim!'

They were 100 metres from the jetty then. McGee
signalled his men to pull the man back on board. They
were not gentle. He ended in an undignified breathless
heap on the deck. A loud rapping on the shuttered
wheelhouse glass drew McGee who did not have to lip-
read. With large frustrated gestures Almeida was demanding an explanation. So was McGee.

'What about Steiner, then? Now you've got your breath
back, senhor, let's hear from you. Come on!'

'Senhor Steiner send me telegram to report to Bluefish
pronto. He tell me you need driver. Me,' he said tapping
his huge chest, 'I am driver.'

'Never heard of Steiner, Mister. Where's the telegram?
Show me the telegram.'

The man looked desperate. He slowly lifted his hand
and felt for the peaked cap he had last seen bobbing away
on the night tide.

'I tuck it in my cap band, senhor. Cap is gone overboard. I have papers in my bag. My driver's ticket,
everything.' He pointed to the battered canvas valise lying
on the deck. 'You want to check my papers, look in there.
You check with Steiner that I am Gilbert dos Santos. He
sent me, why you don't check with him?'

'What did Steiner tell you about us, dos Santos? What did he say in the telegram?'

'Senhor not say much. Steiner he never say much. He told me report to Bluefish, Luderitz Harbour, pronto.'

'That's all?'

'Sure that is all. Why should I tell you lies, for what reason? You no want me on board, take me back, okay. Why treat me like this?'

It was a good question, if the man was genuine. The papers in his valise looked good. Almeida was delighted when he saw them.

'Of course he's genuine,' the skipper said. 'Why shouldn't he be? We both know that Senhor Christie asked Steiner for a driver. So now we get one, and for this I am happy. I check him out later, but don't worry, Captain, dos Santos's okay, I am sure.'

It seemed all right. Almeida was happy, and he was the skipper.

'I'll be watching him,' McGee warned. If dos Santos was a plant and their security had been blown, the Angolans would be waiting for them. They could not abandon the mission on a surmise.

Using the radio to check on Dos Santos was out of the question. The radio frequencies used by the trawlers were constantly monitored. They had agreed on radio silence, but for a few laid-down and specific codes to be used in stipulated circumstances. McGee took his night binoculars to the bridge and turned them towards the jetty and the car park. All he got was swirling fog . . . Bluefish continued outward bound.

Soon they were off Seal Island, the black ugly sentinel to Luderitz, and the first ocean-sized swells were surging by. Bluefish was meeting the challenge without fuss, but there were many on board whose idea of a long voyage was a punt across the Cuito River. Their smiles were looking a little stretched as they tried to adjust to the gyrations of the deck beneath them. Some of them, thought McGee, were going to be very sick, very soon.

Work, he decided, would get their minds off things. He went to look for big Hosi and found him seated on the hatch of the fish hold. He listened to McGee's orders, then looked up at his Captain with disbelieving eyes. No one could be expected to work in those conditions. The Capitao thought otherwise. They had two .50 Browning heavy machine-guns on board. It was time to mount them.

'I want,' said McGee, 'a tripod fixed right on top of the wheelhouse roof, and one,' he rapped the heavy metal coal scuttle aft of the galley, 'right here.' They would be using gas to cook with so the big bin was empty. 'Get everyone on to it, Hosi. I don't want to see anyone without a job.'

With a 12v porta-drill, coach bolts and a lot of raw effort, the heavy machine-gun tripods were brought up and anchored. The life-rafts from the roof they shifted sideways, standing them and binding them with fencing-wire to camouflage the job. The coal scuttle's quarter-inch metal sides needed to be trimmed with an acetylene torch to lower the profile of the mounting and provide the weapon with a more efficient traverse. Dos Santos volunteered himself for the task. He was obviously an expert with the welding torch and did a much better job than McGee would have been able to do on that pitching deck. The man had not said another word since his earlier treatment, but McGee was watching his reactions to their preparations closely. When they opened the crate containing the heavy machine-guns the man's eyes widened, as did his mouth. It did not look like an act.

In those conditions it required four men a piece to lift the heavy guns on to their mountings, then lower them carefully into place and secure the locking lugs. More often than not a man would have to dash to the side, but before dark they had the guns bedded, had checked the mechanisms and were ready to test fire. Bluefish wouldn't classify for a rating in Janes Fighting Ships, but she had a sting to her now.

McGee invited Almeida to see what they had done to

316

his vessel. 'If you want to come and have a look, I'm test-firing the machine guns. It won't do any harm to know how they operate.'

'Sure,' Almeida said, 'I like that. I like that very much.' He throttled back and locked the wheel. Hosi had the belts fitted when they got back, big shiny brass shells flexing up from their boxes to the breech. McGee gave the honours to Hosi on the wheelhouse and Denga in the stern. 'Ready,' he commanded . . . '*Fire!*'

Those who deal in death enjoy the odds being dealt in their favour. By these men, a .50 Browning was considered to be an ace in the pack. Five hundred rounds a minute it fired, which by modern standards wasn't fast. But what rounds they were! Half-inch steel missiles, that flew at their targets at a velocity of nearly 900 metres a second. Anything not shielded by a solid chunk of armour plate didn't have a chance. It was a weapon that had authority.

Hosi was firing his gun in conservative bursts of five. Denga, at the stern gun, was more flamboyant in his approach. It was quite a fireworks display, with a stream of tracer zipping off into the dusk, and the hammering, ear-busting explosions. Almeida, of course, wanted a turn. Whooping like a teenager at a fun fair, he swung the barrel all over the ocean.

'Jesus, let them come!' he roared to the night sky. 'I take on the whole bloody MPLA army right now.' It was wishful thinking, but that was the sort of thing a .50 did for one.

The test was a huge success. The guns were cleaned and put to bed beneath tarpaulins. It was time to do the same with the men. McGee wondered how many of them would have joined the stampede to come had they known of the ordeal *mal de mer*. He was not feeling so good himself as he joined Almeida in the wheelhouse. It was midnight and his watch was from midnight to four.

'Hold bearing three four zero,' Almeida instructed. 'Engine keep at thousand revs.' The skipper glanced at a

317

battered wrist watch. 'Wake me at four or, if any problem, okay.' It was all that had to be said.

An icy nor'-wester was beginning to blow in earnest. It was going to be a long, cold watch. Bluefish at those revs would be doing something like nine knots, but that was not her true speed. To get that you would have to add the speed of the north-thrusting Benguela current. Their true speed would be about 15 knots. With the nor'-wester coming at them, spray from the bow wave was showering the wheelhouse windows constantly. McGee hardly noticed the cheerless conditions. He had plenty to occupy his thoughts and no less than any other factor, the strange arrival of Senhor dos Santos the driver. The time passed quickly.

The following morning saw a jumble of preparations aboard Bluefish. None of McGee's men had yet found their sea legs, but no one seemed to be staggering any more, and there were not so many jaundiced eyes or heaving stomachs. The superstructure was the first thing that required work, the big white panels being overpainted in marine teal. The next area to receive attention was the vessel's name and serial number. Bluefish went and in its place the name PERSEVERANCA was stencilled, with the corresponding number borrowed from Angola's Official Register of Commercial Vessels. They had an impromptu christening ceremony, then continued with the work.

The dinghies they would use were inflated and lashed down, the stores and equipment checked. Once the painting was complete the miscellany of SWAPO, MPLA and Cuban gear was issued. Some of the clothing had holes that could have been bullet-induced but all of it had been laundered and was clean. McGee slipped on his Russian camouflage tunic, a garment of superb quality, with four small magenta stars on the epaulettes that identified him as a Soviet infantry kapitan. He had brought with him his own pair of American canvas jungle boots. By the time all this had been done it was midday and McGee was pleased to notice many of his men standing in the chow line, appetites restored.

Personal weapons were tested again. McGee's choice for the operation was an East German AKM. He fired with it from the deck until a bobbing coke can at a few hundred metres was a first-time cinch.

Some time that afternoon a little spotted mongrel put in an appearance. Where he had come from no one knew, but the gunfire did not seem to disconcert him one bit, he seemed to enjoy the noise, running up and down the deck, barking sharply at the shooting men. They named him Ukongo, the hunter. At nightfall they took him with them to their quarters. By supper time Almeida calculated that they had travelled 450 sea miles, which placed them well over half way to their destination. There were no complaints when he announced an early stand down. They would be in Angolan territorial waters before the next morning, he told them. He was almost right. By daybreak the wind had settled and the air temperature was slipping into a polar decline.

'Fog,' predicted Almeida, 'soon, I think.'

They were soon due off the Kunene estuary; the riverine border that separates Namibia's coastline from Angola. After that they would be in enemy waters. The big east-bound rollers just seemed more heavy, blue grey and surly without the wind to liven up their crests.

The real change was occurring on Perseveranca. On the trawler a slowly escalating human tension insinuated itself in and around them with a chilliness that had nothing to do with the air temperature. Conversation became a mouth-to-ear affair as men, who crossed on foot into enemy territory almost as a way of life, considered their new operational environment. They did not like it.

It was not much of a fog, more a gloom. In the greyness of it the rumble of the big cat engine which had become a forgotten thing startled with its roar. The creaking hull, the swish of the bow wave, the friendly sounds of yesterday now sounded at best unwanted; at worst, an ill-boding dead give-away.

They stayed well out to sea, making use of the radar until the mist belt ended. The skipper then set a heading of 50 degrees they began their run in towards land.

Almeida was seldom far from the radar, constantly bobbing down to examine the display screen, now and then correcting the course. At mid-day he straightened from the instrument and, with a casualness that was alarming, announced, 'There are other vessels nearby. They could be pilchard trawlers but they seem too fast . . . Maybe we got trouble.'

It was a prophetic understatement. At that moment the engine faltered; briefly burst back into life; then shuddered sickly. The rev-counter needle was vibrating so fast it was a blur, the oil pressure gauge plummeted.

'Mother Mary, not now!' Almeida flicked the switch that connected the engine-room speaker but before he could say a word Perseveranca's engines gave a last violent lurch, then stopped. That was it. But for the slapping of the rollers on the hull, there was a total and unwanted silence. Almeida moved like a man stung. He flew from the wheelhouse, stamped down the steps to the deck and through the engine-room hatch. McGee followed, to be greeted by dos Santos with a spanner in one hand and the countenance of a man at a wake. The normally boisterous green-painted engine lay as still as a coffin. They were in trouble. How big was the trouble?

The conversation that ensued was in a brand of rapid Portuguese that McGee had no chance of following. The gestures, however, told the story. The fuel-line had fractured at the elbow, and would have to be repaired. That did not sound so terrible. Could it be done quickly? Yes, it could be done quickly by cutting away the damaged brass section and clamping a rubber hose in its place. Better and better. Did we have such a hose? No, we did not have such a hose. *Disastero*! Almeida stood on the engine bed for a moment, assessing the situation. Could they rob a suitable hose from the bilge pump motor? 'Sim,' said dos Santos. That could be done, 'but . . .'

'Do it,' instructed the skipper, already scooting back up the engine-room ladder. McGee watched the driver for a while as he did the repairs. The man had a mariner's sheath knife, a wicked-looking gully with a heavy blued blade which he used to chop the ancilliary hose to size. It was overkill but it did the job.

McGee told his men to keep their weapons out of sight and to change back into civvies. They were about to get visitors. Back at the bridge Almeida gave him the news. 'They send two vessels to look us over.' He tapped the radar display. 'Look here.' The Furuno set that Perseveranca was equipped with had what was known as a relative unstabilized display screen. This simply meant that the observer had to regard himself as being at the centre of the screen, bearing straight ahead. The successive positions of a target-echo with that type of display depended on three factors: the target's course and speed, the observer's course and speed, and any alteration of course by the observer. With Perseveranca stationary but for the effects of the current, to read the display required no calculations. There was some central sea clutter and a shadow sector to the south, but bearing down on them from about 150 degrees were two closely spaced true echoes. 'They be with us in under half hour,' warned Almeida. There was nothing anyone could do about that. Dos Santos was busy in the engine-room. You could hear the sound of his file screeching. It was a job for one man only.

McGee did a last quick tour of the deck with Ukongo trotting happily at his heels. Through his binoculars he could just make out the silhouettes of the approaching craft. They were big boys and showing a fair turn of speed. If he could see them, they could see him. He sought the cover of the wheelhouse companion-way. At Almeida's knee level he could see, but not be seen.

The trawlers were closing in, bold red Soviet merchant

flags scudding from their stern posts. One of them could have passed as a fishing vessel. The other, the bigger of the pair, was anything but that. It was a 178-foot OKEAN-class vessel, about 680 tons of it, and many years had passed since it had dragged a net. Its super-structure was bristling with antennae, scanners and about every other nautical eavesdropping device the Soviets could possibly have crammed it with. The NATO term of reference for such a vessel was Soviet Merchant Navy Intelligence Gatherer. Almeida had a more succinct term for them. 'Fucking snooper,' he commented in ventrilo-quist talk. 'Fucking Commie snooper.' Almeida certainly had a way with words.

Suddenly a loudspeaker crackled and they were accos-ted in atrocious Portuguese. 'Ahoy, Perseveranca, you are off route. Are you in trouble? Why have you shut down your engine?'

The big vessel was abeam of Perseveranca, not more than fifteen metres away, the sound of her 800-horse diesel strident as her reversed screw churned up her bow water. She was innocuously named LINZA, but the stoic overalled crew men on deck did not suit the name at all. From the bridge several pairs of steady binoculars were surveying them. Almeida was magnificent. Every bit the skipper of the high seas, he strolled on to his bridge. He did not have the luxury of a loud hailer: he did not need one. Cupping his hands to his mouth he bellowed: 'No problems, no need to worry about us. You are the ones off route.'

It did not satisfy the Russians.

'Perseveranca is registered in Luanda. Why are you so far from your fishing grounds?' The other trawler had taken station now, starboard and some distance away, content to await big brother's instructions.

The comrades were taking a chance, McGee thought, and said as much to Almeida. 'Get a bit cross,' he told him. 'Don't take their shit.' The skipper did not need prompting. He lit a cigarette as though he did not have a worry in the world. Flicking the dead match to the wind he took in a lungful of smoke, then answered.

'In these waters I go as I please and do as I please. I am leaving now and you are obstructing me.' He had timed it to the second. Dead on cue Perseveranca's engine thumped into life. It was magic. The skipper sauntered into the wheelhouse, took hold of the spokes and thrust the control lever through the gate to forward. He gave full ahead and she responded with 188 solid horses. McGee's men waved a cheerful goodbye, and they pulled imperiously away.

From somewhere on the deck Ukongo sounded his triumphant bark. Score number one for the good guys, thought McGee. But the whole episode had held them back disastrously. They were late now, very late. They held full revs all afternoon.

Chapter 20

They passed Baio dos Tigres eight miles out to sea, the beacon, flashing in bursts of three with eleven-second intervals, visible in the gloom of the early evening. 'We very close now,' said Almeida. 'The next light is Porto Alexandre; should be visible from seven miles out.'

It came up just over two hours later. Porto Alexandre's beacon was near the end of the cat's tail sand-spit. Almeida saw the light first. Making a considerable adjustment to their heading, he brought Perseveranca around to east of north east. With the light dead-ahead and their stern to the swell, they ran for land.

They were late, two hours behind schedule on a trip in the order of 700 sea miles. That, in normal circumstances, might have called for a bit of back-slapping. The circumstances, however, were not normal. They were too late for the high tide Almeida needed to take Perseveranca into the bay. There was a landing-party to put ashore, and no bay to shelter in . . . They were in for a long wet paddle in the dinghies.

How long and how wet? Almeida must have read McGee's mind. 'We are here.' His broad finger prodded the chart. 'I take you.' The finger did a slight waltz around the cat's tail spit, 'right here.' It looked fine to McGee. Almeida had decided on a spot some 500 metres from the shore where, according to the Admiralty chart, he would have some 10 metres of water beneath him.

'Is best place,' the old skipper said. 'If wind holds then sea will stay flat.'

'It will hold.' There was more sanguine expectation than meteorological knowhow backing McGee's statement. Nevertheless Almeida found the optimism of the soldier contagious. He smiled and watched the big man make his way to the foredeck. The dinghies were down there – lashed, inflated, and ready to launch – so were his Angolan mercenaries. Did they ever stop cleaning their weapons? McGee squatted down in the bows and chatted with them. The Capitao and those lithe hard-faced fighters were as close as any men could get.

McGee gave his final orders in the confines of the crew's quarters. It was the strangest Order Group he had ever called. In the cramped area all his men had taken to their tiered bunks to give him the centre space. He felt like some modern-day Henry Morgan with the whirling shadows of the hanging lamp, the creaking of the hull timbers and the smell of old paint and tar. It occurred to him that Sir Henry would have been astonished at the amount of lethal fire-power the latter-day Cubans could summon up compared with their Spanish ancestors. He spoke slowly and deliberately. They would have but one bite at the apple. There would be no second chances, no reinforcements to patch up any blunders. As he unfurled a map of Objective Number One all conversation came to a stop.

'We,' he began, 'are just off Porto Alexandre, just about here. You have seen the green light that comes from the end of this long sand-spit that curls around the bay. There are no known enemy troops at Alexandre. It is not much more than a fishing harbour with a few processing plants, some of them not in use. It does have a hospital and it does have a woodworking factory. It has only one access road which leads north to the harbour town of Mocamedes. There is an airstrip, too. What Porto Alexandre has that we require is a safe port for Perseveranca and a car population that will provide us with transport to Mocamedes.'

He produced a second map. 'This is Baia de Mocamedes. It is ninety kilometres from Alexandre and is joined by a coastal road that is used by standard civilian motor cars. It's probably in poor condition but we will use it tonight to get from Alexandre to Mocamedes. We have two bridges to cross; bridge one over the Curoca river; bridge two over Rio dos Flamingoes.'

All McGee was really doing then was giving names to their objectives. They had gone over the execution of their mission a score of times before in training without knowing the exact geographical location of those objectives. The effect of his words brought a ripple of excitement, many 'I told you so' looks and almost an end to two weeks of speculation; almost, because though they now knew the where and the how they still did not know why. McGee kept them waiting on edge.

He pinned up a large hand-drawn map of Mocamedes, the town and the harbour. To the raiders he issued identical maps. 'Mocamedes . . . population four thousand five hundred. Angola's third largest port. Logistical link for SWAPO's western and central front. Railhead for the iron ore mines at Casinga . . . heavily defended. This is the entrance road from Alexandre and this is the route we follow . . . This is the Camera Policia, the old police station and cells. SWAPO now run it as a detention and 're-education' centre. It has thirty cells and in one of those cells is the person we have come to Angola to rescue. Now . . . Look carefully.'

The last instruction had been superfluous. He pinned up two head-and-shoulder blow-ups of Patricia. One crystal-clear colour shot he had taken of her himself in Pretoria, the other from the fuzzy Press release shot that Angop, the Angolan Press agency, had put out. He made no attempt to cut short the buzz of excited conversation behind him. For a full minute he stood alternating his gaze at the shockingly contrasting pictures of the woman he loved. Then when he turned back to them the hush told him that they had guessed. They knew.

The rest was routine, information that they knew by heart; expected enemy strength, dispositions, routes, the breakdown of his two teams. 'It's obvious that the enemy have got more than enough troops and a hundred times more fire-power than they require to wipe us out, if they can pin us down. To pin us down, however, they first have to find us. The way we've planned it, that will never happen. We will be off with the tide in the morning while MPLA and SWAPO are still running around in circles.'

With any luck that was the way it would go. McGee was not prepared to speculate on the consequences of poor luck or no luck. Soldiers never did, not those ones who wanted to survive. There were but few questions. It was time . . . The dinghies were waiting.

They launched them to the lee side of Perseveranca. Flabby dark grey behemoths, they belly-flopped into the sea, then nudged like baby mammals against their mother ship. Instead of sustenance the mother ship gave them men, weapons and equipment.

'Keep your bums down.' The last-minute advice from the voice on the bridge raised a laugh. It was a soldier's expression. 'Try to keep together,' McGee called. 'Let's go.'

The two dinghies pulled away simultaneously, six willing paddles apiece pushing them through the choppy black water. Almeida had taken them to within 500 metres of the shore. It should have been easy and would have been but for the grasp of an unusually strong rising current and the deceptiveness of the swell. The rowers had a rhythmical chant going and they were keeping up the stroke.

Soon the sound of Perseveranca's retreating engine dwindled, and over the chant a new sound could be heard – the pounding of surf. They quickened the stroke and the extra thrust was marked, but Alexandre's beacon, which should have been just to their right to bring them straight into the bay, seemed to be slipping away into the night. Then, without further warning, they were among the breakers.

'Keep the stroke, keep paddling!' McGee yelled. Clearly in the brilliant moonlight he could see silver-crested combers striking into a false bay to his right, causing a side-flanking wave to rear up near the beach. To swing obliquely now would be disastrous and that was exactly what was happening to the other dinghy, Hosi's craft. The side wave struck them and even as they bent their backs to the blades he saw it toss them broadside into the path of the main breakers, the dinghy banking grossly, thrusting men and equipment to one side, its super buoyancy their enemy now that the centre of gravity was awry. Then McGee could not watch any more. His craft bucked as a large wave pushed underneath them and onwards. It was worse than anything he had expected. A deluge of salt water caught their stern and washed on board. He yelled at them to paddle. They were simply going too slowly and the backwash was sucking them to a standstill. Massive oncoming surf rushed up again, lifting them and this time thrusting the dinghy ahead. They were riding it, the paddles now superfluous. The surf would do with them as it willed. He could see the other dinghy rearing up to capsize, before being righted by the same breaker and propelled towards the white sand ahead.

Friendly remnant ripples chuckling alongside beached them in about six inches of water and they waded ashore, everyone and everything drenched. They ran the dinghies up the beach, hid them in the dunes and took stock.

It was not a total disaster, but one major item was missing, a kitbag containing plastique, cortex, primers and detonators. They had duplicate packs so divided the contents between the two groups. Hosi's team was to remain at Alexandre, seal off the place, hold it and await the return of McGee. McGee's team's task was to make their way overland to Mocamedes, raid the jail there, release Patricia Christie and return with her. By the look of the distant beacon, in their battle with the sea they had been tossed some four kilometres further up the coast than they had planned. It was nothing. Fifteen men had set out from Perseveranca and fifteen men had landed. They split up under their respective leaders and set out at a steady jog for the harbour. The sound of dogs yapping up ahead warned them that they were not far off course.

Porto Alexandre, wind-chapped, bleached and rusty,

looked a beaten town. The place did not even seem to possess that ability some towns have, to shrug off ugliness under the clement glow of moonlight. It had a foreshore that stretched for about five kilometres. There was a straggle of homes, warehouses, some home-grown factories and a boat-builders' yard holding the bare-ribbed carcass of a long unfinished fishing vessel. There was not much going for Alexandre. The warehouses were mostly empty, with fractured windows and rusted doors banging in the wind. The sand dunes that had once been pushed aside to make way for the town were shouldering back in from every direction as though determined to bury the place. McGee hoped that one day they would.

Alexandre was not in total darkness. In a few houses lights were glimmering and, outside a general dealer-cum-garage-cum-bar, a single dangling light bulb illuminated a faded sign that read Sousa e Irmao Limitada, some petrol pumps and half a dozen cars. Among them were a Peugeot station-wagon and a Chevy van, both of about middle-Seventies vintage, and both with their keys invitingly in their ignitions. From Sousa e Irmao came the typical hubbub of raucous conversation that characterizes such establishments the world over. To add to the ruckus, a radio was playing local heavy rock, and playing it loud.

No one heard the car doors open. Nobody heard the starter motors turn. The only people to bid farewell to McGee and his raiders were Hosi's men in their MPLA uniforms, and they did not have time for much in the way of niceties. They watched the tail-lights of the two vehicles disappear to the north, then went to work. They had a road-block to set up, a bridge to secure, and the local constabulary, if any, to neutralize, all in the space of a few hours. The Capitao would be back at dawn, all being well.

So far, for the Capitao, all was well. He was finding road conditions better than expected. They crossed the Curoca river within twenty minutes of leaving Alexandre. A single-lane cantilever with twin pylons, the bridge soared over a wide expanse of tidal estuary and was made to be blown. Also there they cut the telephone cables from bank to bank.

Thereafter the road veered into the interior and remained surprisingly smooth. Now and then there were stretches of sand and rock but generally it was good. The dunes marched inland for about twenty kilometres, then flattened into desert scrub, where the road seemed to disappear into a multitude of parallel tracks, the whole desert seeming one wide road. In the starkness of the full moon McGee could afford to outrun his headlights. He did so, pushing the Chev to the edge of its limits. The Peugeot, he noticed, was keeping station a few hundred metres behind.

Further inland they were met by a rocky escarpment where the Portuguese engineers had had to make a few cuttings, but mostly the route just wound and undulated and generally found its own way. They were forced to ease up as the road deteriorated into bumps, suspension-jarring dips and sharp bends. At half an hour before midnight they reached the bridge spanning the Rio dos Flamingoes and there they stopped, switched off, and climbed from the cars. They had made up all the time they lost at sea and their ETA at Mocamedes was back on schedule.

McGee clambered down into the dry river bed and surveyed the bridge. This was a Bailey construction, a cheap thing made from prefabricated box girders bolted together. The Portuguese had erected hundreds of them throughout Angola. Unfortunately they were hell to demolish. There were no anchorages to get at, the ends simply resting on each bank. He decided to go for the road sections, the heavy concrete beams fitting between the girders that took the traffic. Working in the glow of a poacher's torch he went to work, packing the putty-like plastique between the concrete and the steel and pressing in the detonators with his thumbs. He led the wires for about fifty metres down the road to a culvert and marked

330

the spot with a small cone of rocks. When he was satisfied that the whole arrangement would work as and when he wanted it to work, he walked back to the cars. There was no further need for hurry.

At just after one a.m. they drove into the outskirts of Mocamedes. At first the inevitable scatter of shanties showed in the headlights, then more sand dunes, the *Muceques* proper, and suddenly they were driving down what was obviously the main street. Wide with a central palm-treed island it was typical of old colonial Portugal. Single-and double-storey plastered buildings, deep veranda-fronted shops and wide pavements gave the place an air of genial *commercializmo*. There were one or two civilians still about as they drove down the Rua but as yet not a uniform in sight. McGee steered the Chev into a side street and signalled Bacar, the other driver, to draw up alongside him. It was not necessary but he just wanted to wish Bacar and his dapper little number two, Teja, good luck. He leaned from his car window. 'Change in plan?' Bacar enquired softly.

'No.'

'Let me make sure of my bearings, Capitao. The street we just turned off was Rua four de Justo or whatever they call it now. The police station is five blocks down. Right?'

'Right . . . Good luck.'

'*Simplicidade!*' Both men gave thumbs-up signs as they drove off. Bacar was right, it was *simplicidade*. Good planning did not need to be elaborate. It required good men with a clear picture of what they had to do, and the guts to do it. All he and Teja had to do was simply take their vehicle, park it, break into a two-storey block of offices and set up a machine-gun on the roof. They were not to initiate any fire but if the shooting started they were to give fire support to the men raiding the police station and then, when they could see the time was right, they were to link up with the rearguard and run for Alexandre. *Simplicidade!* – until the bullets started flying . . .

Carlos and Felix liked to do everything together. If you

331

saw one, the other was sure to be near. They claimed to be brothers, twins in fact, but then blacks introduced their most distant relatives as brothers. What difference did it make? McGee kept them as a squad; they were his decoy squad. Their task was to get past the harbour patrols and into the dock area, locate the inevitable fuel storage tanks or anything else that would go up with a good bang, then set their limpet mines to go up at H-hour plus fifteen minutes. They would then link up with Bacar and Teja. It was simple enough – if you were prepared to discount a battalion of well-trained MPLA militia, their dogs and their searchlights, their barbed wire and alarm systems. His watch gave him 02.20. H-hour was set for 04.45. That was when the strike would take place.

McGee started up the Chev van that now carried the rest of his team, his snatch squad, Oliviera, Denga and Kimbo; the three men he would lead into the prison with all the arrogance of a Kapitan in the Russian Army with the forged papers ordering the release into his custody of the prisoner, Patricia Christie.

First, though, they had to meet the man who would walk into the old Camera Policia, shoulder to shoulder with the snatch team, a certain Cuban-hating SWAPO officer by the name of Msimba Maduro, of late a guest of the South African Security Branch. Christie's doubts were about to be put to the test.

Comrade Maduro would be waiting alone for them at a rendezvous, the State cemetery located about a kilometre north-west of Mocamedes. McGee placed his silenced Walther on the seat next to him and drove off. If Maduro had turned, now was the time they would know about it. He did not believe that would happen, however. There were too many things going for Maduro in South Africa.

Msimba Maduro did not arrive until 03.00, the outside limit set for the rendezvous. In fact he almost did not make the rendevous at all: McGee nearly shot him.

Maduro did everything he should not have done. He was driving a jeep, a little Steyer Puch, in which he roared up the long drive to the cemetery as though the devil was at his tail. Completely ignoring the recognition signals, without even switching off his engine, he ran past the big gates and sprinted up the Path of Remembrance. Then, as though suddenly realizing what a crazy thing he had done, he stopped short, suddenly nervous. He called out in a faint voice, 'It is I, Maduro.' It was all wrong, of course, but it saved him.

Maduro had had a reason for his recklessness. 'I rushed here,' he said, 'because I hope there is time for you to change your planning. The girl you want is no longer at the police station.'

McGee felt as though he had been hit in the solar plexus. For a moment his mind would not function properly, then the questions came: 'Where is she?'

'There was an Angop Press conference this afternoon at the cinema – Press, television, the lot. Miss Christie, of course, was there. The whole purpose of the thing was to put her on show. After it was over the SWAPO detachment commander, Buseddi, from the training camp Giraul, decided to throw a party at his base . . .' Maduro was being too long-winded.

'Where is she?' snapped McGee.

'At camp Giraul.'

'Where is camp Giraul?'

'About eight kilometres north of us.'

'Can you take us there?'

'Of course. There's a good road to the oil refinery. Giraul is just the other side of it.'

'What is the pattern of these parties? How long do they last? When it is over, will she be returned to the jail?'

There were too many questions; then McGee needed too many answers to compute his plan. Suddenly his mind was working like a machine. He needed data and he needed it quickly.

'Buseddi enjoys his booze,' Maduro said. 'They might go right through until dawn, but it's more likely the thing

333

will soon wind down. Buseddi won't take her back. Mazambaan goes everywhere with her. He will take her back in Buseddi's Ulyan jeep.'

Mazambaan alone with Patricia! More data for his brain. 'How well guarded is camp Giraul?'

'By your standards not well guarded at all, but currently it is full with a detachment undergoing desert training; probably about four hundred men with about twenty Cuban and some Russian instructors.'

Four hundred men-plus, thought McGee, and an unpredictable psychopathic ape called Mazambaan. It would be a monstrous risk to go in. Had the SWAPO troops there been the worst, most ill-trained men alive, there would still be a massive pattern of crossfire. There had to be an alternative.

'How well do you know Buseddi? Do you have any influence with him?'

'That depends on what sort of mood the man is in. If he's in a good mood, the whole world is his friend. What do you want me to do?'

McGee did not answer. He almost had it right in his mind. There were still a few points to be appreciated. They still had the powerful element of surprise on their side and that would remain their trump card until such time as Carlos and Felix's limpet mines went up. If Patricia was not in their hands by that time, the mission would be a tragic write-off.

They had one and a half critical hours left in which to pull it off. Of course Maduro could be setting them up. They would have no way of finding that out until it was too late. McGee studied his ex-enemy for a moment: Maduro the renegade; a handful against more than four hundred. The odds were sufficient to make allegiance a somewhat flimsy issue. Still, he believed he could trust him.

He needed the fire power Bacar and Teja could provide. Somehow they had to be recalled. 'Listen,' he said, 'this is what I want you to do, Maduro . . .'

* * *

If the gulf of Mocamedes could be visualized as the abdomen of a maiden's body, then the salient of ponta do Giraul was her ripe breast hanging into the bay – but that was where the softness ended. Giraul was in reality a scrub-dotted, shingle-spread plateau cut away from the sea by six ugly kilometres of sheer sharp cliff. On that inhospitable terrain SWAPO had established a training base.

McGee, once on top of the water tower near the refinery, did not think Giraul seemed badly defended. On the contrary, the camp looked extremely formidable. In the bright moonlight he hardly needed his night glasses to tell him that the thinly wired-off strip running all the way round the circumference of the camp was a minefield, nor that the black slits like humped little crocodile eyes protruding here and there were extremely well-sited machine-gun bunkers. Trying to penetrate a defended minefield under a night sky like that would be suicide.

If it was not to be the minefield, then it had to be the front door which was guarded by a single sandbagged sentry post where the road ran in. Behind that was a gate, and behind that the vehicle park, where an assortment of about twenty heavy ZIL and GAZ-66 trucks were neatly parked.

He could just make out what appeared to be the snouts of some BTR armoured personnel carriers. Buseddi's Ulyanosvk jeep was nowhere in sight. However, being the commander's vehicle, he had probably driven it right up to his quarters, in which case it would be obscured by the central block of tents.

There were also what appeared to be some corrugated asbestos huts dotted more or less at random throughout the central area. Some of them were lit.

McGee lowered his binoculars and eyed the camp some 300 metres away. Buseddi ought to have had a sentry up on the water tower. It was the only high point for miles around. Denga and Maduro, seated on the ledge next to him, were looking down intently.

'I think the party is still going on,' Maduro said. Indeed it was. There was the distinct thrumm of reggae coming from inside. 'The lecture hall where the party is being held, is the third one. Can you see it?'

McGee swung his glasses back. Yes, there was movement there. He had been consistently watching that hut since they had climbed into position. Now he could see two people silhouetted against the square of light at the entrance. Strain as he did, however, they remained anonymous. The interior showed movement but it was just a blur. McGee had seen all that it was possible to see from his perch on the water tower. He had a good idea of the layout of Giraul and he knew there was only one way in. They knew their objectives, and once inside, they would take the cards as they were dealt them. That was all the planning he could do. 'Let's get down,' he said. The time was 04.10.

Soon afterwards Bacar and Teja were brought in from the police station ambush. They had driven past the harbour, they said. There had been no sign that Carlos and Felix had been discovered; no vehicles, no running troops, no excitement at all. Of the twins there had been nothing to be seen. All he could hope for now was that in the confusion that would follow the attack and the explosions, it would be possible to find them. It was a long shot. In the meantime there was a party to go to.

The pug-nosed little Steyer Puch, carrying Buseddi's uninvited guests, did not seem to arouse much interest from the gate guards at Giraul, perhaps because it was such an innocuous-looking vehicle with its little tyres and mini-jeep chassis. One guard held up an indifferent hand. The other did not even cover his comrade. They recognized Maduro and saluted. The Russian Kapitan and the other two FAPLA troops seated on the back bench were hardly troubled with a glance.

Suddenly, however, the whole thing started to go wrong. It was not that the sentries were suspicious of the men arriving at Giraul at that hour – quite the opposite, in

336

fact. Number one guard, mumbling something about 'Comrade commander's party,' simply waved them on. Number two guard had the gate open and was saluting before Maduro had said a word. It had all happened too quickly. The man who had swung the gate open was now standing about twenty paces inside the camp waiting expectantly for them to drive in. Guard number one was standing next to the Puch wondering why that had not already happened.

The sentries were now standing too far apart to be dealt with simultaneously and had not crowded the vehicle as sentries normally do. They had not wanted to see any papers or passes or do anything that McGee had been sure they would do, that he had banked on them doing.

Maduro stalled the jeep, put on the hand brake and climbed out. Did they have a torch, he asked. Yes, they had a torch. An open car bonnet is an irresistible invitation to most men. The guards were no exception. Both of them came forward to look, and both of them were shot with McGee's silenced Walther as they leaned forward over the engine.

McGee beckoned into the empty desert and Oliviera, Denga and Kimbo rose up and came jogging down the road. A sharp-edged full moon was reaching for the western horizon, touching the ground with ice-white light. You could see their long shadows running with them.

With Denga remaining at the gate, six men in the Puch broached Giraul. The first stop was the vehicle park. McGee was forcing himself not to think of the proximity of Patricia. If emotions got in the way now they would all be dead, the girl included. The next move was to annexe a truck that could take a bit of punishment, something that would not fall to bits when a few bullets hit it. He had plenty to chose from. A dozen were GAZ-66 four-tonners and the balance big ZIL 151's with six driving wheels and power enough to tow the QE 2. The ZILs would take a lot of stopping but they did not possess the speed of the GAZ-66's. Speed would be vital. They picked out an almost new vehicle and sounded the tank. It was full. Bacar had driven such a truck many times before. McGee summoned him. 'How does she look?'

'Easy.'

'Right, you know what to do now?'

They stripped sandbags from the wall around the fuel depot and barricaded them against the tail-gate of the GAZ. It seemed to McGee as though they were making noise enough to wake the dead, but time was of the essence. Teja climbed up into the back and settled himself with his machine gun, giving his cheerful thumbs-up sign.

'Everyone ready? ....Right, hit anything that moves from now on.'

'You don't worry, Capitao,' someone said. 'Nao te preocupes.'

By the time the GAZ was prepared it was 04.45 and McGee turned his other men loose on the other vehicles. 'You've got two minutes to chop as many ignition wires as you can; two minutes, then be back here.' It was not much time to do an important job, but there were only a few minutes before Felix's limpet mines were due to start exploding. They did what they could, before there was a scramble for the sandbagged GAZ. Bacar ground the starter motor and the engine coughed loudly into life. They drove from the vehicle park, Maduro in the Puch with McGee alongside him, the GAZ truck about ten metres behind. Maduro knew where to go and the truck kept station. They had six minutes to spare when they stopped outside the lighted Nissen hut. Buseddi's Ulyanosvk jeep was parked there, as were some civilian cars.

Happy sounds were coming from inside the big hut. Glasses were clinking, hands were clapping and there was a lot of laughter. A guitar was being strummed with typical African virility. Outside, in the fading moonlight, McGee's raiders were not unhappy either. They knew they were about to join the party.

Chapter 21

Someone, Patricia Christie thought, had done his revolutionary best to invest the long, bare-ribbed interior of Buseddi's lecture hut with a gala air. The asbestos side walls had been garnished with *boer-hate* posters. A big blue, red and green flag was stretched across the end. The blackboard at the other end carried the message, THE STRUGGLE CONTINUES – THE VICTORY IS CERTAIN. Yesterday's lesson on mine-laying mistakes was still vaguely visible too. A photograph of a broad smiling Sam Nujoma gazing down from above the door gave the party the rubber stamp of approval.

To the desperately tired woman sitting there the whole effect seemed garish and frightening. It was obvious that the whole revolutionary façade had been dreamed up as an excuse for a drunken binge – and then what? It was a nightmare. But then everything that had happened to her over the past week had been a nightmare. It was just a matter of degrees of frightfulness. That day had been bad.

She had awakened to find Mazambaan with her, crouched, smiling. He never seemed to lose that cold hard smile. His face had been inches from hers; Sun-rival on the neck thong swinging past her eyes as he rocked so slightly against her. It was, he had reminded her, the day of the Press Conference. She had not needed reminding. Another thing Mazambaan never seemed to be without was the presence of a saucer-eyed little girl. She was his shadow. If you saw Mazambaan you could be sure that somewhere close at hand, wide-eyed and silent, the girl would be following. Her name, Patricia had learned, was Kaghonda.

Kaghonda never did anything, never said anything but

was always there. She had been present that morning, standing with one arm resting up against the door-post, biting a finger tip impassively, watching.

Patricia had watched her in return, had turned her head away from the face above her and pleaded with her eyes for the girl not to go away. She had seen Kaghonda's black pupils slowly lift and focus on Mazambaan, had felt his weight shift uncomfortably on the mattress. Then as the gaze had not wavered Mazambaan had stood. It was not the first time Kaghonda had intervened, and Patricia knew that the time would come when the girl with the eyes that haunted Mazambaan would not be there.

She was not there now . . . The Press Conference – what a mockery that had been! Flanked there by Mazambaan, Buseddi and another comrade hero, a despicable liar by the name of Msimba Maduro, who, if his citation was to be believed, had caused the destruction of the better part of the racist South African army and their running dog puppet partners in one afternoon's work; had been caught, imprisoned and tortured by the Pretoria racists, only to escape in spectacular and heroic fashion to rejoin his comrades on the western Namibian front.

Comrade Mazambaan was next in the spotlight. He had squashed the latent racist turncoat insect Nakwindi; a man who, to the revulsion of the world, turned his back on the struggling Namibian people, and decided for iniquitous reasons to grasp the bloody hands of the puppets of Pretoria. Comrade Mazambaan had been aided and abetted in the escape by . . .

The glare of the lights had been blinding as they had swung on to her. Yes, a few questions would be permitted. A faceless inquisitor had begun – but there had not been any questions. What had happened was that she had been bombarded with distorted and untrue statements, so cunningly prepared that it had made hardly any difference how she replied. It had been an exercise in gutter propaganda that anyone could have seen through, standard communist anti-South African rhetoric.

That day, it seemed, would have no end. A soldier with a guitar was strumming a monotonous repetitive melody that she had not heard begin. It had just emerged hypnotically into her awareness, for nothing seemed to have a beginning any longer, nor an end. There were no compartments in the passage of time. One day simply faded into the next . . . She would emerge one morning, she knew and be horrified that it was morning, and that an entire tortuous day lay ahead. Perhaps then the spark of hope that smouldered constantly within her would die or be quenched or filter away, or do whatever it was that occurred to unsustained hope. Dear God, she would rather be dead than be without hope. In the meantime it was a kindness of time that it should just drift by. She was so very tired.

Suddenly Patricia found herself wide awake, alert – and puzzled. The beat had picked up but it was not that. To the sound of hand-clapping from the onlookers some of the camp women were performing a dance. Linked in a chain, hand to shoulder, they were undulating like a writhing python. She looked round carefully and slowly so as not to arouse any interest.

Mazambaan was standing next to Buseddi. He caught her glance and smiled that smile . . . but it was not him. Patricia could feel the hairs beginning to rise on her neck. She looked round once more trying to see what it was. There was nothing, nothing if you did not count a burning conviction, almost voicelike in its insistence. Watch! it said, *watch* . . . Nothing had changed that she could put her finger on. The place was still crowded with men, mostly soldiers, some civilians, all of them drinking – standing, sitting or leaning against the tables – but drinking.

No, there had been a change! Msimba Maduro was in the room and he had not been there all evening. Was that it? Was that all there was to it? Had her sixth sense alerted her to the presence of that evil little man? Buseddi was swaying on his feet, his face under the stark electric light a

341

doltish drunken mask. He had his ear cocked and appeared to be concentrating on what was being said to him by Maduro. Then he was smiling, nodding his head and grinning broadly as though comrade Maduro had just told him a very funny story, very funny indeed.

It could not be just that. Maduro had left Buseddi and was walking then, very deliberately towards her. Her whole body was starting to prickle. She shifted her weight until she was poised on the edge of the chair. He sat down opposite her. His eyes, like little brown spiders, seemed to crawl into her own. He seemed to want to talk to her. His head was close, his hand on her shoulder, insistent. She could take no more. She reached back to strike out.

Lightning flashes, a dozen in the space of a squeezed second, ripped through the hut, shocking the mind, dazing it, freezing all reaction. That was what stun bombs did; they stunned. Then shooting men were pouring into the hut and Maduro was dragging her to the floor. McGee had come, she knew it. She screamed, 'Here I am! Here I am!' and whirled, striking with the hatred of a caged leopard at the man on her. With broken glass for claws she gouged for the eyes and for a moment she was free and running. 'Here I am!'

Her shout was beaten flat by the thunder of automatic weapons. Then hands of steel had her, the wrong hands – those of Mazambaan. He had her and was lifting her. He would have to lift a leopard. A man tumbling backwards with the dead weight of a corpse struck them heavily, and she was free again, scrambling on the bloody floor, and screaming McGee's name over and over again. But all you could hear, see or smell was smoke and the crashing, flashing fire of the guns.

Then it was all over. Outside a machine gun was tearing apart the night air but inside were just the animal cries of hurting, bleeding men. She was being lifted and the arms at last were those of her man. 'Here she is.'

Matthew McGee, blackened like a devil, was speaking to her in quick clipped tones. 'Trish, listen to me. There's a long way to go.' He was holding her hand, squeezing it in emphasis. It was like listening to a stranger. 'Men will be with you . . . overland . . . desert . . . fishing boat.' She wanted to hold him, wipe away the blood that was staining him. 'When I say, "Go", you run for that truck. I will be right behind. Ready?' They crouched by the door. There was a lot of shooting outside now. A pane of glass smashed and pieces of asbestos wall were flying everywhere. 'Go! Go! Go!'

Out of the choking smoke, and two short paces from the truck a good man died. Kimbo's hands were reaching for the tail-gate when he gave a little cry and fell away. Then she was up and aboard and they were gathering speed. 'Down!' said the man there, then returned to his machine gun, hammering short bursts here and there. 'Down! Down!' It was the only English word he had been taught for the occasion. 'Down, down, down!'

Kimbo was dead and the camp a smoked hornet's nest. Everywhere there were muzzle flashes, stabbing the dark, and the crack of bullets was constant. The moon was low, however, so the GAZ, in spite of its bulk and the spitting flame of Teja's tail gun, drew little direct fire as it accelerated into the desert. Perhaps the enemy's problem was lack of direction: there was plenty of shouting but none of it in the voices of command they had come to know.

Maybe that was the reason the Steyer jeep made it safely to the gate. It could have been that or it might have been because at that critical moment for the defenders of Giraul, dawn was suddenly precipitated in a terrifying fashion. Across the bay there was a flash, a towering rising fireball of flame, then a concussion like devil's thunder shook both air and ground. The twins had worked the miracle.

It was a matter now of picking up the rearguard, pinning back their ears and going for it. Denga was at the gate. That would be the simple part. To find Carlos and Felix in the town, that would be dangerous and difficult.

McGee's prediction, as it happened, was reversed. The volume of fire down at the gate suddenly became venomous. Denga had to sprint like a jack-rabbit for his life. On the other hand, Carlos and Felix were waiting at the Peugeot in comparatively tranquil conditions, both totally relaxed in the knowledge that Capitao would come, that Capitao would find them. He did.

They took in the enemy Puch at a glance, then swung themselves casually aboard. McGee had one regret as the fire at the bay of little fishes diminished in his rear-view mirror, just one. It was that from the dead men at Buseddi's party, one face had been absent . . . Mazambaan's. He didn't remain with that thought for long.

About forty kilometres from Mocamedes, McGee became aware that they were not the only ones using the Alexandre road at that hour. Behind them now and then one could see the glow of headlights. Someone was in pursuit.

The Puch jeep was sure-footed as a mountain goat, a real cliff climber, but no greyhound. Bacar's GAZ-66 had shown them a clean pair of heels and now the oncoming headlights looked brighter. They were being steadily hauled in by what were bound to be some highly vindictive troops. He leaned across to Maduro and shouted above the engine noise, 'You know the bridge over Rio dos Flamingoes?' Maduro nodded, yes he knew it.

'It's about seven kilometres ahead,' McGee continued. 'When we reach it switch off your lights and drop us there. Turn off the road about one hundred metres the other side of the bridge. Find some cover and wait for us.'

Maduro figured the distance to be less than McGee's estimation and he was right. Without headlights and without the moon it was totally black and he let the Puch nudge its own way ahead in the wheel ruts.

McGee sprang off and groped around until he had located his explosives. Using the wires as a guide he trotted along the road to his marker. In the distance he could make out the growl of heavy engines. There was no time to waste. 'You in position, Denga?'

'Sim, Capitao, I'm in the high ground.'

The icy morning air gave a crisp edge to their voices. 'Okay, Carlos, Felix?'

'Can't see much up here, but we're in position.'

They would all see everything there was to see soon enough. Their sites had been selected on the inward trip when vision was good. McGee scrambled for the little kopje where the wires ended. The vehicles were closing in. He counted five flashes as they breasted a hillock to the south. One more valley and they would be at the bridge. The first set of lights was bearing down on the bridge. It looked like a BRDM scout-car. McGee rested his rifle and felt for the terminals of his hand generator; his fingertips clumsy and numb with cold.

The scout-car was slowing to negotiate the bridge, then there was the sound of concrete grating on steel as the structure took the ton and a half. It was there, silhouetted now by the vehicles following. You could make out its stubby 14.5 gun and the squat turret. McGee waited for the scout-car to cross right over, waited for the following vehicle, a BTR armoured troop carrier, to reach the bridge centre. Then he screwed the generator handle. For a mili-second there was daylight as the plastique detonated, shearing cleanly away six metres of concrete and the front half of the BTR.

McGee lifted himself, with debris still raining down. The enemy vehicle was ablaze from end to end. Now for the scout-car, by then in the culvert beneath them. A rocket flashed down from Felix's position bursting in its heart. There was some screaming. That was all.

The bridge was blown and the coffin of the scout-car was blocking the road. Heavy fire was feeling for the raiders from the convoy. Voices were shouting and troops were running. It was time to move again. Maduro was not with the Puch, where he was supposed to be. They found him lying crumpled nearby with a huge piece of steel debris across his neck. He could not have known what had hit him. It was a strange thing but McGee had come to like that little renegade. 'Go well,' he said and hoped it would be adequate. There was no time for more; an empty river would not hold back the hunting pack for long.

In the light of the burning personnel carrier McGee had taken note of what the enemy had thrown at them, what was still left to contend with and he was shocked. There were three more vehicles on the opposite bank, all streamlined, big-wheeled BRDM scout-cars, probably Cuban-crewed. They mounted a big and quick-firing 14.5 millimetre machine gun, and could travel at a handy 100 kilometres an hour over the type of terrain lying ahead. He was out-gunned and out-paced.

He started up the Puch and skidded into the road. There was desert ahead, relentless open plains. If the chase ended there, they would not have a hope. The Curoca bridge, with Hosi slamming the back door, was his idea of a happy ending.

It was 06.55 and the sky was whitening. They had a high-tide rendezvous with a fishing trawler, for which they were already late. McGee kicked the accelerator flat. With one man less they were lighter and the jeep was quicker for it.

Hosi had had all night to prepare the ambush and had not rushed. First he had attended to the Curoca bridge, packing plastique under the near-side cantilever arm so that the blast would implode. As McGee had done, he had run out his activating wires back to the high ground, in his case a ridge of tall sand-dunes dominating the estuary. There, over a front not much longer than twenty paces, his men had dug themselves in and sited their machine-guns and rocket launchers.

Once that step had been taken his team moved to the far bank and laced the area just off the road with all kinds of mines. Having dusted out their tracks and give-away marks, they returned to their trenches on the dune ridge. By that time it was almost H-hour. Everyone listened for the distant explosion that would signal the attack but with the surf pounding on the nearby beach, how could you be sure? All of them cheered the hour, anyway.

As soon as it was light enough, Hosi walked back down the road and scrutinized his night's handiwork. There was little to be rectified and by the time he returned to his position he was a satisfied man. The killing ground lay below him, as innocent as milk. He squeezed snugly back into his fox-hole and took up his binoculars.

Young sunbeams were jumping from crest to crest across the sand dunes. There was not much else to see until he spotted the army truck bearing down towards them. He had been in the business long enough to recognize the brick-square outlines of the Russian GAZ-66 at a glance. He did not need binoculars for that, and judging by the rattle of safety catches being released all around, neither did his men. The order, 'Prepare to fire,' was superfluous. Leaving a trail of dust a kilometre long, an enemy transport was tearing into their killing ground.

The order 'Fire!' never came. A man was leaning from the passenger-side window waving a handkerchief. The driver was pummelling the hooter, the headlights were flashing.

A great shout went up from the dunes then as Hosi's men broke cover, stood up and cheered them in. Bacar crossed the bridge and Hosi lumbered down the sand slope, grinning, big fists lofted in triumph. They were all smiling, all except the woman. She was just standing there on the open back, staring into the stone-cold wasteland they had just traversed. Her lips were firm without a smile. When at last she glanced around she seemed almost surprised to find herself where she was.

What could he say to her? He hardly knew a word of her language. 'No worry.' That brought a sad smile. 'Capitao, for sure he win.' The smile deepened. Then she spoke to him.

'We're not going to leave without him, that I promise. I don't care what happens, we're not leaving him here.' Hosi nodded his head in agreement. Her words he had not understood. Her meaning was abundantly clear though. He agreed completely. 'Tenha confianca mim,' he said. 'Nao o vamos deixar.'

It was about this time that McGee acknowledged to himself that he was going to be forced to make a stand. Thirty kilometres of flat desert remained between them and Hosi's position at the bridge and the dust cloud he had been observing during the last little while was no longer a smudge: it had split into three distinct plumes, thrown up by three distinct scout-cars running abreast of each other. The machine gunners with the heavy 14.5s would be in range before long but apart from keeping his foot flat on the accelerator there was absolutely nothing he could do about it.

The ground was alternating now between deep sandy sections followed by bedrock and gravel. One instant they would be snaking in the grip of sand, the next crashing over rock ridges and humps. He recalled the stretch from the inward trip. Somewhere nearby there was a T-junction with a branch road heading directly inland away from Alexandre, but also away from the coverless open desert and towards the nearby foot of the rocky escarpment.

It came up suddenly but he was ready for it, swinging left almost without slowing. Overhead came the unmistakable whip-crack of passing bullets. For more than two kilometres the sound urged them onwards. Here and there dust fountains would suddenly burst up as high explosive bracketed them. There was also plenty of incoming tracer. Then the track dived into a valley, winding and coiling. It was Puch country again, the little jeep taking the corners as though on rails. His pursuers would have to slow down now and come on in single file. The problem with these tactics was that they were drawing him rapidly away from Alexandre, Perseveranca and their high-water deadline. Then McGee thought he saw his chance.

Over the past few kilometres the road had twisted further towards a river valley, probably the upper reaches of the Curoca. At that moment they were following the course of the almost dry river cutting into the mountainside with a four-metre sheer drop to the river bed. At a dog's leg in the river, water crosion had caved the roadway in. McGee swung the jeep right off the road, down the rubble and into the green shallow water. They waddled across, nuzzling the Puch into the crook of the dog's leg. They were obscured, but not hidden.

McGee's orders came fast. 'Denga, grab the shovel and throw river sand on to the jeep. Haul up some of those reeds and use them too. Carlos and Felix, take the RPG over to the rocks. Get yourselves into the water. We're going for the last vehicle as it passes. We're going to block the road with it.'

He did not know how much grace they had been given. Budgeting for five minutes, McGee took the PKM machine gun, quickly fed in a new belt and mounted it on Denga's sand castle. Then he waded up stream and checked the position. Carlos and Felix were in the water between some slimy boulders. They would have to kneel to fire but there was no alternative. The jeep, up to its axles in water, was still being buried by Denga but looked disturbingly like what it was: a jeep heaped with sand at a bend in a dirty river.

They needed another few minutes. It was not to be. The first scout car was pushing its snout around the dog's leg towards the road-slide. Battened down and moving cautiously, they would not be underestimating the opposition again. McGee dived flat into the slime and leopard-crawled for the Puch and his machine gun. It was the riskiest, most unlikely, most exposed ambush he had ever commanded, but it might work: if the first and second scout cars passed them by unobserved and if they could blast the tail-end car, and thus block the pass, then they might just still make it, and be back for breakfast on deck.

The first BRDM negotiated the road-slide, then the second was nosing round the bend. The third vehicle was preparing to dip into the caved-in road – and still they hadn't been detected. The machine-gun mount swung their way for a moment, then the BRDM was climbing back to the road. It was now or never. 'Ready!' McGee was almost scared to raise his voice. The scout-car was presenting them with its departing backside then . . . 'Fire!'

Carlos and Felix rose up like swamp monsters. A rocket flashed from the launcher towards the scout-car, clipped the road verge and burst on the cutting above the vehicle, blasting rock in every direction. It was a calamity. They tried for a second chance. Ten seconds were needed for Felix to recharge the launcher. That was how long it took to screw in a fresh propellant and feed a fresh rocket into the muzzle.

The Cubans knew that, too. Their gunners were traversing rapidly. Felix lost the race. The 14.5s opened and tore into McGee's position. Water spouts as big as a man were churning up the river. Bullets were whining everywhere. The machine gun was a joke against those monsters. McGee abandoned it and ran; with Denga at his side he rushed for the cliff of dead ground on the opposite bank, unpinning a phosphorous grenade as he went. He reached the cover. Denga did not, but above him, Felix made amends with his second rocket, striking the scout car square in the rump. The grenade was superfluous.

The middle car's crew tried to make a fight of it, shunting the blazing vehicle backwards to get at them, but the smoke was too thick, the heat at furnace level. There was an open road ahead so the scout-cars used it. McGee had gained nothing. Denga was lying face down in the water, only now it was not just weed-green; it was red. On the far bank one of the twins lay crumpled. Brother Felix, sitting next to him, was crying like a baby. The Puch was

350

incinerating quietly under its muddy jacket. McGee kneeled down, hung his head and vomited till his head was bursting . . . That time they buried their dead.

When he and Felix first heard the oncoming engine, they had not gone far. At first they thought it was the surviving scout-cars returning for the kill but the sound came from the wrong direction. It came from their front, not from their backs, where the fight had taken place. Nevertheless it had to be enemy. They clambered down the road-cutting, drew themselves against the bank and waited.

Whoever it was approaching was driving in a hell of a hurry, with much hectic revving and skidding. The vehicle shot over the top of the rise ahead and roared down the cutting, a shower of shale chips raining down on them, then it was past. It was an Ulyanosvk; four-by-four like Buseddi's jeep. From the glimpse they got of the fast retreating rear-end they could see that only the driver was in it.

Without a single word McGee and Felix clambered up to the road and at a run took off after the Ulyan. The jeep would be able to progress no further than the wrecked scout car and that is where they would take it. There was but a short distance to back-track.

The dog's leg bend was thick with smoke. Both men veered off the road climbed the culvert, then keeping the high ground ran on.

The Ulyan was parked and empty, the driver gone. He was not in the smoke haze of the burning scout-car and the opposite bank showed nothing except the still smouldering Puch. It was only when the wind shifted, puffing away the smoke-screen, that McGee realized how foolish he had been.

'Look out! Down!'

His shouted warning came almost too late. A burst of quick shots crashed into the high ground and whined away.

Both he and Felix had been guilty of assuming that they

351

would be the hunters, that the Ulyan driver would be standing around wide-eyed and gaping at the carnage. He was not. The man now slipping over McGee's sights looked anything but surprised. While they had been seeking him at the ambush site he must have been working his way back to his vehicle and was now bounding, spring-heeled, over the river rocks towards it, firing from the hip as he ran.

Felix's rifle cracked. The shot was wide. Then the wind changed back again, the smoke swirled in and once more they could not see. They could hear, though. They heard the starter motor of the Ulyan grind and the engine burst into life. The vehicle would take a second to turn – a second was all the time it took them to sprint towards the smoke-free ridge above. McGee reached it first. He had a clear shot and he placed it as deliberately as a hunter. Even as he stroked the trigger and his weapon kicked he had the satisfaction of knowing he would score. The driver made a bared-teeth attempt to hold himself upright, to keep the wheel. Twice he almost drove over the verge as he zigzagged in shock. Then slowly he crumpled. Pilotless, the Ulyan, its engine roaring, buffeted its way in a storm of shale along the cutting, then slowly toppled on to its side and stalled. It was all over. They now had a vehicle, and more. They had Mazambaan.

Mazambaan! A chorus of hate seemed to be echoing through every corner of McGee's mind as he advanced on the man. '*Mazambaan*! . . .' Was it he calling out like that? *Mazambaan*! He had not shot him to kill him. No, he wanted the man, to see him, to recognize him. He had things to tell Mazambaan. Mazambaan had things to tell him.

'Don't die, Mazambaan. I don't want you to die yet.'

The man looked at him. In agony or hate . . . ? It was hate. 'You've got something of mine,' McGee said. 'It's time to give it back now.'

By the time they had righted the Ulyan, bandaged the captive and pointed the Russian jeep's nose towards

Alexandre they were so late that unless a miracle was in store, there was no way they could be in time to catch Perseveranca. The trawler with Patricia and his raiders on board should, if Almeida had followed the admiral's orders, be well over the horizon by then. McGee did not believe in divine intervention, but that did not stop him from trying. He tramped the Ulyan's accelerator viciously; to the limit.

It was almost midday by the time they reached the coastal dunes, Hosi's vacated ambush site and a white-grey fog quilt that overlay everything on the other side of the bridge ahead. So they were gone, and that was that – in fact that was how it had been planned. The mist closed in as he took the Ulyan on. Vision was down to about fifteen metres by the time he reached the harbour. He knew they were gone, still he sprinted to the jetty's end.

McGee had never felt more alone. Below him he could discern the wavelets of the bay as they slapped on the pylons, just to his back the stolen GAZ, cold and wet with dew . . . Seawards – not a thing, not a light, not a silhouette, just a blank, grey swirling world of fog.

So they had won, they had achieved their objective. Why then, he asked himself, was he feeling so bloody empty? Why was it such an effort to pick up his feet, turn his body shorewards, and make for the jeep? He was tired to death . . . Too tired to move. That was, until the firing started, so close that he could feel the percussion, see the flashes. Three spaced shots hammered the fog asunder and wrenched McGee's over-stretched reflexes back into action. He brought up his rifle and sprinted towards the Ulyan and the deadly smell of cordite. Then he heard a voice straight from heaven, 'Capitao! . . . Capitao!' it called. It belonged to big Hosi, Archangel Hosi.

Chapter 22

A mile from the shore the shots sounded mournful and
flat as they thudded through the mist. Nevertheless, to the
listeners on Perseveranca's decks they were a signal for
jubilation, cheering and singing. Now the soldiers had no
more doubts. Their symbol of invincibility was returning.
They had a leader. Patricia, her eyes streaming, hugged
and kissed every black cheek. She was dancing. She was
aflame.

It was unthinkable that they would not make it. No-one
seemed concerned about the hundreds of metres that lay
between the shore and the ship, the razor-barnacled
rocks, the in-driving surf; no-one except Almeida, and he
had another worry. A blip had appeared on his radar
screen, coming in from the deep water, a rather solid and
fast-moving blip that would, if it continued on its present
heading, be on a collision course with his vessel. He
answered Hosi's signal with three long blasts on the
foghorn and wondered who would reach Perseveranca
first, friend or foe.

Three more shots came from the shore. They were
launching. To draw in the dinghy, the foghorn was to be
sounded in continuous bursts, and from then on that was
the only sound to be heard from the trawler. But a dozen
pair of eyes were focused into the swirling grey void, alert
and expectant. Patricia climbed to the wheelhouse. There
was something she had to do.

'Skipper, thank you! Thanks for what you did. For
waiting.'

In the dark glow of the wheelhouse roof light the man
looked exhausted. He shrugged his shoulders. 'You were
the one! Senhora, the Capitao is a lucky man.' He pointed

owards the shore, wagging his finger. Almost schoolmas-
erly, he cautioned, 'There are still the rocks and the sea
o beat. It will be hell in that little dinghy. The Capitao is a
ough one, though. That I know. Maybe he can do it.'

'Oh, yes,' agreed Patricia.

'We will see.'

Patricia thought the old man a pessimist, not the sort of
person she wanted to be near just then. She clambered
back down the ladder to the deck and joined the watchers
on the lee side.

But Almeida was not really a pessimist. He had not
mentioned to Patricia the oncoming radar blip, which had
now firmed up into something definitely way beyond the
size of a fishing trawler. If McGee did not reach Perseveranca within the next half hour, and the other vessel was
what he thought it was, they were going to have to shut
down the foghorn or they would be homed in on like a
killer shark. That was not pessimism, that was acoustic
reality. They waited . . . Twenty minutes passed, and they
waited. Almeida's eyes were stinging with sweat. He
switched off the wheelhouse light, pressed his foghorn
again – and waited.

Okongo saw them first, his gruff little bark rising to an
excited yap. There was something there, all right, a dark,
growing smudge in the curtain of mist. The people on
Perseveranca were quiet, waiting to see what sort of toll
Angola had extracted. A few called encouragement.
Names they left alone. Then the shape of the dinghy rose
out of the fog. They were close enough to count the sea-
drenched gasping men and nobody said much more . . . A
rope splashed across, and they hove to.

If any of the men helping at the gunwale had turned
then, they would have seen a young woman, standing well
back to the stern, her lips drawn taut in a deep bow of
emotion, her cheeks wet with more than just the soaking
mist; and then, not wishing to be seen like that, straightening her shoulders and tossing back her head, she walked
slowly forward to claim the man who would be the last one

355

on deck. But nobody turned, so nobody saw her until she had reached him, was holding him, supporting him with possession so patently strong that not another arm was needed.

Perseveranca's head was around even before they had the dinghy aboard. They had two options: they could skulk close inshore, which would make it hard to be detected by radar – but Perseveranca would in that case be pushing against the strong inshore Benguela current chopping their speed down considerably; or they could run at full revs for deep waters and hope that the fog would be thick, wide and enduring. Full revs meant pushing the big caterpillar V8 to a thundering 1300 r.p.m – and Almeida did just that. The heading was west of south west; head-on to the Atlantic rollers. The trawler shuddered for a second or two, waiting for the torque the engine would deliver. Then the propeller bit hard, and Perseveranca rose to the sea. By that time the little acid-green blip was disturbingly close, and closing.

Any doubts those on Perseveranca's tiny bridge may have held about the impulse their antenna was returning to them were dispelled within the short time it took them to make deep water. The other vessel was pursuing them. It was faster than they were and bigger. They ran west of south west until 14.00, as did their pursuer. Then they rounded out and steadied on their southwards run. Perseveranca could cope with 12 knots. It was not enough. The craft on the radar display had at least five knots on them. They were being hauled relentlessly in. What could they do but keep going?

Perseveranca was steering now parallel with the line of the swell. There still was no wind but she was rolling a little more. McGee, who had the wheel, had vertigo staring at the rouletting compass card and an awful nausea spilled up from his stomach. It was hard not to sound grateful when Almeida said, 'I take wheel now. Okay? You better look at radar.'

He looked at the screen and what was disclosed on it

iveted him. The afterglow of the blip was almost dead central to the screen. The enemy ship was virtually abreast of them.

'If fog breaks now . . .' Almeida's tone was tight with agitation; he cleared his throat, 'we got big trouble.'

McGee did not hear him. He was making purposeful tracks along the deck for the machine-gun positions. Both gun crews were alert. The long heavy Browning barrels pointed rearwards into the fog. He corrected them. 'The bastard is somewhere to our right, almost twelve o'clock. He's waiting for a break in the fog to hammer us. Just make sure that does not happen.'

'You think there may be a break, Capitao?' It was Hosi's voice, and from where McGee was standing, amidships, he could not even see the men on the wheel-house roof. The fog looked heavier than ever. 'Just be ready, Hosi. Let's get in first. They're hot on the trail.'

Hosi, as always, took it calmly. 'Don't worry, boss, we're going to hose those niggers down, cool them off a bit.'

The laughter was quiet, but the humour was genuine, and good to hear. Those boys of his were quite something but if the vessel on their beam was what he feared it to be, they were going to have Hell's own scrap on their hands.

The Angolans had about a dozen naval craft of various origins, mostly ex-Portuguese with a few Russian Zhuks thrown in. What Perseveranca would probably be facing up to before long was one of a pair of 136-foot Argos-class patrol craft that was stationed at Mocamedes. Ex-Portuguese Navy, their armament comprised two 40mm Bofors, one fore and one aft – enough to chew the trawler's wooden hull to splinters within seconds, and at a range that totally out-reached their .50 Brownings.

If Perseveranca had left when she should have left, they would not have had the problem they were now faced with. McGee clambered through the fore-deck hatch to the crew's quarters. He wanted a chat with the woman who had blindly spurned an Admiral's sailing orders.

She was working together with D'Oliviera, the medic on a saline drip when McGee lowered himself down th swaying steps. The subject of their attention was lyin dead still on one of the lower bunks. They had him pile with blankets and freshly bandaged, but his eyes wer open, darting black agates, taking in every move. The followed McGee as he came up to Patricia, put his arm round her shoulder and asked, 'How's he coming?' Sh made a final adjustment to the drip-tube valve, the looked up. 'Blood pressure's good, temperature's good pulse rate improved. He'll make it.'

'Do we have to . . .'

She did not let McGee finish. 'Yes, we do have to. Yo brought him aboard and regardless of who he is, what he' done, I can't leave him to die. Anyway, I don't think you really want that, or why did you bring him in?'

Why indeed? McGee could not think of a single reason that made sense. 'I don't know, Trish, but the only time this bastard won't be dangerous is when he's dead. Oliviera must watch him every second.' He turned to the medic. 'Oliviera, watch him. I mean it. If he makes one move he shouldn't, kill him.' McGee leant right over Mazambaan, accepting the man's cold glare, holding and returning the pure naked hatred of the look. Patricia drew him slowly back.

'Matt, Matt, we've got him now. He's in our hands. We can't deny him the care he needs to live. I can't, you can't.' She came to McGee then, holding him tightly. But he had more that he wanted to say and steered the girl to the ladderway. 'Come up for a moment, Trish. You've been buried down here since we sailed.'

On deck the fog looked patchier. They were never out of it but now and then, the air round them lightened ominously. They walked to the bows; holding each other warmly. They had not really kissed until then and when they did it was something simple and tender, so caring and seemingly so desperately out of place with the instant, that he hardened his heart and fought it. The air had such a smell of death in it that to love would be pressing fate to its limit.

Survival was all he was prepared to think about. Quietly he said to her, 'We're not out of it, I think you know that. Your father is waiting on the south bank of the Cunene. There are South African troops there and helicopters with him. The plan was to call out the choppers to lift us off Perseveranca as soon as conditions were good. Instead now I'm praying that the fog does not lift. We've got the People's Navy tracking us and they're close, somewhere over there.' She followed the direction of his gesture. 'Everything depends on the fog. So listen to me, Trish. If the firing starts, I want you to keep below the water line, you'll be safest there. Move quickly but don't run. You'll have time before they range on us. Put on the life jacket that's there. Come, I want to show you.'

McGee demonstrated how he wanted her to lie, made her don the life jacket. 'Keep it on now. Every man on board's got one.' He tried to get her to stay a while but she would not. She had things to do, she said. She hesitated then. 'Mazambaan's got a handcuff on his ankles. What happens to him if the worst comes to the worst?'

'If we start going down?'

'Yes.'

'Under no circumstances is he to be released by anyone but me.'

'Matt, there's something I must tell you right now . . . Sun-rival was stolen from me.'

'I know. Zietsman told me. I knew all about the burglary. They gave me your statement to read.'

'Mazambaan took the ring.'

'Yes, I knew that too.'

'He used to wear it on a thong round his neck. He had it on that night.'

'Yes.'

'I've searched him, Matt. He hasn't got it any more.'

359

'I know. I've got it, Trish. I took it off him after I shot him. It was still round his neck.' McGee opened his shirt at the neck. 'Here.' He lifted the thong. 'You take it now.'

She took it. She held it for a happy moment, then thoughtfully let it drop back into the valley between McGee's chest muscles. 'Not yet, Matt.' She kissed him. 'I know exactly the time and place where I want it back.'

There was no arguing. Patricia hugged him again, turned and disappeared into the forward hatch. With a shock he realized that he could actually see that far, see her climb down the hatch. The weather was changing.

Even the for'ard bollard was visible. Almeida warned: 'It's breaking up,' and fifteen minutes later they burst into the unwelcome sunshine of a glorious winter afternoon. At that same moment, on their starboard beam, with less than a quarter of a mile to separate them, was revealed a patrol craft, Argos class, flying the Angolan colours.

Perseveranca's guns, ready for aggression, were the first to crash into action. McGee could see the water below the sharp prow of the patrol craft spouting up. But with the rolling platform the trawler was providing for its gunners, most of their rounds were going into the sea. The team in the stern position were quicker to correct. They were anticipating the roll now and frequently on target. The best fire, however, was from Bacar and Teja. They had their light machine-gun perched on the gunwales and were hammering out continuously accurate bands of tracer, engaging both enemy Bofors guns in turn.

It was not enough. The Bofors were traversing quickly and relentlessly to target them. Through his glasses McGee could clearly observe the enemy gunners laying their weapons and soon heavy stuff came screaming past, 300 rounds a minute per gun.

'Left, turn left.' Almeida had anticipated McGee's command. They were swinging to present their stern. Both of Perseveranca's point five's could still bear, however, and both were pouring it in.

Then the commander of the patrol craft made an error.

He decided to chase his enemy, turn his vessel and run straight at them. Either he had no confidence in his gunners at that range or he underestimated the little trawler's fire-power. Either way, it was a mistake. His stern Bofors became totally blind and, with his high prow, his for'ard gunners were only getting brief snatches at their target. Both of Perseveranca's Brownings, however, were crashing away. A remnant of the fog belt lay shorewards so they scooted for it shrugged themselves in and cut power.

Blind man's buff, thought McGee. He knew enough about radar to realize that their enemy had problems. The sea was smooth and that was good for the Angolans. There would be no clutter from a rough, breaking surface and Perseveranca had a high profile for their radar impulses to bounce off, but that was not all there was to it. The trawler had moved quite close inshore and would benefit from the land shadowing and false echoes. Moreover the track of Perseveranca's motion-line across their pursuer's screen didn't indicate the exact direction in which the trawler was steaming: if Almeida kept slightly shifting direction it would hardly be apparent on the enemy display. They could play it that way, but for how long?

Perseveranca's brass chronometer read 16.40. The aqua sounder gave them fifty-five fathoms and they swung south again. The main thing was to keep moving southwards. They were deep inside what remained of the fog belt and bound for the Cunene. That was when the enemy commander called their bluff.

'He's cut inside between us and the shore,' McGee observed from the radar. 'We must stand out on his screen now like a bloody beacon.'

Almeida swung further to port, bringing down his revs. It did not really help. The enemy bloodhound was on to them. They had to cut inside again.

'More?' The skipper wanted to know, spinning the wheel still further.

'Yes, more.'

The aqua-sounder was beeping back thirty fathoms . . . twenty fathoms. McGee imagined he could hear surf to the east. Almeida complained, 'We not making headway so close in. Current too strong here.'

'Take it a bit further out, then.'

'Is what he wants for radar picture. Nothing we can do.'

It was true. The patrol craft commander had them in a cleft stick. They had to bear southwards and try to avoid an engagement. They had to keep within the skimpy shorewards fog belt. A thunderous burst of gunfire buffeted the fog asunder. The enemy commander was bringing new tactics to bear – dangerous tactics.

'He'll do it again,' yelled Almeida.

And he did, several times, sometimes coming in so close they could pick up sounds from the patrol boat's deck; fire orders from the bridge; the metallic sound of the ammunition clips being clamped home. They could even feel the very percussion of the Bofors guns as they fired.

For a while they survived it, on occasions shutting down the engine, bringing Perseveranca's head into the sea and waiting, not even breathing, until the hostile Maybach diesels had purred away and faded into the mist. But they came back. They always came back. They were better than McGee had imagined and they were always so close. It was blind man's buff all right, but with the patrol boat's Bofors guns to feel the way.

It would have been playing into the enemy commander's hands to retaliate. What they had to do was to keep slipping southwards; keep hoping that the blindfold of the fog would not lift.

It was too much to hope for . . . suddenly there was no more fog. As though the gods had swept it away, it was gone. It was perfect flying weather; the precise conditions their plans had been based on – and now the very last thing they wanted!

'There they are!'

There is nothing sweet about the lines of the Argos-class patrol vessel with its high boxy superstructure and turretless guns. But from the bridge of the wooden-hulled fishing trawler well within range of those guns, aesthetics were irrelevant. 'We got fucking big troubles.' Almeida's comment, as usual, summed it up. The Angolans were cruising about a mile ahead of them, the feather of their bow-wave hardly lifting as they patrolled across Perseveranca's intended course. The Angolans had them, there was no urgency for the enemy commander now.

'Maybe we get more fog.'

'Yes,' said McGee. Maybe later they would. Right at that moment, at that lattitude, there was nothing to be seen but the bluest of afternoon skies above, a flat sea below, and two ships; diametrically opposed in every way. 'Yes,' McGee said again, but he was agreeing with his own thoughts, not with Almeida's speculations. They were in for a fight.

'You want we turn back to the fog?' the skipper asked fatalistically. The Angolans were keeping their distance. They were not about to repeat their previous mistake and allow themselves to be drawn into hand-to-hand contact. They would take the troublesome little trawler on their own terms, at a range that suited their potent guns and not an inch closer.

'No,' said McGee. 'If they chase us back up the coast it's going to be worse for us in the end. Anyway, the fog's lifting everywhere.'

'Okay, I hold course southwards then. We give them hell, Capitao.'

'Yes . . . We give them hell,' McGee lied.

Perseveranca would now only be able to bring to bear the roof-mounted Browning and even that would be stretched. The patrol craft commander, with his position, his superior speed and his heavy weaponry, could take them apart whenever he wanted to. And that was exactly what he tried for: swinging broadside suddenly, he hit them with both forty-millimetre guns blazing. There was no alternative. McGee yelled, 'Let's get 'em!' The old cat diesel thrashed out full power and with the roof Browning spitting defiance and incendiary shells, they bore down on the People's Navy.

All around them now the water was being thrashed up into towers of hissing foam. The air was alive with the harsh screech of passing metal, but Perseveranca pushed on and on. It could not last. In stunning, blinding succession, three cannon shells ripped in. One high on the stern post twisted the metal clamps and blew the kari wood beam to matchwood; one carried away a ventilator and part of the fish hold hatch; and one struck the donkey winch below the wheelhouse. Coils of anchor chain flailed out in fury – men went down.

They were hurt and bleeding. They had been shaken to the keel, but were still afloat. A great smouldering hole had been torn from the head of the foredeck and the stern post was just a memory. But, the V8 was still thumping. Hosi's Browning was still pelting out incendiary. Patricia and Oliviera were already on the foredeck, working medical miracles – and suddenly McGee had the wildest thought that they could be winning. A minute later his field-glasses confirmed it. They *were* winning!

Perseveranca's company had terrible problems, but at least they were not ablaze. The patrol craft was. A haze of white smoke hung over the vessel and men were scurrying across the deck with hoses. Only the aft Bofors was still fully manned and the shooting was becoming desultory. On the bridge the enemy skipper, black-bereted and swarthy, his arms frantic, his mouth working, ducked as another hail of incendiary shot caught them. Suddenly, as though touched by lightning, his craft began to burn. The People's Navy were in a lot of trouble – McGee gave them another long burst of raking fire then left them to their life rafts . . . Perseveranca turned away to lick her wounds.

What wounds they were! There were four men on the after-deck, shoulder to shoulder in death, as they had been in life; four irreplaceable men who had lived and laughed and fought together. They were gone, but those who were alive were glad to be alive, and that was the way of it.

Beneath the trawler's scarred deck beams you could see right into the crew's quarters. It was too dark to call in the choppers, and if any sort of blow materialized, there was no way they would be able to run against it. They would have to repair Perseveranca as best they could.

The Atlantic could not have looked more innocent, the darkening sky benign. A smoke column from the destroyed patrol craft on the horizon was being teased by alternate gusts of breeze, now warmly from the land, then from the west, and all the time Perseveranca was ploughing gamely onwards to the south and safety.

McGee had worked out a plan to repair the foredeck. It meant jemmying away the planks from the crew's bunks, then relaying them over the damage. Everyone helped, even fat dos Santos. He brought up crow-bars and hammers and worked with a will. By the time they had finished Mazambaan's was the only bunk left intact in the quarters, but the deck had been restored. It looked what it was, a patch job, but standing on the deck you could no longer see past the scarred beams into Perseveranca's guts. Day was closing by the time they had banged home the last nail.

'Mae de Deus . . . protege nos do mar,' prayed dos Santos. If the Atlantic turned ugly, at least they would have Mother Mary to show the way; there was not a man who did not say Amen to that . . . Well, maybe one.

But for the whitest of white moons stirring a trail of quicksilver across the sea it was dark. Standing by the rail, McGee saw no enchantment in it. In fact, though his eyes were following it, he did not even see it. The fine spray from the bow-wave was wetting him but he did not feel that either. He had never felt so exhausted. Fetters of lassitude were dragging him down. And who can observe or feel when numb from killing and drenched with the blood of friends? He hardly noticed the woman at his side. She was there, he was there and they held each other affectionately like old people for a while. Then concentrating on every step McGee turned silently away and climbed to the wheelhouse.

The brass chronometer there, after he had focused for the third time, gave him five minutes before eight. It was time for his watch. Four hours and it would be midnight; four hours and if they were on schedule it would be all over and he could go to sleep for a year.

Almeida was fussing with a pair of dividers and a protractor over an Admiralty chart. He must have guessed what was going through McGee's mind. 'I think,' his word came out 'theenk', 'maybe we one hour late, no more. Baio dos Tigres light we pass at twenty-one hundred. We one hour late.'

'Zero one hundred then and we'll be there,' McGee was not sure whether he had spoken the words so he said again, 'Zero one hundred and we'll be there. Nothing can stop us now, skipper.'

Excepting the sea, thought the skipper but was superstitious enough not to comment. 'Hold course, one hundred seventy,' was what he said. 'Keep revs full.'

Almeida checked the barometer as he had done five times in the previous hour. It had dropped considerably. Above, high-flying cirrus lockets were rushing past the moon. The wind had turned round completely and was now coming strongly off the land; warm, almost hot from the compression it had been subjected to on its arduous journey down from the inland plateau. Thrusting against this berg wind the swell crests were being sliced off and blasted into contrasting icy spray. There was something pretty ugly brewing, but West Coast storms at that time of the year were usually slow-moving heavyweights; hard-hitting but ponderous, they telegraphed their blows.

He watched the bow-wave roll away, alive with phosphorescence. A few hours more. That was all they needed. He watched McGee at the wheel. The man was getting a grasp of it now, feeling the ship under his hands, and with a deft touch checking untoward movement even before it began, keeping the wake stretching white and luminous astern as straight as a tow line.

Almeida could taste the grit from the sand dunes that the wind was bearing the full twenty miles from the shore. He ground his teeth on it reflectively and for the first time since they had sailed from Luderitz Almeida gave Christie's purse money a measure of optimistic consideration. A man with his sea service should have known better.

At midnight the slumbering giant of the South Atlantic, having borne the ire of the berg wind to the limit, asserted its power, hurling back from the south west a blow of full gale force, and its surface awaiting just this change in command, seethed into instant madness. Dark with rage the swell tumbled down upon them.

Almeida took the wheel and held Perseveranca's head as southerly as he dared. The trawler, rolling massively, was scooping aboard volumes of surly black water. An immense wave rose ahead of them and climbing and cresting it they took the full blast of the oncoming wind, salt-spray hitting them like shot from a blunderbuss. Then they were plunging down into the trough, the gale heeling them like a yacht. Almeida fought it, bringing the wheel round as they slipped to leeward in a slide that, willy-nilly, was carrying them landwards.

Suddenly McGee felt so nauseous he could hardly stand. He pushed his way to the wheelhouse door, slid it open and vomited, the wind whipping it away from his mouth like a scarf. Then they were in a trough again, towering mountainous seas running on every side. Completely disoriented, he slammed the door, and fell back on to Almeida.

A giant wave flexed up on the starboard bow, broke and raged down on them, smacking the fragile bows and teeming aboard. The deck light flickered. Perseveranca shrugged loose. Leaden, the bows came up but miraculously the planks held.

Without any thought other than that he wanted to be

with Patricia, McGee found himself clambering down the bridge steps. He had three metres left to traverse before he could scramble down the forward hatch and that was nearly too much. He waited for a trough, then ran. Like a giant demon the wind dealt with him, slamming him back against the superstructure. The deck was pushing up violently. They were climbing again. He threw himself full length towards the hatch and made it.

Inside it was another world. Patricia saw him on the ladder, and smiled with her lips. Her eyes were round with terror. They were in the belly of the beast, oily green calf-deep water slopping up and down and the place reeked of bile. McGee plodded his way across to help, reached out for the support of a stanchion but did not make it. The deck nosedived, leaving him groping. Like a drunk man he tumbled to the bows. For a lifetime Perseveranca just hung there, head down while the Atlantic poured past the planking. Then with the main timbers screaming, they came up. He added to the vomit there and this time there was no wind to excise its foulness. Then they were plunging again.

He wanted her out of there. It was not the most rational thinking perhaps. If Perseveranca went down, they all went down. The good would drown with the bad. For some reason, though, McGee saw it differently.

He pointed to the ladder and said, 'Up.'

Patricia pointed to Mazambaan. 'Unlock him, Matt. You can't leave him chained, not now.'

It would have been impossible to carry her bodily to the upper deck, but McGee would have tried it. She read him, jutted out her jaw and firmly held on to a stanchion.

'Hosi!' McGee ripped off his shoulder lanyard. There was a single key on the clasp. 'Take this, but don't let that bastard loose until you know you have to.'

Patricia reached for the ladder. Perseveranca juddered from another crushing blow. Then together they began to climb.

'You do silly things . . . yes?' Almeida squeezed in a

368

nile between waves. 'I do same for girl like that.' The heelhouse was if anything a crazier place to be in. High bove the main deck, every savage roll Perseveranca ndertook was exaggerated there. At times they were anting to their beam ends, at times it seemed they must eet the sea. Bracing his body, McGee helped Patricia to edge herself between bunks, then using every handhold ere was he fought his way back to help the man at the elm. Another wave drove headlong into them, jolting aem violently. McGee glanced quickly back but Patricia as secure.

They climbed a smooth bank, then dived, wild water eating at them again. 'While you down there I bring the hip up into the wind, slow engines to steering way.' 4cGee made him repeat what he had just said. The noise f the gale was thunderous.

'We're into the wind, no longer headed home?'

'Yes. Yes. That is what I do.'

'We're taking water below deck,' McGee shouted. 'The rew's quarters are swamped!'

Almeida thought about that, his solid hands working he wheel. He drew in his breath to shout again. 'I reckon ve off Praia dos Esponjas now, maybe five miles out.'

'How far from Cunene?' McGee demanded. 'How far rom the border?'

'Six miles, maybe eight, no more.'

'Can we make it?'

Almeida's answer was to point to the foredeck. Water from the last encounter was draining to the stern as Perseveranca heaved up, but not all of it. Some of their makeshift deck had staved in and much of it was swirling down the slit. Almeida was already bringing down the helm, swinging the ship round.

'Only one chance now,' he yelled, 'Praia dos Esponjas.'

You did not have to be a sailor to see what had to be done next. They were on their knees. They had to run with the wind or go down within the next few blows.

Turning for land in those seas would leave the trawler

beam-on to the gale and hopelessly vulnerable while t
manoeuvre was being brought off. A wave, not even a b
one, clapped against them, heeling Perseveranc
broaching the gunwales and washing across the dec
Then they were in a corridor and turning slowly, to
slowly. A jade-black avalanche tumbled on to the
turning the very air to spume. Perseveranca heeled in
possibly. Almeida's huge hands were flung off the whee
Pitching sideways, he struck McGee and both me
crashed into the wheelhouse door. It held. They we
being shaken like dice in a giant's fist. Somewhere gla
was splintering, salt water was crashing in, but once mo
they came up sixes.

Slowly and in great distress, wonderful Perseveranc
righted herself, shouldered her mass free from the bu
lying sea and came around stern towards both wind an
water. Then she was making headway. Slowly, until th
next massive wave picked them up, she wallowed on th
crest, struggled there for a moment then sickening
pitched back. The impetus of the next brute held them
bit longer, dunked them a bit deeper, then crashed b
blackly.

Then suddenly they were surfing, fast, at a much greate
speed than the trawler's Nordic hull had been designed to
take. Trying to reassure no-one but himself, Almeid
shouted again, 'Beach at dos Esponjas is best chance.' I
had better be; they were aimed dead at it. The wav
dropped them and another took them up.

So near, so bloody near! Six sea miles further and the
would have been able to run Perseveranca right up th
Cunene estuary and into Christie's waiting arms. Al
meida, McGee suddenly realized, had been talking to hin
for some time. It was quieter there in the wheelhous
now; there was not the incessant hail of pelting spray and
the older man's voice was hardly raised. 'You call every
one up on deck now,' he told McGee. 'We close to beach
now.' There was no question about it, the waves were
getting tighter, steeper. Perseveranca was surfing in quick

uffeting surges. There were many things that had to be
one.

Almeida had opened the diesel to maximum revs. The
xhaust was roaring as he had never heard it roar as he
crambled to the deck. Then what occurred happened so
ast that, to McGee, the sequence of events was just a wild
umble. All at once the deck plummeted sickeningly. He
elt himself tumbling to the bows, fighting for a hand hold:
uddenly he was in a maelstrom.

Perseverança was nose-under. She had sharply pitched
down a wave face. Her water-laden bows, digging in, had
pried the stern clean out of the sea. The vessel hung there
punch-drunk, the engine over-running, no man in control,
hen pitched back. The blades bit in hard, much too hard;
he propeller sheered from the shaft as easily as a blossom
s twisted from its stem. 370 pounds of brass sank like a
stone and, mortally stricken, a grand old lady swirled into
the pounding, merciless surf.

Almeida had intended to run them on to the beach, to
drive headlong on to the Praia. It was not to be. Like so
much flotsam the undertow pulled them, the breakers
pushed them. They were dumped into the shallows,
scraped off and then dumped again, broaching with every
wave.

McGee hauled himself up, discovered he was at the
mast step and looked around. The beach, gleaming like
shot silk under the intermittent moon, was clearly visible
some forty metres away. It might as well have been a mile.
In that demented surf no one could have reached it. A
wave heaved them up and he held fast as it broke. Shards
of salt water scoured him like broken glass. Then suddenly
they were ploughing beam-on through the surf, higher
again and higher, then down with a keel-snapping crash.
Perseverança had broken her back. The raping Atlantic
had fulfilled itself and they were fast on the sand less than
twenty metres from dry land. McGee ran to the wheelhouse as dazed men began to emerge on to the canting
deck.

371

Patricia was shaken but unhurt. Almeida had not fare
so well. Blood was streaming all over him from a slash of
his scalp. He was slumped groaning in one corner of the
wheelhouse.

McGee told Patricia what had to be done. 'We'
twenty metres out, Trish. That's not far, but none of me
boys knows how to swim. I think Perseveranca will break
up so I'm going over the side with a rope.'

To back McGee's misgivings a wave slammed up an
over the superstructure. Somewhere deep down there
was a splintering screech that was more than just timber
in spasm. It was Perseveranca's scream as her heart gave
up. She gave a massive shudder and tilted still further
McGee dashed for the deck.

All he could remember of the swim was the feebleness
of his efforts, the utter futility of his strokes. In second
he had been thrashed under into a mute, glacial, brutal
world where the sea did with him as it wished; which was
around he was he did not know. He was conscious of the
solitude of his struggle, the dumb bestiality of it. His
shoulder struck bottom and he pushed away, flailin
desperately for a surface that was not there. He lost air
God, he had to have air! Lungs screaming, he clamped
hand to face but wherever the surface was now it was to
far. He needed air, had to breathe that instant. His head
broke surface, his shoulders, he could stand! He wa
gasping sweet air – but the undertow ripped his leg
away, powerful surf pummelled him under. He gripped
the sand, held on and on until the Atlantic rushed in
again and threw him retching on to the edge of the Praia
the beach of sponges.

A flit of moonlight showed Perseveranca to him; i
must have showed him to Perseveranca because he could
hear cheering. Even the thunder of the breakers could
not drown it out. He was on the beach, firmly anchored
in the sand to take the strain of the next man. It was
Felix, the smallest of them. Hitched to the rope with a
nylon garter, McGee pulled him straight out. He threw

ff his life jacket, gasping. 'Welcome,' McGee greeted im, 'to Praia dos Esponjas!'

Bacar was next, then a very shaken dos Santos, bringing ith him McGee's clothes. Teja followed and it was easy fter that. With four strong men drawing the lifeline and dos Santos's massive bulk anchoring the whole thing, Baptisa was hardly in the water before they had him on dry land.

Then Patricia . . . anything less like a Botticelli Venus you could not have hoped to see: she came out of the waves with the grace of a beaching walrus. bringing with her a bewildered and shivering terrier . . . Hanja brought he medical kit. Then it was Almeida's turn. They had to drag the old man from the surf and up the beach but a long sip from the medical brandy flask worked its age-old magic. Soon his huge hands were on the rope too.

Big Hosi and Oliviera, the medic, still had to come through the surf. The man next in line, however, was to be Mazambaan. They waited and watched, bending to make their bodies smaller against the freezing wind.

You could see the wreck from the froth of white water breaking on it. Sporadically, when the moon burst through, you could count the broken deck planks on the listing deck, see the life-line firmly tied. Of any of the men still on board, though, there was not a sign. Tugging on the line brought no response and there was no sense in shouting though some of them did . . . Something had gone very wrong.

Chapter 23

It was during one of the dark spells that Felix, who ha[s]
never let go of the line, shouted, 'Someone is pulling[']
and so it was. Someone was giving the signal. They fe[ll]
upon the rope and hauled Mazambaan . . . Only it wa[s]
not Mazambaan. It was Hosi, holding his neck as h[e]
waded up the beach. He was speaking through pai[n]
clenched teeth and McGee knew, word for word, wha[t]
he was about to hear. Mazambaan had hit Hosi as h[e]
bent to release the manacles. 'He hit me as I was ben[t]
forward. He must have had a steel bar or something.[
] went out like a light.' Oliviera was dead. 'I found hir[m]
with his throat cut.'

Mazambaan had escaped. 'I could not find him any[-]
where. I searched the ship.'

They had a fire going in the shelter of a dune ridge[.]
There they gathered. 'Oliviera's knife and his life jacke[t]
were missing,' Hosi concluded. 'He must have take[n]
them and jumped into the sea.'

'He'll drown, then.' The statement came from Al[-]
meida. 'Undertow will have drag him out to sea.'

He should have killed Mazambaan! Rigours of col[d]
shuddered through McGee, shaking him until his teet[h]
rattled. The skeleton-white driftwood was roaring as the[
] flames took it, but the heat was caustic; skin-deep . . .
He should have killed Mazambaan, Hosi's eyes told hir[m]
that; buried him in the sand of the Curoca river. He ha[d]
not done so and another good man had died.

He had not done so because to have ended it like tha[t]
with the speed of a bullet would have denied him the[
] knowledge why . . . why two men's lives, two men's des[-]
tinies had met like tendrils and entwined so tortuously.

374

e had to be rid of Mazambaan but not leave the riddle of
m coiled to himself in death, like a cut vine.

Mazambaan had not died in the sea. He knew that with
solute certainty. Mazambaan would neither drown nor
eed nor meet death in any form other than that inflicted
y the man ordained to kill him.

It came to him on that raw praia that he had known it all
long. Ever since that savage day at Quimbo 333 his life
ad not been his own, nor would it be until he had
ivested himself of that cause, that nightmare quest he
as bound to.

He would do it. The man could not be far. He walked a
ew paces from the fire, then a few paces more. Hosi saw
im beckon and followed. 'Hosi.' McGee's voice sounded
ollow and distant to his own hearing, like the voice of a
tranger, calling from afar. 'Hosi.'

'Capitao?'

They walked together until the glow of the fire did not
ouch them. 'Hosi, you will lead everyone towards the
order. The Cunene river is seven or eight miles to the
outh. Admiral Christie is there and a contingent of
oldiers. You have a water-bottle. You have a rifle. It will
e an easy walk for all of you, excepting old Almeida.'

'And you, Capitao?'

'I will guard your rear,' McGee lied. 'I will be two or
hree hundred metres behind you. There must be no
urther halts. You must press on until you reach the
order. It is not far.'

'No. Seven or eight miles is not far.'

'Go now.'

'Sim, Capitao.'

He watched the silhouettes as they broke away from the
fire. He saw the hesitation of the woman, saw her turn and
stare into the gloom, then they were gone . . . Somewhere, quite close by, along that stretch of sand a man had
staggered from the surf, then turned and made his way
towards the north. He was on the move. The man could
not be far ahead but tracks in that moving sand would be

as transient as footsteps in a stream. There could be n
more vacillating. I'm coming, he answered the summor
of his mind, *I'm coming* . . . He turned and strode quickl
to the north.

Ahead an endless stretch of hostile seaboard lay, for
saken by Satan himself. Here ceaseless territorial wa
raged; marching sandhills of boundless desert slippin
beneath the seething South Atlantic, but ever advancing
Written into the sand at the right place would be a minut
trail of man-tracks. That was what he wanted. He trotte
then, aware only of the rhythm of his breathing and th
natural contours of the wave-washed moonlit beach
Crabs as big as a man's splayed hand were scootin
helter-skelter from his path.

The right place came up about a thousand paces furthe
north. Like a crocodile trail, a black spine of rocks ran th
full width of the beach, tapering into the sea. He wa
certain he would pick up the spoor there, and he did
Right at the base of the tail, where the sand had beer
blasted to a salty crust, he found the tracks.

Not one careless step had been taken. In spite of hi
wound Mazambaan had moved with the lightness of a
gecko. It took more than eyesight to betray those tracks
There was the green smell of bruised succulents. That was
where the trail began. He had used some dune plants to
step upon but underneath them lay his prints. He had
climbed a sandhill and faded into the valley.

There was no panic to be read in that moonlit spoor;
every footstep had been considered. The trail led parallel
to the coast for a while. Then holding to the massive
curving valleys of sand, perhaps with a thought for the
water wells in the high Sera Techamalinda, it worked an
inland course. The gale was now at his back, and the track
ahead, visible for only a few short paces as the wind
roared through the desert canyons and over the crests,
scourging the massive inland sandhills into a passion of
hissing, blistering grit. The sand was everywhere, in his
nose and mouth, his ears and eyes, robbing him of his

vision, eroding his senses, and every step was a metre of yielding, dragging, sliding punishment. Mazambaan was not far ahead, a recent definition in the spoor had spelt that out and the man's tread was shortening with fatigue. How far he was ahead was the question. But now the desert was lightening and soon there would be some answers.

The world was changing colour with the dawn and the contrast was incredible. From a blotting-paper landscape of ink-stained shadows, to a flooding monochrome red gold blaze, all in the space of less than a thousand man paces . . . In the brilliance of the morning sun the south-easter blustered for a while, then resignedly blew itself out. Red mountainous sandhills rose from the dust on all sides and a heaven as blue as God's own lake washed overhead.

In the middle distance, perhaps within the range of a sharpshooter with a good rifle scope, he saw his quarry. He did not have such a weapon though, and did not want one. When he struck out to kill it would be within the range of the long keen blade on his hip. He wanted to close the range and do it.

As if sensing the presence of his persecutor, Mazambaan turned and looked towards him. McGee was conscious of the utter quietness of the moment, the total stillness. There was not a whisper from the outside to disturb the concentration of engulfing hate, not a single sound besides his own harsh breathing. Then a peaceful breeze whisked a veil of sand from a smallish dune between them and both heads turned to regard it for a moment, no longer. Then their eyes traversed again to meet in a focus of loathing. He felt his arm raising, his finger extend accusingly, unwaveringly as it pointed at the man over the sea of red sand. The man in the distance turned away and without a backward glance resumed his course.

The sun was reaching for its winter apex by the time they saw each other clearly again. The Sera Techamalinda was closer, too, no longer just a hazy violet daub on the eastern horizon. Now it was tumbled granite with deep purple valleys and slashed slate-grey ribs. From its foot a massive mirage lake lapped wetly right up to the desert's edge with lesser hills and rocky koppies rising like islands from the phantom water. That was where Mazambaan was standing, on the edge of the forged lake. Just standing there, watching him again. Shimmering, rising, heat waves warped light and proportion; vision was a lie.

The desert was stonier where they were. Random rock formations, wind-blasted and grotesque, reared up between long drifts of white bleached sand as soft as finest talc. And, flowing over all else, were the dunes, bank after endless bank, massively forbidding and as hot as they were red. As though carved from the terrain, the two men stood, watching, assessing, loathing each other. Then, as though by some accord, both moved off as one towards the mountain range. Both men's paces were shorter and much slower than they imagined.

The chase had gone much further than McGee had expected. Now thirst had become his enemy. His insides were drying, calling for water.

If only he could hold his mind from the thought of water, he would win. In the Techamalinda there were rising springs. A Tjimba nomad had told him that once. Deep and cool they were with bubbling water as sweet as Omutati dew. To think of water was madness, to evict the thought impossible. He walked, relentlessly following the spoor. That was all he had to do.

Around him he knew the dunes were alive with creatures that could survive on the moisture of the desert dew or never drink at all; creatures that could draw water where none existed. In that incinerated land the quest for water was ceaseless . . . The heat was rising through his soles and beating through his brain. He felt his body being pressed dry, squeezed by the furnace doors of sky and earth. Man was no match for these conditions . . . He was man.

The tracks wound on and he followed, or was he

following? Was he giving chase or was he being inexorably dragged like some roped animal? The pursuer or the pursued?

He crossed a rocky ledge and suddenly, as though borne away on wings, the spoor was gone. He had lost concentration and with it the trail. Furious with himself, he turned and the horizon turned with him, and just kept on turning. He felt himself lurching, saw the sky, then the ground, then the man.

It was not Mazambaan. This man was a Bushman, an old hunter, cactus-skinned, sun-wrung and wrinkled. He was squatting lightly on his haunches, frowning, observing him. There were no Bushmen in south western Angola but that did not bother him. The fact that he had not once seen this man's tracks occurred to him but did not disturb him either. Worrying him was the realization that he knew this old Bushman, but his mind was denying him access to that segment of recognition.

Of more importance was that he had to have water then – or die. If there was water to be had the Bushman would know where to find it.

Together they climbed into the soft-bellied dunes, the sand spilling away in rivers beneath their feet. Knee-deep they waded into a valley and there it was, as ugly as a tangle of barbed wire – a !Nara bush with its precious life-giving melons.

Now he had water. Tangy sweet water flowing into his gut; his limbs. He drained it, chewed the !Nara pulp, then stood up. The Bushman gestured in that gentle way he knew so well . . . He was to follow.

They walked from the !Nara bush to the north, recrossing his earlier tracks, crossing the tracks of Mazambaan with hardly a glance, then onwards. They walked until the shadows began to lengthen. The mountain grew closer and the desert flatter.

They were heading towards a rock, massive even at a distance, pointing upwards like a remanding finger, when the old tracker stopped, stiffened, and lowered himself to

379

a watchful crouch . . . There on the desert floor was the spoor the Bushman had taken him so far to discover.

A lion had passed that way, a huge old Tau. The pug marks in the sand were deep on the front left, smudged on the right, their direction exactly towards the finger rock. He bent down and examined the drag-foot trail with his guide, the sensation of *déjà vu* descending again. His eyes had seen it all before, his mind would not unite him with the knowledge he owned.

He felt the leathery touch of the man's hand on his forearm, saw the fingers span the drag-foot pug, then he looked up – the Bushman was gone . . . He was alone. Bushman games? Did it matter? He was alone but the big finger of rock seemed to be sternly beckoning . . . He responded.

The rock was bigger, much bigger than he had imagined, its strata gouged and grooved by a million years of driving grit, its pinnacle sheer and towering inaccessibly into the sky. He had reached the place where he had to go, everything told him that.

How tired he was: mortally tired. He wanted it all to end, for his old Bushman friend to come and together they would steal away from that beautiful, frightening place . . . The gentleness plucking at his spirit, though, had no place there. In the encounter with his enemy it would kill him.

Enemy or enemies? The Bushman had indicated that it was the lion, when he knew with certainty that it was Mazambaan? If it was both, then he was done . . . Mazambaan was close. He could feel it. The hatred that had been his earlier, he needed that venomous infusion now.

He found a spot; a craggy knuckle of black limestone boulders. There he could see and not be seen. From there he would attack. He clambered up and waited. The breeze had dropped and the air hung in a heavy hot curtain. He waited. The sun blazing from the western sky had melted the desert into a blood-red sea. He shaded his eyes and searched it, and waited . . .

The realization that he, too, was being watched did not come jolting in. It came to him slowly, insidiously, with the stealth of a stalking boomslang. He felt his testicles draw, his whole body tauten. The grip on his long knife became a vice as he spun round, slashing in a wide defensive arc through the air . . . the empty air.

No – not quite empty. He wrinkled his nostrils and sniffed. In the stillness it barely reached him, but there it was again, just a waft of it, just enough to tell him exactly what it was that had melted into the desert twilight. Somewhere among that massive pile of rock a far more gifted killer than Mazambaan was at work, watching him with burning amber eyes and twitching tail. But now a shadow had touched the rock – a man shadow; stretched by the setting sun to a monstrous length.

He was coming. His black features were exhausted . . . Mazambaan! Mazambaan, the murderer, the people's hero, the freedom fighter. Mazambaan, figure of a thousand nightmares . . . Ten more paces and he would be beneath the knuckle. Four more paces and McGee would drop on him like a leopard. Two more and the long knife would open him from gut to gizzard. Then, whoever he was, whatever he was, it would be over.

The last step was never taken. Instinct, perhaps, or a fleeting shadow or sound – something had alerted the man. Mazambaan halted in mid-stride and, committed, McGee landed short of his target in the sand. The upwards slash meant to have gutted his adversary and ended it missed by a hair's-breadth, and in an instant Mazambaan had his knife drawn. It was Oliviera's bayonet, blue-bladed, oilstone sharp. The two men faced up like male fighting scorpions, and the feinting, fending, lunging death dance began. The soft under-belly had to be found; the chink where the sting could sink in.

But if either man thought his salvation lay in the death of his antagonist, they were wrong. There would be but one survivor in that arena and it was surprising that neither of them had seen it: the huge Kalahari lion, the drag-foot lion with the mind of a man.

It had seen them. It was crouched on the open sand, not one hundred paces from the contest, as though cast from gold. Now and then it moved. Its jaws would quiver, its tail slap irritably on the desert floor. Once it looked about to charge. Instead it slipped silently forward massive muscles bunched and sliding under a skin that had one major flaw, a festering sore beneath its mane.

The black man appeared to be tiring the faster. Gripping the bayonet clumsily and holding it too far from his body made his attack predictable. Perhaps it was his shoulder wound that caused him to adopt those tactics; one arm doing the work of two. Twice he lunged and found his antagonist further than he had expected.

The white man was letting the fight come to him, but there was an unbeknown advantage for the Owambo in that. With every backward pace the man took he closed the gap between himself and the tau. It could not go on much longer.

Mazambaan lunged again but this time his opponent did not recoil. McGee side-slipped, hardly shifting his stance and suddenly he was inside, close to the man he had come so far to kill, the long knife going for the strike.

That should have been the end of it. Instead it was the snarling moment of the charge. This time the tau made no mistake. One, two, three gouging blows in no more than a moment crushed its old enemy. Fangs like daggers went for the throat.

Mazambaan could have run, then. The lion seemed to have momentarily forgotten him. It was circling the kill, sniffing nervously as though surprised at the ease of victory. The way to the Sera Techamalinda was open and he was still strong enough to make it. He did not run.

Perhaps there was recognition for him in that moment, too; perhaps he saw the chance to end his own personal hell. Most likely he simply wanted to twist the bull's tail one last glorious time. The long knife was at his feet.

382

McGee seemed dead, but then he had looked dead once before. Mazambaan threw himself forward.

The lion did not hear him, did not see him. It felt Mazambaan, though: it felt the long knife sear between its ribs and enter its heart. Then it reared and gutted Mazambaan with one murderous blow.

The Owambo seemed puzzled for a moment; perhaps there was something at odds with his theory of life . . . Then he appeared to gain a princely dignity as though everything had become suddenly clear. He bent forward, seeking out the white man's face as though he had some secret he wished to impart. Perhaps he whispered something as he fell, as they lay there face to face.

As the sky turned from orange to cobalt a sigh of wind from nowhere passed by them. It teased the flaxen mane of the dead tau, ruffling it with a joyless hand, lifted a light shroud of sand over those lying there, then fled. The coldness of the desert night crept in.

Like a child in the depths of a dream gone bad, he tried to will himself awake, to free himself from the cataleptic tethers binding him. He had done it before: you had to persevere to drag upon your eyelids until like pillories they unlocked and parted, and you were free.

There was a sound intruding into the languor, a whirring inside his mind, insistent and aggravating. He wished that whatever it was would leave him. Go away. He tried to say the words but they remained a thought only; so he left it, sank back, uncaring, into the deep dark void. But there, too, it followed him. It became louder and he got angry with it. The spent fire of his body flamed momentarily and his eyelids flickered.

There were dragonflies, two of them, flying almost parallel to him, inches from his face it seemed. They disappeared and the noise with them. Then he looked up into an infinity of morning blue. Suddenly he knew where he was; who he was: McGee, lying in a broken body. McGee was dying and he did not want to die.

He cursed with his mind his paralysed body that would not move, would not rise, would do nothing but lie there covered in desert dust like the carcass of some drought-claimed beast. He *had* to move.

First, his eyelids. He forced them back still further. Then his eyes . . . There was a rock towering above him. His eyes progressed to the pinnacle, and an avalanche of memories tumbled into his consciousness. *!Xai – Mazambaan – the killer lion*. If he could only turn his head he knew it would all be there. He *had* to move.

He did turn, but the dead face that should have greeted him was *not* there. Now more than ever he had to raise himself. Whatever thin thread was holding him to life, he clung to it then. He hauled himself first to his knees, then to his feet . . . There was nothing there but the soft desert floor, the towering column of rock and his own footprints.

Little whimpering noises were rising into his throat. Mazambaan! He tried to scream the name. Perhaps his mouth moved but that was all. Mazambaan! !Xai, !Xai would hear him, !Xai!

There was no answer. How could an empty desert answer . . . ? But there was something; the breath of a whisper in his mind. *Ondoktola*, it said, *Ondoktola meme okua fia . . . Okua fia*. Our mother is dead . . .

If there had been one drop of water to spare, in mercy, his body would have given it for a tear then. But there was nothing . . .

There is a time when there is no more hope. He had fallen back on to his knees when the dragonflies came again. They were flying out of the sun, transparent wings beating red-tipped haloes in the sky . . . But they were not dragonflies. They did not have wings – they had rotors . . . They were helicopters . . . He wondered if they would ever find him.